Praise for the novels of Susan Mallery

"Mallery brings her signature humor and style to this moving story of strong women who help each other deal with realistic challenges, a tale as appealing as the fiction of Debbie Macomber and Anne Tyler."
—*Booklist* on *California Girls*

"Mallery's authentic characters and their refreshing summer escapades are sure to resonate. The emphasis on the power of friendship and the joy of new romance make this sparkling novel a sure hit with women's fiction fans."
—*Publishers Weekly* on *The Friendship List*

"Susan Mallery never disappoints and with *Daughters of the Bride* she is at her storytelling best."
—Debbie Macomber, #1 *New York Times* bestselling author

"Mallery's latest novel is a breath of fresh air for romantics, a sweet reminder that falling in love is never how you plan it and always a pleasant surprise."
—*Library Journal* on *The Summer of Sunshine & Margot*, starred review

"The characters will have you crying, laughing, and falling in love.... Another brilliantly well-written story."
—*San Francisco Book Review* on *The Friends We Keep*, 5 stars

"Heartfelt, funny, and utterly charming all the way through!"
—Susan Elizabeth Phillips, *New York Times* bestselling author, on *Daughters of the Bride*

"Heartwarming... This book is sweet and will appeal to readers who enjoy the intricacies of family drama."
—*Publishers Weekly* on *When We Found Home*

"It's not just a tale of how true friendship can lift you up, but also how change is an integral part of life.... Fans of Jodi Picoult, Debbie Macomber, and Elin Hilderbrand will assuredly fall for *The Girls of Mischief Bay*."
—*Bookreporter*

"Mallery combines heat and sweet in a delicious tale destined for beach blankets."
—*Publishers Weekly* on *The Summer of Sunshine & Margot*

"This engaging story explores the power that lifelong friendship and unconditional love have to help us through life's challenges. Told with a style as authentic as it is entertaining, this book is for the author's many fans as well as those who enjoy Debbie Macomber and Susan Wiggs."
—*Library Journal* on *The Friendship List*

SUSAN MALLERY

the stepsisters

mira

mira™

Recycling programs
for this product may
not exist in your area.

ISBN-13: 978-0-7783-3180-3

The Stepsisters

This is a work of fiction. Names, characters, places and incidents are either the product
of the author's imagination or are used fictitiously. Any resemblance to actual persons,
living or dead, businesses, companies, events or locales is entirely coincidental.

This edition published by arrangement with Harlequin Books S.A.

For questions and comments about the quality of this book, please contact us at
CustomerService@Harlequin.com.

Mira
22 Adelaide St. West, 40th Floor
Toronto, Ontario M5H 4E3, Canada
BookClubbish.com

Printed in Italy by Grafica Veneta

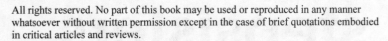

To Kelly, MSN, CRNA. You know who you are!

Thank you so much for your help with my research.
You helped define Daisy's work life, which helped define
who she was as a person. You were so patient with me.
Any mistakes with the technical mentions of anesthesiology are mine.

And to stepsisters everywhere. It's not always an easy relationship,
but I hope that with patience and understanding,
it's a wonderfully supportive one.

Last but not least, if anyone actually owns an Hermès Birkin crocodile bag,
please post a picture on my Facebook page. I would really like to see one
out in the wild! www.Facebook.com/SusanMallery

the stepsisters

one

"Mom, I think I'm going to throw up."

Daisy Bosarge felt the fear that was universal in the parenting world when Krissa uttered those eight little words. Even more concerning was the fact that her son was already home with stomach flu.

She'd known better than to let her daughter go to school this morning, she thought ruefully, but Krissa had begged and Daisy had been late for work and it had just seemed easier to say yes. A decision that was getting ready to bite her in the butt as she drove as fast as she could, given the traffic on the road.

"Ten more minutes," she said, glancing at her eight-year-old in the back seat. "We'll be there in ten minutes."

"I don't feel good."

"I know, sweetie. I'm going to get you home."

At least cajoling her daughter was better than trying to avoid looking at the ominous Check Engine light that had popped on right before Daisy had arrived at the school to pick up her daughter. Yet another problem she didn't have time to deal with.

Priorities, she told herself. Get Krissa home and in bed, look in on Ben, then make an appointment to take her Mercedes to the dealership. After that, she would—

"Mommy, I'm going to throw up now!"

Daisy held in a moan. She carefully checked her mirrors before pulling to the side of the road.

"Just a second," she murmured, knowing at this point there weren't any words in the world that would keep the inevitable from happening.

Seconds later her day took yet another unfair turn as her daughter threw up all over herself, the back seat and the carpet. The smell and the sound of Krissa bursting into tears hit her at the same time.

She put on her flashers and raced around to the passenger side, where she helped her daughter out onto the sidewalk. Cars drove by so close, Daisy felt the whoosh of air as they passed. She kept hold of her daughter as she circled to the trunk, where she kept her emergency tote filled with paper towels, wipes and a shirt for each of her kids.

She cleaned off her daughter's face, then reached for the hem of her T-shirt.

"Let me get this off you," she said. "I have a fresh one right here."

But Krissa stopped her, tugging the shirt back in place.

"No!" she shrieked, looking around frantically. "I'm outside. Someone will see."

Someone who? Krissa was eight and the car was between them and the traffic, with Daisy blocking their view.

"Can you change in the front seat?" she asked, trying to sound reasonable, instead of close to losing it.

"No." Tears spilled down her daughter's flushed cheeks. "Mommy, no!"

The headache that had started a little before noon clicked up a level or two, with a steady pressure building right between her eyes. She ignored the pain and put her hand on her daughter's forehead, feeling the heat there. Before she could figure out what to do, Krissa threw up again, this time down the front of Daisy's scrubs and on her shoes.

Krissa's tears increased and at that moment, Daisy really wanted to join in. She'd had a bad day at work, both her kids were sick, she was never getting the vomit smell out of her car and just because there wasn't already enough crap in her life, her husband had moved out two days ago. To "give them both space to think," as he'd phrased it.

In a text.

Jerk, she thought, feeling the familiar fury tinged with a hint of panic. Although the real word was closer to *asshole* than *jerk*. How could he have done that to—

One step at a time, she told herself. First, she had to get Krissa home, then the car, then—

Out of the corner of her eye, she saw a dark blue BMW slow as it drove past. She wanted to yell out something vulgar to the voyeur, but knew that would set a bad example, so she instead forced a smile.

"Sweetie, let me clean the back seat so you can get in. You can change your shirt in there, and no one will see. All right?"

Krissa nodded reluctantly.

Daisy planted her where she could see her, then cleaned up the mess as best she could. In the eighty-plus-degree weather that was spring in Los Angeles, the interior of the car was already heating up. The smell nearly made her gag. Blood she could handle just fine. Open up a body and she was okay with that, but this? A nightmare.

She finished her work and coaxed Krissa closer to the car only to notice the BMW driving by again, but with the sun hitting the side window, she couldn't see who was driving.

Better to ignore them, she told herself, slipping off her daughter's school uniform polo shirt and putting on a T-shirt with Elsa from *Frozen* on the front. Sadly she had nothing for herself to change into. She wiped up her pants and shoes and was about to try to buckle Krissa in when the BMW pulled up to the curb behind her car.

Daisy told herself not to panic, even as she wished for lethal training in some kind of karate. Or a can of pepper spray. Was that legal in Los Angeles? Before she could decide, the driver's door opened and a tall, beautiful blonde woman stepped out.

Daisy silently ran through all the swear words she knew, created a few unique combinations, then wanted to know why God currently hated her because there was no other explanation for Sage Vitale to be walking toward her, looking as fabulous as only Sage could in skinny jeans and a flowy top that made her appear sexy and ethereal at the same time. Four-inch-heel boots completed the look. Daisy, on the other hand, had been up since four, hadn't showered since yesterday and hey, the vomit.

Last she'd heard, Sage was in Italy, married to a count. Because that was Sage's life. Race car drivers and counts and being tall and skinny and beautiful. Daisy was smart and had a sparkling personality. It just wasn't fair.

Sage looked from her to her daughter. "Daisy? I thought that was you when I drove by. Are you okay?"

No. No, she wasn't. Any idiot could see that. Her kid was obviously sick, Daisy had puke on her pants and shoes, so no. Not okay.

"We're fine," Daisy said, trying not to clench her teeth. Her dentist had told her that if she didn't learn to relax, she was going to have to wear a mouth guard at night to stop herself from grinding her teeth. She felt her bedtime routine already lacked a certain sex appeal and she sure didn't need a mouth guard adding to the problem.

"You don't seem fine," Sage said, her nose wrinkling, no doubt from the smell.

"Who are you?" Krissa asked.

"I'm, um, I'm…"

"This is Sage. She's my stepsister." Or at least she had been, once.

Krissa rubbed her suddenly running nose. "So you're my aunt?"

"No," Daisy said firmly. "Please buckle up so we can get home."

For once, Krissa didn't complain or talk back. Instead she buckled her seat belt, twisting her head to keep looking at Sage. Daisy thought about warning her of the danger of that. Sage was like the sun and if you stared at her too long, there was permanent damage.

Later she would think about what quirk of fate had her former stepsister driving by at the exact moment she was at her lowest. LA had a population of what, eight million people? What were the odds? Although she supposed they did live close. Sort of. But still!

She forced a tight smile. "Thank you for stopping. It was very kind."

"I couldn't believe it was you, standing there on the side of the road," Sage admitted. "I knew you had kids, but seeing you with your daughter… It's just strange."

"We haven't really kept in touch," Daisy said, inching toward her door.

"Right. We haven't seen each other since your wedding."

Daisy stared at her stepsister. Really? Sage had gone there? "Yes, my wedding twelve years ago, where you announced to everyone in the room that you were still in love with the man I was marrying. It was great."

Sage flushed. "It wasn't *exactly* like that."

Oh, yes it was, but Daisy didn't want to stay and chitchat. "Thanks again."

She waved and ducked into her car.

"She's really pretty," Krissa said admiringly. "I like what she's wearing."

"It's jeans and a shirt," Daisy snapped before she could stop herself. "Sorry. I'm tired. Let's get you home."

In the rearview mirror she saw Sage get back in her car. Their eyes met briefly in the mirror, then Daisy focused her attention on starting her car. She pushed the button to engage the engine…and nothing happened. The dashboard lights came on, along with the red Check Engine light, but the engine stayed silent.

Daisy grabbed the steering wheel with both hands and tried not to scream. She didn't want to scare her daughter and possibly herself by giving in to the crazy building up inside of her but why did this have to happen?

Someone knocked on her window. She rolled it down.

"You okay?" Sage asked.

"Not really. My car won't start."

"Want me to take you home?"

Daisy thought about saying she would call an Uber or Lyft or something, but figured that fate was messing with her and she might as well simply surrender. The sooner she got through whatever hell this was, the sooner it would be over. Later, when the kids were in bed and she had showered, she would review her life and try to decide where she'd messed up so much that she had to be punished. But for now, she had a sick kid and someone willing to give her a ride.

"Thank you," she said through clenched teeth, looking into the beautiful green eyes of the one woman on the planet she hated more than anyone. "That would be great."

"How long have you known my mom?" Krissa asked, suddenly sounding significantly better than she had five minutes ago. Yet more proof of Sage's endless powers, Daisy thought bitterly as she buckled her seat belt.

"Since we were young," Sage told her. "I think we were eight or nine."

"I'm eight!" Krissa's tone indicated there was magic afoot. "But I don't understand. You were stepsisters. So Grandpa was married to..."

"Sage's mother," Daisy explained. "For about six years. Do you remember Aunt Cassidy?"

"I don't think so." Her tone was doubtful. "Is she pretty like Sage?"

"Yes." Annoyingly so. "Cassidy is our half-sister. My father, your grandfather, is her dad and Sage's mother is Cassidy's mom. I'm sure you've met Cassidy at least once."

She glanced over her shoulder and saw Krissa's face scrunch up, as if she were trying to work it all out.

"She's your aunt," Sage offered.

"Then why don't I know her?"

An excellent question, Daisy thought. One of the answers might be that since the divorce all those years ago, Cassidy had made it clear she preferred Sage to Daisy and once Cassidy had turned eighteen, she'd taken off to explore the world. She stayed in touch with Wallace, their mutual father, but not with Daisy.

"You don't hear from her?" Sage asked, driving through one of the open gates that marked the entrance to Bel Air. "I'm surprised."

Are you really? But Daisy didn't actually ask the question. What was the point? In a battle of the sisters, she had always come in last. When she'd been a child herself, she hadn't understood why she and Sage couldn't be friends. Unlike many only children, she'd been delighted when her father had told her he was marrying Joanne and giving her a stepsister. She'd imagined having someone to play with, a friend to confide in. She'd wanted a connection, a best friend, a closeness that always seemed to exist between sisters she read about or saw on TV.

But Sage had rebuffed every overture. Even when she was friendly for an afternoon, the next day, she would be cold and distant. At school, she delighted in mocking Daisy. Sage might have been the new girl at their exclusive private school, but Daisy was the one who had felt left out.

Sage glanced in the rearview mirror. "Your aunt Cassidy is a travel writer. She goes all over the world and writes about interesting places and people. Right now she's in Patagonia studying a group of women selling textiles."

Krissa's eyes widened. "She sounds cool."

"Even saint-like," Daisy murmured under her breath, before pointing to the street on the right. "It's just up there."

Sage smiled. "I remember where the house is."

"I wasn't sure."

It had been a long time—over twenty years since Wallace and Joanne had divorced, although they'd shared custody of their daughter. Cassidy had gone back and forth between the houses right through high school. Sage had probably dropped her off or picked her up more than once.

Daisy instinctively pointed toward the long driveway. Sage laughed and repeated, "I know where I'm going."

Which made Daisy feel foolish—a usual state of being when Sage was around.

"I'm surprised you're in Los Angeles," she said, mostly to distract herself. "Aren't you living in Italy?"

"Rome," Sage corrected. "I was."

"You live in Rome?" Krissa's disbelieving tone made it sound as if her almost-aunt had a pied-à-terre on Jupiter. "That's in the EU."

"It's very beautiful there." She glanced at Daisy. "I came home a couple of weeks ago. My mom was dealing with a cancer scare."

And just like that, all Daisy's mad deflated, leaving her feeling small and mean-spirited.

"I'm sorry," she said. "If you'd like a recommendation for an oncologist, I can get you some names."

Something flickered across Sage's perfect face. "Thank you, but it turned out just to be a scare. She's fine now."

She reached the end of the long driveway and stared up at the big house.

"It looks the same."

The inside was different, Daisy thought. They'd updated the kitchen and family room. The master bedroom and bath had also been redone, a remodel completed when Wallace had moved out, allowing Daisy and Jordan to live in the big house. Not that she was going to discuss any of that with Sage.

"The neighborhood hasn't changed much," Daisy said as the car came to a stop. "There have been a few tear-downs but mostly we like to keep things as they are around here." She unfastened her seat belt and drew in a breath.

"Thank you for stopping. You didn't have to."

Sage frowned. "Of course I stopped. I wasn't going to just leave you there, on the side of the road."

Information Daisy found surprising. Until thirty minutes ago, she would have absolutely assumed Sage would drive by without a second thought.

She helped Krissa out of the car. "Thank you again."

Sage waved and pulled away from the house, while Daisy helped her daughter up the stairs leading to the double front doors.

Once out of the rarified Sage-infused air, Krissa seemed to

fall back into whatever flu had claimed her. She sagged against Daisy and wrapped her arms around her belly.

"I still don't feel good."

"I know, sweetie. Let's get you to bed."

She was about to dig out her key when the front door opened. Esmerelda, the housekeeper-slash-nanny-slash-glue that held them all together, waved them inside.

"What happened?" She reached for Krissa and pressed a hand to her forehead. "I knew you would get what your brother has. You threw up, didn't you?"

Krissa's eyes filled with tears. "In the car."

"That's not good." Esmerelda hugged her close. "Poor you. You're home now and I'm going to take care of everything."

Krissa leaned against her, the tears slowing.

Esmerelda glanced toward the front door. "Where's your car?"

"On the side of the road. After I pulled over when Krissa threw up, it wouldn't start again. I need to call the dealership."

"Then who drove you home?"

"Sage."

Esmerelda had started working for the family long after the divorce, but even so, her brown eyes narrowed and her mouth thinned.

"The stepsister?"

Her tone indicated she had as much love for Sage as for cockroaches.

"She stopped to help out. Under the circumstances, I was grateful." Confused, but grateful.

"Mommy, I—"

That was as much as Krissa managed ahead of another wave of vomit. Esmerelda was nimble enough to get out of the way and the marble floor would mop up easily, so Daisy hoped that maybe her luck was changing.

She reached for her daughter. "I'll get her cleaned up and settled. If you could bring up some ginger ale, please."

Esmerelda nodded, already texting to ask one of the daily housekeeping staff to clean up the mess. Daisy made a mental note to tell the bookkeeper to give everyone a bonus that week, what with all the extra laundry and the kids throwing up everywhere.

Daisy had barely taken two steps when Sheba and Lucky came racing down the stairs. They made a beeline for Krissa, sniffing frantically. Lucky gave her a worried look, before glancing at Daisy, as if seeking confirmation that something wasn't right.

"She'll be fine," Daisy assured the yellow Lab. "Just like Ben."

By the time Daisy had cleaned up her daughter and gotten her into a nightgown, Esmerelda was waiting in Krissa's bedroom, the covers on the bed pulled back and a mug on the nightstand. Daisy fluffed the pillows behind Krissa. Lucky climbed onto the foot of the bed, as if prepared to guard her against all comers.

"Do you think you can sip a little ginger ale?" she asked.

Krissa nodded.

As she took a few shallow drinks, Daisy studied her daughter's flushed face. The bug seemed to last about forty-eight hours. Hopefully she would start to feel better in the next day or so.

Krissa handed back the mug and slipped down onto the pillows. "I'm tired."

"I bet you are."

Daisy gently smoothed her hair off her forehead. The color, a deep, dark brown, came from both her parents, but her hazel eyes had been inherited from her father, as had the shape of her face and her mouth. She had Daisy's sturdy build, something she would resent later in life.

At least Krissa was able to talk and say what was wrong. Daisy remembered the terror of the first time her oldest had gotten sick. Ben had spiked a fever at four months, sending her into a tailspin of fear and panic. Telling herself to suck it up and be strong hadn't made a difference.

Jordan had handled the situation like a pro. He'd confirmed what to do with the pediatrician, then had given Ben Tylenol and a sponge bath. Within a couple of hours, his fever had dropped and he was sleeping comfortably.

"But I'm a nurse," she'd said, feeling inept and useless. "I should have handled it."

"You're a new mom. It's normal to panic. When it happens again, you'll be fine."

He'd been right. Ben's next fever hadn't thrown her at all. But that first time had been a nightmare. One she wouldn't have survived without her husband at her side. They'd had it all together once—where exactly had it gone wrong?

She turned to her housekeeper.

"If she can keep the ginger ale down, give her the children's Tylenol in twenty minutes. It will help with the fever." She smiled at Krissa. "Esmerelda already put out the baby monitor. Just call if you need something and we'll come running."

Krissa managed a faint smile. "No running in the house. It's the rules."

"You're right. Try to sleep, baby girl. I love you."

"I love you, too, Mommy."

Daisy and Esmerelda stepped into the hallway.

"I'll stay close," Esmerelda promised. "Twenty minutes and Tylenol."

"Thank you. I'm going to check on Ben."

Her son's room was across the hall. Like Krissa's room, it

was large, with big windows and high ceilings. The en-suite bathroom was larger than most master baths—one of the realities of living in a fifteen-thousand-square-foot house. There weren't all that many extra rooms, but the rooms they did have were huge.

Ben was still in bed, but sitting up and reading on his tablet, Sheba already back in her place in the middle of his bed. Simba the cat stretched out against her favorite dog.

Ben smiled when he saw her. "Hey, Mom."

"Hey, yourself."

He was ten, with sandy brown hair and the same hazel eyes as his sister. More serious and intellectual than Krissa, he'd always been older than his years.

"Your sister is sick. You have powerful germs, young man."

He grinned and flexed his right arm. "I'm super strong."

"You are." She sat on his bed and kissed the top of his head. "How are you feeling?"

"Better. I had soup for lunch and toast. Esmerelda says I can come downstairs tonight." He looked at her. "Mom, I want to do my homework. If I don't, I'll fall behind."

"I think the odds of you falling behind are incredibly slim." She glanced at her watch. "All right. You can get up and sit at your desk for an hour, but only an hour. Then back to bed."

He grinned and scrambled to his feet. Sheba watched to see what was happening, then when Ben only went as far as his desk, she settled back to sleep.

Daisy looked around the room. When Ben had been ready to leave the nursery and move into his "big boy" bedroom, she'd redone the whole space. The neutral, masculine colors would carry him through college. The bed and dressers were new, but the captain's desk was old—salvaged from an eighteenth-century sailing ship. It was elegant, with just enough scars to be interesting.

This had been Sage's room, she thought, trying to remember what it had looked like back then. The furniture had been lighter, the drapes more frilly. She remembered a big dollhouse in the corner. A dollhouse that had been relocated from the playroom to Sage's personal space—something Daisy had always resented.

But her father had reasoned that the move had been hard on Sage. She was leaving everything she'd known to come live with them and it was up to Daisy to make her feel welcome. It hadn't taken long for Daisy to realize that the only person who didn't belong here anymore was her.

Even after the divorce, things hadn't gotten much better. Because of the joint custody arrangement with Cassidy, Sage and her mother had moved into a house in the area and Sage had continued to attend the same private school. Daisy couldn't escape Sage's reign as queen of the mean girls. Being smart didn't matter if you were also overweight and anything but pretty.

"That was a long time ago," Daisy whispered as she walked out of the bedroom. These days she and Sage were practically strangers. She didn't need to dwell on the past. Running into her former stepsister had been a onetime thing. What were the odds of it happening again anytime soon? A million to one, she promised herself.

two

After making arrangements to have her car picked up and taken to the service department at the dealership, Daisy checked on Krissa one more time before heading to the opposite end of the second floor. The master suite was large, encompassing several rooms, including a study she used as her home office, along with his-and-her bathrooms and closets.

She grabbed jeans, a T-shirt, fresh underwear and a bra before heading into her bathroom. She pinned up her hair and then stepped into the steamy shower.

Alone for the first time all day, she allowed herself to think about Jordan. At some point she was going to have to let him know that now Krissa was sick. He was, after all, their father.

Bitterness welled up inside of her. Yes, he was their father and he was also the man who had walked out on his wife and kids two days ago, with no warning. She'd finished her shift, gone to her locker and had found a text from him saying that he was going to be moving out for a few days. Just like that. No conversation, no explanation, just him gone.

She'd been stunned, hurt, outraged and scared. Fortunately outrage had won, allowing her to hold it all together. Because while he'd been in a hotel somewhere, she was left with everything else, including letting their kids know their father was gone.

She'd told him it was unfair to scare them with what was happening. He'd agreed and they'd decided to tell Ben and Krissa that he was away at a conference. But that excuse would only last for so long, she thought as she stepped out of the shower and grabbed a towel. At some point she and Jordan were going to have to talk about what was happening in their marriage. Easier said than done considering she didn't know herself.

Oh, sure they fought from time to time and for the past few weeks, he'd seemed quiet. And lately they'd both been busy and hadn't had much time for each other, but that was normal. Life got in the way, then they worked on fixing the problem. Only Jordan didn't seem interested in fixing so much as going for the dramatic gesture.

As she dressed, she tried to figure out what he was thinking. Resentment kept clouding her judgment, making her want to grab him by his shirtfront and shake some sense into him. Given that she wasn't especially strong and that he was a good eight inches taller, the odds of that happening seemed unlikely.

She slipped on flats, then grabbed her phone. She should let the school know she was keeping—

I'm moving into an extended-stay hotel later today so it's easier for me to have the kids over while we figure out what's going on with us.

She stared at the text. Fury overtook outrage. "No you didn't."

She hit the call button and waited, knowing there was a better than even chance he wouldn't pick up. The phone rang and rang. She wasn't sure if he was avoiding her or with a patient. She was about to hang up when he answered.

"You got my text," Jordan said by way of greeting.

"Yes, I did. Really? Is this how you wanted to tell me what was happening? By text? You couldn't face me in person or call? Let me answer the damned question. What's going on with us is you left. You just walked out with no warning, leaving me to pick up the pieces. Has it occurred to you that your inability to communicate might be part of the reason we're having problems in the first place?"

"Why do you always get like this?"

The unfair statement nearly left her speechless. "You moved into a hotel. You didn't talk to me, you texted me. When I tried calling, you wouldn't pick up. I still don't know why you left. It was supposed to be for a few days. Now you tell me, again by text, that you're checking into a long-term-stay hotel. Not that we've talked about anything. You're just gone. And you want to know why I get like this?"

"I can't talk to you when you're unreasonable."

Anger built up inside of her, accompanied by a big dose of fear. Because somehow that was always what happened—no matter how things started, he found a way to shut her down. If she shrieked back at him, which she wanted to do, she was proving his point. What was the right response?

"Krissa is sick," she said instead. "She's throwing up and she has a fever. Ben's better, but obviously he passed what he had along to her. Is it unreasonable to ask you to check on your kid?"

"Your sarcasm doesn't help."

"Neither does you blaming me for everything and then walking away. If you want to have a conversation about what we're going to tell our children about you moving out, then I suggest we get that on the calendar."

"I'll be there after work."

"Great." She opened her mouth to say more, but he'd already disconnected the call.

★ ★ ★

Much like the moneyed streets of Bel Air, the private school Sage Vitale had attended from third through twelfth grade was surprisingly unchanged. The wood paneling still gleamed, the students still wore black pants and white polo shirts as their uniforms. The computers appeared sleeker, but otherwise, she could have easily thought she had stepped back in time. Even Mrs. Lytton wasn't that different. Her short, sensible haircut had a bit of gray in it, and reading glasses perched on the edge of her nose were a change, but otherwise the stern head of the languages department looked as she had twenty years ago.

"You're late," Mrs. Lytton said as Sage walked into her office and took a seat. "By nearly half an hour. I shouldn't have to remind you that our students are expected to be prompt and those around them are expected to set an example. Especially our tutors."

As a teenager, Sage would have slumped in her seat, allowing her posture and her eye roll to demonstrate how little she cared what Mrs. Lytton thought of her. Older and (hopefully) wiser Sage knew that attitude would get her nowhere.

"I am late," she said, offering her best smile. The one that nearly always worked on difficult clients. "I stopped to help someone with car trouble."

Mrs. Lytton's thin mouth pressed into a flat line. "Really, Sage? Is that the best you can do? You were always so inventive with your excuses. My favorite was the time you claimed to have stopped to rescue baby ducks from a bobcat prowling the streets of Bel Air."

"I was helping Daisy," Sage said. It was early to play such a powerful card, but Mrs. Lytton had left her no choice. "Krissa threw up in the car and Daisy had to pull over. I saw them and stopped to help. Then her car wouldn't start, so I drove them home. That's why I'm late." She offered a forgiving smile.

"You're welcome to check with her, if you'd like. Apparently Ben got the flu first and now poor Krissa has it."

Mrs. Lytton's eyebrows rose. "Well, if you were helping Daisy, then of course it's all right. I didn't know you two were still close."

They weren't. Not back when their parents had first married, not after the divorce and certainly not now. If Sage went the rest of her life and never saw her former stepsister again, she could die a happy person.

"We're family," Sage said simply, comfortable with the lie.

"All right, then let's get to it." Mrs. Lytton opened a folder on her desk before saying in Italian, "I understand you lived in Italy for nearly three years. Are you conversational?"

Sage answered in the same language. "Yes, and I have a basic understanding of grammar. My French is better. I lived in France nearly fifteen years. I'm fluent in both languages."

Mrs. Lytton switched to French. "Your first husband was French?"

"Yes." The third had been Italian. She didn't talk about the second one.

The department head ran her through a series of grammar drills, had her read from a book of French poetry, along with an Italian fashion magazine. When they were done, the older woman leaned back in her chair.

"You have a decent enough understanding of both languages," she said, her tone faintly grudging. "The pay is twenty-five dollars an hour with a thirty-minute minimum. We'll get you set up on the school's app and students can book you when you're available."

Her gaze dropped to the Prada handbag Sage had set in the chair next to her own. "Are you sure you want to do this, Sage? Aren't there other things you would rather do with your time?"

"I've been giving English lessons in France and Italy since I moved to Europe. I think it will be fun to switch things around."

"You're not going to get rich doing this."

Sage kept her smile in place as she said, "Yes, I know. But sometimes the joy of giving back is more than enough payment."

Mrs. Lytton made a sound that was suspiciously like a snort. "Very well. I'll walk you over to the front office, where we'll get you set up on the app. You should see bookings right away."

Sage followed the other woman down the long hallway. She was sure her willingness to tutor rich kids in French and Italian didn't make sense to anyone but her, and sometimes she wasn't sure about it, either, yet here she was.

The idea, born on the long flight from Italy to Los Angeles, had surprised her, not only with its arrival but with her own willingness to actually do the work to make it happen. She knew the reason was that tutoring was very close to teaching and lately she'd been thinking that maybe it was time to see if she could do that. *Maybe* being the operative word. Finding a rich husband while she still had her looks probably made a lot more sense. But every now and then a girl had to do something crazy, right? So she would tutor a few kids, conjugate a few verbs. If it got too tedious or she met someone interesting, then she could dump the whole thing. No one, least of all Mrs. Lytton, would be shocked if it turned out she had no follow-through.

By seven o'clock, Daisy thought she might have all the crises in her life a little more under control. Krissa hadn't thrown up since the afternoon, and Ben was definitely on the mend. She leaned against the kitchen counter and debated whether to eat dinner or simply have a glass of wine and call it a night. The sensible choice was to eat something and she was mostly a sensible person. But she also had to face Jordan sometime in the next hour or so, and right now she was feeling ill-equipped.

"When is Mr. Jordan coming by?" Esmerelda asked, wiping an already clean counter for the sixth time.

"He didn't say."

Daisy had already told the other woman about the phone call. Despite the size of the house, there weren't many secrets—not from Esmerelda. The housekeeper had figured out Jordan had left before Daisy had. She'd seen the empty hangers in his closet and the suitcase missing from the shelf.

"I have a nice pork chop for you," she said. "With the green beans and almonds. Or I could make you a salad. I roasted the golden beets you like."

"I can get myself dinner."

"You can do a lot of things, but that doesn't mean I'm not standing here, wanting to do my job."

Daisy smiled. "You're very sweet to me."

"You're family."

Employer/employee, but also family. Esmerelda's older cousin had been Daisy's nanny when she'd been growing up. Daisy had hired Esmerelda shortly before her wedding to Jordan. Esmerelda managed the house and helped with the kids. Daisy would be lost without her.

"Jordan's moving into a long-term-stay hotel," she said.

Esmerelda's concerned expression didn't change. "For how long?"

"I have no idea. He's on his way over so we can figure that out along with what to say to the kids. I'll eat after I talk to him," she said.

Esmerelda pressed her lips together. "After you talk to him, you won't feel like eating."

"So, hey, a new diet program. We could make a fortune."

Esmerelda murmured something Daisy couldn't hear and started pulling packages out of the refrigerator. She placed a small bowl of olives, several slices of cheeses and some crackers at one end of the massive island. While Daisy poured herself a glass of red wine, Esmerelda cut up an apple and added a few clusters of grapes.

"So the wine doesn't go to your head," she said, adding a cloth napkin.

"You are wise, as always."

On an empty stomach, Daisy was a total lightweight. Better to deal with Jordan with all her faculties intact. He was better at fighting than she was. She'd graduated from UCLA with a 4.0 GPA but she lacked the killer instinct to be a really good street fighter—at least when it came to her marriage.

As she picked up a slice of Brie and put it on a rosemary cracker, she supposed not being good at the emotional dig was something she should be happy about. If only she wasn't always the one getting gut-punched and left on the side of the marital road.

She was just polishing off her snack when Jordan arrived. Esmerelda let him in while Daisy considered pouring a second glass of wine.

"Not the best idea," she murmured as she braced herself for the upcoming conversation. Figuring out what to tell their children about their separation wasn't going to be easy. She should have made some notes beforehand. They needed a strategy.

Jordan breezed into the kitchen. In the past, the sight of his tall, lean body and easy stride would have had her stomach doing cartwheels. Several years into their marriage, he'd still had the ability to make her heart beat faster. Just not lately. As her gaze met his, she felt only dread and a longing for when it had been, if not easy, then at least comfortable between them.

"How are the kids?" he asked, pouring himself a glass of wine.

"Better." She pointed to the back staircase. "You want to go see for yourself?"

He took a big swallow, put down the glass and went upstairs. She followed, wanting to know what was said. A realization that didn't speak well of the trust between them.

He went into Krissa's room first. Their daughter opened her eyes and smiled at him.

"Daddy, you're back! How was the conference?"

He sat on the edge of her bed and smoothed her dark hair off her face. "More important, chipmunk, how are you? Mom said you got sick."

"Uh-huh. Ben had a virus."

"And he shared it with you? We'll have to talk to him about that."

She sat up to hug him. Lucky must have heard his voice because the yellow Lab came racing into the room, tail wagging. Sheba jumped off the bed and wanted her share of attention. Even the normally aloof feline Nala seemed relatively pleased to see Jordan. At least that was Daisy's interpretation of her tail flick.

Jordan petted both dogs and spent a few minutes rubbing ears and accepting kisses, then he gathered Krissa in his arms and stood.

"Let's go see your brother."

Daisy started to tell him that Krissa should stay in bed, then reminded herself that doing so would cause father and daughter to give her that look they shared, the one that said she hated when they had fun. Which probably wasn't what they were thinking at all, but was what always came to mind for her.

They all trooped into Ben's room, the dogs leading the way. Ben, in bed, playing on his tablet, looked up and grinned when he saw Jordan.

"Dad! You're back."

Jordan put Krissa down and hugged Ben. "My man, how are you feeling?"

"Better. Krissa's sick now."

"That's your fault," Krissa told him, climbing onto the bed and slipping under the covers. Lucky climbed up next to her and Sheba settled on the foot, making the full-size bed suddenly a little small.

Daisy sat at the desk chair, figuring they would all talk for a bit, then she and Jordan would excuse themselves to discuss the next step, so she wasn't prepared for Jordan to say, "I want you to know we love you both very much."

She stood and stared at him. "What are you doing?"

He waved his hand in her direction without looking at her, as if brushing her off.

"You know how sometimes there's too much going on and you need quiet time in your room?" he asked.

Both of their children stared at him, wide-eyed. Ben nodded slowly.

"Jordan," Daisy said, walking toward him. "We need to talk first."

"I've got this." He smiled at the kids. "Sometimes parents need a time-out, too."

She swore silently. "Jordan, they're sick. This isn't the time."

Tears filled Krissa's eyes. "What are you s-saying?" Her voice cracked. "Daddy, no!"

"It's okay," he told her.

Ben's lower lip trembled and he glanced between them. "Mom?"

She moved close and offered what she hoped was a comforting smile. "It's okay. You're going to be fine. We love you, like your dad said. The thing is…"

She paused, mostly because she didn't know what the thing was at all.

Krissa's crying turned to sobs and Ben had to brush his eyes. Daisy thought longingly of being strong enough to cuff her husband on the back of his head—an immature and unhelpful wish, but one that was heartfelt.

She shooed Lucky and Sheba off the bed, then sat down and held open her arms. Both kids flung themselves at her.

"Your dad is going to be staying nearby for a little while," she said, furious that they were winging this rather than deciding what to say in advance. But that was how Jordan rolled—create a problem, then leave her to clean it up. "You're going to see him all the time. Once he and I talk some things out, we'll go back to how it was."

As she spoke, she glared at him, silently daring him to contradict her. He only shrugged.

"Are you getting a divorce?" Ben asked.

"No. Goodness, no. We haven't talked about that at all."

Which was true. They hadn't talked about anything.

"You're going to stay right where you are," she continued. "Going to school, hanging out with your friends."

"You'll be here?" Krissa asked earnestly.

Daisy kissed her. "I will."

"And Esmerelda?"

Jordan stiffened at that question.

"And Esmerelda," Daisy confirmed. "This is just for a little while. Like I said, you'll be seeing your dad a lot. And you can always text him on my phone."

Jordan approached the bed. "I love you guys. You know that, right?"

The kids released her and stretched out in the bed. They looked at their dad and nodded. Daisy stood, motioning for the dogs to resume their places.

It took another fifteen minutes of quiet conversation and reassurances for order to be restored. Krissa insisted on staying in Ben's bed and for once, her brother didn't object. Proof of their upset, Daisy thought bitterly as she and Jordan finally went downstairs. Once they were in the kitchen, she turned on him.

"How could you just blurt it out without us talking first? Dammit, Jordan, they're kids. This is not a problem they should be dealing with. I said you and I should talk, not that you should drop a bomb on our kids. We should have had a plan."

He drained his wineglass. "Sometimes life happens, Daisy. You're the one always telling me how busy you are. I was just trying to help you get through your to-do list so I can get out of your way. No need to thank me."

The casual cruelty of his words shocked her. Jordan could be difficult, but he wasn't usually so mean to her.

"You were wrong and you know it," she snapped. "You can try to distract me by being a jerk, but that doesn't take away from what you did."

Instead of fighting back, he gave her a half smile. "I'm wrong so much around you that I wouldn't know what to do with myself if I wasn't."

"So none of this matters to you? We're all a joke?"

The smile faded. "You have no idea what I'm going through here. You don't know what it's like dealing with you and your life. I'm last on your list every time. The only joke around here is me and you go out of your way to make sure I know it."

With that, he walked out. Stopping him wasn't an option

because she couldn't speak. Or breathe. Or understand what had just happened.

He wasn't a joke—he was her husband. They were married and she had no idea why he was acting this way. Something was wrong—she got that—but she had no idea what.

She sank onto a stool by the island and poured herself another glass of wine. She was tired and sad and scared and a thousand other emotions she didn't want to name. She had work in the morning and for the first time maybe ever, she didn't want to go.

Esmerelda walked into the kitchen. "He's gone?"

Daisy nodded. "He told the kids." She felt her jaw clench and consciously relaxed.

"I thought you were going to come up with a plan together."

"Jordan isn't a fan of my plans."

Esmerelda stepped close and put a reassuring hand on Daisy's shoulder. "You're strong enough to handle this."

"I don't feel very strong right now."

"That doesn't matter. The truth is, you'll get through this because you have to. Your children need you."

Daisy knew at the very least, she had to fake holding it together. The alternative was to start screaming and that wouldn't end well. "Why do you always know the right thing to say?"

"I'm blessed with wisdom." Her humor faded. "Daisy, I worry about you."

"I'm fine." A lie, but what choice did she have? She was the one they all depended on. As her housekeeper had pointed out, holding the family together had always been her job. She forced a smile. "I mean it. You're right. We'll get through this."

"Good. Can I get you something to eat?"

Food was the last thing on Daisy's mind, but she knew she needed to pretend normal for as long as she could. "Yes, please. Let's go with the pork chop. That sounds delicious."

three

Sage did her best to ignore the dull ache in the small of her back as she drove home from work. Standing on her feet all day was no big deal, but doing it in four-inch heels was more of a challenge. Ten years ago, she hadn't given it a second thought, but she was closer to forty now than thirty. An incredibly depressing thought, so one she told herself to ignore.

She glanced around as she waited at the light, noting that while it was still chilly March in the rest of the country, in balmy Los Angeles, it was seventy-five and sunny. She'd missed this, she admitted. Paris was exciting, but could be so dreary in the winter, and Italy, while stunning, wasn't home. At least not since her husband had asked for a divorce. She was back—a total failure in every aspect of her life—but at least she was back where the sky was a perfect blue and being emotionally shallow was expected rather than frowned upon.

She drove into the neighborhood she and her mother had moved to all those years ago after Joanne and Wallace had divorced. The solidly middle-class homes were only a few miles from the refined enclave that was Bel Air, but they were light-years away in class and comfort. Bel-Air-adjacent, she and her friends had always joked.

The house had been part of Joanne's settlement. Wallace

had come into the marriage with family money that Joanne hadn't been able to touch, but he'd been a successful internist, and his salary and part ownership in the medical practice had been fair game. Joanne had used every tool at her disposal to get not only the house, but as much alimony as she could guilt him into paying. Joanne had resented the divorce and the fact that Wallace had continued to provide for Sage, despite the fact that she wasn't his daughter. He'd covered her ongoing tuition at the private school she'd attended during the marriage and had put aside some money for college. That money had funded Sage's move to Europe the summer she turned nineteen.

Sage pulled into the driveway and parked next to her mother's Lexus. They might be scrambling to pay their property tax bill, but they drove nice cars. An LA thing, she thought as she collected her handbag and the heels she'd kicked off as soon as she'd gotten in the car. Having money was always better, but even if you didn't, it was important to look as if you did. Around here, appearances mattered more than anything.

Sage got out and locked her car before heading for the front door. For a second, she paused to study the one-story ranch-style house with its big front window and small front porch. So different from Daisy's mansion, she thought. Joanne's entire house could fit in the kitchen and family room of Daisy's house with a few square feet to spare. Here there were only three bedrooms and two bathrooms. The backyard was a decent size, for the area. It was a normal, everyday kind of house. Nothing to be ashamed of, yet she had been. After the divorce, she'd been horrified at the thought of moving and had never brought friends home after school. How could she? They'd all seen Daisy's house.

Funny how time and distance changed things, she thought

as she walked inside. These days she was grateful to have somewhere to stay. Sure, she had to pay her mother a thousand dollars a month for the privilege of her room, but it was worth it. At least for now.

"It's me," she called, closing the front door behind her.

The rarely used living room led into an average-sized kitchen, with the family room to the left of that. The master bedroom and bathroom were off to the right and the two spare bedrooms and guest bath were on the other side.

"In here," her mother answered.

Sage found her mother in the family room, reading a magazine. Joanne glanced up and smiled at her.

"How was your day?"

"Good. I spent the morning doing inventory."

The annual accounting of stock had required her to start her day at eight, allowing her to leave at four. Of course she'd spent the first three hours without the chance of earning commission, so that sucked.

She was about to go back to her room to change when she recognized the red silk blouse her mother had on.

"Interesting top," Sage said dryly. "Did you go through my things?"

"I just wanted to have a look-see. This one is especially nice. Is it silk?"

"Yes. It was nearly four hundred euros."

"I do love quality." Her mother smiled. "I know you don't mind. We're practically the same size."

Joanne was in her late fifties but could pass for ten years younger. She worked hard to keep in shape but she was nearly two sizes bigger than Sage and the way the blouse pulled at the buttons and stretched at the shoulders illustrated that. Not that Sage would mention it. Instead she would be grateful that there was no way her mother could squeeze into her pants, and most of her dresses wouldn't fit. Her shoes were also safe, what with Joanne's feet being a size and a half smaller.

Her handbags were in danger, but Sage had only brought a few home with her. Joanne didn't know about the half dozen locked in the trunk of her car or the twenty or so that were carefully stored with a trusted friend in Rome. As far as her mother was concerned, Sage only had the one Prada that she used.

In the next few weeks, Sage was going to have to figure out a way to get the bags from Italy so she could start selling them for cash, but not until she had a safe place to store them. No way she could leave them in the house—not with her mother around.

"If you're going to keep it, I'm taking three hundred dollars off this month's rent," Sage told her.

"That's not fair. I needed a pick-me-up." Joanne sighed. "Anderson and I aren't seeing each other anymore."

Sage rubbed the small of her back. "Anderson is the current boyfriend?"

Joanne pouted. "Not anymore. He said he didn't see any reason for us to take things to the next level. He was happy with how they were."

"So sex but not marriage."

"Men are such pigs." Joanne tossed the magazine onto the coffee table. "He's nearly seventy. Frankly, he's not going to do better than me, but I guess he has to figure that out for himself."

Translation—Joanne had been dating Anderson because he was rich and old. A delicious combination for her mother, who strongly believed in marrying for money. She'd never gotten the big settlement she'd dreamed of, but she'd done well enough.

Never give your heart. That was Joanne's motto. Sage had

lived by those words, not that they'd served her especially well. Here she was, back where she'd started—working in retail and living with her mother. It was depressing enough to give a girl wrinkles.

"I'm seeing a couple of friends tonight," Joanne said, glancing at her watch. "We're going to get cocktails and see if we can find someone to buy us a nice dinner."

"Good luck with that."

Her mother smiled. "Don't wait up."

Sage nodded, then walked back to her bedroom. The space, crowded with a bed, dresser and desk, was much messier than when she'd left it early that morning. Several of her dresser drawers stood open, as did the closet doors. Clothes were strewn across the bed and chair. Her neatly arranged shoes had been pushed to the back of the closet.

Sage told herself there was no point in getting upset. Her mother was never going to change. Reality sucked and hers more than most. She'd been living in Europe for the past eighteen years. She had no credit or job history in the US, which made qualifying for an apartment tricky. Buying a small condo was out of the question—she didn't have the money.

Her only way out of the mess was to rent a room from her mom for a year, hold down a job and build up her credit score. She wasn't going to screw with her plan over a silk blouse.

She changed into jeans and a T-shirt, then cleaned up her room. By the time she was done, her mom was gone. Sage went into the kitchen and filled a tumbler with ice and water. She took it outside and sat on one of the lounge chairs in the shade. After taking a few deep breaths, she closed her eyes and tried to tell herself everything was going to be fine. She wasn't a big, fat failure with nothing to show for her life beyond a few handbags and a couple, or three, failed marriages.

She'd nearly convinced herself she would be all right when

she became aware of a steady clicking sound and opened her eyes. The house on the right was hidden behind a tall cinder block wall, but the one on the left was separated only by a low wooden fence. She could see the trees and the lawn, along with the covered patio where a man sat at a folding table, typing on a computer.

Sage grimaced, feeling violated by the presence of the neighbor. Why did he have to work outside when all she wanted was a little time alone? At least he hadn't spoken to her.

She closed her eyes again and tried to relax. She knew the house next door. Her friend Adam had lived there back when they'd both been in school. She had no idea what had happened to him.

She opened her eyes and studied her neighbor. He was about her age, with blond hair, like Adam's. Only it couldn't be him, could it?

The man glanced up and caught her staring at him. He smiled.

"Hello, Sage."

"How do you know who I am?" She supposed her mother could have told him but Joanne wasn't the type to be friendly with the neighbors.

"I've known you since we were thirteen." He pressed a hand to his chest. "You've forgotten me. I'm devastated."

It couldn't be him, could it? "Adam? Is that you?"

He smiled. "Bingo."

She grinned. "Bingo? Did you just say that?"

"It's my word when I'm surprised."

"You need a different word." She shook her head. "I can't believe it's really you." She took in the broad shoulders and chiseled face. "You look different."

"And you're exactly the same."

She sipped her water. "If only. So you still live at home?" That was sad. Hadn't he ever wanted a life?

Adam smiled at her. "No. I bought the house from my mom after my dad died and she moved to Vegas. Of the two of us, you're the only one still living at home."

She had no idea how he meant to deliver the words, but they landed like a slap. She offered him a tight smile as she grabbed her glass and stood.

"And here you are, back in the neighborhood," she said as lightly as she could. "It was really great to see you, Adam."

"Sage, wait," he said, coming to his feet. "I didn't mean it like that. Please."

She waved as she walked to the sliding glass door and stepped inside.

Once she'd locked the door behind her, she hurried to her room and sank onto the bed. She wasn't a failure—she *wasn't*. Nor did she care what someone as ordinary and stupid as Adam thought of her. She didn't care about anyone. She never had. It was safer that way. And being safe was the most important thing of all.

By Saturday, Ben and Krissa had both recovered from the stomach flu. They rose early and started the morning with a loud rendition of Marco Polo in the pool. By the time Daisy had dried them off, fed them and walked the dogs, it was time to get Ben to soccer practice. Jordan would be meeting them at the practice to take both kids for the day.

Daisy did her best to act casual, as if splitting their time between their parents was no big deal, but on the inside, she was a mess. Her stomach churned, she was tired from not sleeping and from one second to the next she wasn't sure if she was going to start yelling at everyone or burst into tears.

Most days she didn't mind the chaos of her life, but lately it was getting to her, no doubt the result of Jordan leaving her. She didn't know what his absence meant for their marriage. Worse, she had no idea *why* he'd left or what it would take to get him to come back. So far they weren't even talking. All communication continued to occur through texts, a practice that unsettled her, although not enough to make it stop. She supposed a part of her was terrified of what he would say if they actually did start having a conversation.

Which made her a coward, she thought, walking down the hall toward the kids' wing. Something she could live with because the alternative was knowing exactly what her husband was thinking and she had a bad feeling there wasn't going to be a "them" anymore.

Where had it gone? Once they'd been so good together. She remembered when Ben had been almost five and had wanted to play soccer. Daisy had confessed to Jordan that she didn't know the first thing about the game.

He'd immediately taken her out into their big backyard and had taught her the basics. They'd continued practicing together for several weeks until she was good enough to play with her five-year-old. Jordan had been sweet and loving and supportive. Where had that man gone?

"You about ready?" she asked as she stepped into Ben's room. He was dressed for soccer and holding a backpack.

"Did I pick the right stuff?" he asked, sounding worried. "Dad said to bring clothes for after practice."

Her stomach lurched. It had already started—the changes in their routine. What next?

She pushed worry away and smiled at her son. "I'm sure you did fine, but I'm happy to check. The thing is, kiddo, you're going to be what? Twenty minutes away? You can swing by if you forgot anything."

He visibly relaxed at her words. "You're right. I forgot."

"That's why you have me."

She looked inside the backpack. He'd put in athletic shoes, socks, jeans, underwear and a clean T-shirt.

"Perfection," she told him, ruffling his hair. "Let's add a couple of bottles of water so you stay hydrated. Remember, if you start to feel woozy or lightheaded, tell Coach. I let him know you're getting over the flu, so you might not be a hundred percent."

"I'm not going to faint, Mom." His tone indicated he found the concept both interesting and horrifying.

"Best if you don't."

They went downstairs to where Krissa was in the family room, both dogs stretched out beside her as she carefully tied a large hat on Sheba. Lucky already sported a black bowler hat on his head, giving him a jaunty look. When he spotted Daisy, he gave her a long-suffering look that seemed to say, *"Kids. What are you gonna do?"*

Daisy smiled at her patient dogs before calling Krissa. "Let's get going."

Krissa carefully kissed each dog on the nose, then got up and walked toward her brother.

"Mommy, is Daddy going to remember we need to eat lunch?" Krissa asked.

"I'm sure he will, but you are welcome to remind him."

"Okay. Can we go somewhere fun?"

"That's between you two and your dad. I'm sure he wants you to have a good time so if you have somewhere special in mind, you should ask."

She collected two bottles of water from the refrigerator and put them in an outside pocket of the backpack before opening a drawer and pulling out a cell phone. She waved it.

"I'm trusting you two with this."

Krissa's eyes widened. "The family cell phone?" Her tone was reverent.

Being given the sacred family cell phone was a big deal. Daisy had resisted the pressure to let her kids have their own phones. She and Jordan had agreed that twelve was plenty old enough to get a phone and their children weren't going to be allowed to have their own social media accounts until they were fourteen.

This being Los Angeles, they were driven everywhere, their school had a security system that rivaled any top-secret military installation, and when they were home, it was a good time to decompress. Cell phones seemed irrelevant.

"Just for the day," Daisy said, putting it into an inner pocket of the backpack and zipping it closed. "If something happens, you can reach me or Esmerelda."

Not that she expected anything to happen, but then she hadn't expected her husband of nearly twelve years to move out, either.

She got the kids into the car. The dealership had fixed some electrical problem and now her car was driving just fine. The detail department had done a great job getting rid of the vomit smell, for which she was incredibly grateful.

She drove to the soccer field, finding one of the last parking places. After giving her a hug good-bye, Ben raced over to join his team while Daisy got Krissa settled on the bleachers, the backpack at her feet. About fifteen minutes later, Jordan approached.

"Can you wait here for a second while I go talk to your dad?" she asked Krissa. "I won't be long."

Krissa nodded, more interested in what was happening on the field than in what the grown-ups might be talking about. Daisy walked over to meet her husband, careful to keep them out of earshot of the other parents.

"There's a change of clothes for Ben in the backpack," she said, pointing to where Krissa was sitting. "If you could help him remember it, I'd appreciate that."

It was only after she spoke that she thought maybe she should have offered some kind of greeting before jumping into the logistics of the handoff.

"I can do that," he said easily. "I'll have them back by five this afternoon."

She nodded. "Krissa wants to go somewhere fun for lunch. With her, that could mean anything."

He smiled. "I'll consider myself prepared."

They stared at each other, then glanced away. Daisy had no idea what else she was supposed to say, or even what she *wanted* to say. He'd moved out without warning, they hadn't talked about it once and now he was in an extended-stay hotel. Shouldn't there be at least one thing for them to talk about?

Worse, she had no idea how she felt. She usually alternated between confused, scared and furious, but seeing him left her feeling only hollow and numb.

"I told Ben to let Coach know if he starts to not feel well," she added. "It's only been a few days since he was sick. Oh, and there are a couple of bottles of water in the backpack. He needs to stay hydrated."

Jordan shoved his hands into the front pockets of his jeans. "Anything else?"

"I don't think so."

"Then I'll see you later."

The obvious dismissal cracked the wall she'd built around her emotions and they all came flooding out. Mad seemed to be winning but terror was right there behind. Didn't he miss her? Didn't their life matter to him?

"Jordan," she began, only to stop when he shook his head.

"Not now," he said quietly, a pleading tone in his voice. "Can we please not do this now?"

"Then when?"

"Soon."

He turned and headed for the bleachers. Krissa waved to him and pointed to the empty seat beside her. Jordan joined her and gave her a hug, then they both turned to watch the game. Daisy walked toward her car.

Once inside, she stared unseeingly out the windshield. Her stomach was a mess and her head hurt and she had no idea how to fix whatever was wrong in her marriage. Even more unsettling, she couldn't even begin to define the problems, which should probably be the first step. Was it her? Was it him? Had they accidentally created something toxic? How did anyone get through such a rough patch in a relationship?

She only had questions and absolutely no answers. More frightening than that was a nagging sense that she might be the only one searching for a solution and if that was true, could there even be a way back?

four

Sage supposed describing the Beverly Hills boutique where she worked as "upscale" was being redundant. In this part of town, money was required. Designers ruled, and in her store, it was all Italian, all the time.

When she'd decided to return to the States—although the word "decided" was a loose interpretation of what had happened—she'd known retail was her best bet. She'd worked in exclusive boutiques in Paris, Milan and Rome. She was used to dealing with incredibly wealthy women who not only expected deference and good service, but wanted someone who understood the pain of being them.

Despite being the new girl in the store, she was doing all right. There were enough walk-ins to keep her busy and the more established sales professionals had taken to passing off difficult clients to her. When that happened, Sage did her best to meet the challenge with style and cunning. Demanding bitches might not be fun, but they often had tons of money and if you tamed one, you had a loyal client for life.

Her theory was currently being tested by a thirtysomething who had come in looking for a dress for a cocktail party. So far Inocencia had rejected eight dresses. Just as thrilling, her ridiculous teacup Yorkie had peed on the rug and wouldn't stop barking.

The black-haired, blue-eyed beauty (Inocencia, not the dog) glared at her.

"You're not helping," she said, her voice rising in volume with every word. "I need something special. Why can't you get that through your thick head? Can you handle this or do I need to get someone with half a brain?"

The loathing in the words was mitigated by the fact that Inocencia was wearing nothing but a thong. She had an amazing body, including perfect breasts, the product of excellent plastic surgery.

Sage considered her options. She was running out of size zero dresses for her client, but really didn't want to lose the sale. It was time to put on a show.

"It must be difficult to find something extraordinary when you already have so many lovely clothes," Sage said in English, before deliberately switching to Italian. *"Sono assolutalmente d'accordo."*

Inocencia stared at her suspiciously. "What did you say?"

Sage blinked innocently, before slapping her hand over her mouth. "Oh, no!" She dropped her arm to her side. "I apologize. I'm still speaking in Italian, I mean. English is obviously my first language, but I've only been back a few weeks." She smiled winningly. "I said I absolutely agree with you."

"You lived in Italy?" Inocencia asked.

"I did. I moved to Europe after high school. First I worked in Paris, then Milan and finally in Rome. It's great to be home, but there are adjustments." She laughed. "I'd forgotten how in LA we all drive everywhere. In Europe, everyone walks to everything. I miss that. And the history. Especially in Rome. There's a beautiful statue around every corner. Here, billboards."

Inocencia relaxed. "You worked in retail?"

"Yes. Designer boutiques. What a thrill to see the clothes created and then produced. Everything was couture. I wish I had a few of those dresses for you." She lowered her voice. "Not everyone who can afford that kind of fashion has the, ah, ability to display it as it's meant to be worn."

Inocencia shocked her by smiling. "A few of my friends try to squeeze into dresses they should *not* be wearing. Get your fat ass to the gym, right?"

Sage moved close and lowered her voice. "There are a couple of dresses in back being held for the exclusive client list, but I think they're a little more your style. Let me see if I can shake a couple loose for you."

Inocencia bent down and picked up her dog. "We'd like that very much. Thank you, Sage."

"Of course."

Sage left the dressing room and went into the back. There were no exclusive client collections—just a few items that hadn't been put out yet. She found two she thought would work. As she grabbed them, her manager walked into the small storage space.

"I heard a part of that," Berry, the boutique manager, said in a low voice.

Sage froze, not sure what the older woman was going to say next. While a case could be made that she was working the sale, the truth was, she'd lied to a client.

Berry smiled. "Well done. Inocencia is notoriously difficult and she's never been a regular. I'd like to see her in here more. If this works out and she wants you as her permanent associate, can you handle her?"

Sage thought of all the women she'd helped over the years. There had been the screamers, the criers, the clients who expected her to get them lunch, massage their feet, clean up after their kids or dogs and deliver a dress to them with thirty minutes' notice on a Saturday night at nine p.m.

"Easy peasy," Sage told her boss.

"That's what I like to hear."

Berry helped her with the dresses. They carried them back to the dressing room where Inocencia sat, texting on her phone. She jumped up when Sage entered, holding the first of the dresses. Berry followed.

"I told Sage she could have these, this one time. Because it's you."

Inocencia preened. "I'm a good customer here. I deserve recognition."

"After you see yourself in these, you're going to think you deserve an entourage," Sage said with a laugh.

Berry excused herself. Thirty minutes later Inocencia and her dog had dropped a cool twenty thousand on clothes and Sage had a new client for her file. All it had taken was a little time and giving up her cell number so Inocencia could "let her know when she wanted to come back in."

Sage rang up the sales and helped Inocencia to her car. She returned to the dressing room to put away the dozen or so dresses that had been rejected, then used the small carpet cleaner to take care of the dog pee. Inocencia was a difficult client, but she spent a lot on clothes, so that made her worth it. Sage told herself that she had a great opportunity here. She needed to pay attention and not mess up—as per usual—and all would be well. She was about to retreat to the break room for a few minutes when Berry waved her over.

"This was delivered to you," she said, holding up a white gift box topped with a bright purple bow.

Sage frowned at it. "Interesting."

"An admirer?" Berry asked, her voice teasing.

"I wish, but no. I've barely had time to unpack, let alone meet someone."

She lifted the box lid and found a bottle of tequila, several limes and a note.

> I was rude. Drinks tonight, so I can apologize in person?
> Adam

He'd included his number.

"You do have an admirer," Berry said.

"I'm not sure I'd call him that. He's my next-door neighbor."

"Proximity can be both good and bad."

"True enough."

She took the box to the break room and studied the note. She appreciated that he'd made an effort and that he'd recognized that he'd upset her, even if her gut told her he hadn't meant his comment to sound so harsh.

When they were kids, Adam had been her friend. She wasn't sure what had changed, and she wasn't sure it mattered. In truth, she was lonely. She didn't have any friends, she'd run home because she'd been out of options and her prospects weren't the greatest. Having someone reach out felt pretty good.

She texted him.

> **Thanks for the tequila. I'm off work at 7.**

Three dots immediately appeared on her screen.

> **I'll warm up the blender. Thanks for giving me a second chance.**

She was smiling when she put away her phone.

★ ★ ★

Daisy walked into the locker room, stretching her neck and trying to release the kinks in her back. The surgery had gone long, with her seven-year-old kidney patient requiring unexpected repair work on her large intestine.

Daisy had worried about the extended time under anesthesia, given her patient's weak condition. But little Molly had come through like a champ. Daisy had stayed with her in recovery until her patient had woken up. Once she'd confirmed Molly was breathing comfortably and not in too much pain, she'd left her in the capable hands of the recovery room team.

She opened her locker, pulled out her cell phone and saw she'd missed a call from her father. She pushed the button to call him back and took a seat on the bench.

"Hey, Dad," she said. "I was in surgery."

"I figured. Everything go all right?"

She smiled. "My patient did great. So, what's up?"

As she asked the question, she found herself tensing. Her father had retired and moved to Hawaii a couple of years ago. He'd quickly realized that he wasn't ready to not work and had joined a small general medicine practice in Maui. He worked a few days a week and frequently came back to LA to visit.

Not now, she thought desperately, knowing that there was no way to keep the situation with Jordan a secret if her father came to town. While he often chose to stay at the Bel Air Hotel, he would still be close enough to figure out there was a problem. As she had no idea what was happening with her husband, she doubted she could explain the situation to her father.

"I'm calling about Cassidy," her father said. "There's been an accident."

"What? When?"

Daisy tried to remember if she knew where her half sister was these days. Cassidy was a travel writer. While her home base was in Miami, she was frequently off visiting exotic places. Although hadn't Sage mentioned something about Patagonia?

Given they were sisters, one would assume Daisy and Cassidy would stay in touch, but that never happened. Despite sharing a father, they weren't exactly close. Eight years younger, Cassidy had initially been tight with Daisy, but after the divorce, everything had changed. Sage had become the beloved, fun sister, while Daisy was merely to be tolerated.

"A couple of days ago," her father said, drawing her back into the conversation. "She fell while hiking in Patagonia. She has some broken bones and maybe a concussion. It's hard to tell exactly, because her doctor didn't speak much English and my Spanish is terrible. Desean was there, so he told me what had happened. He's going to stay with her until she's on the plane back home."

"Who's Desean?"

"Her boyfriend." Wallace sounded surprised she didn't know. "I'm not sure that's how she'd refer to him, but they've been seeing each other on and off for a while now. I met him the last time I visited Cassidy. He's a good man. I like him. He said he would get her onto the plane I'm chartering."

"To fly her back to Miami?"

"No, to Los Angeles. She's going to need round-the-clock care and somewhere to stay. I'm assuming I can have her brought to the house."

Daisy held in a groan. There was only one house in their family and she was living in it.

While her father knew in his head that she and Cassidy hadn't gotten along in years, he'd always wanted them to be closer. They were "his girls," as he still called them. Even after the divorce, he'd stayed in touch with Sage and had visited her a couple of times in Europe.

"Dad, no," she began, then stopped. There was no way to refuse. The house was big enough and Cassidy was family. Wallace wanted to take care of his daughter—end of story.

Dozens of thoughts flashed through her head. Things like wondering how long she could keep the separation a secret and what she was going to tell the kids and how mean Cassidy was going to be, but she ignored them. Instead she told herself to suck it up and said, "When is she arriving?"

"In two days. I'll email you the particulars, including some ideas about nursing care. I can't get away for a couple of weeks. I have too many patients scheduled. But I'll get there as soon as I can."

"There's no need to rush, Dad. We'll be fine." A lie, but the last thing she needed was her father showing up, as well.

"Thank you for doing this, Daisy. I'm going to let Joanne know. If you'd tell Sage, I'd appreciate it. Do you have her number?"

"I don't think so."

"I'll text it to you, along with the flight information when I get it. I'm not happy Cassidy was hurt, but I'm glad you three girls will have a chance to hang out together. It's been a long time since that last happened."

It had never happened, she thought grimly. Daisy and Cassidy had been close and then Cassidy and Sage had bonded.

An uncomfortable thought occurred to her. What if Cassidy and Sage were still tight? That would mean if Cassidy came to stay, Sage would follow. Unless she'd already gone back to Italy, and wouldn't that be nice.

"Is Sage still in LA?" Daisy asked. "I thought she lived in Rome." That was what she'd told Krissa.

"Not anymore. She's back in Los Angeles and living with Joanne."

Oh, joy, Daisy thought.

"I'll let Esmerelda know," she said, keeping her voice light. "I think the upstairs guest room would be best. There are big windows and lots of space."

"I agree that's a good choice. They're emailing me a copy of her records. I'll forward them to you as soon as I get them. Once you look them over, you'll have a better idea of what she'll need. Esmerelda can get it all in place."

"No problem, Dad. We'll figure it out."

They spoke for a few more minutes before hanging up. Daisy stared at the blank screen, wishing there had been a way to say no. But she'd been unable to—

"Dammit, Dad!"

She stood and shoved her phone into her handbag as she dealt with the fact that she'd just been played. There had been no reason for her father to ask her to tell Sage about Cassidy's accident. According to him, Sage was living with her mother and he had said he was calling Joanne. No doubt Joanne would tell her daughter about the accident. But he'd made Daisy promise to get in touch with Sage.

She heard the beep that alerted her to a text message. Probably her father forwarding Sage's contact information. And because she'd said she would, now she would have to call, because not keeping her word wasn't an option.

She was thirty-six years old and her father was still messing with her life. One day she was going to have to deal with that, although in truth, the more pressing issue was the fact that her half sister was about to move in. Daisy would be forced to deal with her injuries, nurses in and out of the house, while living with someone who disliked her. And trying to hide the fact that her husband had moved out. The same husband who had once been engaged to her former stepsister—and that same stepsister had loudly promised to love Jordan forever right in the middle of his wedding to Daisy.

"Later, there will be wine," Daisy promised herself. "And possibly chocolate."

Because some days, that was all that stood between her and madness.

Sage arrived home to an empty house. Grateful she wasn't going to have to deal with her mother, she went to her room and quickly changed into jeans and a T-shirt. While she was willing to admit to a little anticipation about her evening with Adam, she didn't want him to know that. And she'd learned the best way to tell a man an evening with him was no big deal was to dress as if it didn't matter at all.

She went into the bathroom to brush her hair before pulling it back into a simple ponytail and tried not to notice the hint of wrinkles at the corners of her eyes. She knew she still looked good, but for how long? Five years? She really needed to start saving up to get some preventative work done. Something she would add to her money to-do list, along with an apartment and possibly putting aside a few dollars for a savings account.

"Not going to think about that right now," she whispered, before returning to her room and collecting the bottle of tequila and the limes.

She walked over to Adam's house and knocked. He opened the door and smiled at her.

"I have the blender ready to go," he said, stepping back to allow her inside.

She held up the tequila and the limes. "Good, because we wouldn't want these to go to waste."

He led the way into the kitchen. She had a brief impression of newish appliances and a lot of leather furniture in the open-concept family room.

Adam was taller than he had been in high school, and broader through the shoulders. He looked like he worked out.

She sat at one of the stools at the kitchen island as he measured tequila into a blender and added lime juice, simple syrup, orange liqueur and ice. While the blender worked its magic, he collected glasses from the freezer.

Less than a minute later, she had an icy margarita in her hand. Adam poured one for himself and sat next to her. He touched his glass to hers.

"To old friends." One corner of his mouth turned up. "By that I mean friends who knew each other a while back. I'm not saying you're old."

"Good, because then I'd be forced to hit you really hard and as you wouldn't hit me back, you'd be stuck."

"You telling me I'm not allowed to hit a girl?"

She grinned. "I'm saying it's not your style." She wasn't sure why she assumed that, but she did.

"You're right," he said with a heavy sigh. "It's a thing."

"Do you want to be able to hit women?"

"No." He sounded shocked. "Why would you ask that?"

"And you prove my point." She took a sip of the drink. "Nice. How did you know where I worked?"

"I asked your mom."

"I'm surprised she told you."

"I threatened to cut off her internet if she didn't."

"Can you do that?"

"Only if I unscrewed the connection at the cable box, which is kept locked. So not easily. But I figured she would believe me."

"And she did." Sage swung her chair to face him. "Now you know where I work, what do *you* do?"

"I put companies on the cloud."

She thought about her phone and how it backed up when she plugged it in to charge. "That's like off-site storage, right?"

"Sort of. Do you want a detailed explanation?"

"Not really."

He chuckled. "Good to know. Companies hire me to get them on the cloud. I'm an independent contractor, which is why I work from home."

"Do you like what you do?" she asked.

"Yes."

"Does it pay well?"

One eyebrow rose. "Looking for a loan?" He winced. "That came out wrong."

She eyed him. "Yes, it did. I'm making adult conversation. It's nice to have work you like that also pays well."

"You're right and yes, it pays well."

He got up and pulled a bowl of guacamole out of the refrigerator, then emptied tortilla chips into a bowl.

"I have chicken taquitos I got from a little place I know, if you're interested."

Her stomach growled. Somehow she'd missed lunch.

"I love a taquito."

He put several on a cookie sheet and set it in the oven, then started a kitchen timer in the shape of a tomato.

"Want to go outside?" he asked.

She nodded and picked up her drink, along with the bowl of chips. He brought the guacamole, his drink and the timer.

His patio was much larger than her mom's, with Mexican pavers and a big covered area. Along with the desk where he worked, there were a couple of lounge chairs, a round table and four chairs. She took a seat. Adam settled across from her.

She turned her head and looked across the low fence. "Why

do houses always look different when you see them from someone else's perspective?"

"It's just a trick of the light."

She smiled, then squinted slightly at the rear view of her mom's house. "Is that my bedroom?"

"It is."

She faced him. "You can see into my bedroom?"

"I can and while I'm more mature now, I will admit that as a teenager, seeing into your bedroom was always the highlight of my night."

She thought about how many hours she'd spent there, doing homework, talking to her friends, changing her clothes.

She swung her head between him and the window. "You were spying on me?"

"And desperately hoping you'd take off your clothes."

"Did I?"

"Sometimes." He leaned back in his chair. "Those were the days. You were my favorite masturbation fantasy." He held up his drink. "I was sixteen at the time, so I say that with knowledge that my behavior was wrong and sexist and I would never do it now."

"Masturbate or stare through my window?"

His mouth twitched, as if he were trying not to smile. "Stare through your window."

An honest man, she thought, knowing how rare they could be.

"So you've seen me naked."

Something flashed through his eyes. "Not in a long time, but yes."

"I'm not sure how I feel about that."

"Flattered?" he asked hopefully. "You're very beautiful. The next naked woman I saw was much less impressive. Of course she was interested in having sex with me, so she could have looked like a tree stump and I would have been delighted."

"Are you more discerning now?"

"I am, and you still remain the standard against which all my lovers are judged."

She winced. "Don't do that. No adult woman should be compared with her sixteen-year-old self."

The timer dinged and Adam went to get the taquitos. Sage wondered what quirk of biology and sociology created a society where women were valued for their beauty and men were valued for strength and power. She supposed it had something to do with procreation, but while it might have worked ten thousand years ago, it was less appealing now.

Adam returned carrying a plate stacked high with the crispy snacks. He smiled as he set it between them.

"Why are you working in retail?"

"Because I don't have the training to be a jet pilot," she said, reaching for a taquito. She thought about mentioning her tutoring, but that wasn't impressive, either.

"Seriously, why? You're rich. You don't need to work."

She licked her fingers as she stared at him. "I'm not rich. Where did you get that idea? I have a small settlement from my ex-husband and that's it. I'm paying my mom rent and I enjoy eating, which means I need to be a working girl." She frowned. "Not in a hooker sense."

"I just assumed you'd married money," he said, then raised a hand. "Not in the hooker sense. Just in the beautiful women tend to gravitate toward wealthy men sense."

"It didn't work out that way. My first husband was a race car driver, but then he crashed and if you can't drive, you can't earn money. My last husband made me *think* he was rich, but he was lying."

And hadn't that been a bitter discovery, she thought, telling herself she'd moved on from the disappointment. She reached for another taquito.

"You have a sweet ride for a working girl," he said, grabbing a taquito and dipping it in the guacamole.

She smiled at the mention of her BMW 3 Series. "She is pretty, isn't she? She cost me a Hermes Birkin crocodile handbag, but she was worth it."

Adam frowned. "I don't understand," he admitted.

"I sold a handbag and bought my new-to-me car with the proceeds."

"No handbag is worth a car."

"You say this as a women's accessory expert?"

His confusion morphed into complete bafflement. "But it's just a purse. My mom has a purse. How can there be one worth thirty or forty thousand dollars?"

"It's a Birkin bag. A crocodile Birkin bag."

"But…"

She patted his hand. "You're going to have to trust me on this. When I leave, you can look them up online and later you can apologize."

He still looked shell-shocked, which was kind of sweet. She liked that the world of high fashion and ridiculous prices was foreign to him. No doubt he would assume that one of her husbands had given her the bag, which was fine with her. She saw no need to tell him how she'd earned it. She might enjoy his company, but she didn't know him well enough to trust him with a secret like that.

"You live a life I can't imagine," he admitted.

"I did, but not anymore. Now I'm just a regular person."

"How does that feel?"

No way she was going to get into that pit of failure. She gave him a bright smile. "I'm ready to be back in the States. I'm not excited about starting over, but this time I'm determined to make better decisions. And that's enough about me. Tell me about yourself, Adam. You live here alone?"

He smiled. "I wouldn't have invited you over for drinks if I was involved with someone." He picked up his drink. "Let me clarify that by saying I'm offering information, not assuming this is anything more than friendly. I'm smart enough to know my place in the universe and mine is not with the likes of you."

She waited for the jab that was sure to follow, but he didn't seem to have anything else to say on the topic.

"What does that mean?" she asked cautiously.

"That you're you and I'm me."

"So not lovers, but we could be friends?"

The smile returned. "Is my luck that good?"

"You're teasing me."

"A little. But in a gentle, supportive way."

"Why aren't you married?"

"I was. She died two years ago."

Sage hadn't been expecting that. "I'm sorry," she said automatically. "That's when you bought the house from your mom."

"It is. I needed a change of scene, as they say. She had an undiagnosed heart condition. One day she stood up at work, had a heart attack and died."

"That must have been horrible."

"It was."

"I've never lost anyone that way," she admitted. "Through death. The closest would be my dad. He just took off and left me and my mom, but that was a long time ago."

"It would have been difficult, though."

"It was. And the divorces."

"Yes, the race car driver and the Italian husband."

There was also Ellery, but she didn't talk about him to anyone. "He was a Count. Or *Conte*, as they say in Italian."

"Making you a Contessa?"

She laughed. "Yes, that was me for about fifteen minutes."

"It sounds exciting."

"In some ways. His family owns a very old house and a lot of land. There was plenty of history to be found, but also leaking roofs, bad plumbing and a chronic rodent infestation." She didn't mention how he dumped her for a slightly older woman with more money than Denmark. A truth that had stung more than a little.

"So only romantic on the outside." He reached for another taquito. "Do you ever see Daisy?"

Until a few days ago, she would have said not since high school and been happy with that amount of distance. While she could still go the rest of her life without seeing her former stepsister, she knew saying so made her sound awful.

"Just last week. Why? Are you two close?"

"Not at all. I haven't seen her since high school."

"She's married with two kids. Right now they're battling the flu."

"Oh, I didn't know you two were in touch. It's nice that you stayed friends. She's great. I always liked her."

Based on what she'd said, he'd made the logical assumption that she and Daisy still had some kind of relationship and it wasn't one that involved wishing each other dead. For some reason she couldn't explain, Sage wanted him to think she was better than she was and now he did. But knowing she'd fooled him didn't sit well with her and while she was enjoying herself, she knew she couldn't stay. Not when she was lying about pretty much everything.

She drained her margarita and stood. "This was really nice, Adam. Thank you for inviting me over."

She half expected him to protest her leaving, but he only smiled at her.

"Thanks for coming over."

She waved and walked through his house and back to her own. When she got to her bedroom, she went to the window and carefully closed the blinds, then sat on the bed and covered her face with her hands.

She could deal with her life being shit—she hadn't expected any more when she'd moved back. What she hadn't counted on was the fact that she couldn't see a way out. Which would have been something she could manage if only she'd been able to pretend that *she* wasn't the problem. Because her being the problem implied the only thing standing between her and happiness was herself, and how on earth was she supposed to fix that?

five

Daisy waited until the kids were upstairs playing after dinner to sit down with Esmerelda.

"I'm going to need your help," she began.

Esmerelda nodded. "I knew there was something going on the second you walked in the door. What is it? Mr. Jordan?"

"No, not him. Cassidy was in an accident."

Daisy explained about the fall and Cassidy being airlifted from a hospital in Patagonia.

"She'll be here in two days. We need to get a room ready for her." She passed Esmerelda a list of medical equipment they would need, including a hospital bed, an adjustable table and a riser with side supports for the toilet.

"I want to put her in the guest room on the second floor. It's large enough to accommodate a wheelchair, if we need one. We'll use the elevator to get her up and down."

Esmerelda read the list. "Good. Because I don't want to give up my main floor room for the likes of her."

Daisy laughed. "Why do you have attitude? You've never even met her." Esmerelda had come to work for Daisy long after Cassidy had moved out.

"I heard about her from my cousin." Esmerelda's expression turned fierce. "I'll do what I'm supposed to do, but I won't like it."

Loyalty came in many forms, Daisy thought, grateful for the support. Esmerelda's much older cousin had been Daisy's, and later Cassidy's, nanny. She had witnessed Cassidy at her best and her worst. While Daisy wanted to think Cassidy had changed, she had her doubts, which would make the long convalescence seem endless.

"I'm sure everything will go smoothly," she lied, knowing her cheerful tone wouldn't fool Esmerelda.

The housekeeper raised her eyebrows. "Really?"

"Sometimes it helps to assume the best."

"Good luck with that." Esmerelda waved the list. "I'll get started on this right away. We'll get the existing furniture taken out and what she needs brought in. I'll need to know if she has any dietary requirements so I can do the grocery shopping."

"I'll get the information to you. She'll have round-the-clock nursing for the first few days."

"Not a problem." Esmerelda smiled at her. "I'm unflappable. And I'll keep my opinion of her to myself."

"Give her a chance. You might like her."

"Unlikely, but I'll wait and see."

Daisy thanked her before going up to the second floor playroom. Ben and Krissa were at the small game table in the corner, a board game between them. They looked up as she came in.

"We're playing *The Game of Life*," Krissa said. "And I'm winning."

Ben made a face that had Daisy thinking Krissa might not be winning all on her own. She had the absolute best kids in the world, something she would have to remember over the next few weeks. Maybe it would help her deal with the reality of having Cassidy move in.

Daisy sat down in one of the chairs and smiled. "So I have some news," she began.

"Is Daddy moving back?" Krissa asked anxiously. "I miss him so much."

Ben watched her, his expression more cautious than hopeful, and didn't speak.

Daisy felt a jab of guilt as she said, "This isn't about your dad. Your aunt Cassidy is going to be staying with us for a little while. Won't that be great?"

"Who's Aunt Cassidy?" Ben asked.

"She's my half sister."

"Sage talked about her the other day," Krissa told him. "Sage is Mom's stepsister."

Ben frowned. "You have a stepsister?"

Daisy nodded.

"Cassidy and Sage's mother was married to your grandfather for a while. Cassidy is their daughter."

"That's confusing," Ben told her, then added, "But I think I met her once, a long time ago. Maybe with Grandpa."

"I think I remember that," Daisy said. "Cassidy was in an accident. She fell off the side of a mountain."

Ben's eyes widened. "For real? That's so cool. I mean, I hope she's all right."

Daisy smiled at him. "She's going to be, but right now she's hurt and she needs help. She'll be staying in the guest room while she gets better. At first she's going to have a nurse to help her."

"Is she going to look scary?" Krissa asked, hunching in her chair.

"She'll be bruised and in a couple of casts. For a while, she's going to be on painkillers, so she might talk a little funny."

"Will she look like a monster?" Ben asked hopefully.

"I'll take a look at her when she gets here," Daisy told them both. "And let you know so you're prepared. Your grandfather is very excited to have her staying with us. He's going to come visit in a few weeks."

Krissa walked over to Daisy, then slid onto her lap. "I don't want to be scared of her."

"I know, sweetie. I'll be right here when you meet her. It might help to remember how she looks isn't her fault. She's hurt. Like when you get a bruise. Sometimes it looks really awful, but on the inside, you're healing."

Krissa snuggled close. Daisy wrapped her arms around her.

"Did you tell Dad?" Ben asked.

"I'm going to let him know next," she said, careful to keep her answer neutral. She would absolutely let Jordan know what was happening, but the how was more of a question. Texting seemed so disconnected, but as they still weren't speaking, she wasn't sure there was an alternative.

"Daddy's very busy with work," Krissa said. "Saving animals."

"Yes, he is."

Daisy was used to the disparity in how their children viewed their work. Being a veterinarian made sense to them. They were less clear on what she did. Anesthesia was a vague concept, at best, at least at their ages.

She set Krissa back on her feet. "I'll let you get back to your game," she said as she leaned in and kissed Ben on the cheek. "Once I know the day and time of Cassidy's arrival, I'll let you know."

They returned their attention to the board game. Daisy went to the guest suite where her half sister would stay.

Back when they'd all been kids, this had been Daisy's suite of rooms. When she and Jordan had moved into the master suite, Daisy had converted them to accommodate guests. Jordan had wanted the rooms for an office suite, but had agreed he didn't need that much space. Instead he'd taken what had been her father's study downstairs.

The living room of the suite could stay the same, she thought, studying the comfortable sofa and the chaise. When Cassidy was more mobile, she might appreciate being able to get out of bed, but still stay in her own quarters.

The large bedroom was at the back corner of the house, with windows on two walls. Even with a king-size bed and large nightstands and a dresser, there was still plenty of room for any other equipment Cassidy might need.

She checked out the bathroom. There was a tub and a separate walk-in shower. The long vanity had double sinks, and a cabinet provided extra storage. Her sister should be happy here—or at least as happy as she could be, stuck in Daisy's house.

Daisy ignored the sense of dread that took up residence in her stomach. She and Cassidy were both adults now. There was no reason to think her sister would be anything but reasonable. Okay, there were lots of reasons, but she was going to ignore them.

She left the guest suite and made her way to her home office. It was a bit of a walk from one end of the house to the other. She remembered how shocked she'd been the first time she'd seen where Sage and Joanne had gone to live after the divorce. Now Daisy knew it was a perfectly nice home in a quiet neighborhood, but all those years ago, she'd been surprised by how small it was. The whole of it was about the size of her and Sage's bedrooms and playroom back here.

All of her friends had lived in houses much like her own. This one had been in her family since the 1950s. It had been built by her maternal grandfather and passed on to his daughter and then to her. She hadn't known the rest of the world wasn't so blessed and the discovery had unsettled her for days.

And speaking of Sage, she thought, sitting behind her ornately carved, Victorian desk. She was going to have to let her know about the accident. Her father would be sure to follow up on his request.

She sent a quick text to Jordan, telling him about Cassidy's injuries and that she would be moving in. When he didn't respond in five minutes, she debated whether to text or call Sage. She knew which option she preferred, but suspected her father would point out that the spirit of his request required that she let Sage know personally.

Holding in a sigh, she pushed the call button and waited.

"Hello?"

"Sage, it's Daisy."

There was a long pause, followed by a surprised-sounding, "Did you mean to call me?"

"I did. I wasn't sure if you'd spoken to your mother yet or not."

"I haven't seen her since I got home from work."

Work? As in a job? Why would Sage have a job? Wasn't she well off from settlements from her divorces?

Daisy shook off the questions and got to the point. "My father wanted me to let you know that Cassidy's been in an accident."

She explained about the fall and Wallace airlifting Cassidy to Los Angeles. "She's going to be staying here until she's feeling better. I'm sure she'll want to see you and your mom."

A truth Daisy had been avoiding, but ignoring it wouldn't make it go away.

"Unless you're going back to Italy soon," she added, trying not to sound too hopeful.

"I'm staying here," Sage said.

Darn and double darn. Her father had been right. "She'll be excited to hear that."

"I'm surprised I didn't hear from her after the accident."

"Dad said she's in pretty bad shape, so I'm not sure she could have called."

Daisy told herself to stop talking. Why was she defending Cassidy of all people?

"He said Desean was with her."

"Desean?"

"The boyfriend?"

"Cassidy doesn't have a boyfriend. She doesn't do boy-friends."

Daisy frowned. "He was with her in Patagonia. That's all I know."

If Cassidy was traveling with a guy, shouldn't Sage know? Weren't they as close as they had been? When Sage had helped her and Krissa the day her daughter had gotten sick, Daisy had been under the impression they were. Was that wrong?

Daisy told herself it wasn't her business and having the in-formation wouldn't change anything. Relationships were com-plicated—she knew that firsthand. Her nonspeaking one with Jordan was plenty of proof.

"Okay, well, I'll text you with the flight info."

"Thanks. Bye."

Sage hung up, leaving Daisy staring at her phone and wish-ing just once she could have the last word.

Daisy traded shifts so she could be home when Cassidy ar-rived. It was the right thing to do, even if she would rather have been wrangling snakes on some snake ranch. Okay, maybe not snakes, but some unpleasant animal-slash-creature. Anything that would keep her away from home for a couple of weeks. Not exactly the mature response, she admitted as she paced by the front door, waiting for the private ambulance to pull up. But an honest one.

"She'll have nurses," Esmerelda reassured her. "You won't have to deal with her."

"She's my sister. There's no escaping her." Daisy shook her head. "I didn't mean that. She's family and I'm glad we're able to take care of her when she's been injured."

While she admitted privately that "glad" was a little strong, she was pleased she'd been able to make the statement without a lightning bolt reducing her to a pile of dust.

She heard a vehicle pull up in the courtyard and walked to the front door. Esmerelda got there first.

"I'm here," the other woman said sincerely. "Always."

Daisy hugged her. "I know you are and I really appreciate your support." She stepped back and squared her shoulders. "All right, let's do this."

They went outside and saw two men carefully unloading a gurney from the back of the ambulance. Daisy had skimmed the medical records her dad had sent her. Cassidy had a broken leg and arm, along with several fractured ribs, multiple contusions and a severe concussion. Daisy had seen plenty of car accident victims, but was still unprepared to see her sister looking so battered and helpless.

Daisy walked toward her.

"Hey, you," she said gently, taking in the cuts and bruises on her sister's face and the casts on her right leg and left arm. Her blond hair was dirty, and except for the vivid color from the cuts and bruises, her skin was practically gray. Gone was the vibrant, energetic woman Daisy remembered. In her place was a seriously injured patient.

Cassidy turned her head and opened her eyes. She blinked several times, as if trying to focus, then physically shrank away.

"Not you! No! What are you doing here? I don't want to see you!"

Daisy instinctively took a step back. The nurse, a tall woman in her forties with short dark hair, smiled at her.

"Hi. I'm Nita. I'll be Cassidy's main day nurse. I flew back with her. She's on some serious medication for the trip, so she's pretty out of it."

Daisy introduced herself, then Esmerelda. She avoided looking at Cassidy, not wanting to endure another outburst.

The men wheeled Cassidy inside. Daisy took them up via the elevator and led the way to the guest suite. The hospital bed and other equipment had been delivered the previous day. Now Daisy hurried ahead to pull back the covers.

"We're going to have to get you into bed," Nita told Cassidy. "It might be a bit uncomfortable, but then you'll get to rest."

Esmerelda, Nita and the two men carefully moved her from the gurney. Cassidy cried out several times, then quieted when she was settled on the bed. Nita examined the controls and began to work the adjustments.

"Tell me what's the most comfortable," she told Cassidy. "I'd like to keep you upright for a little bit."

Cassidy clutched the front of her shirt. "Is she still here?"

Nita looked confused.

"I think she means me," Daisy told her. "She and I weren't especially close when we were younger."

"Sage," Cassidy called. "Sage, where are you? Sage?"

As if summoned from the great beyond, Sage stepped through the sunlight streaming into the room and was briefly in silhouette—her long blond hair flowing around her, her well-fitting dress fluttering at her knees. Daisy half expected a cadre of woodland creatures to scamper at her feet.

"I'm here," Sage said, hurrying to her sister's side.

When Sage was close enough to actually see her, she came to a stop and covered her mouth with her hand. Her shock and distress were visible. Unable to help herself, Daisy moved closer.

"She's actually in better shape than I expected," Daisy said quickly. "The bruising on her face will fade and she's recovering from her concussion. The breaks are healing. The ribs are the most painful but she's young and healthy. She's going to be fine."

Sage nodded, then moved close to Cassidy. "Hey, little girl. I'm here."

Cassidy opened her eyes. "Is it really you?"

"It is."

Cassidy glanced around wildly. "She's here. Daisy's here. Make her go away. Please? Don't leave me with her."

Daisy felt herself flush. The two EMTs busied themselves with the gurney while Nita glanced between Cassidy and Daisy, no doubt wondering what the story was.

Not knowing what else to do, Daisy turned and walked out of the room. When she was in the hallway, she leaned against the wall and tried to tell herself everything was going to be fine. Cassidy was on a lot of medication and she'd just endured a long flight. She was tired and overwrought. Tomorrow would be better.

Which sounded fabulous but was, of course, a total lie. When it came to her sisters—step and half—it was never better. It was only ever worse.

six

Sage watched Daisy rush out of the room. As much as she hated to feel bad for her, this time she couldn't help herself. It was never fun to be the least liked person around.

"Don't be a pill," she told Cassidy. "Daisy's letting you stay in her house. You have to be nice to her."

Cassidy clutched her hand tightly. "She's horrible. She was always telling me to do my homework and making me put my dirty clothes in the laundry. What was Dad thinking, sending me here?"

Sage remembered being on Cassidy's side all those years ago, but now hearing her sister's list of complaints, they sounded pretty pathetic and immature.

"I'm so glad you're here," Cassidy continued, sounding desperate. "I didn't want to come here, but I didn't have anywhere else to go. I thought maybe Dad would fly me to Hawaii, but he said he doesn't have the room and he's busy with work." Tears filled her blue eyes. "I know Mom wouldn't want me around."

"Of course she'd want you," Sage lied. "But you know how small the house is. The only place your hospital bed would fit is on the patio. That would be really uncomfortable when the sprinklers came on."

That got her a slight smile, but Cassidy continued to cling to her hand.

"It's just awful. *She's* awful. I hate her."

"You don't hate her. Cass, you've been out of the house for ten years. We've all changed. Give Daisy a chance."

"Since when did you take her side? You always hated her, too."

Sage didn't want to admit to that.

She tugged free of Cassidy's grip and pulled a desk chair close to the bed. The nurse wasn't in the room, but Sage assumed she was giving them privacy while staying close.

"What happened?" she asked, taking her sister's good hand again. "You really fell off a mountain?"

Cassidy closed her eyes. "I didn't mean to. I was backing up and suddenly there wasn't any ground under my feet."

"Backing up from what?"

"I don't want to talk about it."

Which meant the "it" was bad or possibly embarrassing.

"I didn't know you were in LA," Cassidy said earnestly. "But I'm so glad you're here."

"I moved back a few weeks ago, when Mom had her cancer scare. She wanted company and I'd just found out I was getting a divorce, so it seemed like a good time to come back."

Cassidy turned her head toward Sage, then winced at the movement. "What do you mean, 'back'?"

"I'm staying in the States. I'm done with Europe and it appears to be done with me." She deliberately kept her tone light.

"Are you okay?"

Sage smiled. "Better than you, kid."

"I think everyone is."

Sage heard the sound of rapid footsteps, then Krissa and a boy a few years older appeared at the open door to the bedroom. Ben, Sage thought. Daisy's oldest. Krissa seemed more cautious than curious, but Ben was obviously eager to come in.

"Ready for visitors?" Sage asked, then quickly added. "It's Daisy's kids. You've met them, right?"

"Maybe once. With Dad."

Sage waved them in. They both circled around the bed and stood by her. Krissa kept her gaze on Sage, while Ben stared at Cassidy, his eyes wide.

"Did you really fall off a mountain?" he asked.

"I did. It wasn't a smart thing to do." She raised her broken arm a few inches. "Things hurt."

"I'm Ben," he said. "I think you're my aunt."

"I am and I'm Cassidy."

Sage leaned close to Krissa. "It's okay. She's not too scary-looking."

Krissa glanced at her, then away. "Hi."

"Hi, back."

Krissa looked at her again. "What's wrong with you?"

Cassidy gave her a faint smile. "That's a really long list."

"She means your injuries," Sage told her.

"Oh, that. Broken arm and leg, fractured ribs. I had a concussion, but that's getting better. A lot of really big bruises."

"Do you have brain damage?" Ben asked, sounding intrigued by the prospect.

"It's hard to tell."

Sage sighed. "That's your aunt being funny. There's no brain damage."

"You don't know that," Cassidy said. "You're guessing."

The nurse walked in, bringing a tall pole with an IV bag with her.

"Hello, children," she said cheerfully. "I'm Nita. I'm going to be Cassidy's day nurse. There will be a different nurse at night and we'll trade off with another pair after a few days."

"Is she going to die?" Krissa asked. Ben nudged her.

"No, she's getting better."

"Are you sure?" Cassidy asked dryly.

Nita ignored the question. "She'll be in a wheelchair in another week or so. But right now, I need to give Cassidy some pain medicine so she can sleep. Maybe you could come back later, when she's had a little rest."

"Yes, ma'am," Ben said, taking Krissa by the hand and leading her out of the room.

Cassidy watched them go. "I like her kids. Is that wrong of me?"

"Not at all. Cass, I'm serious. Let the past go. We're adults now. It's time to start over."

"Do you really believe that? Are you saying you *like* Daisy? That you're *friends*?"

Sage pulled free and leaned over to kiss her forehead. "No, but there's no need to be bitchy, okay?"

"You're leaving? Don't go. You can't leave me here alone."

Sage eyed the IV. "In about twenty minutes, you're going to be asleep. I'll come back later."

"You promise?"

"Yes. Now get some rest."

"If you really loved me, you'd take me home with you."

Sage ignored that. She waved and walked out into the hallway. Ben and Krissa were standing there.

Ben looked at her. "You knew my mom when she was a little girl, didn't you?"

"Yes. Daisy was seven and I was eight when our parents got married. We used to be stepsisters."

"But you're not now."

"No. Our parents got a divorce."

Ben and Krissa exchanged a look, but Sage had no idea what they were thinking.

"It was nice to meet you," Ben told her, sounding far older than his years.

"You, too."

He and Krissa walked down the hall to what had once been the old playroom. Sage wondered if it still was.

She took the same route, but kept going until she reached the wide staircase that took her down to the foyer. She wondered if she should say goodbye to Daisy. Not that she had any idea where she was, or what else they would have to say to each other. Plus, what if Daisy was with Jordan—that would be a whole new level of awkward.

She let herself out the front door, then walked to her car. As she drove down the long driveway, she thought about how so much about Daisy's house was still the same. Sage had lived there nearly five years and had never felt it was her home. She'd always been the awkward guest—not quite family and not a stranger—existing in a half-life world.

After the divorce, she and her mom had moved to the house Joanne was in today. Yes, it was smaller and somewhat depressing by comparison, but at least there Sage had known her place. The downside had been that Wallace continued to pay for her education, sending her to the same private school she'd attended during the marriage. Unable to escape her now former stepsister, Sage had gone out of her way to make Daisy's life as miserable as possible.

Daisy had been quiet, shy, studious and slightly overweight. Any one of those characteristics could have been overcome with a little effort, but combined, they were deadly—especially when there was a popular mean girl in residence.

Sage had been Daisy's opposite. She'd been outgoing, social, fun and beautiful. She'd made friends easily and had always been one of the most popular girls. While none of her relationships had been particularly close, she'd made up for intimacy by substituting volume. Anytime things got a little dull, there was always Daisy to pick on. And she had. Relentlessly. Not a memory to make Sage particularly proud of herself.

Things had gotten better in high school, she thought, pausing at a red light. She'd fallen for Jordan and he'd occupied most of her waking hours. Hanging out with him had been way more fun than tormenting Daisy. Sage supposed she'd loved him, as much as she'd been able to love anyone. But her love hadn't been enough for him.

No, she told herself. That wasn't fair. He'd been right— they'd been too young to think about getting married. She could say that now, all these years later, but back then... He'd hurt her, she thought, remembering how damned earnest he'd looked when he'd told her he wanted to put their future plans on hold. He'd sworn he still loved her, but he wanted to wait on marriage.

Sage, feeling the weight and importance of the ring he'd put on her finger, had reacted badly. Hardly a surprise to anyone. Yes, her mother had egged her on, telling her if Jordan really loved her, he would want to marry her as soon as possible. But the fault of the breakup had been Sage's. She'd screamed that she would never forgive him and two days later had, in a fit of drama, left the ring and a goodbye note on the front seat of his car. She'd taken a predawn flight to Paris and had vowed to never look back.

Heartbroken, she'd been determined to make her way in Europe. She'd promised herself there everything would be more glamorous, more interesting. She would let rich Frenchmen seduce her. She would marry into money, have a country château and a city pied-à-terre, knowing Jordan would regret losing her. At least that had been the plan.

Funny how her life had gone so wrong. Looking back she could see where she'd made bad decisions at pretty much every opportunity. Unlike Daisy, who had seemed to get it right all the time.

Sage drove toward her more modest neighborhood and smiled. At least her genuine wish that Daisy and Jordan were happy together spoke well of her as a person. If she wasn't all bad, then maybe there was hope for her after all.

Despite the distance between Daisy's small home office and the guest quarters, she was acutely aware of Cassidy's presence in the house. She might not be able to see her or hear her, but she knew she was there, which made it difficult to concentrate.

She worked her way through the monthly bills, then picked up her phone and studied the dark screen.

She missed Jordan. Sometimes her emotions leaned more toward wanting to bash in his head with a heavy object, but today she just plain missed him. They were married, this was his home and he should be here. Only he wasn't, and if they didn't start talking, that was never going to change.

She still didn't know why he'd left or what his grievances were, a frustrating truth she couldn't ignore. She was trapped between indecision and fear, worry and loneliness.

She put the phone down, then picked it up again and texted him.

We need to figure out what's going on. Not talking doesn't solve any of our problems. To be honest, I'm not sure what our problems are.

She wanted to say more but decided that was enough of an opening. Seconds later, three dots appeared.

I agree.

His quick response told her he was at his desk, rather than

with a patient. She reached for her phone again, this time intent on calling, then drew back. What if she called and he didn't pick up? While she didn't want to believe that would happen, she wasn't sure, and the not knowing made her sad. Shouldn't she expect her own husband to take her calls?

The dots appeared again.

Counseling?

She stared at the single word, not sure if he was asking or suggesting, then deciding it didn't much matter.

I think that's a good start.

Why don't you pick one you like and set up an appointment? You know my schedule. Tell me when and where, and I'll be there.

Was he leaving it all up to her because her work schedule was more changeable than his or because he wasn't that interested in seeing a counselor? Did their marriage even matter to him?

All really good questions with no answers. She and Jordan were dealing with something and she had no idea what it was. Getting help made the most sense.

I'll find someone and get a meeting set up.

Thanks.

She wasn't sure what to say to that. "You're welcome" was too formal and anything else would be… She wasn't sure, but nothing good came to mind.

It shouldn't be this hard, she thought grimly. She and Jordan had been together over a decade. Shouldn't they understand each other a little better than they did? She had no idea what he was thinking or what he wanted. For all she knew, he was done with her and was simply going through the motions so he wasn't the bad guy. Maybe he'd already decided he wanted a divorce and was trying to find a way to tell her.

"Or I could stop assuming the worst," she murmured.

Counseling was a start. With a disinterested third party in the room, they would have the chance to say what needed to be said so they could get on with repairing whatever was broken.

Sage counted out the ten hundred-dollar bills she'd gotten at the bank. When she and her mother had come to terms about Sage renting a room in the house, Joanne had been clear—she only wanted cash. Sage was sure a thousand dollars a month was way too much for what she was getting, but without a credit history, most people considered her a less than good bet. Besides, the location worked for her and with any luck, her mother would meet some guy and disappear for a few weeks.

Joanne pocketed the money and smiled. "Now I can schedule that laser treatment I've been wanting. Getting old sucks."

"You're beautiful, Mom," Sage said automatically.

"I wish." Joanne glanced at herself in the mirror in the living room. "I look old."

"You really don't."

Sage crossed to the small table by the door and went through the mail piled there. One of the envelopes looked like the new credit card she'd been waiting for. She tucked it into her handbag to study later. With luck, she could get started using it right away. Part of her plan was to charge everything, then pay off the bill every month, to build her credit history.

"Have you seen Cassidy?" she asked when she'd finished with the mail.

Her mother stared at her blankly. "Why would I go see her?"

"Because she's here. In Los Angeles. Remember, she fell off a mountain and is recovering at Daisy's house?"

Joanne shook her head. "Oh, right. That was why Wallace called me a few days ago. He was only interested in giving me the information about her accident. I tried to get him to talk more, but he wouldn't engage." She sighed heavily. "Too bad. I really miss that man."

"So that's a no?" Sage asked.

"To?"

"Visiting your daughter."

"I'll get there in a few days. It's not as if she's missing me. Cassidy was only ever close to you."

True enough, Sage thought, but wanted to point out the reason might have been that Joanne had been an indifferent mother at best. After the divorce, she'd fallen into a depression that had lasted for months. She'd ignored everything but her own pain. Once she'd started feeling better, she'd been far more intent on getting a man than caring for her two daughters. Cassidy had been five, so looking after her had fallen to Sage, who had barely been a teenager herself.

Her mother looked at her. "You've been over to the house?"

No need to ask which house she meant. "Yes, a couple of times. Cassidy's doing a little better."

"Did you see Jordan?"

"No. I have no interest in Daisy's husband." She emphasized the last word on purpose.

"You could take him from her in a hot second. Jordan wouldn't care about her family money. I know he thinks letting you go was the dumbest thing he ever did."

There was too much to respond to, Sage thought, suddenly tired from her long day and the family drama she didn't want to deal with.

"While I appreciate the support, Mom, he has Daisy now, and his kids. That's plenty."

"You don't know that for sure. Maybe he'd like to start up with you again. Wondering what could have been is very powerful."

"I'm not interested in a married man," Sage said flatly.

"That's smart. It never ends well. Although if you guilt them enough, the gifts can be nice."

Her mother returned her attention back to her own reflection. "Laser surgery it is. I'm going out in a bit. It's ladies' night at that bar I like. I'm meeting friends."

"Have fun," Sage said as she walked toward her bedroom.

Once inside, she kicked off her shoes and collapsed on the bed. Her feet hurt from work, her head hurt from dealing with her mother and her heart hurt from all the messes in her life. If she had friends, she would love to meet them at a bar, or pretty much anywhere. Sadly, she didn't have anyone she was that close to. She hadn't been home long enough to make new friends and her old ones, well, they'd never stayed in touch.

She forced herself to her feet. After pulling her blinds closed, she changed out of her work clothes and thought briefly about getting something for dinner, only she wasn't very hungry. If she didn't eat, she should at least—

Her phone buzzed. She picked it up and smiled as she read the text.

Why are you shutting me out? I thought we had something, but it's not going to work if you don't communicate with me. I know you're going to say you are, but all I see is a blank wall.

Sage chuckled, then texted back.

Sometimes I need to be alone with my thoughts. And to get undressed. Not everything is about you.

Don't you think it should be?

No. It should be about me.

Adam sent back a laughing until crying emoji, followed by, **Can I buy you a beer? I have a new six-pack in the refrigerator.**

If you include chips in that offer, I'm in.

I can do better than chips. I can make us burgers.

A man who cooks and plies me with alcohol. You're my fantasy.

If only that were true. The front door's open. Let yourself in.

Sage crossed the front lawn and let herself into Adam's house. She walked through the kitchen and out onto the back patio, where there were two open beers on the round table and a bowl of sliced limes between them. In the second before he saw her, she had a chance to admire his broad shoulders and strong body.

He looked capable, she thought. Like a man who could handle himself in a crisis. Ellery had been the same way—without the blue eyes and square jaw.

"Why are you laughing at me?" he asked, turning toward her.

"I'm not laughing, I'm admiring."

He walked over to pick up a beer. "Admiring?" His tone was both teasing and disbelieving.

"Sure. You're a good-looking guy who offered to cook me a burger. Where's the bad?"

He didn't look convinced but motioned to a chair, then took one opposite her.

"How are things?" he asked.

She squeezed a lime slice into hers. "Good. Busy. Did I tell you Cassidy's back?"

He frowned. "Cassidy is…"

"My baby sister. Half sister. My mom, Daisy's dad."

"Ah, the offspring. I remember her hanging out with you when she was here for her custodial visits. You were her favorite."

"She was a little clingy."

And still was, Sage thought. Every time she visited, Cassidy begged her to stay longer. Things were going to get uglier when she was able to start texting.

"She fell off a mountain."

Sage explained about the accident.

"She has round-the-clock nursing while she recovers. She's pretty battered, but her nurses say she's doing well."

He looked at her. "How awkward are the visits?"

"They're fine. Why would you—" She wrinkled her nose. "You're talking about Jordan."

"You two were hot and heavy for a long time. Weren't you engaged?"

"Yes."

For nearly a year, before he'd dumped her and she'd punished him by going for France. Although "dumped her" was a bit of an exaggeration. With the wisdom of hindsight, she could see that he'd been right to suggest they put off getting married. He had still been in college, on his way to veterinary school, and she'd been drifting, not sure of what she wanted in her life beyond Jordan. They had been kids playing at being adults. Not exactly the best way to start a marriage.

"I haven't seen him," she admitted. "Which I'm okay with. He's married to Daisy and I want them to be happy."

Adam studied her. "You sound like you mean that."

"Of course I do. Daisy and I were never close, but I wouldn't wish her ill." She might have, back in high school, but she liked to think she was a better person now.

"I genuinely don't have time to deal with any more drama in my life."

"Then I will regale you with humorous stories."

"Such as?"

"I looked up Birkin bags."

She smiled. "Did you faint?"

"Yes. Luckily, I didn't hit my head when I collapsed. Do you know what they cost? They're a handbag. A damn handbag."

"I think it's way more than a—" she made air quotes "—'damn handbag' if it was worth a car."

"Point taken. You get enough of those together and you can buy a house—even in this crazy LA market."

"Sadly I only had the one."

"Still, your husband must have really loved you."

She sipped her beer, not sure how to respond to his comment. For some reason, she resented the obvious assumption that the bag had been a gift.

"I earned it, Adam. No one gave that bag to me."

He stared at her. "Do I want to ask how?"

"What does that mean? Why wouldn't you want to know—" She set down her beer, leaned back in her chair and started laughing.

He studied her cautiously. "I didn't mean for that to be funny."

"You think I'm a hooker."

"What? No. Of course not. I think that it's possible rich men enjoy spending time with you and buying you things."

"I told you I wasn't that kind of working girl." She put her hands flat on the table and stared at him. "I earned it in a perfectly legal way. When I was in Italy, I met several wives of incredibly rich men. Old-fashioned men who didn't want their wives to know too much about what was going on, so they conducted business in English."

She reached for her bottle of beer. "I'm talking slightly older women who would never download a language app. Once I figured out the problem, I offered to be their instructor. On the surface, we were just friends, spending the afternoon together, having a little girl talk. In truth, I was giving them intensive classes in English. Their husbands made sure they didn't have access to a lot of cash but they encouraged shopping. Lots of shopping."

He swore under his breath. "They paid you in handbags."

"Unusual currency, but one that works for me. I know a few reputable places to resell the bags. They're my nest egg for the future. They're in excellent condition and I have all the documentation. Once I figure out where I can store them, I'll have them shipped over to me."

"They're not with you now?"

"Only a handful of them are. I can't keep them in the house."

Adam raised his eyebrows. "Because you're concerned your mom would take them?"

"Yes, and she would sell them without doing the research so she would get a ridiculously low price. This way is safer."

"You're a constant surprise."

She didn't ask if he meant that in a good way or a bad way.

"I'm doing my best to figure it all out," she told him.

"I feel bad about those women in Italy."

"One of the consequences of marrying money." She smiled. "I'm talking serious money. Like a different planet level."

"You're saying they got what they wanted?"

"I'm saying when you marry money, you earn every penny."

"Wasn't marrying money your plan?"

"When I was younger. I like to think I've learned my lesson."

Her mother never had and watching Joanne prowl for yet another wealthy benefactor was depressing.

"We need to change the subject," she said firmly. "Do you date?"

"No."

"You don't want to think about your answer?"

He flashed her a smile. "I don't need to think about it. No."

"Is it too soon?"

"Somewhat. I work at home, I'm not a guy who enjoys clubs. It's tough to meet someone."

"Want me to keep a look out for single women?" she asked, only half teasing.

"No, thanks. I can get my own girl."

"You just said you couldn't."

"I take it back."

She wondered what Adam would be like on a date. Thoughtful, she decided. Unexpectedly funny. She was fairly sure he would kiss, but did he expect more on the first date?

"You're speculating about something," he said.

"Do you expect sex on the first date?"

"No."

"And if it's offered?"

"If I like the woman enough to want to go out with her, I'm not going to say no to sex, but I'll be disappointed."

"In her performance? Isn't that judgy?"

"No, in the fact that we got there so fast. It doesn't bode

well for the relationship. I don't want to be with someone who thinks she has to use sex to keep me interested. Or someone who's only in it for sex."

"Did you just say *bode*? No one uses that word."

"I do. It's a good word."

"You're so weird."

She kept her voice light and teasing because she didn't want him to know his words had hit her hard in her tender underbelly. How many times had she used sex to get and keep a man? Maybe the easier question was, how many times had she not?

"Remember back in high school there would be the word of the day?" he asked with a grin. "We were expected to use it in sentences throughout the day. We all complained it was a totally lame idea, yet how many of those words got into our personal lexicon?"

"*Lexicon* being one of the words?" she asked.

"I assume so."

"I avoided the words of the day."

"You were a rebel."

She smiled. "And you were..." She frowned, remembering that while they'd hung out in ninth and tenth grade, by their final two years of high school, she and Adam hadn't been friends anymore. She had no memories of doing anything with him or even seeing him much after school, despite the fact that they lived next door to each other.

"What happened to us?" she asked. "In school. We were tight and then one day, you were gone."

His gaze slid from hers, as if he knew exactly what she was talking about but didn't want to admit it.

"Nothing happened."

"Something obviously did, and you don't want to talk about it. Why did we stop being friends?"

His gaze locked with hers. She read indecision there, along with something she couldn't name. Something that made her stomach tighten, even as she said, "I want the truth. Don't worry about hurting my feelings."

Because for some reason, she really did want to know what had gone wrong between them.

He set down his beer and shrugged. "You got mean."

seven

After Daisy got the kids into bed, she debated retreating to her own room for a little mindless TV. She could stream a new series or check out whatever the Food Network was offering. But instead of walking purposefully, she hesitated.

She really should check on Cassidy—not that she wanted to. Spending time with her sister wasn't exactly pleasant and it wasn't as if she *needed* to be checked on. There was literally round-the-clock nursing care and her physician father was a phone call away. Cassidy was fine. Daisy should get on with her evening. Maybe she could finally figure out how to make a soufflé that didn't fall, or she could spend a little time trying to figure out what was going on with her marriage and her husband—both of which seemed to be missing from her life.

But she'd been raised to do the right thing, so despite the voice in her head screaming at her to run, she turned toward the guest suite. With a little luck, Cassidy would be asleep and she could slip out without waking her.

But Daisy's luck had apparently run out. Not only was Cassidy awake, she was sitting up in bed, her hands over her face as she cried into several tissues.

Daisy stood in the doorway to the bedroom, not sure what to do. Her instinct was to run far and fast. Her compassion told her to find out what was wrong and the rest of her just wanted a big glass of wine and a brownie.

"What's wrong?" she asked, doing her best to keep her voice low and comforting. "Are you late on your pain meds?"

Cassidy lowered her hands and stared at Daisy. "What?" she asked, wiping her blotchy face.

"Are you in pain? Should I get the nurse?"

"No." Cassidy sniffed again. "I told her to take a break. She's downstairs, I guess." The tears returned. "Nothing hurts more than usual. It's my life that's screwed up. I mess up everything I touch and I'm a failure."

Daisy reluctantly walked into the room and took the bedside chair. "That's the drugs talking. You're not a failure. You're a travel writer with a great life. You get to see the world, you live in Miami. What's not to like?"

Cassidy pulled more tissues out of the box and blew her nose. "No one cares about me. I could die tomorrow and no one would miss me."

Daisy did her best not to roll her eyes. "That's a little dramatic, don't you think? People care. You have family."

She wanted to say that she cared, but she couldn't quite spit out the lie. She and Cassidy hadn't been close in decades. Come to think of it, Daisy didn't much like Sage, either. Which probably meant she was a horrible person.

"I don't know your kids," Cassidy wailed. "I should know them."

It took Daisy a second to catch up to the conversation. "You don't know them because you don't spend time with them and you live across the country. That's circumstances, not a statement about who you are as a person. You're welcome to get to know them, if you'd like." Although she honestly hoped Cassidy was just in a mood and the need to bond with Ben and Krissa would pass.

Cassidy nodded. "That's true. I could do that. I wonder if they'd like me. Do they know I never liked you? Did you tell them?"

Daisy reminded herself that this, too, was the drugs talking and that she shouldn't take the comment personally, but before she could figure out how to respond, Cassidy kept talking.

"Did that come out wrong? I don't mean it in a bad way."

"Of course you didn't."

Cassidy didn't seem to get the sarcasm. "It's just you were always monitoring me, like you were my mom or something. You're not my mom."

Daisy felt the first flashes of anger and did her best to ignore them.

"No, I'm not your mother. I was always clear on that. Did it ever occur to you that I was looking out for you because I cared?"

Cassidy stared at her blankly. "No."

She'd wanted them to be close—to be sisters who had a real bond between them, but after the divorce Cassidy had only had room in her heart for Sage. Everyone else had come in second—except for Daisy, who didn't even get a ranking.

"I was trying to take care of you because I didn't want you to feel alone or scared. You were a little girl and your family was being torn apart. I thought that might upset you so I tried to make sure you were all right."

She thought about pointing out she knew exactly how it felt to be rejected in her own home. When Wallace had married Joanne, Daisy had been so excited to get a stepmom and a stepsister. She'd fantasized about how they would all do things together when it wasn't just her and her dad. But that had never happened.

On her best days, Joanne had been indifferent, and on her worst, she'd taken great delight in tormenting Daisy—sometimes physically. Joanne spoke fluent French and had taught the language to Sage. The two of them would have long conversations, excluding Daisy, except when they said something she couldn't understand, pointed at her and laughed.

At school, where Daisy struggled to make friends and fit in, Sage had instantly become one of the popular girls. There had been a simple rule—you couldn't hang out with Sage if you admitted to liking Daisy. There'd been no escape when the school day ended because Sage had taken great delight in inviting Daisy's tormentors home to play. Daisy had been alone in her room, listening to them having fun.

When Cassidy had been born, Daisy had hoped to finally find, if not an ally, then at least a friend, but that hadn't lasted.

Cassidy balled up the used tissues and tossed them on the floor. "Don't pretend that you're nice, because you're not. You never were."

"Is this where I point out you're convalescing in *my* house, sleeping on a hospital bed I rented specifically for *you*, cared for by nurses I hired? Hmm, wouldn't my actions be the definition of nice?"

Cassidy stared at her blankly.

"Why do I even try?" Daisy asked aloud as she stood. "Good night, Cassidy. I hope you feel better soon."

With that, she retreated to the other end of the long hallway and shut the door behind her. She told herself she was an adult, with friends and resources, and what did it matter if Cassidy didn't like her? It didn't hurt—not at all.

But there was no comfort in the lies.

Sage wanted to be patient, but she was tired, hungry and thinking that coming back to Los Angeles had been a really stupid idea. She should have started over somewhere no one knew her. Then she wouldn't get her feelings hurt by some stupid guy, and her sister wouldn't be texting her every fifteen minutes for the past two days, begging Sage to come see her. Which she had. Again.

"You have got to stop," she said, letting her irritation show in her voice. "I mean it, Cassidy. This is ridiculous."

It was nearly nine in the evening. Sage had worked a full day and she was due back in the store by eleven the next morning. With Vivian on vacation, Sage was getting more hours, which meant more chances to make commission.

"But I need you here," her sister said, grabbing her hand. "Please stay with me for a little bit."

"I need to get home and eat something. I have to be back at work in the morning."

"Esmerelda can make you something," Cassidy told her. "She won't mind. Then you can stay with me."

Sage seriously doubted whether Daisy's housekeeper would want to do anything for her.

"I still have to work," she said, pulling her hand free of her sister's tight grip.

"Jobs are stupid."

"Yes, they are, but I'm not a trust fund baby like you and Daisy. I have to work to pay my bills."

"Sage, you have to stay. Pretty please?"

With her blue eyes wide and pleading, and the note of whine in her voice, she looked and sounded as though she was eight instead of twenty-eight. Sage held in a sigh.

"You're making me insane."

"I know. Isn't it great?" Cassidy reached for the walkie-talkie on the high table by her hospital bed. "What do you want to eat?"

"Nothing. I'll get something when I get home." She shifted in the chair next to the bed and eased off her heels. Her feet were killing her—the pain almost enough of a distraction to keep her from being seriously annoyed with her sister. Of course if she got over that, she might have to think about what had happened with Adam and she didn't want to. Not only had his assertion stung, she really disliked that she was still thinking about it.

His blunt comment that she'd "gotten mean" had caught her off guard. That was the only reason his words had made it past her defenses. She'd managed to act as if she hadn't cared, then had stayed a few more minutes before excusing herself. To make sure he didn't think she was sulking, she'd changed into a cute dress and had driven away, only to discover she had nowhere to go. Hitting a bar by herself was beyond grim, so she'd walked around Beverly Center for an hour before returning home and hiding out in her room, all the while trying to figure out what his words had meant. Beyond the obvious.

Not that she cared what he thought. He was just some guy she used to know. It wasn't as if they were actually friends, or dating. She needed to get over it and move on.

"Sage!" Cassidy glared at her. "Pay attention to me!"

Sage stared at her sister. "When did you get to be a brat?"

"I'm not. I'm so bored. Things don't hurt as much, so my nurses are weaning me off the painkillers. That means I'm not sleeping all the time. There's nothing to *do*."

"You have a television. Watch something. Read a book. Learn a new language. I'm not your personal plaything."

"Entertain me! You're the fun one."

"I'm not feeling fun right now."

She started to stand. Cassidy grabbed her hand again.

"Wait! I need to tell you something. Desean proposed."

Sage sat back down. "Who's Desean?"

"The guy I've been seeing. Kind of seeing. It's been an on-and-off thing for a while now."

"I didn't know you were seeing anyone."

Not that she and Cassidy talked all that much, but they texted on occasion and she was pretty sure she would remember her sister mentioning keeping a guy around for any length of time.

Cassidy didn't do relationships—not ones that lasted past a weekend. She was pretty enough to get anyone she wanted, but she had no interest in keeping the man of the moment around past the time it took for her to have a couple of orgasms.

"Is it serious?" she asked.

Cassidy tilted her head. "He proposed."

"So you said. That only means it's serious for him. You're the one I'm asking about."

Cassidy waved her unbroken arm. "No. Maybe. I don't know. I like him, but lately he's been pushing me to, you know, commit. I can't do that. I've told him and told him, but he won't listen." She wrinkled her nose. "He's sweet and all. Smart. Funny. Really good-looking, with muscles to die for, but I couldn't marry him."

"You could. You simply choose not to."

Cassidy's lower lip trembled. "That's kind of a mean thing to say."

There was that word again, Sage thought in annoyance. She was about to snap at her sister only to think that maybe she hadn't been exactly supportive. Despite the healing bruises and the fact that she had more energy, Cassidy was still recovering from a serious accident. Maybe a little more patience was called for.

"How long have you been off-and-on seeing him?" she asked.

"A couple of years." Cassidy pressed her lips together. "Maybe three."

"Years? You've been seeing a guy for three years and I'm just now hearing about it?"

"It's not a thing."

"It is to him." Sage softened her tone. "Cassidy, if he's all that you say, why not give him a chance? A real chance."

"Because it will all go to shit. You know it will. No marriage is successful. I mean on TV and stuff, but not in life. Name one person you know who's happily married."

Sage rolled her eyes. "Seriously? How about Daisy and Jordan? They've been together what? Ten years? Eleven? Twelve?"

Cassidy's mouth widened into a smile. "You don't know. Of course you don't. It's not like she would have told you." She lowered her voice. "He's moved out. They're separated. Ben and Krissa come see me every day after school and they told me. It's been a few weeks now. He's moved into a hotel. I don't think it's an apartment." She wiggled her eyebrows. "You should so go after him. It would serve her right."

"Cassidy, stop it," Sage said, mostly to buy time.

Daisy and Jordan separated? She wasn't happy about the news—in truth it should be meaningless to her, except for some generic regret that any marriage had failed. Only she felt more than that. For reasons she couldn't explain, her stomach felt a little queasy and she had the strangest desire to bolt from the room.

"Well, I hate her. It's not my fault."

"You have no reason to hate her. She's taken you in, even though you're difficult and disrespectful."

"I don't care if she likes me. Dad is the one who wants me to stay and she'll always do what he says."

"Why do you hate Daisy so much? When we were kids, she cared about you."

"I just do. Besides, you and Mom were always awful to her. This isn't on me."

Sage wondered if that was true. She and her mother had been pretty awful—yet another piece of her past she would like to do over. Had Cassidy learned to disrespect Daisy from them?

"We were wrong," Sage told her. "I'm sorry about Daisy and Jordan. I hope they work things out." She smiled. "Then I could give you an example of a successful marriage."

"But until then, we don't know a single one, which means I can never marry Desean. Not that he would want me now. I look awful."

"You look fine and do you really think he cares about a few bruises?"

"No." Cassidy sighed. "He loves me. That's why I fell off the mountain. He was proposing and I was backing away and suddenly there wasn't any ground and I was falling."

"At least you have a good story to tell." She rose. "Stop texting me. I have to work and I need my sleep. If you don't stop, I'll turn off my phone."

Cassidy flashed her a confident smile. "You'd never do that to me. You can't. You love me."

"Less and less each day, kid." Sage kissed her cheek. "I'll see you in a couple of days."

"Come back later. We'll watch movies and talk all night."

"No."

"Sage, please?"

"Goodbye, Cassidy."

Sage spoke as firmly as she could. If Cassidy continued to bug her, she was going to have to make good on her promise and turn off her phone.

"But I need you."

Sage paused to look back at her. She smiled and said, "Read a book."

Despite not having to be at the hospital until close to noon, Daisy woke at six in the morning, as per usual. One of these days, she was going to learn to sleep in.

She showered, pulled on jeans and a sweatshirt, and shoved

her feet into a pair of Uggs. She checked her phone, hoping for a text from Jordan, but there was nothing. She'd seen him last night when he'd taken the kids to dinner, but a three-second "Hi, how's it going" did not a marriage make.

She missed him. No, she missed *them*. She missed sitting across from him at dinner and hanging out as a family in the evening. She missed sleeping with him, and sex, not that they'd been doing much of that lately. Something she didn't want to dwell on because it made her wonder if he was doing it with someone else and the thought of Jordan being unfaithful made her sick to her stomach.

The morning routine was familiar. She let the dogs out first thing. Esmerelda fed them and the cats later, after getting the kids breakfast. Theirs was a well-oiled machine and Daisy knew she was lucky to have so much help. Her schedule was constantly changing, but with Esmerelda around, she didn't have to worry about things like getting her kids to school on time or making their lunch.

She opened one of the French doors off the kitchen and both dogs ran into the yard. She closed the door, turned and nearly jumped out of her skin when she saw Sage sitting at the table by the windows.

Daisy pressed a hand to her chest in a futile attempt to slow her heartbeat. She glared at her former stepsister.

"You scared me! What are you doing here?"

Sage turned to her. "Sorry. I'm trying to gather the strength to go home."

Sage looked exhausted. There were dark circles under her eyes and her normally sleek and shiny blond hair seemed dull and in need of a good shampoo. Her clothes were wrinkled, her skin was pale.

"You look terrible," Daisy blurted before she could stop herself.

Sage offered a faint smile. "I feel terrible, so hey, that's something."

"Are you sick?"

"Of our sister." Sage rubbed her eyes. "Cassidy's been texting me constantly. I mean every fifteen minutes. She wants me to come over and keep her company. If I don't answer her, she calls and calls. I'm not getting any sleep, I'm dead on my feet at work, and if this doesn't stop, I'm going to kill her and throw her body in the river." She paused and looked at Daisy. "Do we have a river anywhere close?"

"Not really."

"Figures."

Daisy wasn't sure what to do or say. Having Sage in her kitchen was surreal. Having her look so broken made the situation even more strange.

"Do you want some coffee?" she asked, going for the safest question.

"That would be great. Thanks. I would have made some myself, but you have seriously complicated equipment in here."

Daisy smiled. "Just the espresso machine. There's a regular coffeemaker in the butler's pantry."

"How silly of me not to check that." Sage stretched out her arms on the table and rested her head on them. "Ignore me. I'll drink my coffee, then leave."

Daisy started the coffee, then went to the refrigerator and pulled out a couple of small glass jars of imported yogurt. She put two slices of bread into the toaster before choosing a ripe avocado and a tomato from the baskets on the counter.

Five minutes later, she placed the yogurt and a plate with avocado toast topped with sliced tomato in front of Sage, along with a cup of coffee and a small pitcher of cream. She took her usual seat at the end of the table.

Sage looked at the food and coffee, then at her. "I'm incredibly grateful. Thank you." She sipped the coffee and sighed. "Exactly what I needed. Now about killing Cassidy…"

Daisy grinned at her. "You don't want to do that. You'd feel guilty."

"Not in the moment. She has got to stop bugging me."

"She's bored and she's never been good at self-soothing."

Sage picked up the toast. "I'm pretty sure she knows how to masturbate."

Daisy laughed. "I meant self-soothing in the sense of entertaining herself when you're not around. You've always been everything to her."

Sage eyed her suspiciously. "Was that you being critical?"

"Just stating facts."

Sage took a couple of bites of the toast. "You're right. When she was with my mom and me, we pretty much let her get away with anything. It was easier. I'm sure you had plenty of rules for her." Sage held up a hand. "I meant that as a fact, as you called it. I wasn't being bitchy."

"There were expectations," Daisy admitted. "I was trying to do the right thing, but all I did was make her hate me."

"She doesn't hate you," Sage said.

Daisy picked up her yogurt without speaking.

Sage sighed. "Okay, yes, she hates you and I honestly don't know why."

While the information wasn't news, Daisy had to admit it stung a little. She'd really done her best with Cassidy—trying to be supportive and affectionate, but once Wallace and Joanne divorced, her little sister hadn't been interested in having anything to do with her.

"I wonder if my mom said anything," Sage muttered, reaching for her coffee. "It would be just like her to warn Cassidy to never trust you."

"Why would she do that? I was thirteen when our parents got a divorce. I wasn't a threat to anyone."

"My mom didn't want the divorce. She loved Wallace and God knows she adored living here." Sage finished her coffee and got up to get more. "She was angry and resentful. She couldn't accept responsibility for what happened, so she blamed you. I wonder if she told Cassidy you were the reason her parents were splitting up."

The unfairness of that cut Daisy to the bone. "But I wasn't the reason and Cassidy was only five. That would be a horrible thing to say to a child."

Sage returned carrying the pot. She poured coffee for each of them. "You say that like rational thought plays a part in all this. It doesn't. My mom only cares about herself."

"But—"

Sage waved the pot. "Daisy, let it go. You can't change the past and you can't change my mother."

Daisy sipped her coffee, trying to make sense of it all. She wanted to accuse Sage of lying, but her gut told her otherwise. She knew Joanne had never liked her and had gone out of her way to make her feel unwelcome in her own home, but would the other woman really act so cruelly?

As soon as she asked the question, she knew the answer.

"Kind of leaves a bad taste in your mouth, huh?" Sage asked as she resumed her seat.

"Yes. I hate that my avocado toast is ruined."

"You'll have avocado toast tomorrow while I'll be dealing with our sister."

"Unless you've killed her."

Sage smiled. "There is that happy thought."

They continued to drink their coffee. Daisy glanced at Sage. "You mentioned you have a job," she said cautiously. "So you're back here permanently? I thought you were, um, married."

"Not anymore." Sage's voice had an edge. "We're divorced. You can get them really quick in the Dominican Republic, plus there's the bonus of a tropical vacation. We'd just wrapped that up when my mom told me she might have cancer. She was fairly hysterical, so I came back here to help. When it turned out to be only a scare, I had to make some choices about my life. For reasons that are less and less clear, I decided to stay here."

"Oh." Daisy didn't know what to say. "I'm glad your mom is okay."

"If you mean that, you're being nicer than she deserves."

"I wouldn't want her to have cancer."

Sage chuckled. "How about a rash?"

Daisy grinned. "I would be okay with a rash." Her smile faded. "Don't take this wrong, but it's very strange having you and Cassidy back in the house."

"Imagine how it feels from my end. Once again I have my nose pressed up against the window, looking at all you have and what will never be mine."

Daisy felt her eyes widen. "Is that what you think this is?"

"No, and I shouldn't have said that. I blame the exhaustion." She waved her hand. "You've done well, Daisy. You have great kids and your family. Dogs, cats. It's all good."

"I'm not trying to rub your nose in anything."

"I know that. It's not your style."

"But you still hate me."

Sage looked at her. "I never hated you and now I don't know you."

Frustration bubbled up inside Daisy. Her parents' money had nothing to do with her. The house had been left to her in a trust, and she had a trust fund from both her parents. She'd been blessed and she got that, but where she lived and how much she had in the bank wasn't who she was.

Sage surprised her by saying, "I really am sorry for blurting that out. It's just things are complicated right now. I'm trying to figure out my future and it's not easy."

"Can I help?"

One corner of Sage's mouth turned up. "I think that would be awkward for both of us."

Daisy knew that was true, but she was glad she'd made the offer. "Where do you work?"

"In a boutique. Very Italian, very expensive."

"You speak Italian, so that should be a big plus."

Sage finished her coffee. "Yes, and I have the right amount of meanness to be successful."

Daisy frowned. "Meanness? Why would you say that?"

"No reason. Never mind. I'm in a mood." She smiled. "A lack of self-soothing, I suppose."

"You and me both," Daisy said, then wished she hadn't, because it would lead to obvious questions that she didn't want to answer.

Sage looked away. "Yes, well, Cassidy mentioned Jordan had moved out. One of the kids told her. I'm sorry about that. I hope you work it out. It would be nice to know at least one person with a successful marriage."

Daisy felt her face heat, not sure what to say. The combination of humiliation and shame made her feel exposed in every sense of the word.

Sage rose. "Thanks for breakfast. Don't take this wrong, but with any luck we won't run into each other again this early, anytime soon."

Daisy nodded because she still couldn't speak. Her throat

was tight and her eyes burned. Of all the people who had to find out about Jordan leaving her, why did it have to be her sisters? Two people that she could never, ever trust to have her back.

eight

Sage pulled into her driveway and admitted to herself she couldn't keep going much longer. Between the nights with Cassidy and the long hours at work, not to mention tutoring, she was in serious trouble. If she didn't get some sleep soon, she was going to start having hallucinations.

She had a couple days off. Her plan was to sleep as much as she could, turning off her phone so Cassidy couldn't reach her. Then she would regroup and figure out what to do about her sister.

As she got out of her car, Adam came up the driveway.

Despite how their last encounter had left her feeling battered, she acknowledged that he looked good. He had an ease about him, as if he was just confident enough to know he could handle anything. She'd been confident once and missed it. These days, she felt like she was constantly finding her way.

She locked her car and watched him. When he was a few feet from her, he stopped and shoved his hands into his jeans pockets. His dark blue gaze met hers.

"I'm sorry," he said. "Despite how things have gone between us, I'm usually pretty good with women. But when I'm around you, I'm that damned awkward seventeen-year-old again. All arms and legs with no self-control and the conversational skills of plant fiber. I can't figure out why. Is it the fact that you're so beautiful? Or am I in the early stages of dementia? Which is not meant as an excuse. I'm sorry I hurt your feelings."

"Plant fiber?" she asked, because asking him to expand on the beautiful part would make her seem shallow.

"It was the best I could do in the moment. See? You leave me inarticulate." His mouth twisted. "Don't be mad, Sage. Please. I shouldn't have said you were mean."

She knew she was at a crossroads. She could punish him for what he'd said or she could be an adult and accept his apology.

"You're right," she said slowly. "I'm not proud of some of my past behavior. I wasn't careful with other people's feelings." Her voice turned wry. "I've learned my lesson. I accept your apology and offer one of my own. I'm sorry for whatever I did in high school to hurt or offend you. I'm sorry we couldn't stay friends."

"That was on me. You never actually did anything to me, but I was afraid you would and that I wouldn't be able to handle it. Getting space was about self-preservation."

Because if she'd known she had power over him, she would have used it and turned him into dust.

He lightly touched her arm. "Have dinner with me? I owe you a burger."

She was surprised to feel a faint tingle where his fingers had brushed against her skin. Was she attracted to Adam? He wasn't her type at all—she preferred men who were all flash and no substance. Adam was a genuine person. Would she know what to do with one of those?

More crossroads, she thought. All the men she'd been involved with before had been so easy for her. Easy to seduce, easy to manipulate, easy to leave. She had no idea what being with Adam would be like. Not that he was asking. Dinner as an apology was a far cry from declaring his desperate need for her.

"It wasn't supposed to be a hard question," he said lightly, his voice trying to conceal the disappointment she saw in his eyes. "Have a good evening."

"Adam, wait."

He paused and glanced at her.

"Dinner would be great," she told him. "But I've been dealing with my sister every night for the past week and working long hours. I need to sleep. Can I have a rain check?"

"Sure. Let me know when you have time."

She had the feeling he didn't believe her about being tired, but there was nothing she could do about that.

"I'll be in touch," she promised.

"Sure. Looking forward to it."

She watched him walk back into his house. Part of her wanted to go after him and explain she really did want to have dinner with him, but she knew there weren't words to convince him.

Later, she promised herself. She would show him she meant what she said.

Daisy tried to breathe evenly to quiet the nerves making her stomach writhe. She was being ridiculous. Jordan was her husband—there was no reason the thought of seeing him should have her on edge. Only she hadn't seen him for more than a few minutes at a time for weeks now. Not that they were having quiet one-on-one time. Instead they were meeting with Ben's school counselor to discuss an ongoing bullying problem. Not exactly a romantic rendezvous.

She resisted the urge to glance at her watch, yet again. Jordan would be here, on time. The counselor had emailed them together to set up the appointment.

As if reading her mind, he walked into the waiting area and sat in the chair next to hers.

"I can't believe we're still dealing with this," he said without greeting her. "Ben's a good kid. This is stressful."

Daisy told herself not to read anything into what he said. He was a concerned father, worried about his son. That was a good thing. So what if he hadn't asked how she was or in any way indicated he missed her. This was hardly the time to get into that. Although she couldn't help wishing that he had.

The door to the counselor's office opened and Paloma stepped out to greet them. She was small and slight, with graying brown hair, and an air of determination that convinced students they needed to listen when she spoke.

"Right on time," she said with a smile. "Come on in."

Jordan rose and waited for Daisy to precede him. They settled in front of Paloma's desk. The counselor opened a file on her desk and slipped on her glasses.

"Ben's grades are excellent and his teachers only have positive things to say about how he behaves in class," she began. "He's well-liked and developing some leadership skills." She looked at them over her glasses. "He's a great kid, but I'm worried about the bullying issue."

"I've asked him about Christian," Daisy said, trying to sound more confident than she felt. "He's worried about his friend."

Christian, a smart, shy boy, had long been the target for teasing. Lewis, a new student, had made tormenting Christian his personal mission. He'd taken things so far, he'd been expelled, but there were the lingering effects of Ben still worrying about his friend.

"We've talked about the buddy system," Paloma said. "Making sure no one is on their own in vulnerable locations. Ben's a great friend. He sticks by Christian's side whenever he can, but I'm concerned about them both."

"The situation needs to be handled carefully," Jordan said. "Ben can't follow Christian around every second of every day. He'll be flagged as weak."

Daisy didn't like the harsh assessment, but she knew Jordan was right.

"We're aware of that," Paloma said. "And yes, we do have to balance things. I have Christian's parents' permission to tell you they're thinking of placing him in a different school."

"That would be hard on Ben," Daisy said. "He and Christian are so close."

"That's why I wanted you to know it's on their minds. Christian hasn't been told yet."

"Then we won't say anything to Ben."

"What about martial arts?" Jordan asked. "Would something like that help Ben with confidence?"

"It might." She glanced at her notes. "Now the other topic I wanted to discuss was Ben's academics. He's doing extremely well and we've been talking about the possibility of having him skip a grade."

"No," Jordan said flatly.

Daisy stared at him. "Shouldn't we hear her out?"

"It's not a good idea." He turned to the counselor. "You're one of the top schools in Los Angeles. Figure out a curriculum that will challenge him while keeping him in his grade. I don't want him being the youngest kid in the room. There are social consequences to jumping ahead a grade or being left behind."

Paloma closed her folder. "Obviously this is something the two of you need to discuss. It's not necessary, of course. And you're right, Jordan. We can come up with other ways to keep Ben engaged. It was just a thought."

The meeting continued for another half hour as they discussed Krissa's performance. When they were finished, Daisy walked with Jordan to the parking lot. When they were by her SUV, she drew in a breath.

"I don't understand why you dismissed the idea of Ben skipping a grade. It does have some advantages."

"Not enough to make up for the problems it will cause."

"What problems? He's a happy, caring, well-adjusted kid."

"He would lose all his friends. Sure, he'd see them, but not the way he does now. He's not a big kid to begin with, so he'd be the youngest and the smallest. That's not an advantage. He's happy now. I think we should leave him where he is. Doesn't he have enough going on without him worrying about starting in a new grade?"

"I agree it would be stressful, but I don't understand why we can't at least discuss it."

His mouth tightened. "I know what I'm talking about, Daisy."

"And I don't?"

"You have no experience with this. Sage was held back a year when her mom married your dad. It was hard on her. When we were together in high school, she still remembered how awful it was for her. She was older than everyone else in her class. She was humiliated and it changed who she was. I don't want that for Ben."

Daisy glared at him. "You're comparing our son being too smart for his grade to your high school girlfriend being left behind a year? How are they the same thing?"

He exhaled sharply, his impatience visible. "Great. Now you're not going to listen because I mentioned Sage?"

"No, I'm asking how her experience has anything to do with Ben. It strikes me as an odd analogy. Why are you suddenly bringing up Sage?"

"It's a relevant point of comparison."

Daisy wondered if that was all it was. "Because you're seeing her?"

"What?" His voice was a yelp. "No. When would I see Sage? Last I heard, she's in Italy."

She desperately wanted to believe him but would have felt better about the entire discussion if he'd said he didn't want to see Sage. But if she mentioned that, they would end up fighting about things that didn't matter.

"Daisy, I really don't want Ben to deal with the stress of skipping a grade. That's all I'm saying. I think he should stay where he is because he's happy and successful. Why screw with that?"

She studied him, wondering if that really was all there was to it.

"All right," she said slowly. "I'm not advocating we change anything, I was only suggesting we consider it. But if you feel that strongly, I'm fine with leaving him where he is and asking his teachers to challenge him academically."

Jordan relaxed. "Thank you. I want our kids to be happy and well-rounded people. Grades are important but so is everything else."

She decided to risk ruining their brief détente.

"Jordan, why are you still in a hotel?"

"Because nothing's been resolved."

"That's because I'm not sure what the problem is."

"You know exactly what's wrong."

"I don't. That's not a fair thing to say. You haven't told me so I'm supposed to guess?"

He looked at her as if he didn't believe her. "Fine. I'll tell you. The problem is I don't matter to you anymore. I haven't for a while. I'm trying to figure out if that's a temporary thing or your way of being done with me."

"You're putting this on me? You move out, you won't tell me what's wrong and now you're saying not only do I know but that it's all my fault?"

"You like my shirt?" he asked.

WTF? "You're asking about what you're wearing?"

"Do you like it?"

"It's fine. What does your shirt have to do with anything?"

"You used to buy all my clothes. You said I had terrible taste and shouldn't be allowed anywhere near a store. Even when we were dating, you would buy me shirts and socks and that first Christmas you got me a leather jacket."

She genuinely had no idea what he was talking about. How was any of this relevant to their marriage?

"Yes, I bought you a leather jacket."

"You stopped buying me clothes a long time ago."

"And you're upset about that? Jordan, I'm a working mom. You moved out because you had to buy your own shirts?"

"No. I moved out because you stopped caring enough to buy me shirts." He glanced at his watch. "I gotta get to the clinic. I have a full schedule."

He walked to his car without looking back. She got in her SUV and watched him drive away, not sure how to process what had just happened.

She hadn't bought him shirts? That was his complaint? Couldn't she just be busy? Did it have to have more meaning than that?

Jordan had many flaws but being irrational wasn't one of them, so there was something else going on. Something he wasn't telling her. Something that was a whole lot bigger than shirts. There was no way he thought she didn't care. They were married. She loved him and he knew that. But having a conversation by herself wasn't going to solve their problems. Men!

She started her car, then realized she didn't know where to go or what to do. She'd traded days to have time to attend the meeting about Ben, giving her rare time off with no one waiting for her return. Her plan had been to spend the rest of the afternoon being productive or possibly self-indulgent. But the thought of cleaning out a few closets or even reading wasn't appealing any longer. She felt restless and unsettled as she drove home.

She parked in the garage and went inside. Esmerelda was out running errands, so except for Cassidy and her nurses, she was alone. Maybe the best way to clear her head was to take the dogs out for a long walk. She could—

"Hi."

Daisy spun around and saw Cassidy sitting in a wheelchair in the hallway.

"You're up," Daisy said, hoping she looked surprised rather than horrified. "Congratulations. Progress."

Cassidy looked better than she had in days. The bruises on her face had faded to faint shadows. Her wavy long hair was pulled back in a neat braid and she wore clothes rather than a nightgown. The wheelchair had a support for her broken leg, which stuck out in front of her, but her broken arm had a smaller cast that allowed her to be more mobile.

"I'm so happy to be out of the bedroom," Cassidy told her. "The walls were closing in." She touched the small joystick on the arm of the wheelchair and moved forward a couple of feet. "Watch out. I'm going to be a menace."

Oh, joy. Daisy kept her sarcasm to herself and started for the kitchen. Cassidy followed, no doubt out of boredom rather than interest or a desire for them to hang out. Daisy held in a sigh.

"I was going to make an espresso," she said, hoping she sounded cheerful. "Would you like one?"

"Yes, please."

Daisy busied herself with the coffees. While the first one brewed, she moved a chair away from the table so Cassidy could get closer. Once the coffees were finished, she carried them over to the table and collected cookies from the ceramic container on the long counter.

They sat in silence, sipping their coffee and eating cookies. Daisy tried to relax and enjoy the moment.

"It's quiet," Cassidy said. "I'd forgotten that part of living here. My place in Miami is great, but I'm right off the pool and I can hear people out there all the time. Not that I'm home much."

"I've never been to Miami. Is it nice?"

Cassidy reached for another cookie. "I like it. It's hot and humid in the summer, but it's always pretty and the people are fun. The beaches are beautiful."

She paused, looked at Daisy, then away. What had been a relatively comfortable silence turned awkward. Daisy searched for something to say and came up with nothing. Ridiculous, she thought. Cassidy was her sister—they had to have something in common.

Despite that, the only topic that came to mind was to ask about Joanne. Had she lied to make Daisy the villain of the divorce? Was she the reason the sisters didn't get along? But Daisy knew better than to start down that path.

"Esmerelda told me you have a job," Cassidy said into the silence. "Is that true?"

"Yes, I'm a nurse anesthesiologist."

"I knew you'd gone to college to study that, but I didn't think you'd still be working."

"I am. I love what I do."

"Huh. Didn't Dad want you to be a doctor?"

Daisy smiled. "Yes. There were many fights about my career choice. He wanted me to go to medical school. While he wasn't excited about me studying anesthesiology, he felt if I had to go into that, I should do it as a doctor."

"But you didn't."

"No." Daisy thought about mentioning that she'd done a lot of research and knew that by going into the nursing arm of the profession, she would have more contact with patients— the part of the job she most enjoyed. But she doubted Cassidy was interested in the politics of medicine.

"He expected a lot of you," Cassidy said, picking up her coffee cup. "No one expected much of me."

"Why would you say that? He loves you."

"I know. He's a good dad. But he never thought I was going to do anything important. Mom always pointed out I didn't have to work, with the trust fund and all. You have way more money than me, so why did you bother to go to college?"

"I need to work because it's important to me," Daisy said, surprised by the question. "Some days it's hard, but it's always rewarding. I help people. I ease their suffering and keep them safe during surgery. It's a responsibility I take seriously. I think it's important to have work you can be passionate about."

Cassidy stared at her. "I'm passionate about what I do, but it's not like your job. No one cares if I write a travel article."

"That's not true. Your work educates people. More important, it transports them to a place they'll probably never go. Last year you had that piece on those women in Kenya. The ones who were starting a food co-op. They'd all lost their husbands and they were starting a new kind of family—one that would bring money into their village. You made me feel like I was there. That's a gift."

Cassidy fidgeted in her chair. "I didn't know you read my work."

"Of course I read it. I like seeing the world through your eyes."

"Sometimes it's hard to see it that way when I'm in the middle of it."

"That's probably true for everyone. Workdays can be consuming. It's only later that we can look back and get perspective."

Cassidy looked away. She was obviously uncomfortable and Daisy had no idea why. She was about to ask if Cassidy was in pain when her sister pulled out her cell phone.

"I'm seeing someone," she announced, touching the screen several times, then turning it so Daisy could see the picture she'd put up.

The man staring back at her was gorgeous, with dark eyes and skin, and long braids. His shoulders were impossibly broad. His half smile made her want to smile back.

"He's impressive," Daisy said.

"His name is Desean. He owns the townhouse complex where I live. That's how we met."

There was a tone of defiance in her voice, which made zero sense to Daisy.

"He's in love with me," her sister added.

"Are you in love with him?"

"That's not the point." Cassidy pocketed the phone. "He's Black."

"I noticed that from the picture. Are you feeling all right? You're not making any sense."

Cassidy's gaze sharpened. "But he's Black."

"What does that have to do with anything?" Daisy asked before a terrible truth occurred to her. She half rose from her chair before sitting back down. "You think I'd care about that? You think it matters?"

Tears filled Cassidy's eyes. "Doesn't it? Don't you want to tell me I can't see him anymore?"

This time Daisy did stand. She took several steps back before answering.

"I get that you and I aren't close, but I'm angry and hurt you would think so little of me. If Desean makes you happy, then that's what's important. Who he is as a man, not what he looks like on the outside. I've never done or said anything to make you think I care about things like that. You're wrong about me, Cassidy. You couldn't be more wrong."

With that, she stormed out of the kitchen and hurried up to her bedroom. She closed the door and leaned against it, waiting until the tightness in her chest faded. But she knew the shock and embarrassment that came with her sister's awful assumptions would take a whole lot longer to go away.

nine

Sage made her way down the wide staircase. Cassidy had texted her at two in the morning, crying about bad dreams and begging Sage to come over. For reasons she couldn't explain, Sage had agreed and now was paying the price for her generosity. She wanted coffee and then sleep. Unfortunately the latter wasn't happening. She was due for work at eleven.

Once on the main floor, she headed for the kitchen, thinking she would make herself a cup of coffee before going home for a quick shower.

But when she walked into the kitchen, she wasn't alone. Esmerelda was pulling food out of the refrigerator.

The woman was of average height, in her fifties, probably a size fourteen, and had short brown hair. She wore an untucked polo shirt over jeans.

Cassidy complained that Esmerelda was totally Team Daisy and had a stink eye that was like a stab to the heart. Until Esmerelda turned and saw Sage in the kitchen, Sage would have said Cassidy was exaggerating.

"Yes?" Esmerelda asked, her tone implying what she really wanted to say was *eat shit and die.*

"I come in peace," Sage said, offering the smile she saved for difficult customers. "I was hoping to get some coffee before I go home. Cassidy was especially needy last night and I'm exhausted."

She watched the battle in the housekeeper's eyes. Would she do the polite thing and agree to the coffee, or rudely tell her to get out? Sage was about to surrender and simply leave when Esmerelda walked into the butler's pantry and returned with a mug of coffee. She set it in front of a stool at the island.

"Cream or sugar?" Esmerelda asked.

"Just black is fine. Thanks."

Sage took a seat and picked up the mug. The familiar smell of freshly brewed coffee brightened her spirits. She took a sip, then sighed.

The housekeeper returned to the refrigerator, where she took out eggs, bell peppers and milk. She'd already collected flour and butter. A food processor stood on the far end of the island.

"What are you making?" Sage asked.

"Quiche."

"Now?" She glanced at the clock. It was not quite six. She'd only made quiche a couple of times, but she was pretty sure the crust had to bake by itself for a little bit and the filling was in the oven nearly an hour. "Don't they have to be at school by eight?"

Esmerelda shot her a dismissive look. "They have a late start today. I wouldn't make a breakfast that couldn't be finished in time."

Aware she'd offended, Sage held in a sigh. "You're right. I should have thought of that."

"Does Miss Daisy know you're here?"

"I have no idea. She's aware I've been visiting Cassidy." They'd had that early morning coffee the previous week. Funny how she'd seen more of Daisy in the past month than in the past twenty years.

"I'm going to tell her you were here and that I gave you coffee."

"I'd expect no less." Sage put down her cup. "You're very protective of her."

"She's my family."

"You're not married?"

Esmerelda measured out the ingredients for the crust. "I was. My husband and children were killed in Thailand in the 2004 tsunami. We were working for a different family back then. My husband had taken my children to the beach. I was up at the house, working. They were swept away and their bodies never recovered."

The stark and unexpected words stunned Sage. She instantly felt sick to her stomach. "I'm so sorry."

Esmerelda flipped on the food processor and ran it until she had created the dough. She turned off the machine.

"I was devastated. When I got back to the States, Daisy insisted I come live here so I could be close to my cousin. She's much older than me, but is still my only family. For six months, I stayed in my room. Daisy checked on me so many times. She brought in a grief counselor. When I was a little better, she helped me find a job. When she married Mr. Jordan, my cousin retired and Daisy hired me. She's my family now."

Sage struggled to understand. So while Daisy had been going to college, she'd taken the time to help out someone she'd never met—literally opening up her home. That same year, Sage had been busy dumping Jordan and moving to France.

Saint Daisy, she thought, trying to find a little disdain in the words, but instead felt only admiration for her former stepsister. It wasn't a comfortable feeling.

As if drawn by their conversation, Daisy walked into the

kitchen. She had on hospital scrubs and her hair was in a pony-tail. She dropped her tote bag on the counter and raised her eyebrows when she saw Sage.

"Cassidy?" she guessed, as she walked to get herself coffee.

"She had bad dreams and called me."

Daisy returned, her expression neutral. "I hope she's all right now."

"She's asleep. That's how I escaped. I'd just started to catch up on my sleep when she called me around two."

Daisy hugged Esmerelda. "You don't have to make them quiche for every late start."

The older woman smiled. "I like to make them happy." She shot Sage a look that seemed very much in the "stink eye" category. "*She* wanted coffee."

Daisy's mouth twitched. "I think it's all right to let her have liquids, but no food. If you feed them, they start expecting it and you can never get rid of them."

"Very funny," Sage muttered.

"I try to be, but I'm not naturally humorous. I wish I was. So the quiche won't be ready for about an hour and a half. I'm happy to make you avocado toast again."

Sage rolled her shoulders, trying to ease the sudden tight-ness there. "Don't be nice to me," she blurted. "We've never gotten along and there's no reason we should start having a relationship now. I really don't want to like you."

Daisy's smile faded. "You never have, so that shouldn't be a problem."

Sage opened her mouth, then closed it. Daisy was right. Sage *had* never liked her, but why? They were about the same age, they'd lived in the same house. They'd both been dealing with the strangeness of their parents marrying.

"Why weren't we friends?" Sage asked.

"You really don't know?" Daisy's tone was incredulous.

"You and your mother made friendship impossible. I reached out to you over and over again, and you rebuffed me. At school, you went out of your way to make my life hell. I don't know why. As far as I can tell, I never did anything to make you so vindictive. It's in the past and I'm fine with that, and while Cassidy is here, you're more than welcome in the house, but don't worry. I'm not expecting us to be friends."

Sage felt herself starting to shake. She put down the mug she was holding before she dropped it.

"That was harsh," she said quietly, not sure why the words stung as much as they did. She knew Daisy was right about all of it. Sage had done her best to repress the memories, but Daisy's words had brought them back in color and 3D.

"Was it?" Daisy drained her coffee. "I have to go. I have surgery in an hour and I can't be late."

With that, she picked up her tote bag and walked out. Sage waited until the door to the garage closed. Then she got up, as well.

"Thank you for the coffee," she told Esmerelda.

The housekeeper didn't bother looking up from the peppers she was chopping. Sage waited for a second, then hurried toward the front door.

Just like everything else in her life, her timing sucked. Daisy was just backing out of the garage as Sage went down the front steps. For a single second, their eyes met. Daisy turned away first, leaving Sage feeling smaller and more alone than she ever had.

Daisy's patient was an eighteen-month-old who had taken a tumble down the stairs. Much like Cassidy, he had contusions and broken bones, along with a possible concussion. The femur break was the worst of them and had required a second surgery.

Two hours of meticulous work by the orthopedic surgeon later, the little boy was in recovery. Daisy stayed with him until he was breathing well on his own, with his pain under control. The second she left recovery and allowed herself to think of other things, a thousand emotions intruded.

She still hadn't made sense of what Jordan had told her, but his words had kept her up more than one night. Or maybe it was the combination of what he'd said and the fact that Cassidy had practically called her racist. Now she got to add a little Sage guilt into the mix, which didn't sit well at all.

She had to wonder if she'd been too hard on Sage. No matter that her stepsister had started the "let's not be friends" conversation, Daisy had allowed herself to get sucked into it and she could tell she'd hurt Sage's feelings. Daisy had many flaws but she didn't think hurting people was one of them, even if the hurt came from telling the truth.

She walked into the locker room. Two months ago she hadn't seen her former stepsister in over a decade. Suddenly Sage was everywhere and no matter how Daisy wanted to say seeing her didn't matter, it did. Old wounds were being ripped open and destructive patterns were being repeated.

Knowing dwelling on what had happened wasn't going to help, Daisy opened her locker. She pulled out her cell phone and checked for messages.

Disappointment fisted in her chest. She'd hoped that maybe Jordan would be in touch to explain. Or possibly ask if she wanted to buy him shirts again. She supposed a case could be made that texting went two ways, only she didn't know what to say to him.

"Relationships suck," she muttered as she grabbed her bag. She closed her locker and walked out into the hallway, only to almost physically run into a short, stocky doctor in his sixties.

"Uncle Ray," she said, surprised to see one of her father's

closest friends and the head of orthopedic surgery at a nearby teaching hospital. "What are you doing here?"

"I'm consulting on a case," he said, "and I took a chance that you might be available to have coffee with a lonely old man."

"Oh, please," she said with a laugh. "You're never lonely."

Uncle Ray had four kids, a wife, a large and successful practice, an active social life and a standing Thursday afternoon golf game. She couldn't remember a time in her life when she hadn't known him and his family.

He hugged her. "I'd still like to get coffee, if you have a few minutes."

Her radar went on alert. Uncle Ray was a busy man who rarely did anything without a purpose. While she believed he *had* actually been consulting with one of the pediatricians at the children's hospital where she worked, she suspected an ulterior motive.

"You're going to annoy me, aren't you?" she asked, linking arms with him.

"Possibly, a little."

They went to the main floor coffee stand and got their drinks, then took them outside to the seating area in the hospital courtyard. About a third of the tables were filled with hospital staff taking a break while family and visitors sat at the rest. They found a small table in the shade.

"How are things?" she asked.

"Good. Julie's doing well and my kids are still amazing. Andrea's pregnant."

"Is she? That's wonderful. This makes four kids?"

Uncle Ray beamed. "Yes. She always wanted a big family and I love being a grandfather. How are Ben and Krissa?"

"Doing well. Ben's excelling academically. The school wanted to talk about having him skip a grade, but we're thinking it would be better to keep him where he is."

Uncle Ray nodded. "If they can challenge him without the move, it's probably for the best. That kind of upheaval can be hard on students."

Daisy held in a sigh. "Yes, that was Jordan's point." Honestly, the more she thought about it, the more she thought he was right, which meant her annoyance at the suggestion in the first place made no sense.

"With the kids getting older, you must have a little more time in your life," Uncle Ray said.

She set down her coffee. "Do not start on me."

His bushy eyebrows rose. "I have no idea what you're talking about."

His tone was innocent enough, but there was a sparkle in his brown eyes.

"My father called you, didn't he?"

Uncle Ray smiled. "It's not too late, Daisy. You could apply to medical school, take the MCATs and be on your way."

And there it was. The reason for the "chance" meeting. Given this wasn't the first time her father had arranged for her to be ambushed, she wasn't even surprised. Note to self, she thought. Later, she would call her dad and tell him he was really starting to bug her, but that wasn't Uncle Ray's fault.

"Has it occurred to you I'm thirty-seven years old? I already have a career and I don't want to go to medical school."

"You'd be a doctor by the time you were forty-two. You've always enjoyed kids, so you could be in a pediatric practice by forty-five or forty-six. That would give you at least twenty years of enjoying your work, maybe twenty-five." He sipped his coffee. "More and more medical schools are seeing nurses applying. You'd get plenty of recommendations and your father and I have a lot of connections at UCLA. Think of how much you already know. It would be a snap."

"Uh-huh. I'm not sure anyone thinks medical school would

be a snap." She leaned back in her chair and held in a sigh. "Why do you do this to me? I love my work. It's challenging, I'm helping people and no two days are ever the same. This is what I want to do. I know I come from a long line of doctors and that my dad wanted me to keep the tradition going, but it's my life and I get to choose. I love you, but get off me."

Uncle Ray smiled at her. "I knew you'd say that, but I promised your father I would try."

"Tell him to stop sending his friends to do his dirty work."

"For some reason he thinks you'll listen to me."

"In most cases, yes. Just not when it comes to this. Now, tell me how Racine is doing. Is she still dating that male model?"

Sage told herself she was stressed from everything happening in her life and a lack of sleep, but the truth was much more uncomfortable. Daisy had hurt her feelings.

There—she'd thought it, now she had to deal with it. Two months ago she would have said Daisy affecting her in any way was impossible. They never saw each other. Daisy was firmly in her past and that was where she was going to stay. Only everything had changed and now she was seeing her all the time. Worse, Daisy had laid bare Sage's past behavior, making Sage feel uncomfortable. No matter how she told herself she didn't care what Daisy, or anyone, thought of her, she couldn't escape an odd sense of shame and sadness.

She did her best to shake off the negative feelings. It was her day off and she had things to do. She went running for an hour, then did laundry and completed several errands. She took her shiny new California driver's license to the local library and got a library card, then checked out a couple of books. She read one of them while she ate a solitary dinner at a little place in Westwood, finishing before the evening crowd poured in. When she returned to the house, her mother met her at the door.

"I'm bored," Joanne announced dramatically. "I need something to fill my life. A man would be great, but right now I can't find one. So let's do something together."

Entertaining her mother wasn't on her to-do list, she thought. Joanne, like Cassidy, had the ability to emotionally drain a person and then complain they weren't fun anymore. And speaking of Cassidy...

"You should go visit your daughter," she said cheerfully, as she walked into the house. "She's up in a wheelchair now, so you two could prowl Daisy's house and annoy her. That would be fun."

She should feel guilty for throwing Daisy under the Joanne bus, so to speak, but she didn't. Not after what her stepsister had said to her.

"I do like the sound of that," Joanne said with a smile, then looked at the books Sage held. "What are those?"

"I went to the library."

"On purpose?" Her mother sounded horrified.

"Yes, Mom. On purpose. I like to read."

"Since when?"

"It's entertaining. You should try it sometime."

Joanne shuddered. "No, thank you. We could go out to a bar." Her mouth turned down. "On second thought, that's a bad idea. You'd be too much competition for me." Her gaze narrowed as much as the Botox would let her. "Do you think we could still pass for sisters?"

Something that had never happened, Sage thought, but her mother had quite the imagination.

"Sure. We always have. Now, about Cassidy——"

"Are you seeing anyone?"

Sage inched toward her room. "No. I'm not ready."

A statement that was true, but not for the reasons her mother would think. Forgetting her ex had taken far less time than it should have. Right now she was more focused on trying to figure out things like what she really wanted for herself and why everyone said she was mean.

"Too bad Daisy and Jordan are still together," Joanne mused. "You and he made such a cute couple. I know he regrets losing you."

"They've separated," Sage said without thinking, then immediately wanted to claw the words back.

Her mother's eyes widened before she started laughing with far too much glee. "Really? They've split up? That's wonderful. Sage, you have to go out with him. Think of how much that will upset Daisy."

Sage took a step back. "Mom, no. I'm sorry I told you. It's not good news, it's sad. They have kids together."

Joanne waved away that detail. "Kids, shmids. Who cares about that? Call him. Do you have his number? I wonder how we could get it. Oh, wait! He's a vet. Just put on something cute and go to his office. He won't be able to resist you."

Sage felt bile rising in her throat. "No. Please stop. Jordan and I haven't been together in eighteen years, Mom. He's married and I have no interest in him. Or hurting Daisy."

That last statement shocked her, along with her mother.

"You can't possibly like her," Joanne said, putting her hands on her hips. "She was wretched. Sneaking around the house, doing everything so perfectly. Ugh. Wallace adored her and I couldn't, for the life of me, figure out why."

"Maybe because she's his daughter."

"Whatever." Her mother turned away. "You're not being the least bit helpful. I'm going out. There must be a man somewhere in this city who wants to buy me a drink."

Sage escaped to her room, hoping against hope her mother

stayed out late. When she heard the front door close and her mother's car start up, she exhaled softly and felt herself relax. Alone at last.

But ten minutes later, she had to admit that she was restless and wanted something to do. She glanced next door, hoping Adam was home, but his house was dark. She read for an hour and still felt on edge. She was nearly desperate enough to go see Cassidy, only that might mean running into Daisy and Sage didn't feel up to a confrontation.

She checked Adam's house again, and this time there were lights on. She went out back, thinking she would see what he was up to before texting him.

From her mother's back patio, she could look directly into his kitchen and family room. She expected to see him cooking a late dinner or something, but instead Adam had his arms wrapped around a dark-haired woman and they were kissing. Seriously kissing.

Sage felt her mouth drop open. Adam was seeing someone? But he'd told her he wasn't. Not that it mattered—he wasn't anything to her, but still, he'd lied and she didn't understand that. Adam had always told the truth.

But the proof was right there in front of her. As she watched, the woman shrugged out of her blouse and reached for the buttons on his shirt. He took care of them for her, then pulled her close again. His fingers fumbled with her bra.

Sage quickly retreated to her room. The blinds were already closed, so she didn't have to worry about him seeing in. Not that he would be looking. Right about now, they would be doing the deed.

The thought was unsettling. Was the strange woman the reason she wasn't seeing as much of Adam as she had been? She'd mentioned getting together for dinner, but he'd put her off, saying he was wrapping up a project. Foolishly she'd believed him, but now she wondered if the real reason was the brunette he was currently screwing.

A sense of loss settled in her stomach, along with annoyance and a weird feeling of betrayal. First Daisy and now Adam. Why was everyone making her feel like crap?

She curled up on her bed, closed her eyes tight and willed herself to be somewhere else. But when she opened her eyes a few minutes later, nothing had changed, least of all her.

ten

Daisy always assumed that using a cookie mix would cut down on the mess in her kitchen, but it never seemed to make a difference. Setting up her two children at opposite ends of the large island and helping them bake cookies was fun, but not tidy. A fine coating of flour and sugar covered the countertop and the front of their aprons. Sheba and Lucky lay on their oversize beds, watching eagerly for any happy accidents. Show tunes blared from the speakers in the ceiling and plenty of conversation and laughter added to the pleasure of the afternoon.

"Is the oven ready?" Ben asked, using the bottom of a juice glass to carefully press down on the three balls of dough to form the head of a teddy bear. When the cookies had baked, they would use chocolate chips for the eyes and the nose.

"It is," Daisy told him, walking over to check on Krissa. Her daughter had chosen to make earth cookies—a simple variation of a sugar cookie. Half the dough was dyed blue and half green. Individual cookies were made with a bit of each. As they baked and flattened, the two colors created what looked like land and water.

"I'm doing good, Mom," Krissa said with a smile.

Daisy touched her nose. "How did you get dough on your face?"

Her daughter grinned. "I'm magic."

"You are."

Daisy enjoyed kitchen time with her kids. The shared activity was fun and she'd learned that when they were focused on something they enjoyed, they often talked about things that didn't come up in regular conversation. It was a lesson she'd learned from her father, who had insisted they make Sunday breakfast together a couple of times a month. A tradition he'd continued after he'd married Joanne.

While Sage had been invited to participate, she'd claimed she preferred to sleep late. Cassidy had joined in until she was seven. About then, she'd declared she wasn't interested in Sunday brunch. That was when things had started going badly with Cassidy in every other way.

She recalled what Sage had mentioned—that Joanne might have a part in Cassidy's unfriendly attitude. If so, the older woman had even more to answer for. Not that they were ever likely to have a confrontation.

When Ben and Krissa had each filled a cookie sheet, she put them in the oven and set the timer. The kids went to work on the second cookie sheets. "I Want to Live in America" from *West Side Story* came on.

"That's one of my favorites," Cassidy said as she rolled herself into the kitchen.

"Cassidy!" Krissa climbed down from her step stool and hurried over to her aunt. "We're making cookies. We do it on Saturday afternoons and it's really fun. Mommy has great ideas for different cookies. I'm making ones that look like the earth. Come see!"

Daisy ignored the knee-jerk resentment that welled up inside of her. In her head she knew why her daughter would find Cassidy interesting and appealing but in her gut, she pretty much wanted to throw up.

Cassidy looked at her, one eyebrow raised. "Still making cookies with the children? You used to do that with me."

Daisy frowned, trying to remember when that had happened. "Maybe once or twice. You weren't a real fan."

Cassidy's expression turned wistful. "I enjoyed it, but, well...it was complicated."

Daisy knew better than to ask why. She wasn't interested in getting another emotional hit from her sister. The comments about Desean had been enough for one month.

"If you wash your hands, you can help me," Krissa said, hurrying back to her stool.

"Thank you," Cassidy said, rolling to the sink. "That's very sweet of you."

Krissa preened at the compliment.

Daisy knew it was good that her daughter was a caring person and she appreciated that Cassidy was being nice about Krissa's attempts to bond. She told herself to accept what was happening with an open heart and to ignore the bitterness from the past.

But she found it difficult not to be resentful. When Wallace and Joanne had split up, Daisy had been worried about Cassidy feeling her life was torn apart. She'd gone out of her way to be caring and supportive. Wallace had hired a nanny to look after Cassidy when she was with him—he'd been concerned about Daisy taking on too much, rather than enjoying her own childhood—but Daisy had still tried to be involved. She'd never wanted Cassidy to feel about her the way she'd felt about Joanne. But no matter what she'd done, there'd been a wall between them she couldn't breach.

Cassidy got into the spirit of the cookie bake. She made a few with Krissa, then Ben invited her to make teddy bear cookies with him. He showed her how to roll the one large ball for the head and the two smaller ones for the ears. The timer dinged and Daisy pulled out the hot cookie sheets and put the second ones in. Ben, Krissa and Cassidy went to work on filling the third set.

Esmerelda walked into the kitchen, looking worried. Daisy smiled at her.

"I swear I'm going to clean this up when we're done," she said.

Esmerelda shook her head. "Miss Daisy, there's a woman here who claims she's Cassidy's mother. Should I let her in?"

The room went silent. Even the show tunes seemed to get quiet.

"Joanne is here?" Daisy asked.

Cassidy's smile faded. "Do you think she wants to see me?"

"I doubt *I'm* the reason she showed up."

Krissa looked at Cassidy. "Do I know your mom?"

"No," Daisy and Cassidy said together.

Daisy cleared her throat. "Show her in, Esmerelda. Once the children meet her, please take them up to the playroom."

"But we're not done with the cookies," Ben protested.

"I'll wrap the dough. You can finish later. Joanne is going to want to have an adult conversation with her daughter."

"But I like adult conversation," Krissa said, a whine in her voice.

Daisy gave them both what Jordan called "the look" and they were instantly quiet. She nodded at Esmerelda, who quickly returned with Joanne.

Daisy hadn't known what to expect. She hadn't seen her former stepmother in what? Twenty-plus years? Joanne was still strikingly beautiful, with blond hair and blue eyes, much like her two daughters, but she was older. Gone was the youthful vibrancy—she was an attractive woman who would never see fifty again.

Wearing slim white pants and a tailored blouse, she swept

into the kitchen as if she were the hostess and everyone else had somehow snuck into the party.

"My goodness, how odd it is to be back here," she said with a laugh, her gaze sweeping the room. She crossed to Cassidy and patted her on the shoulder. "Darling, you look wretched. How are you feeling? You should have called me. I would have stopped by sooner."

"Hello, Mother," Cassidy said, her voice cool.

It was only then that Daisy realized Cassidy had been back in LA for nearly three weeks and this was the first time Joanne had bothered to visit.

Ben stood his ground at the counter, but Krissa sidled close to Daisy.

Joanne glanced at the children, then smiled. "Well, isn't this nice. You're baking together. How very domesticated."

Daisy forced herself to relax. "Hello, Joanne. Nice to see you. These are my children. Ben and Krissa."

Joanne glanced at them, swept her gaze up and down Daisy before returning her attention to the kitchen itself. "I see you've updated the place. Not what I would have done, but I suppose one has to work with what one has."

Daisy did her best not to stiffen. She nodded at Esmerelda, who walked toward the children.

"Are you my grandmother?" Krissa asked as Esmerelda took her by the hand.

"No." Joanne sounded genuinely shocked by the question. "I'm not old enough to be a grandmother."

Ben's expression morphed from curious to doubtful. "But if Sage is your daughter and she and Mom are the same age," he began, obviously doing the math.

"They're not the same age," Joanne snapped.

"She's right," Cassidy said with a smirk. "Sage is a year older."

That earned her a look that was nearly a death ray. Cassidy immediately shrank back in her chair. For a second, Daisy almost felt sorry for her, then reminded herself Cassidy didn't need her pity.

Esmerelda ushered the children out of the room. Daisy offered Joanne a tight smile.

"While it was great to see you, I'm sure you and Cassidy have lots to talk about." She looked at her sister. "Did you want to take her up to your suite, or—"

"Oh, this is fine," Joanne said, taking a seat at the island. "We can catch up, as well." She shook her head slightly. "I would have thought you'd be dressing better, Daisy."

Daisy told herself not to take the bait. "How have you been?"

"I'm not the interesting one." Joanne's gaze was speculative. "Let's talk about you instead."

Daisy had the thought that her former stepmother wasn't here to see Cassidy at all. Not possible, she told herself.

The timer dinged. Daisy pulled the cookies out of the oven, then glanced at her sister.

"Cassidy, tell your mom about your trip to Patagonia," Daisy said quickly.

Cassidy opened her mouth, then closed it. Joanne dismissed her with a wave.

"Daisy, so how are you *really*?"

The emphasis on the last word was confusing, but she knew enough to sense danger.

"Joanne, you and I aren't friends, so I'm not sure what's going on here."

"Why would you say that? We were family." Joanne gave a false laugh. "We loved each other."

"No, we didn't. You weren't the least bit interested in me. You went out of your way to make sure I knew you didn't want me around. I've never understood why. I was just a little girl. I was so excited about having a stepmother."

Daisy hadn't meant to say any of that, but she was telling the truth.

Joanne raised her eyebrows. "That is an interesting perspective. You were just a child, my dear. You can't possibly remember enough to offer an informed opinion. I loved your father and I enjoyed being your stepmother. We were a team."

"No, we weren't. You and Sage were a team and I was the odd person out."

Joanne smiled. "Not at all." She looked around the kitchen. "I did love this house and being married to your father." She glanced at Cassidy. "And you were the happy result."

"Yay, me."

Joanne ran her hands along the quartz countertop and sighed. "Such a beautiful house." Her gaze returned to Daisy. "You inherited it from your mother?"

Daisy nodded cautiously.

"How fortunate for you. I'm sure Jordan had mixed feelings about moving." Her mouth curved in a cruel smile. "And how is darling Jordan? I haven't seen him in years."

Daisy's whole body tensed. Inside her head, she heard warning sirens and sensed that Joanne knew that Jordan had moved out. She looked at Cassidy, whose expression of guilt told her where the information had come from. No doubt Ben or Krissa had mentioned their dad had moved out. Cassidy told Sage and Sage told her mother. Even after all these years, she couldn't trust any of them.

"He's fine," Daisy said, knowing there was no way to protect herself from what was coming. She squared her shoulders and told herself she was an adult who was capable of handling whatever Joanne threw at her.

"Still pretending you were his first choice?" Joanne asked

with false concern. "Poor Daisy. How hard it must be for you to know he always regretted letting Sage go."

"I can see time hasn't mellowed you in the least," Daisy said, feeling her control snap. "You were mean to me when I was a little girl, which makes you a monster, but going after me after all these years makes you pathetic." She looked at Cassidy, who sat wide-eyed in her chair. "I'm sorry, but your mother is no longer welcome here. If you want to see her, we'll figure something out, but it won't be in my house."

She swung her gaze back to Joanne. "Get out. Now."

Joanne rose slowly. "I don't remember you being dramatic, but we all grow and change." She smiled at Cassidy. "I hope you're feeling better."

Joanne walked toward the front door. Daisy followed to make sure she left. She was grateful to see Esmerelda, ready to offer backup or throw Joanne out herself.

But Cassidy's mother left without saying anything else. Daisy carefully locked the door behind her and sucked in a breath. Her heart was racing and her hands were sweaty.

"That woman is a nightmare," she said. "If she shows up again, don't let her in."

"Gladly."

Daisy returned to the kitchen and was surprised to find Cassidy hunched over in her chair, crying as if her heart were shattered. The harsh sobs, the shaking shoulders all indicated that Cassidy was near the breaking point.

Daisy paused, not sure how to comfort her. Under normal circumstances, a hug was called for, but she doubted her sister wanted anything to do with her, which left Daisy in the awkward position of hovering and trying not to ask, "Are you all right?"

She went into the half bath in the hall and grabbed the box of tissues, then offered them to Cassidy.

Her sister pulled out several and cried into them. Daisy retreated to the other side of the island and began moving cookies to the cooling racks. After a few minutes Cassidy blew her nose and looked up at her.

"Is she gone?"

Daisy nodded, not sure if Cassidy would think that was good news or bad. Her sister's eyes filled with more tears.

"I don't have anyone," Cassidy said, her voice trembling as she spoke. "She doesn't care about me. She never has. I was just a way to stay in touch with my dad. And while he takes care of me, we all know he loves you best." She covered her face with her hands. "It's been all this time and she never once came to see me and today her visit was just about hurting you."

Daisy had no idea what to do. After a few seconds, she decided to risk rejection and crossed to Cassidy's wheelchair. She pulled a kitchen chair close and sat down, then tentatively patted Cassidy's shoulder.

"I'm sorry," Daisy murmured, knowing the words were useless.

Cassidy raised her head and sniffed. Her eyes were red, her face blotchy.

"She used to say I had to choose. That I could only love her or you and that she was my mother and if I picked wrong, I would pay for it for the rest of my life."

Daisy drew back. "What? She said that?"

Cassidy nodded. "After the divorce. When we moved into that house. She said you were the reason for the divorce and that I'd better be careful around you. That you could make my dad not love me. Sage was all I had."

Daisy wanted to say that wasn't true, but she had no reason not to believe Cassidy. Even more important, she knew Joanne was more than capable of being that mean and vindictive.

"I'm sorry," she repeated, wishing she had something more

comforting to say. "I'd never do that. Even if I would, Dad loves you because you're his daughter. That will never change."

"Sometimes I believe that. It's just I really didn't belong anywhere." She twisted the tissues in her hands. "She doesn't care, and Dad was busy with his life. Sage was gone. I don't have a lot of close friends and I'm scared to love a guy."

Cassidy cleared her throat. "I'm sorry about what I said about Desean. I know you don't care that he's Black."

"You implied I was a racist."

Cassidy ducked her head. "I know. I'm sorry. I was wrong." She looked at Daisy. "Thinking you're awful makes it easier for me." Tears rolled down her cheeks. "If you're not someone terrible, then I picked wrong. If you're not mean, then we could have been sisters and I would have had someone, somewhere, who cared about me."

The sobs returned. She cried into her hands, the sound of her pain hitting Daisy right in the heart.

How had everything gotten so complicated? She didn't want to think Cassidy had been suffering all this time, and she wasn't comfortable feeling sorry for her or wanting to like her. She had no idea if Cassidy could be trusted. Only she couldn't help wondering if even thinking that made her an awful person.

Daisy decided to take a chance. She leaned close to Cassidy and wrapped her arms around her. Cassidy hugged her back, her good arm squeezing tight.

"Look at the bright side," Daisy said, hanging on. "You get to blame your mother. Not only is this all her fault, making her the bad guy is trendy."

Cassidy gave a strangled laugh. "I'll try to remember that." She drew back. "I'm going to go to my room for a bit."

"Sure." Daisy pulled the chair out of the way. "If you need to talk, I'm here."

She regretted the offer as soon as she made it, but didn't take it back.

"Thanks."

Cassidy rolled out of the kitchen. Daisy wished she could simply accept what her sister had said and assume they were going to get along better now. But she'd been burned too many times to be able to open her heart. Maybe it wasn't fair, but Cassidy would have to earn her way in.

Sage had barely set down her purse and slipped off her shoes when her mother burst into her bedroom.

"Finally, you're back! Where have you been?"

"At work. I have a job, remember?"

"Oh, that." Joanne waved a thick envelope. "This is so much more important. You have to go and you have to take me. I insist."

Sage took the envelope, noted it was already opened, and held in a sigh. She glanced at the return address, surprised to see it was from her high school. Why would they be mailing her anything? They communicated with her via email.

"Well, open it," her mother told her. "Hurry."

Sage pulled out an invitation. "It's for a reunion," she said, trying not to wince at the number of years she'd been out of high school.

"They have it every year," her mother said eagerly. "You have to RSVP and I'm your plus-one."

"Why would you want to go with me to my high school reunion?"

"Because it's not just yours. Former students from every class will be there, including some very rich older men who might be looking for a new trophy wife."

Sage had the uncharitable thought that the man in question

would have to be really old to consider a woman in her fifties a trophy wife, but she kept that thought to herself.

"I want to go," Joanne said firmly. "I've wanted to go every year but I couldn't without you. You owe me, Sage."

"I don't know if I'm going," Sage began, then stopped when her mother glared at her.

"It's one of the big social events of the year," her mother told her. "Everyone who is anyone is there. We're going."

Sage tossed the invitation on her bed. She was tired and her feet hurt. Giving in seemed easier than fighting.

"Fine. We'll go."

Joanne beamed at her. "Wonderful. Now I have to go see if I have something to wear. I want to look elegant but sexy."

Still talking to herself, she wandered down the hall. Sage closed her bedroom door and shut the blinds, then changed out of her work clothes. She was about to try to figure out what she was doing about dinner when her phone buzzed.

She picked it up and saw a text message with the beer mug emoji and a food emoji.

She and Adam hadn't seen each other since she'd asked for a rain check on their dinner. Plus there was the issue of the brunette.

Her mother swept into her room without knocking, then twirled, showing off a dark blue cocktail dress.

"What do you think?"

"It looks great, Mom. I'm going over to Adam's."

Her mother twirled again. "I have no idea what you see in him."

"We're friends."

"Whatever."

Sage made her escape.

Adam opened his front door and smiled at her. "So that's a yes?"

She grinned. "It is. Assuming you're alone."

He walked with her to the kitchen. "Why wouldn't I be?"

She sat at the kitchen table. He got them both a beer. When he was seated across from her, she leaned toward him and lowered her voice.

"You had a woman over last week. I didn't know you were dating anyone."

She kept her voice light and teasing so he wouldn't suspect she was mildly hurt by the idea of him seeing someone else. A ridiculous admission, but true.

"It's not that," he said, looking mildly uncomfortable. "It wasn't a date. Okay, it was, but not—" He glanced away, then back at her. "I met her on Tinder. It was a one-night thing."

"You hooked up with some random woman?"

"Why do you sound surprised?"

"I just am. You don't seem the type to just get laid."

He leaned back in his chair and smiled. "Sage, all guys want to get laid. The difference is whether we want it to matter or if we're just getting off."

"And the brunette was about getting off?"

"Yes."

"Isn't it better when it matters?"

"Of course."

"Then why aren't you dating someone?"

Emotions flickered in his eyes, but disappeared before she could figure out what he was thinking.

"I'm not ready," he said at last.

"Because you lost your wife?"

"Mostly."

She wanted to point out that had happened two years before, but doubted he needed reminding of the passage of time. "I know you miss her, but in a way I envy you," she admitted. "To have loved someone that much is meaningful. I never have."

"Should I point out the obvious?"

"That I've been married?" She sipped her beer. "I didn't marry for love."

"Have you ever been in love?"

She wondered about telling the truth, then decided there was no point in lying. "No. Surprised?"

"A little. And sad. Love can be great. You should try it sometime."

"Maybe." Envying him was one thing but risking her heart was another. She didn't think she would ever be comfortable giving someone that much power over her. She liked the theory of love but not the reality of it.

She smiled at him. "Change of topic, please. Are you going to the reunion?"

"Maybe. I usually do. It's for charity and it's fun to catch up with people. Are you?"

"My mom wants me to take her so she can find a rich man."

Adam nearly spit his beer. "Seriously?"

"She's very serious."

"Is that your plan, too?"

"No." It had been, when she'd been on the plane, flying home after yet another failed marriage. But since being back, she'd started to think there might be another path.

"Because I know some tech guys with serious scratch."

She laughed. "Scratch? Is this you, old man, all hip with the slang?"

"Hey, we're the same age."

Sage sighed. "Alas, no. I'm a year older."

"For real? Wow. That changes everything." He raised his beer. "For what it's worth, you look good."

"Thank you. Now are you feeding me or was that just cheap talk?"

"I know better than to lie to my elders, so I'll feed you." He glanced at the clock on the wall. "If we hurry, we can get to the restaurant in time to get the senior special."

"I'm going to have to kill you now, aren't I?"

He chuckled. "I'll stop. For now. So do you have any dietary restrictions? Should I worry about your teeth?"

"Just for that, you're taking me somewhere expensive and we're ordering wine."

"Oh, I had no doubts about that, Sage."

They left their half-finished beers on the table and walked out to his car. As she fastened her seat belt, she had the thought that it had been a very long time since anyone had teased her just to be funny rather than to wound. Her mother might dismiss Adam as not worth her time, but Sage knew she was wrong. Adam was turning into a rare find.

eleven

Daisy spent Saturday running errands. She had a haircut at one, then hurried home to see her kids and get them started on making more cookies. They were spending Sunday with Jordan and she wanted to have the evening to hang out. Krissa and Ben had a movie picked out and she would be making kettle corn—a rare treat, what with all the sugar. She would also be making dinner—another weekend tradition. While Esmerelda cooked the rest of the week and would be happy to prepare something for Saturday and Sunday, Daisy liked to make those dinners herself. Usually the kids hung out with her while she prepped the meal.

Since Jordan had left, Daisy had let the tradition lapse, but she was determined to start it up again. Maybe she would invite Cassidy to join them, although she was less sure about that idea. Since her sister's breakdown, they hadn't spent much time together. Daisy was still trying to take in everything she'd been told and she would guess Cassidy was processing a lot of emotions herself.

Families were complicated, she thought, following a florist's van down the street. Surprisingly it turned in to her driveway and she followed, parking by the garage rather than pulling in. She walked over to the van.

"Can I help you?" she asked the driver, sure he was lost. While she would love to think that Jordan was sending her flowers, the odds seemed exceptionally slim.

"I have a delivery for Cassidy Allyn."

"Oh, she's inside. I'll take them if you'd like."

"Thanks."

While he went around to the back of the van, she fished a five-dollar bill from her wallet and handed it over. In return he gave her a large spray of flowers in a big glass vase. The arrangement was beautiful and heavy. She hung on to the cool, wet glass, trying to keep it from slipping as she used the keypad to let herself in.

After setting the arrangement on the counter, Daisy studied the roses, orchids and lilies. Someone had spent some serious money. She would guess Desean.

She went back outside to put her car in the garage, then carried the flowers up to Cassidy's room. But her sister wasn't in her suite.

Nita, the day nurse, looked up from the book she was reading. "Are those for Cassidy? She's in the playroom. Hanging out with the kids."

Daisy set the flowers on the coffee table. "Thanks. I'll let her know they've arrived."

Nita closed her book and stood. "I spoke to your father yesterday. Cassidy no longer needs full-time nursing care and it's silly for him to be paying for us to be here. Someone will come in every morning for a few hours, but otherwise, she's ready to be on her own. Cassidy's physical therapist has been helping her learn how to get herself in and out of bed and get dressed. Once her casts come off, she'll be able to head home."

"Yes, well, I'm sure she's looking forward to that," Daisy murmured.

A week ago she would have said she was, as well. That getting her sister out of her house and out of her life would be a happy day indeed. Now she was less sure of everything.

Cassidy's confession about her twisted relationship with her mother had caused more than one sleepless night for Daisy. She'd never much liked Joanne, but had never seen the other woman as a vicious monster. Now she wasn't sure about that, either. Apparently the rock-solid foundation of her worldview was just an illusion.

Daisy took the envelope tucked into the arrangement and carried it to the playroom. As she approached, she heard Sage's voice, which was a surprise, but not nearly as much as the fact that she was speaking French. Instantly, Daisy remembered being ten or eleven, sitting in the kitchen for an after-school snack while Joanne and Sage chatted in French, occasionally motioning to her and laughing. She had no idea what they were saying, but even at that age, she'd known they weren't being kind.

She forced herself to unhunch her shoulders. She wasn't that little girl anymore—she could take care of herself and protect her children. What Sage or her mother thought of her was meaningless.

She found Sage on the floor, with Ben and Krissa on either side of her. They were staring intently at a children's book, following along as Sage spoke slowly, pointing to each word as she pronounced it. Cassidy watched from her wheelchair.

Krissa saw her first. "Mom! Sage is reading to us in French. It's really fun. I want to learn to speak French."

She scrambled to her feet and ran to Daisy, who hugged her. "Languages start next year, sweetie. You can pick French, if you'd like."

"I'm learning Spanish," Ben said importantly. "But I'm going to see if I can learn French, too."

Sage smiled up at her. "I came by to visit Cassidy and she

was in here with the kids. I didn't know all my old French books were still here. They're so beautifully illustrated." She paused. "You got your hair cut. The style is pretty on you."

Daisy waited so see if there was a punchline after the compliment, but Sage seemed to be done, so she forced out a slightly grudging, "Thank you," as she did her best to ignore how great Sage looked in jeans and a blouse. It seemed no matter what she wore, she was amazing. Was it because she was annoyingly thin or was it just an unfair skill she'd been born with? Daisy wasn't sure she wanted to know.

Ben stood and stretched. "Can we have some fruit and cheese?"

"Sure. Esmerelda left a plate for you in the refrigerator. Want me to help you?"

Ben shook his head. "I'm ten, Mom. I can get a snack for Krissa and me."

"So grown-up," she teased.

He flashed her a grin before he walked out, his sister at his heels.

Daisy turned to Cassidy and held out the envelope. "Flowers came for you, along with this."

Cassidy turned away. "Throw them out. I don't want to see them."

"They're very beautiful and I already put them in your room." She lowered her voice. "At least read the note."

"What does it say?" Cassidy's tone was defiant.

Daisy instinctively took a step back. "How would I know? I didn't read it."

Sage scrambled to her feet and took it. "I'll read it." She ripped open the envelope and cleared her throat. "Cass—I can't stop thinking about you. I love you and I'm sorry. D." She looked up. "Who's D and why is he sorry? Oh, wait. Is this fall-off-the-mountain guy?"

Daisy didn't understand. "Desean was with you in Patagonia?" She asked the question before remembering her father had mentioned him being there.

Cassidy nodded slowly. "He came with me on the trip and stayed with me until the helicopter came." She looked away. "He proposed."

Daisy felt her eyes widen. "In Patagonia."

"On the mountain," Sage said, her tone amused. "Our little sister freaked out so she backed up to get away from him and, plop. Off the mountain she went."

Cassidy glared at her. "It's not funny."

"Now that you're recovering, it's a little funny. If a guy that good-looking proposed to me, I'd say yes in a hot minute."

"Then *you* marry him." She pointed to the note. "Tear it up. And throw out the flowers. It's never going to work out between us." She brushed away tears. "Relationships never work out. Not the romantic ones."

"The man obviously cares about you," Daisy said before she could stop herself. "He's in love with you and you've been seeing him for a while. That has to mean something."

History was important. At least she hoped it was. Right now history was all she and Jordan seemed to have together.

"Whatever," Cassidy muttered. "You're so bossy. Fine. I'll keep the flowers, but I won't like it."

"Pointing out he's in love with you hardly qualifies as bossy."

"She's right," Sage said cheerfully. "It was just information. Possibly redundant, but I think her heart was in the right place."

Daisy eyed her. "Is this you being funny?"

"If you have to ask, probably not, although that was my goal."

Daisy felt a subtle shift in the energy in the room. For the first time in possibly ever, she and her sisters were having a somewhat normal conversation without spiraling into accusations and loathing.

"I do miss him," Cassidy admitted. "A little. But it would never work and it's better that I ended things. Oh, Daisy threw Mom out of the house the other day. Did she tell you?"

And just like that, the moment passed, Daisy thought, trying not to feel disappointed.

But instead of jumping on her, Sage only looked mildly curious. "No. She didn't say anything. What happened?"

Cassidy wiped her face and grabbed the note from Sage. "She was her usual bitchy self and Daisy stood up to her. Oh, and she knows about Jordan moving out, which means you told her. Come on, Sage. You told Mom?"

Sage winced. "Crap. I didn't mean to." She looked at Daisy. "I swear, I didn't do it on purpose. It just kind of came out."

"Like at the wedding?" Daisy asked sharply. "Where you announced you would love him forever?"

Sage held up both hands. "That was bad. I admit it. It's not my fault the music stopped and the room went silent, just at that moment. But I was drunk, so there's that. I'm sorry. Really. I swear."

Daisy looked at her skeptically. She wasn't sure anything Sage was saying fell in the truth column.

"What do you want from me?" Sage asked. "I said I was wrong and I've apologized. I don't have anything else. Was I upset you were marrying Jordan? Kind of. I guess it never occurred to me he would ever get married. Which, when I think about it, is crazy, right? I mean, I married someone else. Only right when you were getting engaged, he was in that bad car accident."

"This is the race car driver?" Cassidy asked.

Sage nodded. "They said he wasn't going to walk again and

it was really tough on us. Then we split up and I was feeling really bad about myself and then I was at your wedding and you looked so beautiful. And during your first dance, Jordan got a hard-on, so I knew he really loved you. It was just too much."

As was this conversation, Daisy thought, feeling her righteous indignation fading into confusion.

"What?" she asked. "How could you remember if Jordan had an erection?"

"I was traumatized. That kind of thing sticks with you. I got drunk and I'm sorry I ruined your wedding."

Daisy smiled. "You didn't ruin my wedding. You don't have that much power."

"Snap!" Cassidy exclaimed. "Go, Daisy."

Daisy looked at her. "Hey, I'm still not trusting you, so don't push things."

Cassidy only grinned at her.

Sage raised her eyebrows. "So you two are friends now?"

"Still up in the air," Daisy said. "But we've worked out a few things." She thought about how a little bit of information could change her perspective. "I know you didn't blurt it out on purpose. It was unfortunate timing."

"It was."

"I'm sorry about what I said before. About us never being friends. It sounded way meaner than I intended."

"I get why you said it." Sage shrugged. "While we're on our apology tour, I'm sorry I was so horrible to you back when we were kids. I can't possibly list all the things I did, so this is to serve as a general apology for all of them." She paused. "I'm not being flip. I genuinely regret how I behaved."

They looked at each other, then away. Tension filled the room, but not the usual kind. Daisy sensed they were in one of those moments when a single action could change the course of their lives, which sounded dramatic but felt true.

Daisy sucked in a breath. "Okay, so I'm going to go start dinner. I'm making carnitas in the pressure cooker and they take a lot of prep work."

"I'll help," Sage said.

Daisy stared at her. "Why?"

"Because I want to and you're too nice to throw me out after I offered to help with dinner."

"But it's cooking."

"I'm clear on the concept."

"You two are weird," Cassidy said, pushing the joystick on her wheelchair and rolling out of the room.

Daisy didn't understand what was happening with Sage, but felt compelled to ask, "Did you want to stay for dinner, as well?"

"Sure. That would be nice."

"Now you're just trying to freak me out."

Sage smiled. "That is very much a possibility. I guess you'll just have to wait and find out if it's true or not."

Sage made good on her word. She helped with dinner, then stayed to enjoy it. Once Daisy had started prepping for dinner, everyone had migrated to the kitchen, even the dogs and cats. It was loud and despite the size of the room, everyone kept getting in the way of everyone else, but it was still fun.

Ben showed Sage how he fed the pets with only minor supervision. Sheba and Lucky were exceptionally well-behaved, waiting patiently for their meals to be placed down on mats in the pantry before devouring every morsel in seconds.

The cats ate in the laundry room. Their dinner—some raw concoction that smelled like liver and blood—had to be measured and then placed onto flat dishes.

"You have to be careful," Ben told Sage. "It's uncooked meat, so there are germs that could make us sick."

They left the cats, then returned to the kitchen, where Ben reported on who had been fed what.

Dinner was just as chaotic as the prep. The five of them sat at the table in the kitchen, the two dogs stretched out under the table and the cats each claiming an empty chair. Conversation flowed easily, allowing Sage to simply enjoy herself. She and Daisy seemed to have called a truce and she was going to enjoy that while it lasted.

After dinner, the kids went upstairs to watch a movie, while Daisy poured Cassidy and Sage more wine. Sage was pretty sure they were on their second bottle, which might mean she was Ubering home.

"How can you not remember Mrs. Pickle?" Daisy asked with a laugh. "I loved math, but I swear she went out of her way to make it as boring as possible. I'd been so excited to take geometry, but when I found out she was going to be my instructor, I actually started crying, I was so disappointed."

"I'm eight years younger than you," Cassidy pointed out. "How would I remember your high school math teacher?"

"I remember her," Sage said as she shuddered. "She was a mean old bat. If I had a nickel for every time she compared me to Daisy, I wouldn't need to work." She looked at her stepsister. "You were so annoying."

"Me?" Daisy asked with a laugh. "I didn't do anything."

"You were smart. Like scary smart. All I heard, all the time, is 'Daisy's so successful at school. Maybe you could learn from her.' If I made the mistake of pointing out we weren't related, I got the pitying looks."

"So my intellect intimidates you," Daisy asked, her voice teasing.

"Oh, please. You were an annoying person to have around in high school. I wasn't ever intimidated."

"You were a little," Cassidy said cheerfully. "I remember that. I wasn't scared of Daisy, but I was scared of this house."

Daisy stared at her in surprise. "Why? It's a great house."

"For you. For me it was just big and cold and I didn't like coming here every other week. That was so hard, going between houses, having different rules. I never knew how Mom was going to be when I got back."

"Why would your mother act differently when you moved back with her?" Daisy asked.

Sage looked at Cassidy, who sighed.

"Because she resented the divorce," Sage said. "She didn't want to live in that tiny house. For what it's worth, I think she actually loved Wallace very much and was devastated when they split up."

"I have a hard time imagining her loving anyone," Daisy said, then grimaced. "Sorry. I didn't mean to say that out loud."

"If anyone knows that happens, it's me." Sage raised her glass. "I give you a pass."

"Thank you."

Cassidy glanced between them. "A—why do you get to say if she gets a pass or not, and B—we were talking about me."

Sage chuckled. "So we were. Continue."

"You guys got to go on with your lives and everything was always the same, but it wasn't like that for me. I was so little when they split up and I didn't know what was happening and then Mom said it was Daisy's fault, so that scared me."

Sage saw the anger in Daisy's eyes.

"I was thirteen," Daisy said, her jaw clenched. "Do you really think I could have caused a divorce?"

"I get that now, but I was five back then. I didn't know

anything." She picked up her wine. "Dad tried, though. He always wanted to know how I was doing and he stayed in touch the weeks I wasn't with him. Mom never did. Sometimes I swear she forgot I was her daughter. She always acted shocked and put out when I showed up every other week."

Sage wanted to say that wasn't true, but she had a feeling it was. Joanne wasn't exactly maternal.

"You were there for me, though," Cassidy said, pointing at Sage.

"I tried to be."

Cassidy turned to Daisy. "I slept with her when I was there. Every night and she never got mad."

"You stopped when you were ready."

"I think I was nine."

She had been, Sage thought. Ready to have a life of her own.

Cassidy leaned toward Daisy. "I think Mom resented you because Wallace loved you first."

"I'm his daughter and he didn't meet her until I was six. Of course he loved me first."

"That's logic. She's not big on logic. My theory is Dad married her to give you a mother and that's not a good reason to get married to anyone, but especially not to her. Mom wants to be adored."

Sage was surprised by Cassidy's insights. "When did you figure all this out?"

"I take a lot of long flights. That gives me plenty of time to think."

"You've put it to good use. You're right about Mom. She needs to be the most special person in the room. I doubt Wallace knew that."

"She was very beautiful," Daisy offered, her tone slightly grudging. "He would have noticed that. I just hope you're wrong and that he married her because he loved her and not for me. As Cassidy said, it's a bad reason to get married."

"There are worse ones," Sage pointed out. "Like marrying for money."

Daisy smiled. "Who does that?"

Cassidy winked at Sage. "You'd be surprised."

"Joanne's looking for a rich husband as we speak," Sage admitted. "She wants to be my plus-one at the reunion with the idea she'll meet someone there." She looked at Daisy. "I assume you got your invitation. You're going, right?"

"I don't know. Maybe. Probably not." She leaned back in her chair and sighed. "Not by myself and I don't know if Jordan will want to go. We always have. Besides, it's always a pain finding something to wear and I never feel I'm dressed right, no matter how hard I try."

"Come by the store and I'll help you find something."

Sage made the offer without thinking, then was surprised to find she meant it. Daisy appeared equally startled, while Cassidy simply drank more wine.

"Do you carry my size?" Daisy asked, "Or is anything bigger than a four or six just too gross to consider?"

Sage raised her eyebrows. "Did you mean that as bitchy as it came out?"

"No. Sorry."

"It's fine. I was just checking. We carry a lot of sizes and I can think of at least three dresses that would look great on you. Make an appointment with me and I'll find you something nice."

"I will. Thank you. Although, and no offense meant, I'm not excited about attending a party with your mother."

"If it makes you feel any better, I'm not, either."

twelve

Jordan arrived a few minutes early to take the kids out to dinner. Daisy let him in, then stepped out of the way as Lucky and Sheba came running, their big feet skittering on the hardwood floors. He greeted them both, then smiled at Daisy.

"I hope these two are behaving themselves."

"They are, but they miss you."

"Next time I drop off the kids, I'll stay a little while and throw the ball for them."

"They'd like that."

She studied him. He looked as he always had—handsome, with broad shoulders and a strong face. He was the kind of man women noticed and speculated about. Daisy'd had a crush on him all through high school, but he'd only had eyes for Sage.

"Ben is finishing up some homework and Krissa is doing her reading. They'll be down in ten minutes," she said, then wondered if she should offer him a drink or take him to the formal living room or what? She felt awkward and unsure of herself, unclear if they were going to stay on friendly footing.

Jordan solved the problem by heading for the kitchen. She and the dogs trailed after him. Jordan sat at the island and smiled at her.

"How are you doing?" he asked.

She took a seat a couple of barstools down. "I'm good. Busy."

"Me, too. We have a spay and neuter event coming up. We're working with one of the shelters."

Several of the local animal clinics offered low-cost spay and neuter days for families on a limited income. Volunteers helped keep things moving. Daisy had helped a few times, but wasn't sure she should offer now.

"The annual reunion is in a couple of weeks," she said, keeping her tone neutral. "Did you want to go?"

His gaze locked with hers. "Did you?"

Why couldn't he just answer the question? Why did he want her to put her feelings out there before he did the same? She suspected it was just a style thing on his part, yet it always left her with a sense of being exposed. Worse, a part of her kept waiting for him to use her feelings against her, which was a very real fear but probably not fair to him.

"I'm not sure, considering how things are between us," she said slowly.

He leaned toward her. "We always have a good time." He reached out and captured one of her hands. "Daisy, I miss you. I miss us."

Tension she hadn't known was there eased. "I miss us, too."

"I'm glad we have an appointment with a therapist. We need to figure this out and we're not getting anywhere on our own."

She had no idea what "this" was. From her perspective, Jordan had simply moved out with no warning. Except for his odd complaint that she never bought him shirts anymore, she didn't know what he wanted or even what had made him so unhappy in the first place. As for them not getting anywhere on their own, they were barely speaking, so the odds of anything changing seemed slim.

But she didn't want to get into that right now, so instead murmured, "The timing of his vacation sucks."

"Yeah. Three weeks? Who goes away for three weeks?"

"Exactly."

The most highly recommended therapist she'd found had explained he was going to be on vacation and then would be catching up with his existing patients. Daisy had been willing to wait, but that had put off their first appointment several weeks. Still, it was scheduled and that was a good first step.

"Daisy, I—" Jordan began, but was interrupted when both kids ran into the kitchen.

"Dad! Where are we going to dinner?" Ben asked.

"I want to go somewhere fun."

Ben sighed. "Not pizza. We always have pizza."

Jordan released her hands and reached for his children. They surged close and hung on to him.

Daisy watched the kids with their dad, each of them telling him what was happening in their lives. Most of the time, she thought they were doing fine with the separation, but every now and then she was reminded this was hard on them, too.

He straightened. "There's a new sushi place on Melrose I thought we'd go to."

Ben and Krissa stared at him with identical expressions of dismay.

"We're having raw fish for dinner?" Ben asked, sounding horrified.

Krissa made a gagging sound.

Jordan laughed. "I'm kidding. We'll go to Island Burger. How's that?" He looked at Daisy. "I'll have them back by eight."

"Thanks."

Daisy walked them to the door, Sheba and Lucky leading the way. She hugged Ben and Krissa.

"See you two soon."

They walked out onto the porch. Jordan paused at the front door and glanced back at her.

"So yes, on the reunion?" he asked.

She smiled. "I'd like that."

"Me, too. See you in a bit."

He closed the door behind him. Lucky whined low in his throat. Daisy petted him.

"I'm with you, big guy. None of this makes sense to me, either."

And while she appreciated that they would be doing something together, she couldn't help wondering why they weren't talking more. Or at all.

Soon, she promised herself. They would be in therapy and maybe then they could get things figured out. Because right now they were living a nonmarriage, which was bad enough, but what really scared her was the fact that every day that went by, she missed her husband just a little bit less.

Late morning on her day off, Sage lay on a yoga mat in her mother's backyard. As she inhaled, she pulled in her core, raised her arms over her shoulders and pointed her toes, then slowly raised herself until she was in a perfect V shape. She held it for a slow count of three, then lowered herself back to the mat, midsection burning.

The air was warm, the trees provided shade. This was good, she thought, raising her arms again. She might have crawled back to LA in defeat, but she was getting her act together. Wallace had sent her a check for a thousand dollars, something he did once or twice a year. She not only appreciated the cash, but she liked the fact that he still thought of her. Wallace was the closest thing to a father that she'd ever had.

"You're killing me, Sage."

She sat up and saw Adam standing by the low fence between their yards.

"How am I supposed to concentrate when you're doing Pilates ten feet away?"

She grinned. "You were inside. I didn't think you'd notice."

He chuckled. "Do I look dead? I don't feel dead. Can you work out in the house?"

"There's no room. Besides, I'm completely covered."

"You're wearing a tight tank top and leggings. I can see everything. It's cruel. Take a class. Please."

"Classes cost money."

He shook his head. "Fine. We'll take a drop-in class together, my treat. Maybe if I'm next to you, I won't notice as much."

She stood up and put her hands on her hips. "Are you telling me you actually do Pilates?"

"I hurt my back a few years ago. The physical therapist recommended it as a way to strengthen my muscles." His smile returned. "Plus, I'm usually the only guy in class. It's a good ratio. Meet you out front in twenty minutes."

"You're incredibly weird," she said, but he was already gone.

She went inside and slipped on flip-flops before pulling on an oversize T-shirt and grabbing her bag. She went out front and saw Adam pulling out of the garage in an older white Mercedes two-seater convertible.

She got in the passenger side. "A very sweet ride."

He smiled at her. "I thought you'd look good in it."

"So do you." She fastened her seat belt. "So you really do Pilates to pick up women?"

"Mostly for my back. It's been nearly four years and it hasn't bothered me at all." He winked at her. "The women are just a bonus."

He drove a couple of miles to a local studio and parked. He registered them both before paying for the class. There were about eight other clients, all women. A couple of them greeted him by name. Sage stored her bag, sandals and T-shirt in one of the open cubbies, then took a mat.

Fifty minutes later, she was sweating, sore and out of breath, but she felt good. Still lying on her back, waiting for her stomach muscles to stop quivering, she joined the group in calling out a thank-you to the instructor. Adam stood with far too little effort and held out his hand. She let him pull her to her feet.

At the cubbies, she slipped on her T-shirt, while he shrugged into a button-up Hawaiian shirt and pulled board shorts over his yoga shorts. He stepped into battered boat shoes before picking up his car keys.

"I'm starving," he said. "Want to get something to eat?"

"Sure."

Adam drove them to a little bistro just off Sunset, close to UCLA. They were seated at a shaded table on the back patio. There were Mexican pavers, climbing vines and a slight breeze.

"Perfection," Sage breathed as she sat down, then tried not to wince when her thighs complained.

"It's a great place with good food and a nice atmosphere. We won't be rushed."

She glanced around at the other patrons. "Lots of college students. Is that appealing?"

He frowned. "Are you asking if I come here to pick up college girls? God, no. They're too young. I prefer someone age-appropriate."

"I was just asking," she said, keeping her tone light. "I didn't mean to offend."

"I'm not that guy."

"I believe you." The information made her want to ask what guy he was.

Their server appeared. Adam ordered a beer while she asked for the blackberry mojito. They agreed to split several small plates, including a mushroom tart, fried cauliflower, polenta fries and a cheese plate.

Sage handed her menu to the server. "You realize we're going to be eating more calories than we burned."

"I know but it will be worth it. How's work?"

"Good. Busy. I'm establishing a client list, which helps. Repeat business means better money. Vivian, the reigning queen of sales, doesn't like me, but I'm trying to win her over."

Adam picked up his water glass. "She's going to like you less when you start outselling her."

"Why would you think I would?"

"Am I wrong?"

She grinned. "No."

"There you go."

She looked at him. "So about the woman you had over a couple of weeks ago," she began.

Adam held up both hands. "I haven't seen her since and I have no plans to see her."

"It really was just sex?"

"Yes."

"Was the sex good?"

He chuckled. "When is it bad?"

"It's not always good for me the first few times. I've never been a fan of the one-night stand."

"Makes sense. You've always been into serial relationships. Jordan, the race car driver. I'm sure there have been others."

More than he knew, she thought.

Their server returned with their drinks and the cheese plate. When she'd left, Sage said, "Tell me about your wife. How long were you married?"

"Eight years." He looked past her, his expression more resigned than sad, then he swung his gaze back to hers. "She didn't want children. She made that clear from our third date. She wanted me to know that if the relationship was going to get serious, she wasn't interested in having a family."

Sage sipped her drink. "Not the usual choice. I know more and more women don't feel they have to have children, but it's still kind of expected."

"Do you want kids?"

The question caught her off guard. "I don't know," she said, knowing she wasn't going to tell him the truth. "I think I've always been afraid I wouldn't be a good mother. I didn't have a great role model."

"It's not too late."

"It's close to too late. Go back to what you were telling me. She didn't want kids. That must have surprised you."

"It did. I'd always assumed I would have a family, so I needed to think about it. I knew enough to know I wasn't likely to change her mind and if we were going to keep seeing each other, I had to be okay with that."

"You decided you were okay with that," she said, reaching for a slice of gouda. "You must have been or you wouldn't have married her."

He nodded. "But after a few years, I changed my mind. I really wanted a family. I talked to her about it and she reminded me she'd been totally clear on the subject."

"Did you fight?"

"No, but things were strained. I was resentful, which makes

me an asshole. She hadn't lied. I was the one changing the rules."

"And then she died and you felt guilty about being mad at her."

"Uh-huh. That's how it went. I sold our house and bought the one I have now. I read a few books on grief and I think I'm sort of adjusted."

"But you don't date. You just find women on Tinder and have sex."

One corner of his mouth turned up. "There is that, yes."

"Why are you avoiding relationships?"

"I don't know. Guilt, maybe. I don't want to be disappointed."

"Are you still in love with her?"

"No."

Why was it other people's problems were so much more interesting than her own? "Adam, you're a single guy with a great job. You're good-looking and funny and very normal. You could have just about anyone. Maybe it's time to put yourself out there. Go on a date. Go on a second date."

He sipped his beer. "That's the nicest thing you've ever said to me."

"I can be nice."

"I know. I'm just surprised you're willing to see that quality in yourself. I know you were hedging before, when I asked about kids. What's the real reason you haven't gotten pregnant?"

Just then their server appeared with the rest of their dishes. Sage busied herself cutting up the tart and scooping some of the cauliflower onto her plate. She'd just taken a bite of a polenta fry when he said, "Sage?"

She grimaced. "I'm not the girl anyone wants to get pregnant. You can't be beautiful arm candy when you're pregnant."

"That's not true."

"It's very true. Ellery was the only one who wanted to have children with me and I just couldn't go there with him. Not when I knew I was going to break his heart."

She'd spoken without thinking and by the time she realized what she'd said, there was no grabbing back the words. Adam looked mildly confused.

"Who is Ellery?"

She took a large swallow of her drink. "My second husband."

One eyebrow rose. "How many have there been?"

"Three. The race car driver, Ellery and the Italian count. Ellery's a professor at the American University in Paris. We met at a market. His French was terrible and he was trying to buy—" She waved her hand. "I guess it doesn't matter what he was trying to buy. I helped him and we started talking."

Adam's gaze was knowing. "Let me guess. It was love at first sight for him."

She nodded.

"You were his princess."

She nodded again. "He loved me. The others wanted me, but Ellery truly loved me. I could never understand why."

"You don't think you're loveable?"

She pointed her fork at him. "Do you really think you're in any position to talk about mental health?"

"No."

"I thought not. Anyway, he was very good to me, but there was an unequal distribution of power in the relationship and that's never good."

"He worshiped you and you enjoyed being worshipped?"

"To quote you, bingo." She managed a smile. "For a relationship to work, people have to care the same amount and it was never going to be that way between us."

"But you married him anyway?"

"I did. I wasn't feeling very good about myself and, as you said, Ellery thought I was his princess. Because of him, I went to college."

His eyes widened. "You have a degree?"

She supposed she could have been annoyed at his obvious disbelief, but she decided to go with finding his reaction amusing.

"Yes, Adam. I do. I can read and do basic math. Some mornings, I manage to dress myself."

"Sorry. That came out wrong." He cleared his throat. "So, what did you study?"

"I have a degree in environmental studies and a minor in world history."

"Damn, Sage, you're the whole package. Smart, beautiful and well-educated. Tell me again why you're not married."

"I think we can both agree I need to let the marriage thing rest for a while."

He slid a piece of mushroom tart onto his plate. "Why do you sell clothes if you have a college education? Couldn't you get a—" He paused, as if not sure what to say.

"Real job?" she finished dryly.

"I didn't want to say that."

"I know." She shrugged. "I wasn't sure what to do with my degree. I know retail and it was easy. I'm still considering my options." Because she wasn't ready to talk to him about her dream of being a teacher. She liked Adam too much to deal with him laughing at her.

"You're a constant surprise," he said, then smiled. "In a good way."

"Then that's how I'll take it."

Daisy stared at herself in the full-length mirror of the large private dressing room. The dark green cocktail dress flattered her in every way possible. The fit-and-flare style emphasized the good parts and covered up the less-good. The sheen of the fabric added a glow to her complexion. Honestly, she looked good—better than good. With makeup and her hair done, she would be able to hold her own at the reunion.

"Knock, knock," Sage said from the hallway. "I want to see."

Daisy opened the door. "I love it."

Sage studied her critically, then motioned for her to turn around. She tugged on the shoulders, then checked the waist before nodding slowly.

"I thought this would be the one. The color is great on you and the plunging neckline is going to get a lot of attention. You have boobs, you should show them off."

"You say that like you don't have boobs."

"Mine are tiny little flat things. Not impressive at all." She met Daisy's gaze in the mirror. "The other two dresses were okay. This one is dazzling. You have to buy it."

Daisy admired the swaying skirt as she moved back and forth. "I do. It's ridiculously expensive, but I don't care. It's pretty and it makes me happy."

"You don't care because you're rich."

The comment was delivered in a teasing voice that made Daisy think maybe Sage wasn't being mean. In fact her former stepsister had been nothing but warm and helpful during the shopping process.

Daisy had been reluctant to meet Sage at her Beverly Hills boutique, but the reunion was rapidly approaching and Daisy literally didn't have anything to wear. She sensed the evening might be a turning point with Jordan and wanted to look really good for him. Who better to help with that than the most beautiful woman she knew?

She'd decided to ignore the weirdness of Sage helping

her achieve that goal—what with their complicated Jordan history—and had made an appointment. Now as she looked at her reflection, she knew she'd made the right choice.

"I'll take it," she said firmly.

"You should." Sage's gaze dropped to Daisy's bare feet. "What about shoes? You're going to want some great high-heeled sandals." She smiled. "And a bit of attitude."

"Shoes, I have. I'm less sure about the attitude."

"Then you're going to have to fake it. Confidence is huge—even if you're only pretending. The way a person walks into a room can affect the rest of their day."

"What would you know about pretending to be confident?" Daisy asked.

Sage smiled. "I did it all the time in high school. Did you really think I believed I was all that?"

"Yes. Absolutely."

"I didn't. I was as scared and nervous as everyone else. I just knew how to pretend better."

"I can't begin to believe that," Daisy admitted. "You were the one who knew what to wear, how to talk. You even intimidated our instructors."

"None of that was real. You were all fooled."

A concept that was difficult to grasp. Sage not the most confident person in the room? Impossible.

"I would try to channel you when I wanted to be brave," Daisy admitted. "All the times I fought with my dad, I pretended to be you."

Sage's eyes widened. "What are you talking about? You never fought with your dad. He adored his annoyingly perfect kid. Every adult I knew liked you way better than they liked me. Other than my mom. Wherever I went all I heard was how great you were." She shuddered. "You were my worst nightmare."

Daisy told herself not to react negatively to the outburst. Although her instinct might be to assume the worst, she almost felt there might be a compliment buried in there somewhere.

"You resented that I was a better student," she said slowly.

Sage rolled her eyes. "I resented you were so damned smart. And such a rule follower. The teachers at school *still* talk about you. It's not right."

"I got along better with adults than kids," she admitted. "With grown-ups, I understood the rules. With my peers, it was more of a crapshoot. I wasn't like you, Sage. I didn't know what to say or how to dress."

"I didn't, either. Like I said, I was faking it half the time. If I wore something someone teased me about, I turned it around and made them the silly one." Her mouth twisted. "Sometimes more cruelly than I should have. You had book smarts, and I had a social intelligence. I was also more outgoing, which made a difference, and I was much more willing to defy authority."

Daisy felt her worldview shifting. "I'm speechless."

"Don't be. Now tell me the truth. Did you really fight with your dad?"

"Yes. About a lot of things. When I was in high school, we mostly fought about my career choice. He wanted me to go to medical school and I didn't."

"But you were smart enough and you come from a long line of doctors."

"So he reminded me, almost daily." Daisy held out her hands, palms up. "I'd planned to be a pediatrician. I got into a special summer program for high school students interested in studying medicine. We rotated through various parts of the hospital. During our surgery rotation, I became fascinated by the anesthesiologist. I thought what she was doing was incredible and so interesting. I did a lot of research and quickly found out that nurse anesthesiologists do a lot more work with patients than doctor anesthesiologists. That's what I wanted. So no medical school for me."

"You defied your father?"

"Yes, and he wasn't happy about it."

"I'm impressed. Weren't you afraid he'd stop loving you if you didn't do what he said?"

The simple question was like a punch in the gut, Daisy thought, as sadness overwhelmed her. Because knowing Joanne as she did, Sage's question made perfect sense. Joanne wouldn't allow any kind of defiance to go unpunished and that was the kind of parental love Sage had grown up with.

"I knew he'd get over it," she said softly. "Although he still hasn't given up." She told her about her recent visit from Uncle Ray.

"You're really brave," Sage told her.

"I'm not, but I couldn't pick a career to make my father happy and I know, deep down, he wouldn't want that for me. I'm not like you. I didn't take off for Europe by myself when I was nineteen."

Sage waved away the comment. "I was young and didn't know any better."

"But you did it. You made a life. You fell in love and got married. You saw the world." She smiled. "I've been living in this same house since I was born. I'm not exactly a risk taker."

"Being one has its disadvantages. Sometimes it's nice to know where you belong." She pointed to the dress. "I want our seamstress to adjust it so it fits perfectly."

"Thank you." Daisy brushed the front of the skirt. "I never would have found this on my own."

They looked at each other for a second. Then Sage gave her a quick smile and left her alone in the dressing room. Daisy watched her go, not sure what was happening. After all this time, was it possible she and Sage were starting to become friends? And if that was true, it was about the strangest happening ever.

thirteen

Daisy nervously adjusted her emerald drop-style earrings. They were nearly two carats each, with diamond accents. She'd inherited them from her mother and while she loved them, she rarely wore them. They weren't exactly something you put on to run to the grocery store.

But the school reunion was different—it was a glamorous event with a charity auction and while the dress code was "cocktail attire" she knew better than to be underdressed— jewelry wise.

She studied herself in her bathroom mirror, not sure if her upswept hairstyle and heavier-than-usual makeup made her look as if she was trying too hard. Most years she wanted to look nice, but tonight there was the added pressure of wanting to look good for Jordan.

She slipped on her Stuart Weitzman strappy sandals and told herself she'd done the best with what she had. As she walked out into the hallway, she nearly ran into Cassidy, who was sitting in her wheelchair at the top of the stairs.

"Hey," her sister said, glancing at her. "You look really good."

"Thank you." Daisy frowned. "You're not thinking about trying to take that chair down the stairs, are you?"

"What? No." Cassidy rolled back a few feet. "I was lost in thought and wasn't paying attention to where I was." A half smile tugged at her mouth. "No need to worry about my mental state."

"Good, because you're getting better every day. Your bruises are gone and you'll be in a walking cast soon."

"Can't wait for that."

Daisy expected Cassidy to wheel away, but instead she stayed where she was, as if she had something on her mind. Daisy waited patiently.

"You're still in touch with your friends from high school?" Cassidy asked.

"Sure. Aren't you?"

Cassidy looked away. "Not really. It's hard to keep up with people when you travel so much. I can't get back for engagements or weddings."

Daisy knew her sister traveled a fair amount but didn't understand why she couldn't take a flight from Miami to LA for a wedding, not that she would mention that. Her détente with Cassidy was still new and fragile.

"Did you want to come tonight?" she asked. "Maybe some of your friends will be there and you can reconnect."

Cassidy shook her head. "Not like this. No one wants to see me broken."

"You're not broken. You had an accident and now you're doing great. You could tell them what happened. It's a wonderful story."

Cassidy's brows rose. "That I was so horrified by Desean proposing that I fell down a mountain? I'd rather not be pitied."

"I was thinking more about how you were writing about the women in the small villages empowering themselves by selling their beautiful textiles online and how the internet has made it possible for women like that to finally have a steady income without being dependent on a man."

Cassidy's mouth dropped open, then closed. "Oh."

"Yes, oh. You don't have to mention Desean at all. You could have just tripped and fallen. It's not graceful, but it's close to the truth." Because Daisy knew all about trying to dodge those who wished her ill.

"I don't want to go in a wheelchair," Cassidy said, then smiled. "Besides, Krissa and Ben have already picked out the movies we're watching tonight after we have Uber Eats deliver the biggest pizza ever."

"You don't have to watch the kids," she began, but Cassidy held up her free hand.

"Don't go there. I like hanging out with them. They're a lot of fun." Her expression turned wistful. "Funny how I never thought I even liked kids, but it turns out I do."

"They like you, too." Daisy hesitated, thinking there was something more she was supposed to say, even though she had no idea what it was.

Cassidy pointed to the stairs. "Go on. Jordan will be here soon. You don't want to keep him waiting."

Daisy took a step forward, then paused. "You've never asked why he left."

"I didn't think you wanted to talk about it." She shrugged. "It's not like I'm good at relationships, so I'm not going to judge."

"The truth is, I don't actually know why," Daisy said, surprising herself and possibly Cassidy with the admission. "We've both been busy, but that's nothing new. One day he just left. He said I should already know why. About the time you took your tumble, he moved into a long-term-stay hotel. We're going to see a counselor in a couple of weeks. I'm hoping that helps."

Daisy had no idea why she was sharing all this—she and Cassidy weren't close. She wasn't even sure she would say she trusted her sister, yet here she was, blabbing all her secrets.

"He shouldn't have left," Cassidy told her. "I hope he's home soon. Running away never solves anything. It only makes things worse."

She moved the joystick on her wheelchair and turned around. "I'm going to find Ben and Krissa and see if we can get some kind of consensus on pizza toppings. You have a good time tonight."

"Thanks."

As Daisy went downstairs, she wondered what Cassidy had been running from. Love? Before she could decide, Jordan walked into the foyer and smiled at her.

"Hi. You look great."

"You, too."

His dark suit emphasized his broad shoulders and lean build. The gray shirt and tie added a touch of sophistication.

Her heart rate ticked up a little in anticipation. When he put his hands on her shoulders, leaned in and kissed her, there was a distinctive flutter low in her belly. His mouth was warm, the scent and feel of him familiar.

He drew back. "Ready?"

Yes, they were expected at the reunion, but what if they didn't go? What if instead of spending the evening with other people, they spent it with each other? They could go upstairs and lock the bedroom door, then make love the way they used to. Slowly, with intention, as if being together was all that mattered.

He grabbed her hand. "I've got my eye on a couple of auction items. A few will close early, so I want to make sure we're there in time to bid."

"I'm ready," she said quietly, telling herself it wasn't his fault he couldn't read her mind. If she wanted to know what he thought about her idea, then it was up to her to share it with him.

But she couldn't. Just the thought of being that vulnerable made her sick to her stomach. She didn't want to see rejection or scorn in his eyes and while she had no reason to believe he would feel either, she simply wasn't prepared to offer an alternative evening. And maybe, just maybe, her reluctance to take a chance on the man she'd married was part of the reason he was gone.

"I don't know," Joanne said, staring at herself in the mirror. She smoothed the front of the black satin dress. The style was simple—a long-sleeved, fitted sheath with a boat neckline and hem length that ended modestly just above her knees. The appeal of the styling was the way it showed off every curve, without giving anything away, and the plunging back that dipped just past Joanne's waist.

Sage had seen the dress for rent online and had known it would look great on her mother. Since it had arrived, Joanne had been vacillating between the rental and her original choice.

"Your blue one is pretty," Sage said, using her best "shop girl" tone. "But this is classic. On the wrong woman, it's boring. But on you, it's elegant and just dangerous enough to capture a man's attention."

"It's plain," Joanne complained.

"It's a showstopper."

Her mother pressed her lips together, as if trying to decide. "All right. I'll wear it. I have those lovely diamond drop earrings Wallace gave me." She looked pointedly at Sage's shorts and T-shirt. "Shouldn't you be getting ready?"

"I've already done my hair and makeup," Sage said easily. "I'll go put on my dress."

Not knowing what the event was like, Sage had gone for simple. Her makeup was subtle. Rather than fuss with her hair, she'd pulled it back into a low ponytail that hung straight down her back. She'd coughed up the money for a good spray tan, so her skin glowed.

Her navy dress, bought gently used in Paris, was a simple slip dress under a cap sleeve, lace overlay. The slip dress came to mid-thigh, while the overlay was three inches longer. She had fake sapphire earrings and gold Jimmy Choo sandals.

She collected her small evening bag, then went out to meet her mother. Joanne wrinkled her nose when she saw her.

"You look nice," her mother said grudgingly. "Once we get there, stay away from me."

Sage knew that her mother didn't want competition, but the comment still stung.

"I'm not interested in meeting anyone," she said. "You don't have to worry." She pulled her phone out of her bag and checked on their Uber.

"The car's about three minutes away," she said. "You ready?"

"I don't know why we didn't get a limo," her mother complained as they stepped outside to wait. "An Uber is so low-rent."

"But inexpensive," Sage said, keeping her tone light. "Unless you're springing for the limo, this is all my budget can afford. Besides, you probably won't be coming home tonight with me."

Joanne smiled. "Wouldn't that be nice."

A black SUV pulled up in front of their house. As they climbed in, Sage glanced toward Adam's place, but the lights were off. She supposed he'd already left for the reunion. It was only after they'd pulled onto Sunset Boulevard that she remembered that she'd never asked him if he was bringing a date.

The unsettling thought made her want to squirm in her seat. What did she care? They weren't dating, and although he'd said he didn't "do" relationships, she'd never met a man who wasn't willing to lie about his past.

Except for Jordan, she thought, looking out the window as they drove west toward the beach. Of course when she'd known Jordan, they'd both been kids. It had been—

She tensed as she realized that he was taking Daisy to the reunion. She'd known, of course. She'd helped Daisy find a dress. But somehow she hadn't realized that they would run into each other. She hadn't seen Jordan since the wedding, and look how that had gone.

No, she told herself firmly. She wasn't going to think about that. She was going to enjoy the evening, get reacquainted with old friends and have fun. If she ran into Daisy and Jordan, so what? She would be friendly and nothing else.

They arrived at the venue—a beautiful old house, overlooking the Pacific. The outdoor space was strung with lights. Wide glass doors stood open, inviting guests to step inside.

Sage got out of the SUV and looked around. There were already at least a hundred partygoers milling around. The sound of the conversation was jarring—she still wasn't used to so many people speaking English at the same time. The parties she'd attended with her various husbands had always been a mix of locals and expats, with conversations in English, Italian, French and German filling the room.

Sage showed the invitation to the teenagers manning the entrance. They were given programs that listed the items available for auction, then waved in.

Joanne looked at her. "I meant what I said. No poaching."

"You go for it, Mom."

Her mother's expression tightened. "Don't call me that here."

"Sorry."

Joanne sniffed, then raised her chin and walked into the party. Her stride was confident, her bearing regal. Several older men turned to watch her, their eyes widening when they caught sight of the back of her dress. Sage had a feeling that if there was a single, straight man over the age of fifty in the crowd, her mother would find him. Sage silently wished them both luck.

She waited a few seconds, then walked in herself. It was only after she'd made her way to the bar and ordered a glass of white wine that she realized the fatal flaw in attending an event like this. Nearly everyone was part of a couple.

She reminded herself she'd been in much tougher crowds and that she should simply do her best to have a good night. So what if she wasn't in a relationship.

She sipped her wine and looked around, trying to find someone who looked familiar. She spotted the ever-stern Mrs. Lytton but decided to save her for later, if things really got desperate. A few men smiled at her, but she ignored them. She didn't see Adam anywhere.

By the entrance, she saw Daisy and immediately moved toward her. Seconds later, Jordan appeared beside her. Sage stilled, not sure what to do.

Daisy looked beautiful. Her updo suited her features and complemented the style of her dark green dress. Jordan wore a suit with an ease that some men never mastered. He looked good, Sage thought. An older version of the man she'd once loved, but no one she knew now.

Too many years and too many miles, she thought, moving into the crowd. Walking up to Daisy was one thing, but approaching Jordan was something else. She wasn't interested in getting to know the man he was today. Yet before she could get out of the way, Daisy spotted her and waved. Daisy said something to Jordan before breaking away from him and approaching Sage.

"You're here," Daisy said with a laugh. "I'm glad and it's weird."

"My mother's here, too, so be warned."

"Thanks. I'll steer clear. Have you seen anyone you remember from high school?"

"Not yet. I was hoping to see Adam. Remember him? He went to school with us and lives next door to my mom. I haven't seen him yet."

Daisy pointed to the bar. "Let me get a drink and we'll go find him together."

Daisy left Sage chatting with a woman they'd both known back in high school and moved through the crowd, looking for Jordan. She found him with several of his guy friends. As she approached, she wondered if he'd seen Sage or if she should mention her. As far as she knew, they hadn't spoken to each other since the wedding.

As she joined him, she wondered if she should be worried about the two of them, or him with anyone else. As they hadn't exactly been talking, they hadn't set up rules for their separation. Something she should have thought about long before tonight.

Jordan smiled as she approached. "There you are." He turned to his friends. "I'm going to dance with my wife."

"Gentlemen," Daisy said, taking the hand he offered.

They stepped onto the dance floor and began to move with the slow song playing.

"Steve says Erica's pregnant again," Jordan said conversationally. "This new one makes four. That's a lot of kids."

"It is."

He glanced at her. "You okay?"

"Why do you ask?"

"I don't know. You seem like you're upset."

"Jordan, are you seeing anyone?"

The question came out a little more bluntly than she'd intended, but she didn't call it back. Knowing, one way or the other, mattered.

"What?" His voice was nearly a yelp. He looked around, then spoke more quietly. "Why would you ask that?"

"Because I want to know. You moved out with no warning and I have no idea what's going on between us. We never talk. It seemed like a logical question."

"No."

He took her hand in his and led her off the dance floor. They wove through the crowd until they were outside. He looked around and headed for a small table in the corner of the huge patio overlooking the ocean. Under normal circumstances, Daisy would have admired the view—just not right now.

Jordan sat across from her, leaning close.

"I'm not seeing anyone. I wouldn't do that."

"Then why did you leave? You said before that you think you don't matter anymore to me, but that's not true. And I know it's not about me buying you shirts. So what's going on?"

He glanced at her, then away. "The shirts are a symptom. It's like date night."

"We don't have date night."

His gaze returned to hers. "I know. We used to. When we were first talking about getting pregnant, we agreed that we would always take care of our marriage. That the kids had to be important, but we were supposed to matter to each other, too. We established date night. About a year ago, you started cooking a big family dinner on Saturday night and date night got lost."

Daisy wanted to protest that wasn't true, but maybe it was. She remembered that they'd gone out together—maybe not every Saturday but a few a month.

"I thought you liked our family dinners," she said. "I never get to cook when I'm working and it seemed fun to all hang out together."

"I like our dinners. That's not the problem. The problem is you stopped wanting to have date night, like you stopped buying me clothes and you stopped giving me cards for no reason. You've checked out on us. That's why I left."

His words stung. "That's not true. Jordan, you're my husband and I love you. I'm busy. You're busy." Part of her wanted to apologize for the things she wasn't doing and part of her wanted to tell him he was being unreasonable. "It's not like you do little things for me, either. I don't get any cards or flowers. You used to put gas in my car and you don't do that anymore."

"I wondered if you'd notice."

She stared at him. "You stopped doing that on purpose?"

"I didn't think it mattered to you one way or the other."

She wasn't sure if that meant he was trying to get her attention or he was being petty, nor did she know which was worse.

He sighed. "I'm tired of coming in last, Daisy. Everyone else gets your attention. The kids, the pets, Esmerelda. Everyone but me. You didn't even notice I moved out of our bedroom."

"You didn't move out. You got sick and wanted to be in the guest room for a few nights."

"I lied."

"How was I supposed to know that? You're upset because I didn't know you were lying?"

"I'm upset because you let me stay there night after night without asking me to come back."

"But you said you were sick."

She genuinely didn't understand. It was as if he was making up rules as he went and she was in trouble for not being able to follow along.

"How can I know what you want if you don't tell me?" she asked. "I feel like everything with you is a moving target."

"You're not interested in me anymore."

"I love you," she said intently. "I've always loved you. Sometimes life gets in the way of me saying that, but my feelings haven't changed. Have yours?"

"No." His gaze locked with hers. "I love you, too, and I want this to work."

Then why was he living in a hotel? Why was this the first real conversation they'd had in weeks? Why did she feel like she didn't know him anymore?

Confusion blended with annoyance and a touch of fear, while a burst of laughter reminded her they were in public, at a fancy event, and this wasn't the time.

"We are incredibly bad at this," she said lightly.

He smiled. "Agreed, but I'm not giving up."

Good to know. "Me, either. So we'll keep things as they are until we meet with the therapist?"

"Right."

"We have a plan." She wasn't sure it was a good one, but at least they'd talked and they were still interested in making things work.

He stood and held out his hand. She allowed herself to be pulled to her feet. They returned to the dance floor. His arms came around her and they moved close together. Daisy told herself they would get through this. In therapy they would get some skills and find a place where they were both happy. Relationships were all about compromise, right?

"Sage, darling, is that really you?"

Sage saw a tall redhead heading her way. In the second it took her to put the face and voice together, her until-this-second good mood vanished and her defensive mechanism kicked in.

"Lana," Sage said, offering a smile much happier than she felt.

They gave each other an A-frame hug and air kisses.

"I can't believe you're here," Lana said, waving a highball glass. "You look amazing."

"*You* look amazing," Sage told her. "Not a day over nineteen."

Lana preened. "Good genes," she said with a laugh.

Or excellent plastic surgery, Sage thought, taking in the faintly too-tight line of her jaw. Lana's brown eyes were a bit wider than normal and her nose was slimmer. Sage would guess there had also been a bit of a nip and tuck on her body.

"Aren't you supposed to be in Monaco?" Lana asked. "Married to someone royal?"

"I was in Italy, but that relationship was over a while ago. After living in Europe for years, I was ready to try LA again."

Lana's gaze turned speculative. "Are you back to claim Jordan as your own? He and Daisy are still together." Lana waved toward the dance floor. "Young and in love. It's a bit treacly for my taste, but you did always have a fondness for him, didn't you?" Her expression shifted to predatory. "Didn't you declare undying love for him at their wedding?" She laughed. "We talked about that for weeks. Poor Sage, losing her man to Daisy of all people."

Minutes too late, Sage remembered that her friendship with Lana had been superficial and based on their shared enjoyment of tormenting the less powerful.

She didn't know what to say about Jordan—any protest would be dismissed and possibly give Lana ammunition for another attack. With Daisy and Jordan both here, the situation could escalate into something unpleasant for everyone. She searched frantically for some distraction, briefly wondered if she should mention the plastic surgery, wished she could faint on command, then nearly fainted for real when Adam walked up and put his arm around her waist.

"There you are," he said easily. "I've been looking for you." He turned to Lana. "Oh, hi. I didn't see you standing there. Sage is back in town. Isn't it great?"

"Peachy." Lana studied them the way a cat studies an injured mouse. "You know each other?"

"She lives next door," he said with a grin. "I'll just say it—I'm one lucky guy."

Lana's eyebrows shot up—as much as they could, what with the Botox. "You're dating?"

Sage put her hand on his shoulder. "We are. Isn't it funny that we found each other after all this time?"

Adam gave her an impressively smoldering look. "It only took me twenty years to get the girl."

Sage laughed. "Um, no. Maybe twenty years for you, but only twelve or thirteen for me."

"Good point." He leaned in and lightly kissed her. "I'm starving. Let's go check out the buffet. Then I want to bid on the tickets to the Rams' season opener."

Sage looked at Lana and sighed. "What is it about men and football?"

"I'm sure I don't know." Lana glanced between them. "I

wouldn't have guessed it, but I suppose you make a cute couple. Have a good one." With that, she walked away.

Sage stayed close to Adam until her heart rate returned to normal, then she faced him.

"You saved me. Seriously. She was going on and on about Jordan, whom I haven't even spoken to, nor do I want to, but I didn't know what to say to distract her. I'm not kidding. You were perfect. Thank you."

"You're welcome. I saw her moving in and knew she was trouble." He gave her a self-deprecating smile. "Every now and then it's important to rescue a damsel in distress." He nodded at something over her shoulder. "Daisy and Jordan are right there."

An odd non sequitur, she thought, refusing to turn around. "You didn't hear me before? I'm not interested in Jordan. That was over years ago. Did you come with a date?"

He laughed. "I told you, I don't date."

"Then do you want to hang out with me tonight?"

Something flickered in his eyes, but she couldn't tell what he was thinking.

"I would," he admitted.

"Good." She linked her arm with his. "I believe you promised me a trip to the buffet, followed by the thrill of watching you spend money on football tickets."

"I did."

"Then let's get started."

fourteen

Sage and Adam spent the rest of the evening together. He lost the football tickets to someone willing to bid a lot more, but won a celebrity chef dinner for six. A little after midnight, she texted her mother to say she was ready to go. Joanne texted back she would find her own way home.

"I'm not sure I want to think about what she's doing," Sage admitted as Adam drove through the quiet streets. "Or who."

"Best not to go there."

"Agreed, and while we're on the topic, does your mom date?"

He winced. "No. No dating. She can have gentlemen callers, but that's as far as I want to go."

"Gentlemen callers? What are you? Eighty? Are you seriously not okay with your mom finding someone?"

He stopped at a light and glanced at her. "She can find as many men as she likes—I just don't want to know about them doing it. Besides, she and her sister have decided they don't need men."

"She was with your dad for a long time. It makes sense she's not ready to fall in love again, but in a few years, she may surprise you."

"As long as she doesn't mention sex, I'm good with whatever she decides." He glanced at her. "Don't judge. It's not like you're okay with it."

She grinned. "I'm fine with your mother having sex."

"Very funny."

He pulled into his garage.

"Wait there," he said as he got out of his car. He circled around and opened her door, then held out his hand.

She took it and stood, expecting him to move back. Only he didn't and they ended up standing right in front of each other.

"I had a good time tonight," he said.

"Me, too. I'm still grateful for the rescue."

"Anytime."

The overhead light turned off, leaving them in the darkness of the night with only the streetlights for illumination. She was aware of him right in front of her, looking at her as if—

Well, damn. She owed him. She'd said it and obviously he believed her. In her experience, there was only one way a woman like her paid off her debts. He expected her to sleep with him.

Disappointment followed the revelation. Under other circumstances, she would be interested in doing the wild thing with Adam, but not like this. Not as an obligation.

"I know what you're thinking," he said quietly.

"I doubt that."

He took her hand in his, then led the way out of the garage. But while she expected them to head to his house, instead he walked to hers. When they reached the front porch, he lightly kissed her before stepping back.

"Tonight was fun," he said. "Thanks for spending it with me."

What? He was leaving? "You don't expect me to sleep with you?" she blurted, unable to stop the words.

He loosened his tie. "Nope."

"Why not?"

"Because I like you, Sage, and I have no interest in using you to get off."

With that he disappeared into his garage. Seconds later, the big door lowered and he was gone.

Daisy had never been to counseling before and didn't know what to expect. She and Jordan had each been emailed pages of paperwork to fill out, asking easy things like how long they'd been married and how many children they had. There were also more difficult questions about what each of them felt was and wasn't working in their relationship. She'd spent most of an evening filling everything out and on the day of the appointment, found herself oddly nervous as she walked into the unassuming office building off Beverly Glen.

She'd come straight from the hospital and was still wearing scrubs as she walked into the nearly empty, well-appointed waiting room. Jordan was already there, looking as nervous as she felt. He sprang to his feet when he saw her.

"You made it," he said. "I wondered if you'd get delayed."

"I had backup," she told him. "You know this first appointment is for two hours, right?"

He nodded. "It's more of a get-to-know-you session, the material said."

"You filled it out and emailed it back to Dr. Braxton?"

His expression relaxed. "I knew you would and I didn't want to be the slacker."

He pointed to the various degrees and certificates hanging on the wall. "You picked a man. Thanks for that."

"I thought you'd be more comfortable that way. With a woman, you'd be worried she was going to be on my side."

"Only a little," he said with a grin.

They sat next to each other on one of the sofas.

"How's work?" she asked.

"Busy. Good. You?"

"Same."

They sat in silence for several minutes until the only other door opened and a tall, thin man in his mid-forties smiled at them.

"Daisy and Jordan, I presume?" he said.

They nodded and stood.

"I'm Carl Braxton. Come on in."

They followed him into a large office. An L-shaped sofa stood at one end, with a pair of comfortable chairs opposite. On the far side of the long room was a small desk and chair. Dr. Braxton motioned to the sofa.

"Please, make yourselves comfortable."

They took seats next to each other. Daisy immediately realized it would be difficult to communicate when they weren't looking at each other, so shifted to another cushion.

"Just so it's easy to talk," she explained.

"Sure," Jordan said, sounding nervous.

Dr. Braxton took a seat in one of the chairs. "I've already reviewed your paperwork. Today is a two-hour session where I get to know you a little bit and we confirm what you want to work on in these sessions."

"Our marriage," Daisy said cautiously.

"Yes, that will be the main focus." Dr. Braxton glanced between her and Jordan. "You've moved out?"

"Yes. I'm at a hotel."

"Do you like being there?"

Jordan looked startled. "Not especially. It's not fun living in a hotel room."

Dr. Braxton turned to Daisy. "How do you feel about Jordan moving out?"

"Uncomfortable. Sad. Angry."

"Why angry?" Jordan asked.

"For a lot of reasons." She moved forward on her cushion. "You didn't tell me you were leaving, you just left. Nearly a week later, you told me you were moving into an extended-stay hotel. By text! Not even a phone call. I hate it when you tell me something important in a text. It's not fair to me and it's rude."

"But everything was fine at the reunion. We had a good time. Now you're saying you're mad? Which is it?"

"What are you talking about? Yes, we had a very nice time together. I enjoyed the reunion a lot, and I chose not to fight with you that night, but that doesn't mean what you did was okay. I understand we have things we have to work out, but from my perspective, that means exactly that. Working them out. Talking about them. Not just running away and talking to each other via text."

His mouth twisted. "You say you want to have a conversation with me, but that's not true. I'm tenth on your list of nine things to deal with. Everything is more important than me, including the pets."

She felt frustration bubbling up inside. "You keep saying that, but it's not true and it's not fair. I've asked you what's wrong and you won't tell me. You say that 'I know.' Well, I don't know and I've asked and you won't be specific. It's maddening and makes me scared you're just playing games. You complain I'm not doing enough for you, that I don't give you cards or buy you clothes. Fine. I'll accept I let those things go. Not on purpose, not with an ulterior motive. It just happened. And you know why? There are a thousand things to do every day. We're really lucky—we have full-time, live-in help, but I still have two children, and a career, and responsibilities around the house. And yes, the pets do require attention. Pets that you brought home, one by one, without ever asking me."

Jordan glared at her. "We have children, Daisy. Kids need to grow up with pets."

"It's not the law, Jordan, and asking me if I wanted another dog or cat would have been nice. But you didn't. You showed up with them, while I was at work, so by the time I got home the kids had bonded and if I refused to keep them, I was the shitty parent and you were the sweet dad just trying to be nice. It's not fair to me or us."

"You're being ridiculous."

Words designed to fuel the unexpected rage bubbling inside of her.

"You're not listening," she said, her voice rising. "I work as many hours as you do but when I get home I still have my other job waiting for me. You waltz in the door and ask what's for dinner. What about doing the little things for me? Oh, wait. You've never done that. You complain that I'm not giving you cards or buying you shirts, yet you've never taken care of me that way. You also don't do anything around the house. God forbid you should change a lightbulb or buy dog food."

"It's not my damned house! It never has been, it never will be. It's your house, Daisy. Why should I worry about it at all?"

The words, almost a shout, hit her like a blow. She felt the air rush out of her body. For at least two heartbeats, she couldn't catch her breath. Her gut reaction was outrage, but that was quickly overwhelmed by an icy cold certainty that Jordan had just blurted out a truth that was going to change everything.

"Daisy, I'm sorry," he said quickly, his voice anxious. "I didn't mean that."

"You did. You don't think of the house as your home."

"Your mother left it to you. It's yours and it always will be. I'm fine with that. I didn't mean it. I'm sorry."

"It's our home," she whispered. "We live there. We've made love there and raised our children there. I thought the house was a part of who we are. Now you're telling me it's not."

He covered his face with his hands and swore. "I didn't mean it like that. Sometimes it's hard knowing you don't need me." He raised his head to look at her. "That makes me feel unnecessary."

"How can you say that? It's just a house, Jordan. It's a place. I thought you were okay with it. You said you were excited about moving in."

"I was but you won't let me be a part of it."

"What does that mean?"

"You want to keep it your house. When we did the big remodel, you never asked me what I wanted. You consulted the designer and your father, but not me."

"You told me you weren't interested! When I asked you about the changes, you said to do whatever I wanted."

"I tried to talk to you about a few things. A big game room in the attic, a workshop for me in the garage, but you dismissed those ideas, so I stopped trying."

She didn't understand. "We already have a media room and the kids have a big playroom. Why start construction in the attic? As for the workshop, I said it was fine and to talk to my dad about the plans."

He looked away. "Yeah, it was fine and I should talk to your dad. Do you get how emasculating that is?"

"No. I don't. When you said you weren't interested, I asked him to help me because it was too big a project to do on my own. I told you that was what I was going to do. Again, you said you were fine. So you're telling me you weren't fine and that you resented my father helping when you wouldn't."

The unfairness of that settled in her stomach like a stone. "What was I supposed to do?"

Dr. Braxton looked at Jordan. "What aren't you telling her, Jordan?"

Jordan shifted uncomfortably. "I wanted something of my own. A space that was mine. Not yours, not your father's, just mine. A piece of me in that big house. But you said no to the attic and I had to go through Daddy to get something in the garage. In the end, it wasn't worth it to try."

She stared at him, trying to hear the words through her anger and bitterness. Maybe his view of the house wasn't so much a betrayal, but a cry to be a part of things. Having space of his own made sense. Everyone needed that. But she wasn't sure she was willing to see his side of things. Not yet—not when he'd hurt her so much and refused to communicate with her.

"I thought you liked the house," she said softly, suddenly fighting tears.

"Sometimes it's not what I thought."

"The house is exactly what it's always been, so what isn't what you thought? Me or us?"

His gaze locked with hers. "I don't know."

Two hours later Daisy felt as if the energy vampire had sucked out her life force. She'd never been more exhausted in her life. Her head hurt, her body ached, and forming coherent sentences and speaking them seemed impossible. As she sat in her SUV, all she wanted to do was go home and crawl into bed.

The session had been grueling. Dr. Braxton had steered them away from the emotionally fraught discussion about the house and had guided them toward other topics, promising they could come back to the house issue when they had more skills. They'd worked out a few logistics about pickups and dropoffs, and they had both agreed that there would be no important issues discussed by text. Anything more significant than a scheduling change would be handled in an in-person phone call or a face-to-face meeting.

Dr. Braxton had also given them homework. They were to have a date before their next session in two weeks. They were also to list ten things they had liked about each other before they got married and ten things they liked about each other now. Daisy would need to calm down a little before coming up with even one.

Jordan's words had cut her to her heart. He'd known she'd inherited the house when her mother had passed away. It had been held in trust until she turned twenty-five or got married—whichever came first. He'd always said he loved the house as much as she did and couldn't wait to live there with her. He'd joked about all the extra money they would have to spend on new cars for him, what with no mortgage payment. They'd been happy in the house—at least, she'd been happy. Now she wasn't sure about anything when it came to him.

She gathered the strength to start her car and head for home. Her home, she thought bitterly. But not Jordan's. He'd made that plenty clear and while he might regret what he'd said, he couldn't take it back and she couldn't ever forget.

Sage walked into a blissfully quiet and empty house. Her mother was still spending time with the guy she'd met at the reunion. Sage hoped their relationship lasted years and that they were both wildly in love. Or at the very least, she would be excited about two weeks on her own. Not that she didn't care about her mother—she did. Just carefully, and from a distance.

She stepped out of her heels and sighed in relief as her hot, sore feet came in contact with the cool tiles. She walked bare-foot into her bedroom and was just about to close the blinds before changing when her phone buzzed.

You up?

She read the text and laughed, then looked out her window. She saw Adam in the yard, waving at her.

She retraced her steps out onto the back patio. They met at the low fence.

She hadn't seen him since the night of the reunion, when he'd saved her, spent the evening with her, kissed her, then announced he liked her too much to sleep with her. The man was nothing if not confusing.

"I still owe you dinner," he said. "I've been marinating chicken and I made macaroni salad and a green salad."

"You're always feeding me," she said with a laugh. "I should cook for you."

"Can you cook?"

"Yes. I can prepare an array of French and Italian dishes. Not that I have any of the ingredients in the house and I haven't looked at my mother's pan collection, so it might not go well."

"I knew it. You're a food tease."

She leaned close. "Honey, I'm all kinds of tease."

He grabbed her by her wrist and tugged until she took that last step forward. Then he leaned in and kissed her.

The unexpected contact surprised her, although not as much as the sudden heat that exploded low in her belly. She pulled free of his light grip and wrapped her arms around his neck. His hands settled on her waist, while his mouth claimed hers in a tender, yet demanding kiss.

She liked the feel of his mouth on hers, the way he seemed to enjoy what he was doing for the sake of it and not just as a means to an end. She liked how he didn't try to touch her breasts or her ass, taking things too fast.

He shifted slightly, kissing along her jawline and nibbling on her earlobe.

"Was that a yes on dinner?" he whispered.

She drew back and laughed. "Yes, please. Let me go get changed and I'll be right over."

He released her. "You're welcome to dine naked, if that's your thing. I'm just sayin'."

"You're so generous," she said with mock sincerity. "Thank you."

"Anytime."

She was still laughing when she returned to her room. She closed the blinds, then stepped out of her dress and hung it before looking over her small closet. Normally she would put on jeans and a T-shirt, but she wanted to wear something a little nicer. Maybe even flirty.

She unfastened her bra, then slipped on a red sundress that dipped low in the front. Usually she put on a little boob tape to keep it in place, but figured Adam wouldn't mind if she flashed him a nipple. She slid her feet into flip-flops.

Adam's front door stood open in welcome. As she stepped inside, she felt herself relax. Being around Adam was always fun. He was interesting and nice. No, she thought, calling out that she was here. Not nice. *Kind*. And kind was way better.

"On the patio," he yelled.

She shut the door behind her and went to find him. He stood by the barbecue, a plate of raw chicken and a pair of tongs on the small table. His gaze dropped to her chest before rising to her face.

"I've got, ah, beer on ice or I can make you a drink," he said, clearing his throat.

She smiled. "A beer's good. I'll get it myself."

When she returned from the kitchen, she sat in one of the lounge chairs and sighed. "Let me know when you want me to set the table," she said, kicking off her flip-flops and wiggling her toes. "Until then, I'm going to enjoy being off my feet."

"Long day?"

"Always."

"You should wear more sensible shoes if you're going to stand for hours."

She sipped her beer. "Sensible shoes don't sell designer clothes. I have to look the part or the rich ladies won't let me help them."

"There is that." He put the chicken on the grill, then closed the lid and carried the empty dish into the kitchen. When he returned, he picked up his beer. "I haven't seen your mom in a few days."

"She met someone at the reunion."

Adam seemed startled by the news. "For real?"

Sage laughed. "She's looking for another rich husband. I may not think hers is the soundest of plans, but I will give her credit for determination. I hope it works out."

"I don't get marrying for money."

"You have a skill set. You never worry about having to take care of yourself. You were never taught it was more important to be beautiful than to be smart."

"Is that what she said to you?"

"Every day. She warned me not to give my heart—that I had to make decisions about men with a clear head."

"Did you listen?"

"Sometimes."

He raised the lid on the barbecue and carefully turned the pieces of chicken, then lowered the lid.

"Is that still the plan?" he asked, watching her as he spoke.

"A girl's gotta do what a girl's gotta do."

"Sage, I hate to break it to you, but you're closer to forty than thirty, so not exactly a girl."

"Ouch. And just a few minutes ago I was thinking that you were kind. I take it back."

As she spoke, she tried to figure out if she was teasing or not. She knew Adam wasn't being mean, but to be told she wasn't a girl anymore… She wasn't sure how she felt about that.

"Isn't there some appeal in being mature?" he asked. "Knowing you've learned lessons and can see your way more clearly."

"There are a lot of assumptions in that statement."

"You don't think you've learned lessons? You can't think you're the same person you were at eighteen."

"No, I'm not her."

"Do you regret that?"

She considered the question. "Yes, but not for the reasons you think. I don't miss being that beautiful, but I do wish I'd expected a little more of myself. I wish I hadn't made so many mistakes."

"We all wish that."

She sat up and swung around to set her feet on the patio. "Saying I'm a girl allows me to think nothing is that significant. That the time for being serious will come later. Being a woman is a whole different level of the game and I'm not sure I want to play there just yet."

She hadn't planned on being so honest, but realized saying the truth was kind of freeing.

Adam smiled at her. "Has it occurred to you that it's too late? That you've already been doing the woman thing for a while now?"

"The woman thing?" she asked, her voice teasing. "What does that mean?"

"I don't know. I'm out of my league. You have to help me."

She stood and crossed to him. After raising herself up on tiptoe, she kissed him. "How about if I set the table instead?"

"That works."

She started for the house, then spun back. "You know I'm not wearing a bra, right?"

She was impressed that he kept his gaze locked firmly on her face. "Yes, I noticed."

"Good."

After dinner, they returned to the lounge chairs. Adam pulled them close together and poured them each a brandy. Sage stretched out on one chair. He sat on the end of the other and pulled her feet onto his lap.

"Have I ever mentioned I give a great foot massage?" he asked.

"You did not."

"So you're about to be amazed."

He put her left foot on his thigh and pressed his thumbs into the pad of skin right below her big toe. Involuntarily, she groaned. He chuckled.

"You were right, I'm amazed," she whispered, leaning back and closing her eyes.

He rubbed hard, going in deep, finding all the places that ached from her ridiculous shoes.

"Do I want to know how you learned to do this?" she asked.

"I took a couple of classes as a birthday present for someone."

She opened her eyes. "Your wife?"

"Yes."

"You must have been a heck of a husband."

"I tried."

"You should start dating again," she told him. "You're not the Tinder type."

"I do okay."

"But aren't you the one who told me the sex was better when you cared about the person?"

"I am, but relationships are tough."

"Are you afraid?"

He smiled. "Are you?"

"Yes. Definitely. I've failed at marriage three times. I'm not sure I loved any of them. I'm back home, living with my mother, trying to figure out my future. Me get in a relationship?" She laughed. "I don't think so."

"You have a lot to offer."

"I'm pretty and I'm good at sex. There's not much else on the table."

Adam shifted to her other foot. "Is that what you think about yourself? You're more than a piece of ass, Sage."

"Yes, I'm a nearly forty-year-old piece of ass, as you pointed out earlier this evening."

For reasons she couldn't explain, she suddenly felt tears burning in her eyes. Tears? WTF. She didn't cry—not ever. Tears were for suckers.

"That's not what I said."

"I know." She held up her hand. "I'm sorry. I guess I'm suddenly in a mood. I take it back. And while I do that, I'll return to my original point. You need to be seeing someone."

"Not happening."

"Why are you so stubborn?"

"You show me yours first," he said. "Tell me what you're really doing back in LA. Why are you living with your mom and working retail? Why aren't you out finding some rich guy to fund your happily-ever-after? There's something driving you and I can't figure out what it is."

She picked up her glass of brandy, then put it back down. After tugging her feet free, she tucked them under her. She thought briefly about slipping off the skinny strap of her dress to flash him some boob. That might be enough of a distraction to make him forget the question.

But instead of doing that or running or a thousand other things, she sucked in a breath and admitted, "I want to be a teacher."

His steady gaze never wavered. "I thought you were already tutoring."

"I am. I mean a real teacher, with credentials and a classroom and students leaving me apples."

"Do kids still do that?"

She smiled. "A metaphorical apple."

"You'd be a great teacher," he told her. "I can totally see it. You have a four-year degree, so what's holding you back?"

"Fear. Logistics. I need to find a certificate program or I can try to get into the LA Unified School District's internship program. I haven't decided which way to go. But before all of that, I need to re-establish my residency and my credit and that takes time."

She picked up her glass again. "I appreciate you not laughing."

"I wouldn't do that. You're pretty amazing, Sage. You can do anything you want."

"You have no idea how much I wish that were true."

"Have a little faith."

She smiled because that was what he expected, but she knew that faith was never enough. Most dreams took hard work, an instinct for timing and luck. So far in her life, she'd managed to avoid having all three at once—whether through circumstances or an unconscious need to self-sabotage.

This time would be different, she promised herself. This time she was going to do better.

fifteen

Daisy wanted to believe that everything was going to be fine. She wouldn't show she was upset. Ben and Krissa were both excited about spending the night with their dad at the hotel, and Jordan had even gotten special dispensation to allow Lucky and Sheba to tag along. Privately Daisy was sure he would regret bringing the two oversize dogs, but that was on him. The bigger problem was not only that both kids would be gone for the night—something that hadn't happened even once—but the lack of conversation between her and Jordan.

Since their first therapy session there hadn't been much more than logistical texts and one quick call when Krissa had wanted to tell her dad she got an A on her history project. Perhaps foolishly, Daisy had hoped for more.

She'd thought they might try to speak more, to start to work through their issues, maybe talk about how long he'd been resentful of the house situation. They still had their date to go on, something neither of them had raised yet. A silly part of her wanted him to mention it first. Ridiculous, but true. But he hadn't and now she was annoyed about that and worried about the kids being gone.

Maybe they could talk for a few seconds when he arrived

to pick up the kids, she thought, adding canned and dry dog food to the tote she'd prepared for Lucky and Sheba.

"Daddy's here!" Krissa shrieked from upstairs. "He's here."

She raced downstairs at a speed that made Daisy's stomach lurch.

"Calm down," she told her daughter. "You've stayed at a hotel before."

"Not like this!" Krissa danced to the front door, then threw it open. "Dad, we're ready," she yelled loud enough to make Sheba wince, and ran outside.

Daisy clipped leashes onto collars, then called for Ben. Her son came downstairs at a more normal pace, his backpack slung over his shoulder.

She smiled at him. "Excited about tonight?"

"I guess. I was going to watch that show on PBS."

Daisy did her best not to laugh. "I'm recording it for you. Have fun. You need to spend time with your dad."

Ben hugged her. Krissa appeared, hanging on to Jordan.

"Hi," Daisy said cheerfully. "Ready to be invaded by the horde?"

"Hey."

His smile seemed half-hearted and his tone was decidedly lacking in enthusiasm. She frowned.

"Everything all right?"

"What? Sure. I'm fine. We're going to stop for takeout. It'll be fun."

He hugged Ben and picked up the small suitcase she'd packed for the kids. "I'll have them back by noon tomorrow."

So much for the private conversation, she thought, ignoring her disappointment.

"Great. Are you sure about the dogs? You can leave them here. It's no trouble."

His gaze avoided hers. "I'll take them. See you tomorrow."

He ushered the kids and the dogs outside and closed the door. Daisy stood in the foyer, not sure what had just happened. Where was the warm, affectionate man who had taken her to the reunion? Or what about the guy who had shown up at therapy, so concerned about their marriage? Or the angry guy who accused her of not caring? Indifference scared her.

"I really don't understand him," she muttered, turning around and walking into the kitchen. They would figure it out. They had to. Her marriage was important to her and she wasn't giving up. The knot of fear in her chest didn't mean anything. They were going to be fine.

She walked into the pantry to get tea. When she stepped out, she nearly shrieked when she saw an upright Cassidy, standing with the help of crutches.

"What are you doing?" Daisy asked, her voice slightly strangled. "You're not supposed to be walking."

Cassidy grinned. "I'm not walking, I'm kind of hopping and as you can see, I have a new cast."

Daisy looked at the bright pink cast that went from mid-thigh to the top of Cassidy's foot. "Is it smaller?"

"A little. I'll get a walking cast in a couple of weeks. In the meantime, I'm allowed to use crutches for a few hours a day. The doctor wants me to get mobile."

Cassidy sounded more upbeat than she had since arriving. Her color was good and she had more energy.

"We should go out," Cassidy told her. "Somewhere casual because I can only wear shorts. Oh, wait. I could put on a dress. Please, I'm so tired of being inside. I need to get out and be with people."

Daisy eyed her sister. "You're not super steady on those crutches, so we'd need a wheelchair. Your electric one would never fit in my SUV. I wonder if we could rent a van with a ramp." She glanced at her watch. It was nearly six on a Saturday night. "Maybe there's some kind of van service I could call because I doubt I could rent one before Monday. Maybe Beverly Center has wheelchairs. I could push you around."

Cassidy's eyes widened. "You'd do that for me?"

"Yes. Why do you ask?"

"I don't think I'd push you around in a wheelchair."

"Hardly a surprise. I've always been the nicer sister."

Cassidy laughed. "You're right. Sage and I are the mean ones. If we could get a van next week, that would be enough. I can stay in tonight. Want me to text Sage and find out what she's doing?"

Two months ago Daisy would have been confounded and possibly revolted by the suggestion, but her life had taken a turn for the unexpected, so she found herself saying, "Sure. We can order in."

Cassidy leaned against the counter and pulled her phone out of her shorts back pocket. She texted quickly, then looked at Daisy. "She's answering. I can't remember how late she has to work today." She returned her attention to her phone.

"She just got home. She'll get changed and come over. She suggests that Chinese place we all like."

"I know the one," Daisy said, returning to the large pantry, where she pulled open a drawer and dug around until she found the takeout menu.

When she returned to the kitchen, Cassidy waved her phone. "You know that stuff is all online."

"Yes, but it's easier for us to look at a menu rather than pass around your phone."

"You're so last century."

Daisy ignored that and pointed to the family room. "Go rest until she gets here. You need to get off your hurt leg or it will get swollen."

"You're bossy," Cassidy called, making her way to the sofa, where she collapsed.

Daisy checked the refrigerator and was pleased to see a couple of baskets of strawberries and blackberries. She rinsed the fruit, then collected sugar and the Vitamix.

"Esmerelda's going to be pissed if you mess up her kitchen," Cassidy told her. "I'd be careful if I were you."

"Stop making trouble. Esmerelda doesn't care if I cook." Not that making cocktails was cooking. "Besides, she's off this weekend."

"So you have time to hide the evidence."

Daisy laughed. "Exactly."

She poured a quarter cup of sugar into the blender and added the fruit, then ran the Vitamix until everything liquefied. She tasted the mixture, added a couple more tablespoons of sugar and ran it again.

She poured the sweetened berry puree into a pitcher, then slowly added a bottle of champagne. After carefully stirring everything together, she got out three champagne flutes just as the doorbell rang.

"I'll get it," Cassidy said, reaching for her crutches.

Daisy shook her head. "Stay put."

"Bitch."

"Ingrate."

Daisy let in Sage. "Your sister's in a mood," she warned. "She has crutches and thinks she's all that."

"Kids today," Sage said with a smile. "What can we do?"

"Lock her in her room?"

"I can hear you," Cassidy called from the family room.

Sage joined her on the sofa while Daisy poured them drinks. She carried them over, along with the takeout menu.

Sage took a sip. "Delicious."

"Berry Bellinis," Daisy told her. "Easy and yummy."

"Thanks for inviting me over." Sage kicked off her flats and tucked her feet under her. "It was a long day. I was looking forward to relaxing, but my mother informed me I had to make myself scarce. Her new boyfriend is coming over."

Daisy didn't understand. "You can't meet him?"

Cassidy leaned against Sage and sighed. "She's too old."

Sage grimaced. "I suspect Joanne is trying to pass for about fifteen years younger than she is. I get in the way of that."

"Buy why lie? He's going to find out eventually."

Cassidy looked pitying. "Sweetie, it's not about keeping him. That's unlikely. It's about getting as much as she can, as quickly as she can."

"It's sad," Daisy said.

"Very." Sage took another sip. "She can't play this game much longer. She's nearly sixty." She grabbed the menu. "Can we order? I'm starved. I didn't get a lunch break today."

"But that's illegal," Daisy told her. "You're supposed to have a thirty-minute break for every—"

Sage held up her hand to stop her. "I know the rules. Life doesn't always work that way. Now let's talk food."

"Something spicy," Cassidy said, shifting away from Sage and propping up her leg. "Like me."

Sage grinned at Daisy. "You were right. She's in a mood."

"Told you so." Daisy grabbed her drink. "Mu Shu pork and spring rolls or dumplings."

"I'm going to be so puffy in the morning," Sage muttered. "Thank goodness the store's closed."

They ordered enough for at least eight people. While they waited for the delivery, Daisy topped up everyone's glass.

Cassidy drained about half hers in a single gulp, then waved her glass. "I'm off pain meds so I can drink again."

"And make up for lost time," Daisy said dryly.

"I'm ignoring that. So first kiss."

"What?" Sage asked, confused. "You want us to kiss you?"

"No, silly. I want to know about your first kiss. Who was it? How was it? And I'm talking a real kiss, like with tongue. Not some silly game thing. I'll start. I was fourteen and the guy was David Green. He's was quiet and smart, but cute. I pretended to have trouble with my math homework and asked him to help me. On our third tutoring session, he kissed me. Really kissed me." She sighed. "Young David had been practicing because he sure knew what he was doing."

Daisy grinned. "Did you two ever date?"

"No, he moved away. I wonder where he is now. Maybe I should stalk him online."

"Or not," Daisy told her. "My first kiss was also a guy from school," she said. "I was fifteen. We were at a party and we went for a walk. It was nice."

"Jimmy Barlow," Sage said. "You dated him like three months."

"How can you remember that?"

"I just do."

"Yes, we dated. Young love." Daisy reached for her Bellini. "Your turn, Sage."

"I'm not playing this game," she said with a shake of her head. "Let's talk about something else."

"What is wrong with you?" Cassidy demanded. "We're just being silly. Why does it matter who you kissed when you were a kid?"

Daisy realized the problem. "Because it's Jordan."

Sage shot her a look. "I doubt you want me to go there."

"You had to have kissed other guys before Jordan," Cassidy said.

"Not in a way that meant anything." Sage shifted on the sofa. "We aren't talking about this."

"It's okay," Daisy told her, a little surprised to find she was telling the truth. "I know you two were serious. You were engaged. He would have been your first everything."

Sage stared at her. "How can that be okay? I don't think it is, so how can you? We're just starting to get along. This is working." She motioned to the three of them. "I don't want to screw everything up because I used to sleep with your husband."

Daisy watched color stain Sage's cheeks.

"That came out wrong," Sage said quickly. "Before he was your husband. I haven't slept with Jordan in years. It's just he feels like this giant elephant in the room. You're married to him, I used to be engaged to him, I said those things at the wedding. It's all too upsetting, so no, I don't want to talk about kissing him."

Daisy was caught up in a bigger truth, one that was nearly as unexpected as an alien landing.

"You like me," she whispered.

Sage glared at her. "What?"

"You like me and you don't want to hurt my feelings."

"I never said that."

Daisy smiled. "It's okay, I know you're emotionally stunted. For what it's worth, I like you, too."

"Oh my God! We're having a moment," Cassidy crowed. "This is incredible. Okay, now let's talk about me more. Best date ever. Mine was with Desean. We were in Barcelona and we had dinner in the Gothic Quarter. Great part of the city with all these narrow streets and alleys. On the way to the restaurant, the shops were still open so we could mark our route, like we turned right by the tea cart and there was a giant plastic cow when we turned left. But by the time we were finished, the stores were closed and someone had put the cow away so we had no landmarks to guide us."

Cassidy smiled at the memory. "We had no idea how to

get back to our hotel. Our ten-minute walk turned into an hour. By the time we arrived at the hotel, we were laughing so hard, we could barely stand up. Some guys would have been mad or frustrated, but not Desean." She sighed. "Then we went upstairs and made love. It was magical."

"Tell me again why you don't want to be with him?" Daisy asked. "He's good-looking and he sounds really nice."

"I'm ignoring that and telling you it's your turn to talk about your best date."

Daisy hesitated, watching Sage carefully. "Maybe this isn't a good idea."

Sage reached for the pitcher. "It's with Jordan. I know and I'm completely, totally, absolutely over him, so tell away."

She filled all their glasses, then set the half-empty container on the coffee table.

"Jordan took me to Hawaii," Daisy said. "We'd been dating a few weeks, but we hadn't, um, you know."

"Sex," Cassidy said loudly. "You're talking about sex."

"Yes. Well, we hadn't yet and I was afraid that meant he didn't really like me. I had a few days off work and mentioned that to him, thinking we might go away for the weekend or something. He surprised me with tickets to Hawaii."

"And?" Cassidy prompted.

"We had a good time."

"Oh, please. That's all you're sharing?"

"Under the circumstances, it's for the best," Sage said. "He waited because you mattered. He wasn't looking to get laid."

"That's so romantic," Cassidy said. "I love this." She turned to Sage. "What about you?"

"I haven't had my best date yet. At least I hope not."

"Interesting," Daisy said. "Good for you. Be optimistic."

"It's that or start drinking to get through the day."

They all laughed at that. Seconds later, the doorbell rang.

Daisy jumped up to get the food. When she returned to the kitchen, Cassidy was setting the table, hopping from place to place with forks and serving spoons. Sage was studying the contents of the wine cellar.

"Any preferences?" Sage asked.

"Whatever looks good to you."

She took a bottle of red to the table. After she set it down, she looked at Daisy.

"Okay, this is probably going to spoil the mood, but I have to know. Does he still shout 'Oh, baby, baby' when he comes?"

Shocked by the personal nature of the question, Daisy was about to refuse to answer. But before she could speak, she felt her lips twitch as laughter built up inside of her. She tried to hold it in, but she couldn't. Sage joined her, leaving Cassidy staring at them.

"You're both so incredibly strange."

Sage grabbed her hand. "So that's a yes?"

Daisy was laughing too hard to speak. She nodded and squeezed her sister's fingers.

"Every time," she managed, gasping for air as tears filled her eyes. "Every damn time."

Sunday afternoon, Sage lay on a lounge chair in Adam's backyard, soaking up the sun. Her hangover had faded. Adam was on a lounge chair in the shade, the Dodgers game playing on a speaker.

Dinner with Daisy had been a lot of fun, she thought, still surprised she and Daisy could enjoy each other's company. The Jordan awkwardness hadn't come between them and Cassidy had been good company. Such an unexpected outcome.

"You're looking fierce," Adam said conversationally. "Are you plotting someone's death?"

"Nothing like that." She dragged her chair into the shade next to his and sat back down. "I like Daisy."

He looked momentarily confused. "Okay," he said slowly. "And?"

"There's no and. I like her. I guess I even respect her. Huh. I like Daisy."

She turned the concept over in her mind and found that it was really true. She liked her former stepsister.

"I always thought I hated her, but I don't anymore." She looked at Adam. "I think we're friends."

"Don't sound so surprised."

"I'm stunned. We've never gotten along. Part of that was my mom, but still. I like her. I feel good about that. Like I can believe in other things."

"Unicorns?" he asked, his voice teasing.

"Maybe."

His smile faded. "Sage, if you're serious about this, be careful. Don't mess it up the way you did with the professor."

Her good mood faded. "What are you talking about?"

"You had a good thing going with Ellery and you couldn't stand it. I don't know why—maybe you don't think you deserve to be happy, or you couldn't deal with him loving you and you not loving him back. Either way, you cheated on him to end things, and from what you've told me he was a great guy."

She swung her feet to the ground and stared at him. "How could you possibly know I cheated on him?"

He shrugged. "I'm guessing. I know you, and confrontation isn't your thing. You get what you want in other ways. You saw him as a problem, so you either took off or you cheated." He lightly touched her arm. "I'm not judging. You were in pain. I'm just saying it didn't end well."

The raw truths were unexpected. She told herself not to

be hurt, that Adam was only trying to help, but there was an element of ouch to the whole conversation.

"Ellery wasn't right for me. The situation with Daisy is totally different."

"I know you're finding your way and I'm sure you're enjoying having Daisy as a friend. I'm just saying watch yourself. You tend to mess up the things that matter most."

His blunt assessment cut through her defenses and right into her soft underbelly. She gave him a tight smile as she stood. "I didn't realize you saw me as that flawed. How can you stand to be around me?"

"Sage, wait. I'm sorry. I wasn't trying to upset you."

"Too bad. You did such a good job of it."

He reached for her, but she pulled away.

"I need to go."

He stepped in front of her. "Wait," he said softly, his dark eyes filled with concern. "I apologize. Everything I was trying to say came out badly. You're no more flawed than anyone else and it was wrong of me to make you think otherwise. I'm sorry." He touched her chin to keep her looking at him. "Please don't leave."

"You hurt me."

"I seem to do that a lot. I'm sorry." His mouth twisted. "Please don't go. I'll be more careful."

"I want to believe you."

"Then do. I care about you. I care enough to tell you the truth. That should count for something."

He had a point, but not one she especially liked. "You care about me?" she asked, mostly as a distraction.

"You know I do." He gave her a self-deprecating smile. "I just wish I knew how you felt about me."

"What? How can you ask that? We're friends. Of course I like you."

"I wasn't sure. I thought it was possible I was just a convenience."

The verbal smack was back. Even knowing he wasn't trying to hurt her didn't take away the sting. "Because I'm shallow?" she asked bitterly.

"Because you're *that* girl and my luck's never been that good."

"I'm not that girl anymore."

"You are to me."

They stared at each other for a long time. She believed he hadn't been mean on purpose and that he genuinely felt regret. In his dumb way, he'd been trying to help with Daisy.

"Okay," she told him, sitting back down. "We should probably start over."

He sat facing her. "Thank you."

"You're welcome." She cleared her throat. "I really like Daisy."

He smiled. "I'm glad you're becoming friends. You can hang out and do girl stuff together."

"What do you consider girl stuff?"

"I don't know. Waxing?"

She laughed. "We don't sit around and wax together."

"I've never waxed. I only know what I've seen on TV. I thought women did everything together."

"Not that." She reached for his hand. "I don't want to mess things up with her. You're right that I tend to make really bad decisions. I'm working on it."

"I only said what I did because I care about you."

His words warmed her. "I care about you, too."

They looked at each other, then away.

"Want to care about me at a movie and then at dinner?" he asked, sounding hopeful.

She grinned at him. "Yes, I would."

sixteen

The link from an interesting article on kids' birthday parties had led Daisy down the rabbit hole that could be Pinterest. She'd gone from admiring cute goody bags to decorations to salivating over gorgeous pictures of bedrooms with elegant chandeliers and beds overflowing with fluffy pillows. Not that she could even consider any of the possibilities. Decorating any part of the house was suddenly fraught with emotional tension, thanks to her lone therapy session with Jordan. On a more practical note, shantung silk drapes were elegant, but not overly practical in a house with cats who loved to climb.

Her phone buzzed with a text. She reached for it while still lusting over a tasseled throw that would no doubt cause the dogs to descend into an "Is this a new chew toy?" frenzy, then glanced at the message.

Just letting you know I've decided to rent a house. Even with therapy it's obvious this is going to take a while and the hotel is getting expensive. I found a furnished one with three bedrooms and a yard, so the kids will have space. I want to start taking them on weekends and a couple of evenings a week.

The words blurred as she felt her heart crack. Shock kept

her immobile as the phone fell from her hand to the carpeted floor in her office.

He'd promised, she thought frantically, fighting to catch her breath. He'd promised no more big announcements in a text, but it hadn't meant anything. It had all been a lie.

She went from paralyzed to sobbing in a heartbeat. Her entire body shook from the pain and disbelief. He'd *promised*.

The wound inside of her grew until she was sure it would swallow her, leaving nothing behind. Her sense of hopelessness was nearly as big as her fear. If she couldn't trust him to keep the tiniest of promises, if he would do this to her, what had become of their marriage?

She brushed the tears from her cheeks, then picked up her phone. It was late afternoon in Hawaii, so her father might still be at work, but she needed him.

She pushed the button to call, then waited. He picked up on the first ring.

"Daisy! How's my girl? How are—"

"Dad, something's happened." Her voice shook as she spoke. "Everyone's okay," she added hastily. "No one's hurt. It's just J-Jordan."

"Tell me," her father instructed calmly.

"He moved out. He left me."

She explained what had happened and how surprised she'd been. She told him about the hotel and finished by reading him the text.

"I don't know what to do," she admitted, the tears returning. "We're in therapy. Only one session, but we're trying. And he said he wouldn't drop any more bombs in a text. But he's got a house and we never talked about it. I don't even know what's wrong. Not really. He's says I'm too busy, but that's not fair. And he said this wasn't really his home, which hurt my feelings. I love the house and he knew we'd be living here when we started dating, so why throw it in my face now? I don't think he loves me anymore."

The sobs overwhelmed her again. She covered her face with her free hand and gave in to hopelessness. Her father was silent until she managed to get control again.

"I'm sorry," she whispered. "I shouldn't have called."

"Don't ever say that. You can always call me. I wish I was there to hug you and tell you everything is going to be all right."

She gave a strangled laugh. "No offense, but I wouldn't believe you on that last one. Tell me what to do. Please. I'm so lost and scared and confused."

"First, none of this is your fault."

Love filled her heart. "Oh, Dad. While that's sweet, it's not true. I'm responsible for at least fifty percent of what happens in my marriage, so this is at least fifty percent my fault."

"Maybe, but he's the jerk who left my daughter, so forgive me if I take your side. I don't think he actually cares about you owning the house. I think that's just a distraction from what's really wrong." He paused. "Jordan always wants to be the center of attention and the most important person in the room. You make more money than him, you deal with the kids, you manage the house. What does he bring to the table?"

His words upset her. "Dad, I love Jordan. I need him and the kids need him."

"He should know that but does he?"

"I've told him. He complains I don't pay enough attention to him. I keep feeling like he wants me to say something or do something, but he won't tell me what it is."

"Do you want me to come early? I can clear my calendar and be there tomorrow."

She knew he would do that for her—cancel appointments with his patients and fly back to the mainland, if she needed him.

"Thanks for offering, but I'm okay." She wiped her face again. "It was just the shock of it. He looked me in the eye and promised not to text anything important. It's been less than a week and he went back on his word. I don't know what to think."

Worse, she wasn't sure what his actions meant. Had he freaked out or was he letting her know that she didn't matter anymore?

"I'm worried about you, baby girl."

"Don't be." She tried to inject certainty into her voice. "I'll be all right. I just needed to hear your voice."

"I love you, Daisy."

"I love you, too, Dad."

"Call me tomorrow and let me know you're all right. I can be there in a few hours."

"Thanks. I'll get through it. Hopefully Jordan and I can work this out." Her first lie of the day, but at least it was for a good cause, she told herself.

Daisy set down her phone, put her head on her arms and gave in to tears. She cried out all her worry and confusion and fear, knowing it wouldn't help but might make her feel better.

"What's wrong?"

Cassidy stood in the doorway to her study. Her sister looked concerned as she swayed on her crutches.

"Nothing. I'm fine."

The automatic response had Cassidy rolling her eyes. "Seriously. What is it?"

Daisy knew there was no keeping what had happened a secret. She would have to tell the kids and they would tell Cassidy, so why not just get it out there?

"Jordan's rented a house." She sniffed and waved her phone. "He told me via text, after promising not to give me any big news that way. We were supposed to be talking about stuff like that." Tears slipped down her cheeks. "I don't think he wants to come back."

Cassidy's mouth twisted, then she pulled her phone out of her shorts pocket and began texting.

Resentment tasted bitter on Daisy's tongue. "Telling the world?"

Cassidy looked at her. "Asking Sage to come over so we can talk about this together."

Daisy was surprised to realize she would appreciate the support. "Oh. Thank you."

"You need to stop thinking the worst about me."

"You first."

Cassidy surprised her by smiling. "I think I can do that."

"I need a beach cover-up," Joanne said impatiently, flipping through the contents of Sage's closet. "Something cute. We're going to Mexico. His friends have a very nice house on the beach and I have to fit in."

She pulled out a Prada sundress Sage had earned giving English lessons, frowned at it, then let it fall to the floor.

"Why are all your clothes so ugly? You're not helping." Her mother spun to face her. "Why can't you be happy for me?"

Sage put her hands on her hips. "Stop," she commanded. "Just stop. I haven't said anything, so don't accuse me of being unsupportive. You barge in here and throw my clothes around, to borrow something without asking, so hey. I'm the only one who gets to have attitude. I'm glad you're happy with the new guy but that doesn't give you license to be a bitch."

They glared at each other. Sage figured there was a fifty-fifty chance that her mother would brush off her comments with a laugh or that they were about to seriously get into it. At this point, Sage wasn't sure she cared which.

Joanne blinked first, bending over to pick up the dress and hang it back in the closet.

"I'm just excited," her mother admitted. "I want things to go well with Peter."

"Me, too." For more reasons than her mother thought.

Sage crossed to her dresser and pulled out two cover-ups that were cute but large enough to fit her mom.

"Try these," she said. "They're flattering and they pack like a dream."

Joanne hugged Sage. "Thank you, darling. You're the best. Now, I'll be gone for two weeks. You'll have to take care of the house and whatever bills come in."

Oh, joy. "Sure, Mom." She heard her phone buzz, but waited until Joanne returned to her own room before checking it.

Daisy's in meltdown mode. Jordan's being an ass. Please come and help.

"What did he do now?" Sage muttered, reaching for her handbag.

She walked into her mother's room. "I'm going out. Are you sleeping here tonight?"

"Peter's sending a car in an hour." Joanne smiled. "So I won't be here when you get back."

"Have a wonderful time, then. I'll see you in two weeks." She paused awkwardly, not sure if she should go hug her mom or not. Joanne decided that for her by retreating to her closet.

Sage texted Cassidy that she was on her way. Twenty minutes later, she knocked on Daisy's front door. Esmerelda let her in, looking worried.

"Miss Daisy's in her study," she said, pointing. "She's very upset."

"Where are the kids?"

"Cassidy's with them. She won't tell me what happened. She just keeps saying Mr. Jordan isn't coming back."

Sage felt her stomach twist a little. "Let's not assume the worst just yet. They're in counseling and that's a good sign. Maybe this is just a rough patch."

Sage hurried to the master suite. She'd only been in here a handful of times, even when she'd lived in the house. Once she entered the open double doors, she had an impression of pale gray walls and light carpeting. Ahead was the bedroom. To the left and right were his-and-her bathrooms, and right by the door was Daisy's study.

Her stepsister sat on the plush sofa, a photo album on her lap, a glass with clear liquid and ice in her hands. The open bottles of vodka and tonic told her what was in the glass.

"Hey," Sage said brightly. "How are you doing?"

Daisy raised her head and stared at her as if she couldn't quite place her. Her eyes were red and her face was blotchy. "Sage? You came?"

"I'm right here. Are you drunk?"

"I hope so."

"But Cassidy texted me like half an hour ago. How did you have time?"

Daisy waved her glass. "I haven't eaten dinner yet." She paused, as if thinking. "I'm pretty sure I didn't eat lunch, either." She pressed her index finger against her lips. "Shh. Don't tell."

"I won't."

Sage took a glass from the shelf and ice from the built-in under-the-counter ice machine, then poured herself a drink and sat next to Daisy.

"Start from the beginning."

Tears filled Daisy's eyes. "He lied."

She explained about the promise and the text. Sage listened carefully, telling herself that wanting to kick Jordan in the balls wouldn't help anyone, although it might make her feel better.

"Why is he being such a dick?" Sage asked.

"I don't know. I thought we were getting better. He said he hates the house."

"What? This house? Why? It's beautiful."

"It's not his."

"Great. So he's being a guy, too."

Daisy turned her attention to the album on her lap. "He's so handsome." She ran her finger along a photograph of Jordan in a baseball cap, grinning at the camera. "I had a crush on him in high school, but he had you and who could compete with that?"

"It was years ago," Sage told her.

"I know, but he was so everything. I kept wishing you two would break up and he would fall for me." She looked at Sage, her eyes wide. "Then you broke up. Did I do that?"

"No. He broke up with me and then I went to Europe."

More tears spilled onto her cheeks. "I would never do anything to hurt you, Sage. You're my sister. I just loved Jordan. I'm sorry."

Sage put her arm around her. "Don't be sorry. You didn't do anything wrong." She flipped to the next page in the album. "You two make a cute couple."

Daisy fell for the distraction. "We were. We met at a party. You'd been gone a couple of years, I think. I didn't know anyone. I can't remember why I went. I'm not really a party person, you know? I guess I'm not very fun."

"You're plenty fun."

"Not like you. Is it wonderful being beautiful?"

"It has its moments."

"I always worried I wasn't pretty enough for Jordan. There's a study that says the key to a successful marriage is for the wife to be thinner and prettier. I'm not prettier than Jordan and I'm not skinny, either. I'm just ugly and f-fat." Her voice broke on the words.

Sage took the drink from her and pulled her close. "Don't say that. You're way prettier than him and thinner. Jordan's lucky to have you. I'm sorry he's being a shithead."

"Me, too. You were smart. You loved him first, before he learned how to break my heart. He never loved me."

"That's not true. He loves you very much. He's just going through some stuff and it's messing with his head." At least she hoped that was all it was.

Daisy finished her drink in one long swallow, then poured another—heavy on the vodka.

She drank half of that before looking at Sage.

"Thanks for coming over. That's really nice of you. It's better now, you and me. Being friends, I mean."

"It is."

"I wish it could have been this way before." She waved her free hand. "Not the Jordan part, but the us part." She pushed the album onto the floor, then angled toward Sage. "I tried a bunch of times. I reached out to you. I wanted us to be friends and sisters."

Sage's guilt was instant. "I know you did."

Daisy's eyebrows shot up. "You did? But why didn't you want that, too? Why did you hate me?"

"A lot of reasons. I was scared. My mom didn't want us to get along."

"I know she resented me." Daisy's lower lip trembled. "I wanted her to be my mom and she wouldn't even like me. I was just a little girl. She was so mean."

Sage braced herself for more tears, but Daisy surprised her by shaking them off.

"Why were you scared?" Daisy asked.

Sage smiled. "Have you seen this house? It's huge. Our little apartment was crappy, but at least it was familiar. One day she married Wallace and the next we were moving. My mom was excited, but I didn't want to leave my friends or my school."

She felt the shame of that time. "They held me back. I was humiliated."

"I don't remember that," Daisy admitted. "I know it happened, but we were in different classes, so I wasn't a part of it."

"You were so smart and all the teachers adored you. Plus, you know, your dad."

Daisy swayed slightly as she frowned. "What about my dad?"

"You were his best girl." Sage did her best not to sound bitter. "He practically worshiped you and while he was great to me, it wasn't the same. I would look at how he treated you and how my mom treated me and I would get mad." She sucked in a breath and risked the truth. "It was easier to hate you than be angry with the person who was actually doing the damage."

Daisy's eyes widened. "Your mom?"

"That would be her." Sage picked up her drink. "It doesn't matter. It was all a long time ago."

Daisy grabbed her hand. "It does matter. You're still in pain—I can feel it. Oh, Sage, I should have tried harder." The tears returned. "I gave up on you."

"Daisy, we were children. You have no responsibility for what happened. You tried to be my friend over and over again, and I pushed you away. I'm sorry. It would have been better for both of us to get along. Plus you had such great toys," she added, trying to lighten the mood.

"What toys? What are you talking about?"

"Mine were sad, worn little things, while you had an entire playroom filled with books and games and dolls. It was like living in a toy store."

"I would have given them all up for us to be sisters."

Daisy was drunk enough that lying would be a problem, which meant Sage had no option but to believe her. How would their lives have been different if they'd figured out how to be friends? If Joanne hadn't come between them so many times they'd stopped trying?

"You're sweet," Sage told her. There was no going back. They were stuck in their muddled present.

Daisy surprised her by giggling. "At least you'll always have Paris."

"What do you mean?"

"You'll always have Paris. You know, from the movie." Daisy drained her drink. *Casablanca.*

"I never saw that."

"What? You have to see it. It's beautiful and sad." She paused. "I think I have to throw up."

Sage guided her to the massive bathroom. Sure enough, Daisy threw up everything in her stomach. When she was done, she leaned against the toilet, her eyes closed.

"I want to die."

"And yet you won't," Sage told her, putting a cool washcloth on the back of her neck. "Are you done or do you need to throw up again?"

"I'll be dead by morning."

"Unlikely. Come on, let's get you into bed. You can sleep it off. I want to say you'll feel better tomorrow, but that seems unlikely. I'll let Esmerelda know you're going to need a little extra care."

Daisy started to nod, groaned and then collapsed onto the

floor. "Leave me here. It will be easier for the paramedics to carry me out."

"I think if you're dead it's the coroner, but that could be from watching too much television."

"You're mocking me."

"A little." Sage helped her to her feet. "In twenty-four hours, you'll be good as new. I'm going to get you a pitcher of water. Drink as much as you can." She eyed Daisy's pale face. "On second thought, I'll bring a little ginger ale, as well. You need aspirin, but you should wait until your stomach calms down."

Daisy leaned on her as they walked toward the bedroom. "You have a lot of experience with being drunk."

"Kind of the story of my life."

seventeen

Daisy spent a miserable night. She'd thrown up enough of the alcohol that she wasn't drunk for very long, but not so much of it that she avoided a hangover. It was kind of the worst of both worlds. She dozed until five, when she got up and showered. Shortly before six, she picked up her phone to text Jordan.

She'd spent much of the last couple of hours trying to figure out what to say. As far as she was concerned, he'd betrayed her *and* them. She didn't know why he'd done it, but she had to confront him. She'd been way too passive when he'd first moved out—immobilized by shock and fear and hurt. This time, she was going to take control because it sure didn't feel like he knew what he was doing.

If we don't have a conversation today, I'm calling a lawyer to make our separation legal.

She waited less than two minutes for his response. **I'm just out of the shower. I'll be over as soon as I'm dressed.**

Daisy ignored the sudden clenching of her stomach. She went downstairs and started coffee. When the pot was full, she poured half of it into an insulated carafe.

"Good morning," Esmerelda said as she walked into the kitchen. "How are you feeling?"

"Awful. Thankfully I don't have to be at work until noon. Jordan's on his way. Would you send him up to my study, please?"

"Of course."

"I don't know how long he'll be here." She paused, not sure what to say. "We have a lot to talk about."

"I'll look after the children."

"Thank you."

Daisy went upstairs. She paced while she waited, ignoring the sense of dread building up inside of her. Yes, this was a complicated situation and she probably should have handled it differently from the beginning. But dwelling on that didn't help anyone. She was going to be more proactive from this moment forward. She would think with her head and not her heart. She would make the right decisions for herself and her children, no matter how much doing that hurt.

Jordan burst into her study about fifteen minutes later. He was stone-faced and waving his phone.

"What the hell kind of message was that? Are you threatening me or did you mean it?"

Daisy ignored him as she walked out into the hall of the master suite and carefully closed the big double doors, then shut the one leading into her office.

"While your outrage is interesting, it has little to do with the problem," she said, doing her best to stay calm as she faced him. "You started this, Jordan. You promised. You told me and the therapist that you wouldn't communicate anything significant by text, but you couldn't even go a week without breaking your word. You promised and I trusted you, which makes me a fool, but it also makes you a liar."

He stared at her, his face comically blank, as if he had no idea what she was talking about.

"I didn't lie," he insisted. "About anything. What are you talking about?"

Now it was her turn to wave her phone. "You texted me that you were moving into a house and that you wanted to take the children for more overnight visits. You don't think that counts as significant? That you're leaving a hotel for a house where you have a lease? You don't think taking that step is something we might have talked about before you made that kind of decision?"

"Not really." He shook his head. "Is that what this is all about? The house I rented?"

"Yes. It's huge. It's a big deal, and don't you dare say it's not."

"It isn't. Why does it matter if I'm in a hotel or a house? The hotel was getting expensive. This is easier. There's more room and it will be better for the kids." He walked to the window, then turned back to her. "It's not like we're fixing things between us. I wanted my own space. I didn't think it was that big a deal."

She could see he meant what he said—that he honestly thought the change was nothing.

"How can you think that?" she asked. "How can you not see this is hugely significant? Not just that you did it, but that you didn't discuss it with me. We're talking about our marriage. You're taking steps that feel permanent and I'm not part of the decision process. You're going to get mail there!"

"What does mail matter? You're not making any sense. I'm still not living here. All that's changing is the location."

"No, it's more than that. A hotel is temporary. A hotel implies you'll be back soon. A house says we're on the road to getting a divorce."

The emotion she'd been holding at bay slammed into her, nearly driving her to her knees. She felt sick to her stomach and not strong enough to deal with what was happening. She wanted to beg him to move back home. The house was over fifteen thousand square feet. He could have an entire wing to himself. Wasn't that separation enough?

"Why do you have to go there?" he asked. "You're making more of this than it is."

"You're making it less."

They stared at each other. His obvious impatience reminded her to be strong. She had to be. Pushing aside her worry and fear, she said, "What do you want from me?"

"I want things back the way they were when I mattered."

"Why do you keep saying that?" She paused to try to keep her emotions under control. "Our marriage is important to me. I want us to be happy together. I didn't like it when you moved out and I don't like that you're taking this next step. I understand there are problems and I want us to work on them, but I can't fix what I don't understand."

"I come in last all the time. I'm not sure you even want to be married to me anymore."

Unexpected anger surged through her. "I just said our marriage is important. Do you think I'm lying about that? I'm not. You're the one who moved out. You're the one who keeps changing the rules. You complain that you don't matter to me but you're the one walking away. I never asked you to leave—I didn't even know you were considering it. Just poof, you were gone. No conversation, no anything. You decided, just like you decided to get a house without telling me. It's like you expect me to read your mind, then you punish me for getting it wrong. I will never know what you're thinking if you don't tell me. I can't guess what you want. Tell me what's different now than it used to be, or at least tell me specifically what you want to change."

"I want to be important to you."

"If you weren't important, we wouldn't be having this fight. Why won't you be specific?"

"I am specific." He crossed his arms over his chest. "You don't get it, do you? You don't need me, Daisy. I'm not sure you ever have."

His lack of cooperation infuriated her. "Maybe that's because I can't depend on you. Here I am, begging you for information, but will you tell me anything? Give a hint? Of course not. You have a house? Great. Stay there until you figure out whatever it is you're dealing with. When you have an answer, let me know."

Something flashed in his eyes. Once again she had the sense she was being tested and that she'd failed.

"This probably isn't the best time for us to be in therapy," he said quietly.

"I couldn't agree more."

"I'll send Dr. Braxton an email and let him know we're not going to make our next appointment."

"Fine."

Without saying anything else, he walked out of the room. Daisy stayed where she was, consciously slowing her breathing. She was still hurt and scared, but under that was a sense of resignation. Or maybe just the first hint of the inevitable. Whatever Jordan wanted wasn't anything he was going to tell her. She didn't know if he didn't know himself, or if he felt she should be able to guess. Either way, she knew they were on the wrong path—one with an almost assured unhappy ending. What she didn't know was how to turn things around before that happened. Or if she wanted to.

★ ★ ★

Sage groaned softly when she opened the front door and heard the television. Her mother wasn't supposed to be home for another ten days. Having her cut her vacation short wasn't good news.

"Mom?" she called.

"Back here."

Sage walked through to the family room at the back of the house. The drapes were pulled and all the lights were off. HGTV played on the TV. Her mother was lying on the sofa, a bottle of rum on the coffee table beside her, a half-empty glass next to it.

First Daisy and now Joanne, Sage thought. Men disappointing women—it was an old story.

"You okay?" Sage asked, wishing she could simply escape without having to speak to her mother.

"No, I'm not. His friends were horrible. They convinced him I wasn't right for him and he asked me to leave." She tightened the belt on her robe and reached for her glass. "Good riddance. He was an ugly old man who couldn't get it up anyway. I can do better."

"You can. You're beautiful and vibrant and he's a fool."

"That's what I said." Tears filled her eyes. "I hate him."

"He's not worth the energy."

Joanne nodded, then motioned to the kitchen. "Be a dear and get me another can of Coke. I need it for my drink."

Sage did as she asked, then excused herself to get changed. Once she was in her room, she quickly texted Adam.

Please tell me you're home and in the mood for company.

A few seconds later, her phone rang.

"We're talking on the phone?" she said quietly, so her mother couldn't hear. "Is that allowed?"

He laughed. "I'm in my car. It can read me texts, but answering them is tricky. I didn't want the reply to translate into something about wanting to buy a cow."

"Did you want to buy a cow?"

"Not all of it. What's going on?"

She told him about her mother's early return and the unhappy circumstances. "I was hoping to escape to your place, but if you're driving, you're not home."

"I'm on my way. In the meantime, you can let yourself in." He gave her the code for the front door.

"You're trusting me with your house," she said, her tone light. "What if I go through your stuff?"

"I don't have many secrets."

"What about that stash of porn you keep under your mattress?"

He laughed. "These days porn is online, Sage. I don't need a stash."

"You're right. I forgot. I'm not much of a porn watcher."

"Me, either. Make yourself at home. I'll see you in about half an hour."

Sage was still smiling when she hung up.

She changed her clothes, then checked on her mother. Joanne had fallen asleep. Sage wrote a note, then quietly left.

She let herself into Adam's house. While she was tempted to go exploring, she instead sat on the living room floor and stretched out her back and hip flexors, then did a few yoga moves until she heard his car pull into the garage.

"Honey, I'm home," he called.

She started laughing. "In the living room."

She scrambled to her feet just as he stepped into the hallway. Unlike everyday Adam who wore jeans and polo shirts, this version of him was in a dark suit, with a white shirt and blue tie. He looked as good as he had at the reunion.

Deep in her belly she felt a little twist of desire—unexpected, but not unwelcome.

"You look powerful and sophisticated," she told him.

"That's the look I was going for." He raised his briefcase. "I can work from home but every now and then my corporate bosses summon me and off I go, to dazzle them in person. How does pizza sound? I've been daydreaming about pepperoni."

"As long as I can do veggies on my half, I'm happy to have pizza."

"Veggies?" He made a gagging noise. "Why would you do that to a perfectly good pizza?"

"You're such a guy."

He winked at her. "I am. Let me get changed, then we'll order."

He walked into what she assumed was the master bedroom. She nearly followed, so they could continue their conversation, then stopped herself. She and Adam weren't at the "you can see me undressing" stage, which meant she should stay in the hallway.

"How's your mom?" he asked, his voice slightly muffled.

"Passed out. Hopefully she'll stay drunk for a couple of days, then move on to someone else."

"Is she going to be a problem for you?"

"What do you mean?"

"Will she steal money from you or take your stuff? Like your Birkin bag?"

"I only had the one and the other expensive bags I have are in the trunk of my car. I don't keep cash around."

He walked out of the bedroom barefoot and shirtless, wearing only worn jeans that hung low on his hips. His chest was muscled, his shoulders broad. As she watched, he pulled on a T-shirt.

"You can keep your stuff here, if you want," he told her, leading the way into the kitchen. "You already have the code to my front door. You can come get it anytime you want."

His generous offer was nearly enough to distract her from the sight of his body and what that visual was doing to her girly parts.

"What if it's a Tinder night?" she asked, mostly to distract herself. "I wouldn't want to get in the way."

He flashed her a grin. "I'll give you fair warning if things head in that direction." He scrolled through his phone. "Pizza, salad and maybe a chocolate lava cake?"

She laughed. "Why bother with the salad?"

"Because then I can pretend my meal is healthy."

"Sounds good."

He placed the order, then got out two beers from the refrigerator. They settled on the big sectional in the family room.

"I'm sorry about your mom," he said.

"Me, too, although I'm not surprised. They got involved really fast. That doesn't usually end well." She took a sip of the beer. "It's so strange. Last night I was dealing with Daisy getting drunk over crap Jordan's pulling and tonight my mom is dealing with something similar. What is it with your gender?"

"Don't blame me. I haven't screwed up."

"I know. I was asking generically." She thought about how upset Daisy had been. "Jordan moved from a hotel to a house and told her in a text. She was devastated."

Adam looked shocked. "That's a boneheaded thing to do. Is he trying to split them up?"

"I don't know. I hope not. They've got kids and she works really hard. With her money, she doesn't need a job, but she has one and it's a big deal. Plus, she's got Cassidy living there. It's a lot and for Jordan to do what he did? I don't get it."

Adam surprised her by smiling.

"What?" she demanded.

"You're being a good friend."

"I know. It's weird, right? I mean all my life, I've hated her and now I don't. I like her. She's smart and funny and a terrific mother. I admire how she is with her children—she's so patient and caring. I wish things had been different when we were kids. Daisy's the kind of friend who has your back." She paused for a second. "I've been thinking about what you said before. About me not screwing up the relationship. You were right about that. I do it a lot—mess up the good stuff in my life. It's as if I want to destroy it before someone else can. As if that gives me control."

She looked at him. "And I did not plan to go down that psychological path."

"It's okay. I'm a modern man and I can handle it. Not like those guys you knew in Europe."

She grinned. "Actually men in Europe can deal with emotions much better than men in America. No offense."

"None taken. Are you happy being back?"

"Yes. It's the right decision, although dealing with my mom isn't especially fun. I do love my shower. The water pressure, the space to move around, the fluffy mat when I get out."

"They don't have bathmats?"

"Not like ours."

"What else is different?"

"Central heat and air conditioning. In older buildings, it doesn't exist." She picked up her bottle. "Oh, grocery shopping. You have to weigh your own produce and in some stores, you have to pay for a cart."

"Why?"

"I don't know. You just do. And the walking. Everyone walks everywhere there. I miss that. Here everyone drives."

"Gotta love LA."

"I do. Have you seen the movie *Casablanca*?"

"Sure. It's a classic. Great script, strong acting. You're not a fan?"

"I've never seen it."

"Seriously? You have to see it. I have the DVD."

"You have DVDs? Haven't you heard of Netflix?"

"I have that, too. But some things need to be on DVD and that's one of them. Want to watch it?"

"I would."

He got up to find the DVD in his collection. She put plates and flatware on the coffee table and got them each a second beer. He'd just put the DVD into the player when the pizza arrived. After they each took a slice, he reached for the remote.

"It's in black and white," he said with mock seriousness. "Are you going to be able to handle that?"

She grinned. "Just start the movie, weirdo."

He chuckled and pushed Play.

Minutes later, Sage found herself caught up in the story. Ingrid Bergman was so beautiful and heartbreaking as Ilsa, torn between the two men she loved. Humphrey Bogart was the perfect swaggering hero. She was mesmerized by the story and kept having to remind herself to eat.

When they were done with the pizza, Adam cleared the coffee table, then sat back down on the sofa and pulled her close. She leaned against him, as he put his arm around her. The feel of his warm body so close to hers was the perfect accompaniment to the movie.

When the final credits rolled, he paused the DVD.

"What did you think?"

"I loved it. I want to watch it again, but I'll do that on my own."

She was going to say more, only just then she realized how

close his mouth was to hers. She put her hand on the back of his neck and drew his head down to hers.

The kiss was easy at first. A light brushing of skin on skin, but then Adam wrapped his arms around her and shifted slightly, angling his head and deepening the kiss.

The first brush of his tongue sent liquid heat surging through her. Need exploded, shocking her with its intensity. She wanted him touching her everywhere. She wanted them both naked and exploring. She wanted to be in his bed afterward, curled up next to him, knowing that the rules had changed and she could stroke and explore and taste at will.

"I should get you home," he said, pulling away. "We both have to work tomorrow."

The unexpected rejection cut her more deeply than she would have thought possible. It was barely nine. She didn't have to be at the shop until eleven and Adam worked from home and made his own hours. There wasn't exactly a time issue. So why didn't he want her?

She sat back on the sofa. "Oh, okay. Thanks for dinner and the movie," she said, hoping her disappointment didn't show. The last thing she needed in her life was pity.

"I'm always up for a rescue," he told her. "You now have my door code. My casa is su casa."

She forced a smile and quickly made her escape. Once back at her mom's house, she checked the family room and saw her mother had gone to bed. The TV was off and the bottle of rum was empty. Sage rinsed it, then put it in the recycling and retreated to her own room. She sat on the bed and pulled her knees to her chest.

She had no idea what had happened tonight with Adam. She didn't know if he wasn't interested in her sexually, if she was trapped in the friend zone, or if he was giving her space. From what she could tell, he wasn't seeing anyone else and he wasn't gay, so why didn't he want to have sex with her? And why on earth did she care so much?

Daisy stood at her locker, trying not to panic. Two people had called out, leaving her taking on a second shift. The extra hours of work weren't the problem—it was her kids. Esmerelda had an emergency dental appointment and wasn't available to pick them up from school. Jordan's office manager had said he was in surgery for the next three hours and couldn't be disturbed. Cassidy still wasn't cleared to drive and Daisy was out of options.

She stared at her phone, started to scroll through her contact list, then stopped herself.

Yes, she and Sage were friends now. They'd found their way through their troubled past and it was great, but trusting her former stepsister with her tender emotions and trusting her with Ben and Krissa were two very different things. Only she didn't actually have a choice.

She found the number and pushed the call button.

Sage answered on the first ring. "Hello?"

"It's Daisy."

"Oh, hi. What's up?"

Daisy hesitated, almost saying "never mind." Then she told herself that she and Sage had come a long way and she should take the step of faith. Plus, she was desperate.

"I need a favor. I'm tied up at work, Jordan's in surgery and Esmerelda had to go to the dentist. Is there any way you could pick up the kids from school?"

"Sure. I'm off today. What time do they finish?"

Relief eased her tension. "Three."

"Then I'll be there."

"Great. I'll call the school so they can tell the kids to look for your car." Daisy pressed her hand to her chest. "Thank you so much. I really appreciate it."

"Not a problem. What time will you be home?"

"Close to eleven, but Esmerelda should be home around five. She'll take care of things from there."

"Happy to help."

"You've saved me."

Sage chuckled. "That seems to be our new pattern. I'm kind of digging it."

"Of course you are." Daisy smiled. "Seriously, thank you."

"Anytime."

After they hung up, Daisy stored her phone in her locker, then went back to work. As she walked through the hospital, she thought about how strange it was for her to turn to Sage and have her stepsister be willing to help. Now she just had to hope that nothing went wrong.

eighteen

Sage felt beyond out of place, waiting in the pickup line at school. While it was certainly an ordinary activity for parents everywhere, it wasn't one she'd ever participated in before. She waved at Ben and Krissa, who ran over and climbed into the back seat.

"You came!" Krissa sounded delighted. "They said you would because Mom has to work and Esmerelda needs to go to the dentist."

"Her tooth's been hurting her for a while now," Ben added. "It's important to take care of teeth. In the olden days, not having teeth was a death sentence."

Sage made sure they put on their seat belts, then pulled out onto the main road. "I'd heard that. How was your day?"

"Good."

"I finished my book for reading," Krissa told her.

Ben rolled his eyes. "I finish all my books."

Krissa stuck out her tongue.

"So," Sage said quickly, capturing their attention as they looked at her in the rearview mirror while she waited at a light. "Do we have homework?"

"I did mine already," Ben said. "It was pretty easy."

"I don't have any. I finished my book."

He looked at his sister. "You already said that."

"I wanted more attention."

Sage held in a smile. "I'm glad neither of you have home-work because I thought we could spend the afternoon doing something fun."

"Like what?" Ben asked, sounding suspicious. "We can't play online. Mom limits our game time."

"Not a computer game. A craft."

The kids exchanged a look. Sage smiled, then returned her attention to the road.

"What kind of craft?" Krissa asked.

"I thought we could make tie-dye T-shirts."

"You can make them at home?" Krissa asked, sounding impressed. "Is it hard?"

"Not really. Cassidy and I used to make them all the time when we were your age. We'll need some supplies, though. I thought we'd go to the craft store and get what we need, then make shirts. You can do one for yourself or your mom or dad."

"Can I do one for Lucky?" Krissa asked eagerly.

"If they have dog shirts. Sure." Sage knew the visit to the craft store would mean a hit on her credit card, but she was pretty sure Daisy would offer to cover the costs and depend-ing on how much it turned out to be, Sage just might let her.

"I want to make a shirt," Ben said, surprising her. "Tie-dye is cool."

"Good. Then that's what we're going to do."

An hour later they arrived home. The three of them trans-ported the buckets, bottles and shirts inside.

"We'll set up in the laundry room," Sage said. "There'll be plenty of room in there."

The kids carried everything in, then went upstairs to change into casual clothes. Sage found Cassidy in her suite watching some daytime talk show.

"Is this what you've been reduced to?" Sage asked, picking up the clicker and turning off the TV.

"Hey, I was into that."

Sage smiled at her. "Really? What was it about?"

Cassidy sighed. "Someone did something to somebody else."

"That's what I thought. Your life is sad and small."

"I'm trapped because of my injuries. Don't judge me. There's nothing else I can do with a broken leg and arm."

"You could be writing a book."

Cassidy blinked at her. "Excuse me? A what?"

"A book. Essays, nonfiction, a sexy romance. You're a writer, so why aren't you writing?"

"I have a broken arm. The cast wraps around my hand. I can't type."

Sage channeled a little inner maternal power and said, "You've never heard of voice recognition software? You don't have to type it. You can speak it. But that's for later. I'm going to teach the kids how to make tie-dye shirts."

"Does Daisy know you've invaded her house and are taking over?"

"She's working a double shift and Esmerelda's at the dentist. I'm in charge so brace yourself."

Cassidy slid to the edge of the sofa and pushed herself to her feet. She swayed for a second, then reached for her crutches. "Nobody tells me anything. How come I'm the last to know?"

"You're too busy sulking. You should think about changing that."

"You're in a mood."

"I am and I like it."

They all met downstairs. The laundry room was as big as Sage remembered—certainly larger than any apartment she'd ever rented. There were miles of counter space and two separate sinks, along with an industrial-sized washer and dryer.

Sage had the kids cover the counters with clean newspaper while Cassidy was charged with taking the tags off the stack of white T-shirts.

"You got shirts for the dogs?" Cassidy asked, holding one up. "Do they know?"

"Lucky loves to dress up," Krissa informed her. "Hats are his favorite."

"He's one good-natured dog," Cassidy muttered.

Sage had everyone put on protective gloves, then showed them how to measure the right amount of dye into the jars, before adding water and shaking it until the dye dissolved. The different colors were poured into buckets, followed by a mixture of water and soda ash.

They wet the T-shirts in the sink and laid them out on the counter. Sage explained how to fold the shirts, or twist them, to get different patterns. She and Cassidy helped them gather the fabric and secure it with rubber bands in the right places. Then they started putting the shirts into buckets of dye.

By five o'clock, all the shirts had been dyed, rinsed and were hanging to dry. The kids each had two for themselves, as did Lucky and Sheba. Sage had made a shirt for herself, for her mother and for Adam. Cassidy had made an extra-large one but wouldn't say who it was for. Krissa and Ben had worked on one for their dad and Esmerelda and had each made one for Daisy.

Sage went in the kitchen to see about dinner. There hadn't been any word from Esmerelda, but Sage knew an emergency dental appointment could run late. She'd just put her hand on the refrigerator when she realized what she was doing.

She was watching Daisy's children. She was responsible for

them, the pets, Cassidy and the house. Okay, Cassidy could almost take care of herself, but the rest of it was on Sage.

While that thought shouldn't have been a surprise, it was—mostly because Daisy had trusted her. She'd been in need and she'd been comfortable enough—or possibly desperate enough—to call her stepsister.

Sage knew they'd become friends, but this was different. This was more than liking someone. Daisy's kids were her life and she'd given them to Sage. Sure, just for a few hours, but still.

A warmth started in her chest and migrated to the rest of her body. She felt good—empowered even. Then Ben asked what was for dinner and the emotional spell she'd been in broke, releasing her back into the moment.

She found the ingredients for a chicken taco salad in the refrigerator, along with fresh guacamole and a bag of tortilla chips. Cassidy helped the kids set the table, entertaining them with stories of her travels, including the time her backpack and all her supplies had been washed away by a flash flood, leaving her with nothing but the clothes she was wearing and, ironically, a formal ball gown.

"Why did you take a ball gown camping?" Ben asked as he set out glasses.

"I was going to a fundraiser at the end of my trip. I hung it up every night so it wouldn't get too wrinkled. It was high enough in the trees that it didn't get swept away, but it was kind of stained from getting wet."

"Did you go to the party?" Krissa asked, wide-eyed.

"I did. In my stained ball gown. Everyone wanted to know what happened and I had a great story to tell them."

They were all laughing when Sage heard the front door open.

"That must be Esmerelda," she said. "Let me go see how she's doing."

Sage walked down the hall and found Daisy's housekeeper cupping the left side of her face in her hand. Her cheek was swollen and she looked to be in pain.

Esmerelda stopped in her tracks, obviously surprised to see her. "What are you doing here?"

At least that was what Sage assumed she was trying to say. It sounded more like *Wha ru dung ear.*

"Daisy had to work a double shift and she didn't want you to miss your appointment so I got the kids. What happened?"

"Root canal."

Sage winced. "That has to hurt. Do you have medication?"

Esmerelda held up a small pharmacy bag. Sage took it and shook out the bottles. There was an antibiotic and a painkiller, both with instructions to be taken with food.

"Go get settled in your room," Sage said firmly. "I'll bring you something to eat so you can take your pills."

Esmerelda shook her head, then winced. *"Inner."*

"I'm fixing dinner. It's taco salad. I can handle it. Go get in bed. I'll bring you a tray."

Esmerelda hesitated, then nodded before walking toward the back of the house. Sage returned to the kitchen.

"Esmerelda isn't feeling well," she began, then wished she'd been less blunt when both children turned to her, wide-eyed.

"What's wrong?" Ben asked.

"Is she okay?"

Sage silently swore, even as she smiled. "I said that wrong. She had a root canal and her mouth hurts. She's fine, but she needs to be quiet. I'm going to fix her something to eat so she can take her medication and start to feel better."

Cassidy used her crutches to head for the pantry. "Ben, help me get the Vitamix out. I'll make her a fruit smoothie with a little protein powder that will be easy to digest. After all the work they did, she's not going to want to chew anything. Krissa, look and see if there's any cottage cheese. That's nice and soft."

Ben and Cassidy made the fruit smoothie while Sage helped Krissa scoop out cottage cheese. Sage put the two pills on a small dish before putting everything on a tray, including an ice pack for her face, and carrying it to Esmerelda's room.

Esmerelda had kicked off her shoes and stretched out on the bed, a few pillows behind her back. She opened her eyes when Sage knocked on the half-open door.

"Here you go. Food and your meds. I'll check back in an hour or so to see if you want some soup." She put the tray on the nightstand.

Esmerelda looked from it to her and back. "Thank you."

"You're welcome. After dinner Ben and Krissa are going to want to come see you, to make sure you're all right. Is that okay?"

Esmerelda nodded. "Don't want them worried."

"I agree." She tapped the smoothie glass. "This should go down pretty easy so you can tolerate your pills." She pulled her phone out of her pocket. "Text me if you need anything. I'm not leaving until Daisy gets home."

"Okay."

Around seven, the taco salad devoured, they checked on the shirts, which were drying nicely. Krissa wanted to wear hers to bed, but Sage explained it had to be washed first. Sage texted Daisy to let her know that everyone was doing well and to tell her about Esmerelda's root canal.

By nine, the house was quiet, Ben and Krissa in bed. Sage and Cassidy stretched out in the family room. They had jazz playing softly and had raided the liquor cabinet, taking a bottle of what Sage would guess was very expensive cognac for an evening treat.

"You made Desean a shirt," Sage said, watching her sister as she spoke.

"No. I tie-dyed an extra-large shirt. There's a difference."

"So now you're going to lie to me?"

Cassidy leaned back against the sofa and closed her eyes. "I didn't make it specifically for Desean, but if I ever see him again, I might give it to him."

"He doesn't strike me as the tie-dye type."

Cassidy opened her eyes and smiled. "He'd wear it for me."

"So the man has it bad?"

The smile faded. "He used to be in love with me."

"And now?"

"I don't know. I haven't talked to him in weeks."

"Not even to thank him for the flowers?"

"No. Not even then."

"Do you miss him?"

Cassidy looked at her. "Why all the questions?"

"I'm curious. You have a great guy madly in love with you and you won't have anything to do with him. What's up with that?"

"You know the answer. I don't know how to make it work. I don't know how to love him back and not have it all fall apart. I believe love's real, but I don't have it figured out."

"Maybe it's hard because when it works, it's amazing."

"You speak from experience?"

Sage thought about her long line of failed relationships. "No. Not even close. I speak from a place of wishful thinking."

"Do you want to fall in love again?"

The real question was did she want to fall in love for the first time, but why go there? "I don't know. Maybe. With the right guy."

"And if he doesn't exist?"

"Then no. Being with the wrong person is pretty awful. I've done that enough in my life."

Cassidy reached for her glass. "I don't think Desean is the wrong guy, I think I'm the wrong girl."

"For him or for anyone?"

Cassidy winced. "Don't put it like that."

"Why not?"

"It's depressing to think I'm not right for anyone."

"But that's how you're acting. As if you can't fit in anywhere. I think you're giving up because the thought of trying and failing is too painful to consider."

"You really think you should be the one giving advice?"

Sage heard the edge in Cassidy's voice and knew her sister expected her to start a fight.

"Oh, Cassidy, don't be like that. I'm just pointing out that if you don't get your act together, Desean is always going to be the one who got away. Regrets suck—trust me on that one."

"Do you regret losing Jordan?"

"No." Sage thought for a second, then repeated, "No. He was right to say we were too young to get married. My actions—running off to Paris the way I did—prove I was too immature to handle marriage."

Cassidy waved her hand. "This could have all been yours. How could you not regret that?"

Sage smiled. "The house is Daisy's so this couldn't have been mine."

"I meant the family stuff. The kids, the dogs."

Sage considered the issue of regret. "Not for me," she said slowly. "Not with him. We've both moved on."

"But at the wedding—"

"I was drunk and depressed. I wasn't missing Jordan. My regrets are more about who I could have been and the fact that at every fork in the road, I went the wrong way."

"Me, too," Cassidy said glumly.

Sage raised her glass. "We are a pair."

"We are, but of what?"

They both laughed. Sage smiled at her.

"I don't say this often enough, or maybe at all, but I do love you."

Cassidy's eyes widened, then filled with tears. "Do you mean that?"

"Yes. You're my sister and I will always love you."

"I love you, too. Even though we both suck at relationships."

Daisy pulled into the garage a little before midnight. She was tired to the bone, but not sleepy. For her entire second shift, she'd been a wreck—worrying about what was happening at home. She knew she hadn't had a choice, that Sage had been her only option, but what had she been thinking, leaving her kids with her? She could only hope that Esmerelda had gotten home early and had been able to take charge again. If not, God only knew what kind of disaster she was walking into.

She hurried into the house and saw that there were a handful of lights left on. Despite her dental surgery, Esmerelda was still taking care of things, Daisy thought, grateful she had her housekeeper to depend on. She was always—

"You're back."

The voice came from the family room, causing Daisy to jump as she spun toward the sound. She saw Sage sitting up and stretching.

"What are you doing here?" Daisy demanded, her tone more harsh than she'd meant.

"Watching over the fam. What time is it?"

"Midnight."

"You did have a long day." Sage blinked a few times, then glanced at her. "You look terrible."

"Thanks. I feel terrible. What are you still doing here?"

"I wanted to stay until you got home. The kids went to bed at nine with no problem. Esmerelda is pretty out of it. She drank a smoothie and ate some soup. She kept down both her painkiller and her antibiotic."

Sage rose and crossed to the kitchen island, stretching as she walked. "Ben made a chart for her so she'll know when to take her meds. All she has to do is follow the times and then X out the boxes once she's taken the pills." Sage smiled. "That kid is a whiz on a computer."

Daisy tried to take it all in. Sage's presence, the need to monitor Esmerelda's medication. She'd only been gone for a few hours and it felt as if everything had changed. "I didn't know it was that serious."

"I think the procedure hit her pretty hard. She should be up and around tomorrow, but she's not going to be eating a steak anytime soon. What else? The kids ate their dinner and we watched a movie, then I read to them in French, mostly because I know it annoys you."

Daisy managed a smile. "Gee, thanks."

"Anytime. They brushed their teeth and went to bed on time. Oh, we made shirts."

Sage started down the long back hallway. Daisy followed, not sure what she meant by "we made shirts" only to come to a stop when she entered the laundry room.

Nearly a dozen tie-dye shirts hung from a portable clothing rack. The predominant colors were yellow and blue, but there were bits of green and a couple done in bright pink. The designs were pretty and the colors bright. She knew it was a good craft project, but despite telling herself it was fine, she still felt a knot in the pit of her stomach.

She remembered all those years ago, when Cassidy had come home from her week with Sage and her mother. Every couple of months, Cassidy had a new tie-dye T-shirt she and Sage had made together, one she wore proudly, as if it was a connection to the ever desirable Sage. Daisy understood the ridiculousness of being jealous of the activity, but even now, she looked at the shirts and felt left out. As if she hadn't been invited to the cool kids' table. Proof she never should have trusted Sage.

"We kind of got carried away," Sage admitted. "They made a couple for themselves and for the dogs." She pointed to a blue-and-green T-shirt. "That's for their dad. I don't know how you feel about tie-dye, but you are now the proud owner of two."

Sage held up a pink shirt and a blue one. "They each wanted to make you one."

Daisy looked from the shirts to her stepsister. "These are for me?"

"Sure. I have one. Cassidy made one for Desean but she won't admit it. Of course I made one for Adam, which is weird, I know, but not weirder than the fact that I made one for my mom."

And just like that, the mad and the worry and the pain were all gone. Sage had managed everything perfectly. She'd taken care of the kids and Esmerelda and she'd helped Daisy's children make tie-dye shirts.

"I was worried," she admitted. "About tonight. About you handling it all."

Sage looked at her. "I wouldn't let anything happen to them. Not ever. I hope you know that."

"I do now."

Daisy's throat got tight. She didn't know what else to say, so she simply threw herself at Sage and hung on. For a second, nothing happened, then Sage hugged her back and they stood there, clinging to each other, for a very long time.

Inocencia shook her head. "Not that one. Why don't you understand? I need a dress for a luncheon." She flicked her hand at the ten discarded dresses scattered around the large dressing room. "These are all awful."

Sage reminded herself that Inocencia was always going to be a difficult client and to accept that was to find peace. As she reached down to pick up a couple of dresses from the floor, Inocencia's little dog lunged at her, teeth bared. Sage pulled her hand back just in time.

"Oh, Royal doesn't mean it," Inocencia said with a laugh. "She can be feisty, but it's all in good fun."

"Of course," Sage murmured, standing. "Let me get you a little more champagne, then I'll go check in back. There have to be some new things waiting to be unpacked. Maybe your dream dress is in there."

Inocencia sighed. "I doubt that."

Sage risked a couple of fingers to grab another discarded dress. As the small dog growled, Sage caught sight of the animal's jeweled collar. It looked expensive, and ridiculous, but it made perfect sense for such a pampered pet.

"Be right back," Sage murmured, backing out of the dressing room.

She hurried to the breakroom and got her phone out of her locker. After opening an app that allowed her to text internationally via the internet, she quickly contacted her friend Gianna, a gifted designer in her own right who made knockoffs and custom clothing. Typing quickly in Italian, she said:

Help! A client is making my life hell. She needs a great dress for a luncheon and hates everything I have. She has a small dog—maybe six pounds. Yorkie mix. If she picks

a dress, can you make a matching outfit for her dog? And can you rush it?

Seconds later three dots appeared on her screen. While she waited for Gianna's reply, Sage searched through new arrivals, settling on a couple including a white bateau neck Oscar de la Renta midi dress. The butterfly print was fresh and would allow Inocencia to wear all sorts of colored gems. She texted a picture to her friend.

This is the dress I'm selling her.

Save me from women like that, Gianna texted. **Yes, I can make a dress and a matching little hat. It is nothing. Three days and then overnight shipping. I'll need the dog's measurements.**

Gianna quickly texted back a sketch of a matching dog dress she'd done, complete with a tiny hat.

Let's say a thousand dollars, US. That way you can mark it up fifty percent and she won't flinch.

Sage grinned. **You're the best.**

So I've been told. Ciao.

Sage carried the dress and her phone back to the dressing room. Inocencia looked up and sniffed.

"Is that the new Oscar de la Renta? I saw it on the runway in New York. I'm not sure."

Sage smiled at her as she hung up the dress. "What I like most about the style is the simplicity. It requires a woman with a great body to show it at its best. But you know who I was really thinking of?" She glanced down at the dog. "Royal."

Inocencia frowned. "What are you talking about?"

"Something custom for her. A little dress and jacket. Maybe with a hat. Oh, we could get you a leash with the butterflies sewn on. Imagine a cute little dress and hat for Royal." She glanced at her client. "You're in emeralds to pull out the green of the dress. It would be too precious for words. I have a friend in Italy who does all kinds of custom work." She lowered her voice. "Don't tell anyone, but she does a fair amount of work for several designer houses. She does things like this on the side."

She showed Inocencia the sketch on her phone. Her client cooed. "It's adorable. She could make the matching dress for Royal?"

"Absolutely." Sage laughed. "In less than a week. She has access to the fabric. Gianna's in Rome, so the quality of the materials is exquisite. And only fifteen hundred dollars for the dog outfit, including the butterfly leash."

"I want it. The luncheon is in two weeks. It has to be here by then."

"Of course. Let's get you in the dress. Then I'll take some pictures of you and Royal, along with Royal's measurements, and text them to Gianna. I'll have the sketches confirmed by this time tomorrow and the outfit within a week."

Sage sold Inocencia the Oscar de la Renta dress, along with two others that would also be getting matching outfits for Royal. After ushering Inocencia to her car, Sage returned to the boutique and found her manager in her tiny office.

"Do you have a second?" Sage asked, stepping in and shutting the door behind her.

Berry's expression turned wary. "Is there a problem?"

"Not that I can think of." Sage took a seat and smiled at her boss. "Inocencia was in today, looking for a couple of dresses."

"Did we have anything she wanted to buy?"

"She did, but the sales weren't easy."

"I know what you mean. She's never satisfied."

"I might have found a way to keep her happy."

Sage explained about the custom dog dresses and showed Berry the picture and drawing Gianna had texted.

"She'll make up the first outfit and get it to us in a week. The others will be here in about two weeks." Sage paused. "Gianna's cost is a thousand dollars an outfit."

Berry winced. "That much?"

"She's using the same fabric as the couture houses and her work is fast and custom. I sold the outfits to Inocencia for fifteen hundred each."

Berry leaned back in her chair and smiled. "That's a great markup."

"I want fifty percent of it."

"What? That's outrageous."

"Why? It's my client, my designer and my idea. For the store, it's pure profit. Why not share?"

Berry studied her. "Can we offer this service to other clients?"

"I'll talk to my friend about that, but if we do, I want my cut."

"If someone else sells the outfit, you'd only get a third of the profit. The other sales associates would need their percentage, as well."

Sage thought about all the rich customers with little dogs and tried not to get too excited about the potential. "I want it in writing. Please draw up a sales agreement. I get fifty percent of my own sales and a third of everyone else's."

Berry smiled. "Done. We'll also need an agreement with your friend."

"I'll get in touch with her right away."

nineteen

The first thing Daisy noticed was a gorgeous floral arrangement sticking out of the kitchen trash. She rescued the display and studied the roses, orchids and lilies, pulling out the broken stems and shifting the remaining flowers to fill in the empty spaces.

"When a man sends you flowers, you should enjoy them," Daisy murmured as she worked, wishing Jordan would send her flowers. She didn't think he ever had. Not that he would now—they weren't speaking at all. A ridiculous state of affairs.

With a little distance and perspective, she was willing to admit that stopping therapy had been a dumb idea. They weren't going to get better on their own, and not speaking for weeks at a time only added to their problems.

She pushed her worries aside and focused on the flowers. Once the arrangement was put back together, she went upstairs in search of her sister. She found Cassidy in the living room of her suite, her broken leg propped up on an ottoman as she read a book.

The bruises were gone, as was the cast on her arm. She would get a walking cast next week. Obviously Cassidy was on the mend, which meant that at some point, she was going to have to return to her life.

"How long are you going to stand there, staring at me?" Cassidy asked without looking up.

"I'm not sure." Daisy took a seat. "I liberated the flowers from the trash can."

Cassidy put down her book. "I have no idea what you're talking about."

Daisy smiled. "I doubt that."

"They're from Desean."

"I figured. The man knows how to pick out an arrangement."

"Whatever." Cassidy rubbed her knee, then raised her slightly wizened arm. "This is gross."

"You'll get back to normal soon enough. Physical therapy helps."

"I just can't be what he wants, you know? Relationships are hard and I've never been able to make one work."

Daisy smiled. "You're very dramatic."

"It's true. I haven't had a single successful romantic relationship in my life. They all end badly."

"Because you want them to. I would guess you walk away before things get close to serious. Your relationships can't fail because you're not trying. Am I wrong?"

Cassidy folded her arms in front of her chest. "You are. Sometimes I fly away."

Daisy smiled. "Very funny, but you're trying to use humor to deflect me. Your relationships don't fail, Cassidy. You sabotage them."

"Fine. Sure. How does that matter? In the end, they don't work and that's the point. Desean is better off without me." She blinked several times. "I don't want to hurt him anymore."

Which was a little closer to the truth, Daisy thought. "And you don't want to get hurt yourself. You don't want to risk falling for anyone because, as far as you're concerned, it's just a matter of time until the guy in question breaks your heart, and you're not sure you could survive that."

"It's better this way," Cassidy whispered, and pulled a folded piece of paper out of the front pocket of her shorts. She passed it to Daisy.

> I love you, Cassidy, but you're sending me a clear message and it's time I started listening. You're done with me. I've been fighting that truth, but there's no point anymore. You and I want different things. So I'm going to get out of your way. You won't hear from me again. I wish you all the best, always, and I hope you find what you're looking for and that it (or he) makes you happy.

Daisy read the note twice before handing it back. "He sounds like a great guy."

Cassidy nodded. "He is. He's very kind and supportive. I wish it could be different."

"It *can* be different. You're the one making all the decisions about what happens with you and Desean. He's obviously willing to do whatever it takes to make you happy. Even give you your freedom."

"And then what?" Cassidy asked, her voice filled with regret. "I tell him I love him and we should be together and then what happens? It's good for a while and then we start fighting or he cheats or we get tired of each other? I can't do that. I won't take the risk. No one ever gets it right."

"People do. There are a lot of successful marriages out there. You don't even have to get married. You could just live together."

"Why do you even care?"

"Because you're obviously miserable without him and the man is devoted to you. Trust me, that doesn't happen all that often."

"I want to believe you, but do you really know what you're talking about? No offense, but you and Jordan aren't exactly happy."

Daisy knew she couldn't argue with that. "We're in a rough patch." She paused and held up her hand. "Okay, fine. It might be a little more than that. But we'll figure it out."

Cassidy didn't look convinced. "Sage has been divorced three times."

"Three? I thought it was two."

"Oh, whoops. I'm not supposed to talk about Ellery."

Daisy reminded herself not to be distracted. "Sage is a special case. Her reasons for marrying aren't traditional."

Cassidy smiled. "You mean she's never married for love? I guess she hasn't, but her relationships still didn't work. And look at my parents. Dad only married Mom to give you a mother, so that was doomed. I think they had me to save the marriage, but that's way too much pressure to put on a little kid. I don't know why Dad decided to finally divorce her, but he did." She paused, as if thinking. "I guess the biggest problem was Joanne loved him and he didn't love her back."

Daisy had planned to dispute Cassidy's assumption that the only reason she'd been conceived was to repair a broken relationship, but found herself saying instead, "You really think Joanne loved Dad? I know we've talked about it but I find it hard to believe."

"I know she did. The divorce devastated her. I don't think she's ever gotten over him, not really. She measures every man against him, and he's a great guy, so no one makes the grade."

"I thought she married him for the money."

"I'm sure that's how it started, but at some point, she fell hard. After we moved out, she would cry herself to sleep." Cassidy shuddered. "It scared me so much, I would go sleep with Sage."

Daisy didn't want to feel compassion for her former step-mother. Joanne had been cruel to her from the start and had—

A memory surfaced—one she hadn't thought of in a long time. Anger and fear fought for dominance as she remembered the sharp pain of being hit over and over, and the loathing in Joanne's eyes as she kept raising her arm to strike her.

No, she told herself. That wasn't the reason for the divorce. It couldn't be.

"I'm sorry it was hard on her," she said stiffly, pushing aside the past. Right now Cassidy had to be her priority. She would deal with the rest of it later.

"Me, too. You got to live here, with your loving father, and I got shuttled back and forth, like an unwanted hot potato."

Daisy leaned forward and grabbed Cassidy's hand. "We all wanted you around. My dad tried to be the custodial parent, but Joanne wouldn't let him. I'm sure she felt the same."

Daisy wasn't completely sure, but she wasn't going to admit that. Whatever Joanne had felt at the time, Cassidy was the one who mattered now.

"I wanted you to live here, too." Which was true—at least until Cassidy had turned on her.

"You did?"

"Yes. Of course. You're my sister."

Cassidy turned away. "And then I blew it by turning into a raving bitch. I'm sorry."

"It wasn't your fault. You were a kid and being told a lot of different things." If anyone was to blame, it was Joanne.

Cassidy squeezed her fingers. "Thank you for saying that. You're really nice to me and I don't deserve it."

"Everyone deserves to be loved."

"We should put that on a pillow."

"Or a T-shirt."

They smiled at each other. Daisy drew back.

"All right, while you're feeling warm and fuzzy, I'm going to bring your flowers up so you can look at them and think about Desean."

"Way to ruin my mood."

"You care about him more than you want to admit. Yes, there are risks in being in a relationship, but imagine how you'll feel if in a couple of years you realize you made a hideous mistake only to find out he's fallen in love with someone else." She stood. "Regrets suck. Which is also something we should put on a pillow."

"You're so bossy."

"Yes, and I'm nearly always right. Don't have regrets, Cassidy. He won't wait forever."

Sage stood in her bedroom doorway and stared at the clothes thrown everywhere, the half-open drawers and the desk chair lying on its side. Under normal circumstances, she would assume there'd been a robbery, but the rest of the house seemed untouched.

She walked down the hall to her mother's bedroom. She knocked once, pushed open the door and then nearly gagged at the smell of liquor, rotting food and body odor.

Her mother lay on the unmade bed. Takeout containers were stacked on the dresser and several vodka and rum bottles were in the small trash can by the nightstand. Her mother's hair was greasy, her robe was stained and she looked a decade older.

Sage stepped over discarded clothes and shoes and grabbed the TV remote. When she'd muted the sound, she looked at her mother.

"What were you looking for?" she asked, her tone abrupt.

Her mother didn't bother pretending confusion or denying she'd trashed Sage's room.

"I don't know. Clothes. Money. Drugs."

Sage thought about the extra money she'd received from the boutique for her dog fashion sales. Thank God for direct deposit. "I don't keep cash around and I've never been into drugs."

"People change."

Her mother's voice was listless, as if she didn't actually care what they were discussing.

Sage put down the remote. "Mom, this isn't healthy. You've got to start taking care of yourself."

"Why? Nothing matters anymore."

"I don't get it. You didn't know Peter long enough to care much about him, so why is this hitting you so hard?"

Her mother's mouth trembled as tears filled her eyes. "What if I never get another man again? What if I'm too old? What will happen to me? I'll be homeless and living out of a shopping cart and I'll be ugly."

She began to cry, little sobs escaping even as she pressed her hand to her mouth.

"You're not going to be homeless because you own this house and you can't possibly be ugly. You don't have the genes for it."

Joanne sniffed. "I hadn't thought of that, but you're right. We come from a long line of beautiful women. It's not as if I look like Daisy."

"Hey, don't say that. Daisy's pretty."

"Oh, please. She's dumpy at best." Her mother sat up and wiped her face. "You're right. I'm taking the Peter thing too hard. I need a plan." She picked up a glass from the nightstand. "Be a dear and get me some ice."

Sage hesitated, not sure if she should enable her mother, then she decided that getting ice was not the hill she wanted to die on.

Once her mother was sipping her drink, Sage spent the better part of an hour putting her room back together. Thankfully, her mother hadn't found her secret stash of jewelry. The fabric bag containing her three wedding sets, a few pairs of earrings and two diamond tennis bracelets was still taped to the bottom of her dresser.

Adam's house was dark, so she texted Daisy.

Want some company?

Love some.

Be right over.

She drove to Daisy's, stopping for a quick In-N-Out burger along the way. Esmerelda let her in.

"They're in the family room," the housekeeper said, smiling at her. "I'm making chocolate martinis."

"Sounds delicious. How are you feeling?"

"Better." Esmerelda hesitated. "Thank you for helping me last week. And taking care of the children. I appreciate it."

"No problem."

"You're not who I thought."

Sage grinned. "I'm starting to get that a lot."

She found Cassidy and Daisy already sprawled on sofas.

"We had pasta for dinner," Cassidy said with a laugh. "We're in a post-carb slump."

"Esmerelda said she's making chocolate martinis," Sage told them, settling into a plush club chair.

"Great," Daisy mock-grumbled. "Sugar. Just what we need. We should take a walk or something."

Cassidy knocked on her cast. "I won't be joining you."

"Then I guess we'll have to sleep it off." Daisy waved toward Sage. "I heard from my dad. He's going to be here in a couple of days."

"He's my dad, too," Cassidy pointed out.

"You are such a little sister. Fine, I heard from *our* dad."

"Better."

Sage laughed. "I heard from him, as well. I haven't seen Wallace in forever. He said he wanted to get together."

She'd been pleased by his request that they spend a little time with each other, but knew she would have to make sure her mother didn't find out. Joanne was already in a bad place—hearing Wallace was in town would send her spiraling down even further.

"We should have a sister reunion," Cassidy said. "Maybe a theme party. Like the 1950s. We could all wear poodle skirts."

Sage looked at her. "Did you have wine with dinner?"

Cassidy grinned. "Maybe."

"No poodle skirts," Daisy told them. "I'll look terrible in them." She turned to Sage. "For the record, we didn't have wine with dinner. Cassidy's just being a brat."

"Go with your strengths," Cassidy said with a laugh.

"Children today," Daisy murmured before reaching out her hand to Sage. "You're the only one with an exciting life. Tell us what's new."

"My mother got dumped by some guy and she's in the middle of a meltdown. It's not pretty."

"Is she okay?" Cassidy shook her head. "Never mind. I don't care."

"You have to care," Daisy told her. "She's your mom."

"She doesn't care about me. She's been to visit me once and that was mostly to torture you. I should hate her, but it's too much energy." She looked at Sage. "What do you think? Should I hate her?"

Sage didn't want to get in the middle of that. "Like you

said." Too much energy. Maybe you can go see her when you get your walking cast."

"Or not," Cassidy muttered as Esmerelda appeared with a tray of chocolate martinis. She passed them out and excused herself.

Daisy sipped hers, then sighed. "Perfect, as always." She set it on the end table. "Sage, do you think your mom was in love with my dad?"

"Not when they got married, but definitely by the time he asked for a divorce. Somewhere along the way, she fell for him. She was very upset that he wanted to end things."

More than upset, Sage thought, remembering her mother screaming and sobbing, begging Wallace to give her another chance, swearing she would do anything to make him happy.

"It wasn't just about the money?" Daisy asked, sounding oddly hopeful.

"Not at the end. They had difficulties for about a year before they split up. He started withdrawing."

"How do you *know* that?" Cassidy asked.

"She told me. As you may recall, our mother doesn't respect boundaries—at least not anyone else's." Sage shrugged. "At first he was a little distant, but then he kind of disappeared from their relationship. She was frantic—she knew he was slipping away. And then, suddenly, he was gone."

Daisy made a sound low in her throat. Cassidy spun toward her.

"What?"

Sage was surprised to see tears in Daisy's eyes.

"It's my fault," she whispered, her voice shaking. "The divorce. I didn't get it until a couple of days ago, but it's on me."

"What are you talking about?" Sage asked. "You were thirteen. It can't be on you."

"She hit me."

Sage stared at Daisy. "My mom?"

Daisy nodded, hugging her arms close, as if even now she had to protect herself. "I'd forgotten what happened. Or repressed it. I just remembered the other day." She sucked in a breath. "It was a couple of weeks before they split up. Joanne and I were arguing in the kitchen and she was so mad at me. She was making a salad and she hit me with a wooden spoon."

Daisy swallowed. "I was immobilized by shock or something, because at first I didn't do anything. She kept hitting me. It hurt so much. Finally I ran and hid in my room, but I couldn't stop crying. My dad found me and saw the welts. He got really quiet."

Cassidy looked between them. "Holy shit!" she said, horror filling her voice. "Are you okay?"

"Now?" Daisy managed a smile. "I've recovered."

Sage didn't know what to say. Her mother had slapped her a few times—mostly across the face, but only with the back of her hand. Never with anything that would leave a mark.

"I was there when they told you about the divorce," Daisy said and looked at Cassidy. "You were so small. You had no idea what it meant but you knew it was bad."

Cassidy swallowed. "I remember," she said, her voice low. "I started to go to you, but Mom pulled me back. She said I shouldn't depend on you anymore. She said you weren't to be trusted."

"Jesus." Sage took a big gulp of her martini. "Where was I when this happened?" She held up her hand. "Never mind, I don't want to know." She turned to Daisy. "I'm sorry."

"Me, too. I know it's not my fault, but it feels that way."

Sage shook her head. "Wallace was already pulling back. By then he had to regret the marriage. Things would have ended between them regardless."

Daisy picked up her glass, then put it down. "Jordan has

said I pull back. He talks about how I don't care about him and that he can't get my attention. He's never specific, which makes it hard to talk about. I wonder if I'm doing to him what my dad did to Joanne."

"No," Sage said firmly. "You're not."

Despite the seriousness of the discussion, Daisy smiled. "You know this how?"

"I know you. You're not passive-aggressive. You do what has to be done, even when you don't want to. Plus, you don't want your marriage to be over. You're upset that he's gone and you're angry that he's putting you through all this. If you weren't still in love with him, you wouldn't care what he did."

"Wow," Cassidy said, her voice admiring. "That's deep."

"I agree," Daisy admitted. "But maybe I do withdraw around Jordan."

"You get mad to my face," Sage pointed out. "Is it different with him?"

"Sometimes it's not worth the fight, but that's mostly when I'm tired. After he texted me he'd moved to a house, I confronted him. Not that night," she added.

"Yes, that was the night you threw up all over me," Sage teased.

"Not on you, just near you." Daisy's smile faded. "The next morning I told him he either came over and talked to me or I was calling a lawyer."

Cassidy's eyes widened. "For real?"

"Yes. I don't want to play games with him."

"Like I told you," Sage said smugly. "You confront him. So not like your dad."

Daisy held up her martini. "You're right. Yay, me."

Healed by good conversation and better company, Daisy went upstairs to her bedroom. She sat upright in bed against the pillows. After staring at her phone for nearly a minute, she told herself to just suck it up, then started typing.

I think we should go back to therapy. It's the only way we're going to get our problems resolved.

She sent the message and waited. Seconds later, three dots appeared on the screen, followed by, **I agree. Could you set up an appointment for us or do you want me to?**

I'll do it.

She waited, but he didn't respond to that, leaving her feeling both relieved and unsatisfied. Could he at least say thank you, or good-night, or something to indicate he'd received the message? She knew they had different communication styles, but why did his have to be so distant and unfriendly? Or maybe he was just fine and she was being too judgy.

"Not knowing those answers is only one of the many reasons we need professional help," she said aloud as she set her phone on the nightstand. "Men and women, trying to live together in harmony. What was God thinking?"

twenty

Sage wove her bike between the pedestrians and skateboarders. Adam was in front of her, leading the way on the boardwalk, his bright blue tie-dye shirt making him easy to spot. They were headed north, with the ocean to their left and beachfront hotels and restaurants on their right. Despite being a weekday, there were plenty of people on the beach.

The concrete boardwalk went from Palos Verdes all the way to Santa Monica. It wove past Marina del Rey and LAX airport. If you timed it right, you could be on the path when all the flights were taking off for places like Australia and Japan. The huge planes roared by overhead, giving the illusion they were nearly low enough to touch.

Sage had been tempted away from her day-off errands by Adam's invitation for a bike ride. Since moving back to LA, Sage hadn't been down to the beach, so she'd jumped at the chance to get a little exercise and enjoy the sunny morning.

Close to noon, they turned in their rental bikes. Adam pointed to a café across the street.

"Want to grab some lunch?" he asked.

"Sure."

He surprised her by taking her hand in his. Their fingers

laced together in a way that made her want to step a little closer.

They were quickly seated at an outdoor corner table shaded by a large umbrella.

"I'm thinking champagne," Adam said with a grin. "We're celebrating."

"Are we?"

"I got a new contract. It's a big one. I've been working toward it for a long time. I'm moving a large medical practice onto the cloud, which could lead to other practices. It's a huge field with a lot of opportunity."

She smiled. "Congratulations."

"Thanks. I'm excited. That's what the meetings have been about the past few weeks."

"Ah, so no more suit wearing. I'll miss it."

He rested his elbows on the table and leaned toward her. "I could wear a suit every now and then, if it makes you happy."

"You do look good in one."

"Thanks. You look good in everything."

She laughed. "I wish that were true."

Adam ordered a bottle of champagne. When the server left, Sage asked, "Are you going to hire more people?"

"It's just me. I want to work hard for the next few years and build my nut."

She raised her eyebrows. "Nut as in a financial goal?"

"Uh-huh. I want to have all the money I'm going to need by the time I'm fifty."

"And then retire?"

"No, but I'd like to slow down and travel." He flashed her a smile. "On the other hand, I'm also toying with the idea of buying a cabin up in the mountains, which would mean working longer to pay it off."

"What does 'cabin' mean?" She made air quotes. "One

room with no indoor plumbing or a fancy house on the shores of Lake Tahoe?"

"Something in between. I want indoor plumbing and lots of solitude, but a grocery store within twenty minutes." The grin returned. "I'm still an LA kind of guy. I don't enjoy peeing in the wilderness."

"At least you get to do it standing up. Women have to squat."

"There is that."

"Is your house paid for?" she asked.

"It will be in six months."

"That's impressive." And slightly disheartening. She didn't have the credit rating to get an apartment and he'd nearly paid off his house.

No, she told herself firmly. She refused to be discouraged. Yes, she wasn't where she wanted to be, but she'd stopped making really dumb mistakes. She had purpose, or at least a plan. Success would follow.

"What are you thinking?" he asked.

"That running off to Europe might not have been the best idea I ever had."

"What would you have done if you'd stayed here?"

"I haven't a clue."

Their server appeared with an ice bucket, the champagne and two glasses. After opening the bottle, she poured them each a glass, then retreated.

Sage touched her glass to his. "Congratulations on the new contract. You're an impressive guy."

"Thank you. Would you have married Jordan?"

It took her a second to remember what they'd been talking about.

"No. I don't think so."

"But you were engaged."

"Until he put on the brakes." She smiled. "Which he was right to do. We would have been a disaster together. Ignoring the fact that we were too young, there's no way we would have made it."

"You're not still in love with him?"

There was an intensity in both his question and the way he looked at her. As if the answer mattered a lot. Sage reached across the table and rested her fingers on the back of his hand.

"I'm not in love with Jordan. He's Daisy's husband. If I wasn't friends with her, I wouldn't give him even a moment's thought. It's been over for nearly twenty years and I'm perfectly happy with that."

Adam relaxed a little. "I just wondered."

"What about your love life?" she asked, her voice teasing. "Is there a woman in your cabin in the woods?"

"Like I keep her trapped there? No."

Sage laughed. "You know that's not what I meant. Don't you want a relationship? Everyone says falling in love can be magical."

"What do you say about it?"

She thought about all the romantic disasters in her life. "I'd like to stop screwing up anything good that comes my way."

"What do you want, Sage? Where do you see yourself in five years? Married? Ruling the world?"

"I don't have the management skills for ruling the world." She considered the question. "I'd like to try making something work, romantically, I mean. I'm not sure I'm a good bet, but I would like to try."

She picked up her champagne. "By the way, I noticed how you tried to distract me. You never answered my question. Tinder forever or something more?"

Emotions flashed through his eyes. "Something more. I'd like to be with someone I could love and respect, who felt the same way about me. I'm looking for something solid." One corner of his mouth curved up. "I know solid isn't fashionable, but it's important to me."

"Actually solid sounds really good."

After a leisurely lunch, Adam drove Sage home. They pulled into his garage. Sage got out of his convertible and stretched. Drinking at lunch always made her want to take a nap. No matter how long she'd lived in France and Italy, she'd never figured out how to manage a glass of wine in the middle of the day.

She walked around the back of the car and smiled at Adam. "I had a great time."

"Me, too."

She stepped closer, expecting him to kiss her. But instead of a casual embrace and the light brush of his mouth on hers, he drew her hard against him so their bodies touched everywhere. One of his hands tangled in her hair, and then the other dropped to her butt, where he squeezed. At the same time, he kissed her with an intensity that stole her breath and made her heart beat faster.

The sleepiness evaporated, leaving her alert and aroused. She looped her arms around his neck and parted her lips so he could deepen the kiss. His erection pressed into her belly, making her insides clench.

He drew back enough to rest his forehead against hers.

"I can't resist you anymore," he admitted, his voice gravelly. "Either come inside and make love with me or slap me and put me out of my misery."

She reached for his hands and placed them on her sensitive breasts. "I thought you'd never ask."

"Is he here? Is he here?" Krissa danced around the kitchen as she asked the question for the eighth time in ten minutes.

"Sweetie, you know he isn't," Daisy said with a laugh. "Grandpa's on his way from the airport. It won't be much longer. Why don't you go wait by the living room windows so you can see him drive up?"

Krissa spun in a circle. "I can't wait to see him. I love him so much. Do you think he brought us presents?"

"It's not your birthday or Christmas, why would he do that?"

Ben glanced up from his book. "Because that's what grandparents do, Mom."

"Is it? I didn't know that."

Ben and his sister exchanged a look.

"I'm going to wait by the window," Krissa said. "I can't stand it."

She ran out of the kitchen. Ben dropped his book onto the island and followed her. Esmerelda laughed.

"They love Mr. Wallace."

"They do."

Her father always took time with each of her kids, making them feel special and loved. He had a gift for that, she thought happily. She was just as excited as her children. Having her dad around always made her feel safe—as if nothing could hurt her as long as he was there to protect her. It wasn't a feeling she'd experienced in a long time, but since the separation, she could use a little more security in her life.

"He's here! He's here!"

The excited shouts drew her to the front of the house. Sure enough, her father was carrying his suitcases up the front steps. Krissa and Ben raced out to greet him. He dropped the suitcases as the children threw themselves against him.

Daisy watched the greeting, happy and relieved to see he looked as he always had—tall, strong and healthy. Her father had thick graying hair and features similar to her own. He wore a Hawaiian shirt and jeans, and looked about fifteen years younger than his nearly sixty-eight years.

As the kids continued to cling to him, he glanced at her over their heads.

"Hey, kid," he said with a grin.

"Dad."

"I missed you."

"I missed you, too."

Ben and Krissa finally released him and Daisy moved in for her hug. The familiar embrace eased tension she hadn't known she was carrying.

"Thanks for coming," she told him.

"There's nowhere else I'd rather be."

Ben carried in his suitcase, while Krissa took charge of his carry-on. Once they were in the house, Esmerelda hurried out to greet him. She offered her hand, but Wallace brushed it away and hugged her.

"How are you doing?" he asked.

Esmerelda smiled brightly. "Very well, Mr. Wallace. I keep watch over your family."

"I know you do."

"Daddy!" Cassidy, more mobile in her new walking cast, made her way down the stairs, then flung herself at Wallace. "I've missed you."

"I've missed you, too, little girl. How are you? Recovering?"

"Yes. I'm nearly back to normal."

Daisy watched them together, aware that for once she wasn't jealous or annoyed to see Cassidy with her dad. Yet one more difference since she and her sister had learned to get along. There wasn't the same need to claim all the attention, to make it clear she was the favorite. Her father loved them both and she was happy about that.

Everyone made their way into the family room. Wallace opened his suitcase and pulled out two ukuleles. The kids fell on them, obviously delighted, while Daisy tried not to wince.

"Really, Dad?" she asked.

He winked at her, then turned back to his grandchildren. "You can go online and take a few lessons," he said. "In the meantime I also bought you a DVD on how to play."

"Can we go watch this, Mom?" Ben asked.

"Yes. Have fun. In the playroom," she added. Thank goodness the house had thick walls. "Dinner is in an hour."

"We'll be ready," Krissa said, running upstairs with her ukulele, her brother at her heels.

"You couldn't get them something quieter?" Daisy asked with a laugh.

"They'll have fun and that's what matters to me."

"You say that now," Cassidy told him. "But you forget your guest room is close to the kids' rooms so you might be in for it, too."

"I'll survive." He glanced between them. "It's nice to see you two together."

Daisy looked at Cassidy. "I'll admit when you first told me she was coming here to recover, I wasn't exactly thrilled. But it all worked out."

Cassidy nodded. "We've found our place in the Universe."

"Had you lost it?" Wallace asked, his voice teasing.

"Some."

Just then Sage walked in. "Hi, everyone."

Wallace stood and crossed to her. "Sage." He hugged her and kissed her cheek. "It's been too long. Thanks for coming over."

Sage smiled at him. "You made it sound like your evening would be ruined if I wasn't here. Something I totally understand, by the way."

Everyone laughed.

They talked for a few minutes, then Cassidy took their father upstairs to get settled. Sage followed Daisy into the dining room, where they set the table.

"Are you really okay that I'm here?" Sage asked. "If it's better to just have a family night, I can come back."

"You are family," Daisy said without thinking, then realized she meant it. Sage was part of her family now.

"When you put it like that." Sage cleared her throat. "Thank you."

Daisy stared at her stepsister. "Something's different," she said, not sure what had caught her attention. Sage hadn't cut her hair and her makeup was its usual, perfect self. "It's your smile. It's very smug. Did you get a promotion at work?"

"I had sex with Adam."

Daisy felt her mouth drop open. She closed it and grabbed Sage's hand. "You did? When? Are you happy? Was it great? I always liked Adam so I want it to be great."

Sage grinned. "It was amazing. He's funny and smart and kind and he gets me. We had a wonderful night. Seriously, I couldn't get enough of him."

Her smile faded. "I like him, Daisy. I haven't liked anyone in a long time and I don't want to blow it."

"Then don't."

"It's not that easy. I tend to screw up every relationship and I don't want to mess up with him."

"Then don't," she repeated, holding up her hand. "Be aware of what's happening. When you get to that place where you see danger, turn away. Ask what I would do and then do that. Not that I have the world's greatest track record, but I don't instinctively run toward disaster."

Sage laughed. "What would Daisy do? I like it. I like it a lot."

★ ★ ★

Sage handed the box to the clerk at FedEx, telling herself it was for the greater good. Despite her mother's promise to come up with a plan, Joanne was still drinking too much and crying throughout the day. Worse, the house was starting to smell like a boys' locker room. Something had to be done.

When she got home, her mother was curled up on the family room sofa, her eyes puffy, her face pale. She'd managed to pull on wrinkled, stained sweatpants and a T-shirt.

"Hey, Mom," Sage said cheerfully. "How are you feeling?"

"Lost. Alone. Old. Useless. Unwanted." Joanne looked up. "And you?"

Sage smiled at her. "I'm sorry you're still feeling down."

"Down?" Her mother gave a humorless laugh. "That's one way to describe it."

Sage ignored the words and the attitude. "I got you something that should help you feel better." She paused until her mother was looking at her. "A week at the Golden Door spa."

Joanne's eyes widened as her mouth dropped open. She sprang to her feet. "Are you serious? You did that for me?"

"I did." The gift had come at a steep price, but desperate times and all that. Plus she was looking forward to having the house to herself for a week.

"Oh my God!"

Her mother pulled herself to her feet and hugged her. Sage tried not to wince at how bad she smelled.

"They're expecting you Saturday," Sage told her, stepping out of the embrace.

"I haven't been there in forever. Not since I was married to Wallace." Her happiness dimmed. "Those were wonderful years."

"And now you get to go back," Sage said, hoping to remind her of her good fortune.

"You're right and it's wonderful." She touched her hair, then scrunched up her face. "I need to take a shower and start a detox. I'll want a pedicure before I go. No need for a facial—I'll be getting one there. This is just so wonderful, Sage. Thank you so much."

"Of course."

Joanne hurried toward her room. Sage spent the next hour picking up the house and cleaning the kitchen. After vacuuming, she glanced outside and saw Adam sitting at his desk in the shade. She walked out to see him.

"Want some company?" she asked, standing by the fence. "Or are you too busy with work?"

He smiled at her, a warm, knowing smile that gave her butterflies in her stomach.

"I'd like a little company," he said.

She went through her house and over to his, then let herself inside. He met her in the family room and pulled her close. As she stepped into his arms, she thought about how right this all felt.

"What's going on?" he asked after he'd kissed her and pulled her down next to him on the sofa.

"I'm sending my mom to the Golden Door spa."

Adam's expression was completely blank. "Should I know what that is?"

She laughed. "Probably not. It's a spa just north of San Diego. Very exclusive, very nice." She sighed. "It cost me three handbags."

He sat up and winced. "Not Birkin-priced bags?"

"No. Just regular designer ones. A week is about ten grand."

"I'll never understand women."

"But, Adam, they have men's weeks, so you could go with one of your buddies."

"That's never happening." He kissed her. "I'd go with you, though."

"Really? I wouldn't have thought you were a spa kind of guy."

"I've never been, but I'm open to the experience." He stroked her arm. "You're doing a really nice thing for your mom."

"She's in a bad place and selfishly, I can't wait to have the house to myself for a week. Plus, I feel sorry for her. She's always defined herself by the man she's with, which means she has no control over anything that's happening to her. That's a hard way to live."

He watched her without speaking, as if he didn't want to say anything. She shifted so she was angled toward him, her legs stretched across his lap.

"I know," she told him. "I used to be like that."

"This is me, not talking."

She smiled. "Yet I can hear every word you're thinking." Her smile faded. "My marriages were about being with a guy and what that would do for me. I wasn't in the relationship for the right reason. I don't want to do that anymore. I don't want to be defined by a man. I want to take care of myself. I want to be strong."

"You've always been strong."

"You're sweet for saying that but I've always been a taker. I take what I want and walk away. Worse, I sabotage myself right before things get really good, but I'm working on changing. I want to get to the place where I'm proud of myself."

He rubbed her legs. "You're impressive as hell."

"Not yet, but I'm working on it."

twenty-one

Daisy arrived home from work to find her father reading in the family room—both dogs at his feet, and Nala and Simba stretched out on the back of the sofa, behind him.

"You draw a crowd," Daisy said as she walked over to hug him. "Probably because you're so nice to come home to."

"I try to be a considerate guest," he said with a smile. "As for the pets, I've always liked them and I think they know that. How was your day?"

"Busy. Long."

He raised his eyebrows. "No details?"

"I'm afraid any medical talk will give you ideas."

He put down his book and rose. "Daisy, I'm done trying to talk you into going to medical school."

"Really? Because you had Uncle Ray make a run at it just last month."

"That was the last time. You're obviously happy in your work and I need to accept that."

"Uh-huh. Why don't I believe you?"

"People change. And speaking of that, go get out of your scrubs. I'll meet you back here where I'll make you a heck of a martini and we'll talk about our days."

There was something in his tone, she thought. "What happened?"

He waved toward the stairs. "I'll see you in a few minutes."

She checked in on the kids before heading to her bedroom. It only took a few minutes to change into jeans and a lightweight sweater.

"What's up?" she asked as she watched her father add ice to the martini shaker.

"You're assuming the worst."

"You're avoiding the question."

He handed her a martini, then motioned to the sofas. When they were seated across from each other, he raised his glass. "Cheers."

"Dad!"

"Fine." He took a sip. "I had lunch with Jordan today."

She hadn't been expecting that. "Well, he is your son-in-law, so it's not totally crazy." She wasn't sure what else to say. Should she ask how he was or what they'd talked about?

Her father smiled at her. "He misses you."

Then he should get his ass back to the house. But she only thought that, rather than speaking it. "That's nice to hear."

"He wasn't very forthcoming about your problems, which I respect. A marriage is a private thing. But I let him know I was worried about you and him and that he could always talk to me." He smiled. "Not that I'm going to take his side. You're my daughter."

"I appreciate the support. So basically he said nothing?" She tried to keep the tension out of her voice.

"He complained you're doing too much and he comes in second all the time. I told him a pity party wasn't a good look and that maybe if he did some of the things with you, they'd get done faster and you two would have more time together."

She relaxed. "An excellent point, although I'm sure he's right. I'm a little like you—when I get unhappy, I withdraw."

"Are you unhappy?"

"Not all the time, but marriage is hard."

"Yes, it is. I'm sure you're dealing with a lot right now. Having your sister in the house, reconnecting with Sage, all the while missing Jordan."

Daisy nodded because that was the response that made the most sense, but on the inside, she was a whirlwind of confusion. Her father was right about everything going on, only all of that had happened after Jordan had left, so it couldn't really be part of the problem. But the more important point, the one that had her head spinning, was that she hadn't thought about missing her husband for a while now. Maybe weeks.

She was pissed, she was worried, but she didn't miss him. Not the way she had at first. She didn't look across the table at dinner and wish he was there. She didn't miss sharing the bathroom with him. Or sleeping with him. And if she didn't miss him, if she wasn't afraid he would stay gone forever, didn't that say something? Only she wasn't sure what.

She filed that thought away to deal with another time. There was information there and she had to figure out what it was.

"Having Cassidy around has been much easier than I thought it would be," she admitted, hoping for a subtle shift in topic. "I wasn't happy when you first asked if she could stay here, but it's worked out."

"I'm glad you two are getting to know each other as adults. You're sisters and family matters."

"It does, Dad. Let me know if you want to move back to the mainland. You'd be very welcome here."

He smiled at her. "Thank you, but if I decide to come back, I'll get my own place."

"Multi-generational living is the new in thing."

"A single man needs his own space."

"An interesting point," she told him. "Why are you still single? It's been a long time since you and Joanne split up. I know there've been a few serious relationships, but nothing that lasts."

"I had my one great love."

"My mom."

He smiled sadly. "From the moment I met her, I knew she was the one. Since then, well, let's just say I've never met anyone who makes me feel the same way."

"Did you marry Joanne to give me a mother?"

His gaze met hers. "Yes, and that was a bad decision on my part. It wasn't fair to her."

"Because she thought you loved her?"

He hesitated before nodding. "In my defense, at the time, I thought love was possible. When I realized it wasn't, I should have stayed more present in the marriage, but I withdrew. She sensed that and it made her insecure and unhappy. You know how it ended."

"Because she hit me? Dad, is your divorce my fault?"

"Daisy, no. Her hitting you the way she did spurred me to action I should have taken months before. I knew she was unhappy and I tried to understand, but what she did to you was unforgiveable. I nearly used it against her to get custody of Cassidy. Maybe I should have."

"I'm sorry for my part in it."

"You had no part. Joanne and I are to blame for the end of our marriage, and most of that's on me."

Daisy told herself the kind response was to feel sorry for Joanne, but the little girl who had been neglected, mocked and beaten couldn't summon the emotion.

"Dad, you shouldn't be alone."

"I'm not. I have my work and my friends. I have my family."

"I wish you had a partner. Someone to take care of you."

His brows rose. "I'm not infirm."

"I meant emotionally."

"Does Jordan take care of you emotionally?"

"Not lately," she admitted.

"Before did he?"

"Sure," she lied, knowing the truth was less tidy. She couldn't remember the last time Jordan had taken care of her and she had a feeling his answer about her would be exactly the same.

Sage disliked being indecisive. Either she had to do it or not do it. There were several ways for her to move forward with her teacher accreditation, but the program that interested her the most was at UCLA. TEP—Teacher Education Program—was an intense, two-year process, focusing on diverse urban schools, something that made sense, considering where she lived. But she wasn't sure how to afford it. The tuition and fees were over seventeen thousand dollars a year, and the program was full-time. So how exactly was she supposed to pay for it and support herself?

Another option was through USC's online program. That would allow her to work a few hours a week while studying for her teaching certificate. The Los Angeles Unified School District had an internship program for people with a four-year degree. That program focused on doing, with prospective teachers learning as a teaching intern.

Each path had up- and downsides. She needed to decide which she liked best and which made sense given her limited resources. Or she could forget the whole thing for the evening and rewatch *The Crown*.

No, she told herself. She had to make a decision because

the alternative to that was working in retail and living with her mother, and neither option would make her happy. A plan meant forward movement and feeling better about herself. No plan meant letting life happen, and hadn't she already done enough of that?

If only things weren't going so well, she thought, aware of the ridiculousness of that statement. Even so, she couldn't shake her sense of unease, as if disaster was right around the corner. She'd never been especially lucky and she'd always screwed up, even when she knew better. While she wanted this time to be different, she just wasn't sure that was possible.

As if offering a distraction, her phone buzzed with a text from Cassidy.

Can you come by the house? I need to ask you something. It's no big deal. Well, it's a little big, but not big-big. Crap! Just come over. Please.

Sage laughed, then grabbed her bag and started for the door. Traffic was light. She made it to the house in less than twenty minutes. She found Cassidy in the family room, with a confused-looking Daisy.

"She wouldn't say what this was about," Daisy told her. "It's all very strange and ominous."

Cassidy wrinkled her nose. "I didn't want to have to say it twice. I just…" She twisted her hands together. "I need help."

"I'll say," Sage murmured.

Daisy grinned at her, then raised her hand for a high five.

"I'm serious," Cassidy told them, her lower lip trembling. "I need you two to fly to Miami. I'm going to close up my apartment and I can't do it myself."

Sage looked at Daisy, who seemed as shocked as she felt.

"You're moving?" Daisy asked. "Why?"

"I can't stay there. It doesn't matter where I live—I just

need to be close to a major airport. LA has that. So does San Francisco or Atlanta. I might even decide on New York."

"Okay," Sage said slowly. "But not Miami?"

"Desean owns my townhouse complex. That's how we met. I can't stay there. It'll hurt too much to see him again."

Sage thought about pointing out that if seeing Desean would cause pain, then maybe Cassidy had been a bit too quick to break up with him, but knew that wouldn't help.

"I've hired movers to take care of the big stuff, but I need you to get my place ready for them and to bring back some personal things. I've made a list of exactly what needs to be done. It should only take a day or two. I'll pay for the flights and everything else."

"I'm sure if you talked to your doctor, she would say you're all right to travel," Daisy offered.

"I don't want to risk it." A single tear fell down Cassidy's cheek. "I just can't. Please. I need your help."

"Wouldn't it be better to face him?" Daisy asked. "To confront your fears head-on? Once that's done, you can get on with your life. Hiding doesn't make anything better."

Sage knew Daisy was trying to help, but doubted that was what Cassidy needed to hear right now.

"I'll do it," she said quickly. "Daisy, come with me. Your dad's here to watch over the kids. Esmerelda will be around to pick up the slack. You could use a few days away. We'll stay at a nice hotel, clean out Cassidy's apartment, have a fancy dinner and a couple of spa treatments, and come home." She added, "I'll pay for my own spa treatments."

Daisy looked stunned. "You mean fly to Miami, just like that?"

Sage hid a smile. "Shocking, but yes. That is what I mean."

"I have to work."

"You have vacation days. Use a few for this. I'll be asking

for time off myself. It's what people do." She glanced at Cassidy. "Our baby sister needs us. Besides, Cassidy's always kept a diary. Now we can find it and read it."

"Don't you dare!"

Sage grinned. "It's the price of doing business, little sister. We do this for you and we get access to all your secrets."

Cassidy flushed. "I can't believe you'd do that."

"I won't," Daisy assured her, then looked at Sage. "Don't read other people's diaries. It's rude."

"And that would bother me why?"

Daisy's lips twitched. "You're incorrigible."

"Yes, I am. So we're going?"

"Let me see if I can get the time off work. If I can, then I'll talk to my dad and Esmerelda."

"I can help with the kids, too," Cassidy told her. "I really appreciate this."

Daisy looked as if she were going to say something about Cassidy facing Desean, but then seemed to change her mind.

"All right. I'll find out in the morning if I can take time off work. Once we know that, we can get tickets and find a hotel and that sort of thing."

"You'll want to stay at the Four Seasons," Cassidy said. "They have hammocks out by the pool."

Sage sighed. "I want a hammock."

"We're going to be busy."

"Not every second. Oh, pack something sexy. We'll want to go to a club."

Daisy rolled her eyes. "We're not going to a club. We're there to work."

Cassidy grinned at Sage. "Don't worry. I'll get you a name."

The only downside to the unexpected trip to Miami was that it came just a day after Joanne left for the Golden Door spa. Sage would have liked to take advantage of the empty, quiet house. But Cassidy wanted them to go as soon as they could and Daisy was able to take the time off work, so three days later, Sage was trying to decide how many bathing suits she'd need.

She had Cassidy's to-do list tucked in her tote. Most of it was easy enough—returning her internet modem, emptying out her refrigerator and mailbox, dumping any liquids so they wouldn't be packed. They should be able to get that done in a day, leaving plenty of time for lying by the pool and maybe a little shopping. Sage was hoping that the time away would allow her to come to some decisions about what she really wanted for the future and hey, maybe even pick a direction.

She walked through the empty house, locking the doors and windows and turning off the lights. It was nearly eight in the evening. She and Daisy were taking the red-eye to Miami. They would go directly to Cassidy's townhouse to work. With a little luck, they would finish up that day and have the remaining two days to just hang out.

She returned to her bedroom, then rolled her battered suitcase to the front door. She'd already packed her tote and handbag. She had about twenty minutes before Wallace and Daisy were due to pick her up, so she hurried next door and knocked.

Adam let her in. "You ready?" he asked, after he kissed her. "I am."

She paused, not sure what else to say. She wanted to tell him she would miss him, but worried that would make her seem too needy or freak him out. They were obviously involved in some way—they hung out a lot and were sleeping together—but she wasn't sure how to define what they were doing, so she didn't know if missing fell in the "me, too" category or was more of a "back off, bitch" kind of thing. Not that Adam would ever think of her as a bitch, which meant the latter was unlikely, but still, it was all so confusing.

"I'll miss you," he said, surprising her, but in a happy way.

She smiled. "I'll miss you, too. A lot."

His expression turned serious. "I know I don't have the right to say this, but I'm going to anyway. Don't cheat on me."

The words shocked her. "Why would you say that?" Which was a dumb question. Obviously he was concerned. "I won't. I wouldn't. Adam, no. That's not what's going to happen."

She wanted to say more, to defend herself, but as she stared into his eyes, she had the sudden thought there weren't words to make him feel better. Given her past, his concern was probably reasonable. The only way she could make him feel better was to get through the trip and come back to him.

He looked away, then back at her. "It's just…"

She put her hands on his chest, then kissed him. "I get it. I won't do that." She wanted to tell him to trust her, but knew that wouldn't help.

"You're so beautiful," he told her, tucking her hair behind her ears. "No guy can resist you."

"Sweet but not true."

She was going to say more, but she heard a car pulling into her driveway.

"That's Wallace and Daisy."

He nodded and walked her out. Together they went into her house and collected her luggage. Sage introduced Adam to Wallace, then kissed him one more time.

"I won't text you when we arrive," she said, her voice teasing. "It'll be about four in the morning, your time."

"Have fun," he told her, then held open the back door of the car. "I'll see you when you get home."

"Yes, you will."

She waved and got inside. Daisy turned around in the front passenger seat.

"What's wrong? You look upset."

"Adam's worried I'm going to cheat on him while we're in Miami."

"How? You'll be with me. It's not like you're going to go off and have sex with someone. Even ignoring the logistics, you wouldn't do that."

"Thanks for having faith in me."

"You're not that kind of person."

Sage didn't bother correcting her. She liked that Daisy saw the best in her, even when it wasn't deserved. They'd come a long way together.

Wallace got back in the car. "You girls are going to have a good time on your trip."

Sage laughed. "I've been informed that now that I'm closer to forty than thirty, I'm no longer a girl."

Her former stepfather smiled at her in the rearview mirror. "You'll always be one of my girls."

"Thanks, Wallace. That's nice to hear."

Once they arrived at the airport, Wallace drove them to their terminal, then helped them unload their luggage. As Sage hugged him goodbye, he slipped a wad of bills into her hand.

"I know you two will be doing some shopping. Buy yourself something pretty."

The unexpected and generous gesture made her eyes burn a little.

"Thank you," she said, hugging him again. "You've always been the best man I've ever known."

He kissed her forehead. "I keep hoping I'll come in second to some nice man you've fallen for." He cleared his throat. "All right. You two have fun and take care of each other."

"We will," Daisy told him.

Once they were through security, they found their gate. They'd barely settled in chairs to wait until boarding when Daisy jumped up.

"Can you watch my stuff? I'm going to take a walk."

"Why?"

"I'm nervous. It helps me burn off energy." Daisy put her hands on her hips. "Does it really matter why? Can't I just take a walk?"

The attitude was unexpected, as were the too-wide eyes and the rapid breathing.

Sage stared at her in disbelief. "You're afraid to fly?"

"What if I am? A lot of people don't like to fly. It's just not natural, you know? Planes are big. They weigh a lot. Big things should stay on the ground."

"There's nothing to worry about. Air travel is safe."

"Which all sounds great until you crash and die in a fiery explosion."

"Technically, I think you die on impact, so the fiery explosion doesn't matter so much."

Daisy glared at her. "Do you think this conversation is helping?"

"Sorry. You know we're in first class and they have sleeper seats. You can sleep the flight away."

"I'm not sleeping. I have to be awake to will the plane to stay in the air."

Suddenly the trip to Miami was looking less and less fun. "Go take your walk," she said. "I'll watch your things."

Daisy returned just as they were boarding. Sage ignored her fidgeting. Once they were seated, Sage handed her a pill.

"Take this."

Daisy eyed her suspiciously. "What is it?"

"Something to help you sleep. It will last until we get to Miami."

"I don't want to be groggy tomorrow."

"I don't want you willing the plane to fly for six hours."

They glared at each other. Daisy blinked first and took the pill.

"It's not going to work," Daisy told her. "I'm too tense."

"We'll see."

By the time the plane backed away from the gate, Daisy's eyes were beginning to close. As they began to speed down the runway, she was sound asleep.

Sage waited until they cleared ten thousand feet, then lowered Daisy's seat into the flat position and draped a blanket across her. Daisy stirred just enough to grab her hand and squeeze her fingers.

"Night, Sage," she whispered, her words slightly slurred.

"You're a ridiculous creature," Sage told her, before lowering her own seat and closing her eyes. *But I still love you.*

twenty-two

"This just doesn't feel right," Daisy said as she opened the front door of Cassidy's townhome. "We're violating her personal space."

"We're doing exactly what she asked us to do," Sage said, following her into the small foyer. "Plus, hello? She gave us the keys."

They were on the ground floor. There was a staircase to their left and a hallway to their right. Daisy shook off the sense of being where she didn't belong and started down the hallway. One door led to the garage while another opened onto an unfurnished guest bedroom with an attached bath and a little patio overlooking a fenced garden.

"This is nice," Daisy said. "Lots of light. The paint and carpet are neutral."

"You're not on an episode of *House Hunters*," Sage told her with a grin. "You're allowed to be bitchy."

"It's an empty room. What is there to be bitchy about?"

They went up the first flight of stairs and found themselves in the main living space. The huge open room had a kitchen at the far end, a dining area and the family room. The ceilings were high, the tile floors a warm beige.

Daisy looked around, searching for some sense of her sister, but there weren't many personal touches to be found. There weren't any books or magazines and there wasn't any artwork on the walls.

"It's more like a hotel room than a home," Sage said.

"I agree. I know she was away a lot, but where's her stuff? A sweater, a pair of shoes, anything that proves she lives here."

"Cassidy's not big on roots."

"There's a difference between that and living as if she's invisible."

They went up to the next level. The large master bedroom was similar to the living room—generic furniture in a comfortable space. The duvet cover was white, as were the pillow shams. The long, low dresser could have belonged to anyone and there weren't any items on top. Even the counters of the master bath were bare.

They retraced their steps and went into the second bedroom on that floor.

"Finally," Daisy said, feeling herself relax. "Here she is."

The bedroom had been converted into Cassidy's home office. There was a big desk in the middle of the room and bookshelves on all the walls. Papers and folders and books were piled on the desk and spilled onto the floor.

The bookshelves were also overflowing with hats, vases, dolls, dozens of framed pictures, and a jean jacket hanging off her chair.

Daisy studied the pictures of Cassidy with people from around the world, photographs of sunrises and sunsets, and several of her with Desean.

Sage looked around. "Her diary's not here. I'm guessing the closet."

"This is the place that makes the most sense. It would be impossible to find in this mess. Besides, why are you obsessed with her diary?"

Sage grinned. "Because then we get to know her secrets."

Daisy groaned. "Grow up. We're not reading her diary." She pulled the list Cassidy had given them out of her handbag. "Let's find the modem first and put it by the door. Then we can start packing up the things we're taking back with us."

"What do you think you're doing?"

The low male voice made Daisy jump. She spun toward the sound and saw a tall, muscled man standing in the doorway to the room. Her head registered that this was Desean, while her fight or flight response loudly pointed out that the man could snap her like a twig.

Sage, much more socially practiced than Daisy, smiled and walked toward him.

"Hi. I'm Sage, Cassidy's sister. This is Daisy. You must be Desean."

His stern expression relaxed. "I've heard about you both. Nice to meet you."

Daisy smiled and waved from the safety of halfway across the room. The man was handsome enough to be disconcerting, she thought, taking in the brown eyes, close-trimmed beard and long braids. His shoulders were nearly as wide as the doorway and his arms were thick with muscles. The Hawaiian shirt was a little incongruous, but also seemed to take him from superhero status to a more normal man level.

"I didn't know you were coming," he said, his voice low and gravelly, with a hint of velvet. "Cassidy didn't…" He shrugged. "We don't talk anymore. But I saw you arrive and come into her place so I wanted to find out what was going on."

Daisy felt her heart sink. Oh, no! He didn't know why they were here and based on the flowers and the note, he was still in love with Cassidy. So finding out they were closing up her apartment would be devastating.

She opened her mouth, then closed it, not sure how to explain without hurting his feelings.

"Really?" Sage asked with a sigh. "You're going to wimp out on me."

"I can't tell him."

"Wiener dog." Sage looked at Desean. "I'm sorry you're finding out this way. Apparently both my sisters are cowards. Cassidy asked us to fly out so we could take care of a few things before the movers come. She's leaving Miami."

Desean seemed to visibly grow smaller. His head dropped. "I thought maybe she'd come back and we could talk. I guess that's not gonna happen."

Daisy found herself hurrying to his side. "She's been dealing with a lot, what with the fall and everything. But she's getting better. Maybe when she has some time to think, she'll reconsider."

He looked at her, his dark gaze intense. "You're telling me that after six weeks stuck in bed, she hasn't had time to think?"

"Okay, not that, but..." She pressed her lips together. "I'm sorry. You seem like a nice guy."

One corner of his mouth turned up. "I am, but that's not enough for Cassidy. Whatever she's looking for isn't me."

Daisy pulled her phone out of her jeans pocket. "She's healed a lot since the last time you saw her." She showed him several pictures of Cassidy.

"Those your kids?" he asked, flipping through the pictures.

"Uh-huh."

"Ben and Krissa, right? She talked about them. She wasn't sure about having kids, but used to say if you could do it, then anyone could." He frowned. "I didn't mean that to sound bad."

Daisy waved away his concern. "It's fine. We didn't used to get along, but we're friends now. I wish I could change her mind about you."

"Me, too."

"Why don't you join us for dinner tonight?" Sage said.

He brightened. "I'd like that. Where are you staying?"

"The Four Seasons."

He nodded. "I know a couple of restaurants nearby. Why don't I pick you up at seven?"

"Perfect," Daisy told him.

They exchanged numbers and walked him downstairs. After returning to the living level, Daisy walked into the kitchen.

"I don't get it," she admitted. "Why is she being so stubborn?"

"Because she's an idiot."

"She's scared."

"We're all scared, but that doesn't mean we don't at least try." Sage leaned against the counter. "He's not going to wait for her forever and then what? She wakes up and realizes he's the one, only he's moved on."

"I know. I worry about that, too." Daisy opened the refrigerator. There was nothing inside. An inspection of the cupboards yielded a few staples and a couple of bottles of vodka, but little else.

"Clearing out her place isn't going to take long at all," Daisy added. "You know, we could get it done today, have dinner with Desean and fly home tomorrow."

Sage smiled at her. "Or we could get it done today, have dinner with Desean, then have a good time."

"What does that even mean?"

"It makes me sad you have to ask. We could lie by the pool, get a massage, go shopping. You know, fun stuff we never do at home because we're both too busy."

"Just thinking about that makes me feel guilty," Daisy admitted.

"Because you're not allowed to have fun? Says who?"

A very good question, Daisy thought. Why was she hesitating? They were already here. Her kids were taken care of, she had the time off work. Why not enjoy herself?

Sage laughed. "I can see you weakening. Good. Why don't you get this level ready? I'll tackle the bedroom and closet. I'm sure her diary is in there somewhere. Oh, and be on the lookout for the modem, so we can drop that off with the cable company on our way to the hotel."

"We're not reading her diary," Daisy said firmly.

"You may not be," Sage told her. "But I am."

Desean took them to a Cuban seafood restaurant that looked deceptively casual on the outside, but on the inside was all white tablecloths and well-dressed diners. They were immediately shown to a quiet table in the back. Nearly every customer turned to watch them be seated and while Sage wanted to think she and Daisy were the reason for everyone's attention, she knew Desean was actually the main attraction.

Even with her wearing four-inch heels, the man still towered over her. He had an air of confidence that, combined with his size, got people's attention. Plus there was the whole hunky-guy thing going on.

"Thanks for inviting me tonight," he said after their server had taken their drink orders. "It's nice to get out. I've been spending too much time alone."

"Missing Cassidy?" Daisy asked, then looked stricken, as if she wished she hadn't said that.

Desean nodded. "I can't help it. I love your sister and I don't know how to get over her."

"Time will help," Daisy offered.

Sage held in a groan. "How about another woman?"

Daisy shot her an incredulous look. "Don't say that. Cassidy's our sister. Why would we want him to be with some-one else?"

"Because she dumped him and he needs to move on."

"That's heartless."

"That's practical."

Desean surprised Sage by laughing. "I can see Cassidy gets her attitude from you two." His humor disappeared. "I'm not seeing anyone and I won't be for a while. I'm not that guy. I want a real relationship with someone I care about."

Which was similar to what Adam had talked about when they were getting to know each other, Sage thought. The difference between getting laid and having it matter.

"I've always been that way," he added. "But Cassidy's the first woman I've been in love with."

Their server returned with their drinks. She and Daisy had each ordered mojitos while Desean had chosen Irish whiskey.

"She's scared," Daisy told him. "After her parents split up, she felt torn between the two families and never comfortable in either place. She's afraid to put down roots. If she's trapped, how can she protect herself?"

Desean sighed. "She knows I'd never hurt her."

"If you stay together, you'll hurt her," Daisy said firmly. "It comes with being in a relationship. Believe me, I know this one. My husband and I are separated."

"He's being a total jerk," Sage said.

Daisy flashed her a smile. "Thanks. I think so, too." She turned back to Desean. "My point is, if you're in a relation-ship, you're going to hurt each other. That's a given. It's what you do when that happens that matters. Cassidy either doesn't have the skills to manage that, or she doesn't trust herself."

"That's very deep," Sage told her.

"Thanks. So how did you and Cassidy meet?"

Desean smiled. "She'd come to see the townhouse. I have

a management company that handles the listing for me, but I happened to be on the site that day, so I showed her around. For me it was love at first sight. I'd never understood what that meant, but I knew from the second I saw her, she was the one."

"Did you tell her that?" Sage asked.

"No. I knew it would scare her away. Hell, it scared me. But we talked and laughed and went out for drinks. Before I knew what was what, we were back at my place." He sighed. "Big mistake. I acted just like every other guy in her life. I should have held out and made her see I thought she was special."

Sage was again reminded of Adam and how he managed the same problem differently. He'd "held out" on her. Amazingly, the tactic had worked. By the time they did the deed, she was much more involved than she'd expected.

"We hung out for a couple of weeks," he continued, "then she took off for one of her assignments, gone a month. I worried I'd never see her again, but when she got back, she moved into her place and we took up where we'd left off. Then she dumped me."

Daisy flinched. "Did she say why?"

"She said it was too much for her. She left again. When she came back, we got back together." He picked up his glass. "That's how things went with us. I started going with her on some of her assignments. We'd get along great, I'd think it was going to work and then she'd end things. When she invited me to Patagonia, I thought this time was real, so I bought a ring and proposed. You know what happened next."

Sage patted his arm. "I'm sorry. She's going to regret losing you."

"Maybe, but that doesn't change where we are. It's been one too many times for me. I'm not going to go running back again. She's made her feelings clear."

Daisy leaned toward him. "Don't give up. You love her."

"Not much help if she doesn't love me back."

Sage and Daisy exchanged a look. Sage had no idea what to say to him.

"She doesn't believe in romantic love," Daisy admitted. "She says no relationship works, so why bother trying. It makes me sad. Jordan and I are in a bad place, but that doesn't make me not believe in love anymore."

Sage wasn't sure she had anything to add to the conversation. She'd never been in love. When she'd been younger, it was because her mother had warned her not to risk her heart. Joanne spoke from experience—the only man she'd truly cared about had broken her heart. Sage supposed she'd loved Jordan, in her way, but they had been kids. Since then, she'd never fallen for anyone—a sad thing to admit after three marriages.

She wasn't sure what she felt about Adam. She liked him a lot—she respected him and enjoyed his company. She looked forward to seeing him and missed him when they were apart. She was still a little rattled by his request that she not cheat on him. It meant he didn't trust her, which made her question her own worthiness.

She looked across the table at Daisy. What about her and Jordan? Were they going to work it out? The separation was going on for a long time and from what Sage could figure out, they weren't even talking. Were they headed for divorce?

She thought about Krissa and Ben and hoped that wasn't the case. Splitting up was devastating for a family. Look how Wallace ending things with her mom had screwed up all the kids.

Sensing her good mood fading, Sage shook off the negative thoughts and told herself they needed to change the subject.

"You won't get a tan if you stay in the shade," Sage said.

Daisy, comfortable in her lounge chair, stuck out her tongue. "Bite me."

"You forgot to add the *b*-word. Bite me, bitch."

"I don't swear."

"You did last night."

"Barely."

Daisy smiled, then returned her attention to the fashion magazine she'd bought in the hotel's gift shop. She had to admit, if only to herself, she was having a great time. She and Sage had finished cleaning out Cassidy's apartment the previous day, then had had dinner with Desean.

She and Sage had gone shopping that morning. She'd picked up a few things for herself, along with stuffed manatees for both kids. She knew Ben would pretend he was too old for a stuffed animal, but that he would enjoy the present.

Now they were sitting poolside, overlooking the bay, enjoying the warm, sunny afternoon. As it was midweek, only a handful of other guests were taking advantage of the perfect weather.

She was a little tired—they'd stayed at the restaurant with Desean until closing and she hadn't slept that well in a strange bed—but oddly happy. Yes, she missed her children and her pets, but getting away was nice. She appreciated the lack of responsibility, the new experiences and hanging out with Sage. Funny how only three months ago, the thought of spending even an hour with her stepsister would have sent her screaming into the night. Now she and Sage were friends. Daisy trusted her and enjoyed her company. Life was nothing if not unexpected.

She turned the page in the magazine and saw an ad for an all-inclusive resort in the Caribbean. The romantic scene showed a couple walking together on a beach. The guy looked a little like Jordan, which made her think of him, which had her realizing that while she'd admitted to missing her children, she hadn't once thought about missing him. Worse, she'd barely thought about him and had only told him about the trip on her way to the airport, via text.

Shouldn't she be lonely? They were married—he was the man she wanted to spend the rest of her life with, at least he had been. Had that changed or was this just a bad patch they would get through?

She thought about her conversation with her father and how Wallace had told her about withdrawing from Joanne. Daisy wondered if she was doing the same thing—pulling back rather than dealing with the situation. Or if it was something worse. Jordan had accused her of not caring anymore. He said she was already gone. Was that at the heart of their problems?

No, she told herself firmly. She wasn't ready for her marriage to be over. She was hurt by his behavior and she wanted things fixed. Plus, she was pissed at all he'd put them through by leaving. The opposite of love wasn't hate. It was not caring at all. So her anger was a sign she still cared.

Twisted logic, but she could live with that.

Maybe things would be better when she got home, she thought. They would be back in therapy and—

"Holy shit! It's implants!" Sage waved a small leather journal, then walked the few feet to the lounge chair next to Daisy and sat down.

Sage grinned. "Cassidy had implants. That's the big secret."

"Stop reading her diary."

"Yeah, because you saying that will make a difference. Come on. You have to have a reaction."

"If they make her feel better, then good for her."

Sage looked disappointed. "I thought you'd be judgy."

"You frequently think the worst of me."

"Not anymore. *I'm* shocked. Why aren't you shocked?" Sage's mouth twisted. "It's because you have boobs, so it makes sense someone would want to get them." She looked down at her own modest curves. "Should I get implants?"

"Only if they would make you happy."

Daisy thought Sage looked great just the way she was. While Daisy wore a tasteful cover-up over her one-piece bathing suit, Sage pranced around in a bikini, her body all lean and strong. It was depressing to think they were the same age. Not that age had much to do with size, but still.

Sage flopped back in the lounge chair. "I'm disappointed in your lack of reaction."

"I'll try to be more judgmental next time."

Sage grinned. "Thank you." She put down the journal and closed her eyes. "This is nice, just relaxing out here. I need a pool in my life."

"You're welcome to use the one at the house."

"Thanks. I appreciate the offer, seeing as I'm unlikely to have the money to get a pool of my own. Right now I'm focused on saving for an apartment and raising my credit score."

Daisy wasn't sure what to say to that. "If you need a loan…" she began.

Sage opened her eyes. "No."

"I'm just offering—"

"I get that, and no."

Daisy had had no idea about Sage's financial situation. She had assumed her stepsister had been marrying for money, but apparently not. Sage lived frugally and Cassidy had paid for Sage's airline ticket to Miami and had asked Daisy to pick up the hotel bill. Sage's clothes were well-made but not new. In fact, Daisy had been the only one doing actual buying when they'd gone shopping that morning.

"Are you broke?" she asked before she could stop herself.

Sage kept her eyes closed. "I have a small nest egg I'm keeping for emergencies or, hopefully in a couple of years, a down payment on a condo."

"So you're saving for an apartment and then a condo?"

Sage opened one eye. "Why all the questions?"

"I'm worried about you. I have money. I could—"

The other eye opened and her look became pointed. "We've already had this conversation."

"It doesn't have to be a loan."

Sage swore under her breath. "You should try to be less annoying. I'm fine. I have a plan."

Daisy waited expectantly. Sage groaned, then said, "I want to be a teacher."

While the confession was a surprise, the reality of it made sense.

"You're very good with my kids," she said. "You're likeable and responsible, plus you went over to Europe initially to teach English. I can see it. To work here, you'd have to be accredited, right? Would you need a four-year degree?"

"I have that."

Daisy smiled. "You never told me. Congratulations."

"Thanks. We weren't exactly speaking at the time."

"So you got it while you were in Europe?"

"The American University in Paris. There's a process to get accredited here and I'm weighing my options. I can apply for an internship through the LA Unified School District, I can enroll in an online program through USC or there's a two-year program through UCLA."

"That's a lot of choices. Which one do you like the best?"

"The UCLA program, but it's expensive and full-time. I don't think I could work, so not that."

Daisy pressed her lips together rather than offer money again. Sage had made it clear she wasn't interested in accepting assistance. Was that about their relationship or did she re-sist everyone who wanted to help?

"I don't want to make the wrong decision," Sage told her. "I mess up a lot."

"That's not true. You're doing great."

"Shall we ignore the divorce that brought me here in the first place?"

"Yes. Completely. Since you've been back, you've been working, hanging out with Cassidy and me." She grinned. "Sleeping with Adam."

Sage's lips twitched. "The sex has been very nice."

"So you like him?"

"I do. Which scares me. Like our sister, I'm wary of rela-tionships. They never seem to work out. She's sabotaging her-self with Desean. What if I do the same thing with Adam?"

"We talked about this, remember? Do what I would do."

Sage looked at her. "Not to send us into a spiral, but you're currently sitting by a pool in Miami, separated from your husband."

"I'm in Miami because of Cassidy. The separation is differ-ent." Daisy sighed. "But no less troubling, I'll admit."

"What's going on there?"

"I have no idea. For all I know, he's seeing someone else."

Sage looked surprised. "Do you really believe that?"

"I don't know. Maybe. Probably not. He could be."

"Have you asked?"

"Once. He said he wasn't at the time. I don't know if that's changed and I'm starting to think I'm not that interested in the answer."

"You don't mean that."

"No, I don't." She pressed her lips together. "I don't miss him. I did at first, but not recently. Sometimes I'm not sure I care that he's gone."

Sage's eyes filled with concern. "You do care. I was there the night after he texted he was moving into a house. You cared a lot."

Daisy nodded. "You're right. But everything I felt before—the anger, the fear—it's all faded and I don't know what that means. I worry that we've been separated so long that getting back together is going to be impossible."

"It's not. You two still care about each other. You just have to decide you *want* to reconcile." Her sister looked at her. "Unless you don't."

And that was the question, Daisy thought. Simple and to the point. Did she want to stay married to Jordan or not?

"I want to fix things."

"You sure?"

Daisy drew in a breath and waited for her heart to tell her the truth.

"Most days."

twenty-three

Daisy and Sage landed at LAX just before nine in the morning.

"What are your plans for the day?" Daisy asked as they waited for their luggage.

"I have to be at work at noon," Sage said, staring at her phone. "Well, that sucks."

"What?"

"Adam just texted to say he needs to fly to San Francisco to meet with a client. He'll be gone three days." Her mouth twisted. "He's on his way to the airport right now. I'm not going to see him until he's back." Sage looked at her. "Why are you smiling? It's hardly good news."

"You like him," Daisy said with a grin. "He matters to you. I think that's really wonderful."

"We had a good time while we were away. Don't ruin it now by making me want to kill you."

Daisy laughed and linked arms with her stepsister. "Such vicious talk. You need to deal with your anger issues."

"What I need is Adam to not be gone when I get home from work."

"You can come hang out with us. My dad's still in town and I know the kids would love to see you, too." Daisy knew that Esmerelda would be preparing enough food for twenty, so one more for dinner wouldn't matter.

"Maybe," Sage grumbled. "I doubt I'll be in the mood."

"We'll make you feel better. Say you'll join us."

"Whatever."

Daisy ignored the sullen tone. "Come straight from work. I'll tell everyone to be expecting you."

They collected their luggage, then went out to meet their driver from the car service Daisy had arranged. She dropped Sage off first and then they went on to her house.

Esmerelda met her at the door and hugged her. "So good to have you back. Everyone is well. Your father is out golfing with some friends and I took Ben and Krissa to school this morning. Cassidy is up in her room. She's been on edge since you left. She thinks you're taking the later flight, and I didn't tell her otherwise."

Daisy smiled. "Good. I'll go see her in a bit."

She and Sage had talked about how best to handle Cassidy. Yes, they'd agreed to do her a favor, but they were also aware that they were enabling her poor decision. Rather than give her any details of their trip, they'd agreed to text her a vague **All is well**, and let her find out what had happened when they were back.

Daisy went upstairs and unpacked. She checked her email and visited with Esmerelda for a while before finally heading toward Cassidy's suite. She found her sister pacing in her room, walking almost normally, despite the cast on her leg.

When Cassidy saw her, she rushed forward.

"You're back! Why didn't you tell me you got back early? I thought you were on a later flight. How did it go? You got everything done? The townhouse is ready for the movers? Did Sage read my diary?"

Daisy took a seat in the living room and motioned to the chair opposite.

"We know about the implants," she said with a laugh. "Sage isn't sure how she feels about them, but honestly, I don't care one way or the other. If you're happy, then I'm happy."

Cassidy folded her arms across her chest. "I can't believe you read my diary."

"I didn't. That was all Sage. She just told me the juicy bits." She paused. "We returned the modem, dumped the liquids and generally got your place ready for the packers."

"Thank you. I'll call them and let them know to put me on the schedule. I'm going to store all my furniture with them until I figure out where I'm going to live."

Daisy took a deep breath. "What is wrong with you? We met Desean. He's fantastic. Thoughtful, kind, funny and possibly the most attractive man on the planet."

Cassidy's lips twitched. "The planet? Really? That's quite the endorsement." Her mouth straightened. "You met him?"

"We had dinner with him and talked for hours. What don't you like about him? Cassidy, have you considered you're throwing away what might be the best relationship you'll ever have? I know you're scared, but come on. Suck it up and act like a grown-up here. Face your fears and take a chance."

Cassidy turned away. "I can't."

"Why not? Are you so afraid of being happy? Yes, there will be bad times, but you get through them and are stronger because of them."

Cassidy brushed tears from her cheeks. "Because you know about this? I'm sorry, but where's your husband?"

"I haven't got a clue and you know what? That's irrelevant. Jordan and I are having problems. Even if we work things out, we'll have problems again. Hopefully the next time, we'll handle them better. But the fact that he and I have messed up doesn't mean no one should ever try to be in a relationship. You and I are getting along right now. We're close and I like it, but do you think that means we won't drift apart at some point? We could. Or we could make an effort to keep what we have and build on it. That's the point. We have choices and we make decisions."

Daisy leaned forward, determined to get through to her sister. "I vow, as of right now, that no matter what, I'm not giving up on you. Not this time. If you run, I will hunt you down and make you be my sister."

Cassidy's eyes widened. "You'd really do that?"

"When have I lied to you?"

"You haven't."

"Okay, then yes, I'd really do that." She exhaled. "Cassidy, give him a chance. No, I take that back. Give yourself a chance. Men like him are rare and you're going to be sorry you let him go. I know you're scared, but some things are worth fighting for."

"I want to believe you," Cassidy began. "But I can't."

Daisy smiled at her. "That's okay, because the only person you have to be believe right now is yourself. You're stronger than you think and as soon as you recognize that, you'll be able to move forward rather than staying stuck."

Cassidy studied her for a couple of seconds. "You really won't let me go?"

"I am with you to the end, kid. Deal with it."

Two days later, Sage arrived home from work to find that her mother had returned, looking happy, refreshed and at least five pounds thinner.

"I had a wonderful time," Joanne said, hugging Sage for the third time in two minutes. "Thank you so much for sending me to the spa."

Sage hugged her back. "I'm glad it worked out. So the spa was nice?"

"It's beautiful and they treat the guests so well, but that wasn't the best part."

Sage stepped out of her heels and tried to tell herself that whatever her mother was going to say would be fine. She'd done her bit, springing for the week at the spa—nothing else was on her.

"I met someone!"

Sage smiled, hoping her dismay didn't show. What her mother needed was a break from the manhunt, not a new target in her sights.

"Did you? Tell me about him."

Her mother led the way to the kitchen where she had all kinds of vegetables laid out on the counter. She picked up a knife and began cutting a red pepper into strips.

"His name is Thomas and you'll never guess."

Sage sat on one of the kitchen chairs. "What?"

"I knew him in high school! We both went to Culver City High, if you can believe it. A few of us went out the first evening we were at the spa. Just to a local place, just for fun. I saw this man watching me and something about him was familiar." Her mother beamed. "He came over and asked if I'd gone to Culver City High School and that was it." She sighed dramatically. "It was like a TV reality show. Honestly I was looking everywhere for the camera."

"That's great, Mom," Sage said, hoping this particular relationship had a happy ending.

Joanne moved on to slicing cucumbers. "He's not rich like most of the men I go out with, but he's well off enough. He owns several gas stations in Escondido and San Diego. He's a widower. His wife died three years ago from lung cancer, poor woman. His kids are grown, of course." She arranged the cut vegetables on a plate. "I like him, Sage. I haven't liked anyone this much in a long time."

"I'm glad for you."

"Me, too." She smiled. "I owe it all to you. Not just for the fabulous spa week but for reconnecting with Thomas. You're so good to me. I want to do something in return. Something special."

"You don't owe me anything, Mom. I'm really happy for you. That's reward enough."

Her mother laughed. "You're sweet to say that, but I'll think of something."

She carried her veggies to the family room. Sage escaped to her bedroom, not sure what to make of her mother's change in attitude. Having a man in her life always made her feel better, but it was a temporary solution at best. Still she would enjoy the relative calm while it lasted.

She changed her clothes, then checked to see if Adam had texted. He was due in that evening and had promised to text her as soon as he was back.

She couldn't wait to see him, which was both good and troubling. She liked him a lot—so much that sometimes it scared her. Not because she was afraid he would do anything to hurt her, but mostly because she wasn't used to being happy with a guy. Unless she went all the way back to high school and dating Jordan, she couldn't remember ever having an uncomplicated relationship. But with Adam there were no red flags, no drama, nothing to make her feel that she should run. He was a good guy who cared about her, which should have delighted her and instead left her uneasy. Happy, but definitely a little wary.

Forty-five minutes later, he texted to say he was on his way home from the airport. She told her mother she was going out, then sat on his porch to wait. As soon as he pulled into the driveway, she was up and hurrying toward him.

He got out of the car. "I missed you," he said, pulling her close, then kissing her. "Six days was too much. Let's never do that again."

He kissed her a second time, making it impossible for her to speak. Not that she minded. Being in his arms, feeling his passion and knowing he'd missed her was plenty.

"How was your trip?" she asked when he drew back.

"Good. Productive. How was Florida?"

"Really fun. Daisy and I had a good time and we got to meet Desean."

"So you said in your texts." Adam's gaze locked with hers. "You said he was movie star handsome."

She heard the slight worry in his voice and touched his cheek. "Yes, he was incredible, but not for me. He's my sister's almost fiancé. Even if he wasn't, I'm seeing someone right now. Someone who's important to me."

His brows rose. "You're seeing someone?"

"I am."

For a second, she wondered if she'd gone too far. Did he think they were also seeing each other, or was it more casual to him?

Panic gripped her, making her want to pull back and possibly bolt for the safety of her mom's house.

He smiled at her. "I'm seeing someone, too, and it's going really well."

The fear faded. "Yeah?"

"Yeah. Now let me get my stuff from the car and we can head inside where I can show you all the ways I missed you."

Daisy told herself that therapy was supposed to be difficult—that if the problems were easily fixed, then everyone would be happy all the time and little cartoon birds would help the world get dressed every morning. But honest to God, if Jordan said he was tired of being last on her list one more time, she was going to throw a lamp at him.

Dr. Braxton glanced at her. "Daisy, I sense tension."

"Not tension," she said without thinking. "Anger. A boatload of it."

Both men stared at her.

"What's that about?" Jordan demanded, sounding defensive.

"It occurs to me that we're halfway through this session and all we've talked about is your feelings. How you don't feel appreciated. How difficult it is for you to deal with my inheritance, which makes no sense to me because it's not like it's new."

She turned to Dr. Braxton. "Here's what I would like to talk about. Jordan rented a house. He moved out of the hotel and into that house without talking to me first." She spun back to Jordan. "Hardly surprising, considering you moved out of our home without saying a word."

She faked a smile. "Oh, wait. You texted me, so I guess that counts as words, just not the spoken kind."

Jordan glared at her. "We've talked about this. Why do we have to discuss it again and again?"

"Why not? We're discussing what bugs you again and again. So hey, let's make it my turn. You promised you wouldn't text anything important. You complain you're last in my life, but here's a news flash, you're not doing anything to make me want to put you first. You've always done exactly what you wanted when you wanted, everyone else be damned."

She scooted to the edge of her chair. "As for my inheritance, I'm not going to apologize for the fact that my mother came from money, or that she left me a trust fund. You knew it when we started dating and you knew it when we got married, so don't you dare complain about it now. I'm sorry if the fact that I earn more than you at my job makes you feel like less of a man, but you need to learn to deal with it because I'm not quitting."

She drew in a breath. "I don't know what you want. Should I give up my inheritance? Sell the house? Would that make you happy? Do you want me to stop working? Because if any of that is true, it seems to me the only way to make you happy is to be smaller than I am and I won't do that. I'm willing to meet you halfway, but I'm not willing to subjugate myself to some antiquated notion you have about what I should be. So tell me, Jordan, what exactly will it take to make you happy?"

He looked away. "I hate it when you're a bitch."

"Jordan, that's not helpful," Dr. Braxton admonished. "I request that you speak respectfully in these sessions. Is Daisy right? Are you uncomfortable with her inheritance and her job?"

"It's not about that."

"Then what is it about?" Dr. Braxton pressed.

Daisy waited, hoping that maybe this time she would get some actual information.

"Daisy's already done with us. She's going through the motions so when she asks for a divorce, she's not the bad guy."

The blunt statement stunned her nearly as much as Joanne's hits had, all those years ago. Daisy stared at her husband in disbelief.

"How can you say that? I've never even hinted I want a divorce. I want this to work. I'm here because I want things to work." She felt tears burn in her eyes. "Jordan, no!"

"It's true," he told her. "You're not in love with me anymore."

Dr. Braxton looked between them both. "How long have you felt this way, Jordan?"

He stared at the carpeted floor. "A while."

Daisy fought her tears. "Why didn't you say something?"

"What do you think I've been talking about all this time? You don't care about me, Daisy." He turned to Dr. Braxton. "I've been asking her to go away with me for the last eighteen months. Just the two of us for a long weekend. She always says she can't get away. Last week she flew off to Miami with her stepsister. It was a last-minute thing. Three days at the Four Seasons." He glared at Daisy. "You don't even like Sage!"

"I do. We're sisters."

"That's new."

Guilt flared, making her feel defensive. She told herself to focus on the topic at hand. Jordan was right—he had wanted them to go away and she'd resisted. She'd claimed to be too busy, or that she couldn't leave the kids, yet she'd taken a trip with Sage.

"I'm sorry," she said. "I understand why you're upset about my trip to Miami. It wasn't for fun," she added quickly. "Cassidy needed us to close up her apartment." Which was kind of true and kind of not.

"That took three days?" His gaze locked with her. "All I wanted was to be the man in your life, Daisy. Nothing more. But I was never enough."

They stared at each other. She felt herself flushing and struggled to figure out what to say. After a few minutes of silence, Jordan rose.

"I don't need this shit," he announced before walking toward the door. "Go to hell."

The door slammed shut behind him, the sound echoing in the silence of the room. Daisy pressed a hand to her chest, feeling as if Jordan hadn't just walked out of their session but as if he'd walked away from any hope of their marriage being healed.

While that should have been the worst of it, she was now going to have to face the very real possibility that the central problem wasn't him leaving but the fact that somewhere in the past few months, they'd each decided their relationship wasn't worth saving.

Sage found a parking spot on the street. She was only having dinner with her mother.

She waited for a break in the traffic, then darted across the street to the trendy bistro. There was outdoor seating and lots of plants. She had no idea what kind of food they served, but at this point, all she really cared about was getting off her feet. Honestly, as long as the place served cocktails, she didn't care if the food was raw, macrobiotic or vegan.

She gave her name to the hostess and was shown to a table in the back. Her mother was already seated, looking even better than she had when she'd gotten home from the spa. Ah, the powers of young love, Sage thought, smiling.

"Cute place," she said as she sat down. "Not in our neighborhood."

Her mother's brows rose. "Sometimes it's important to try new things. How was work?"

"Busy. Lots of customers, not so many sales. I feel like I spent the whole day carting clothes from the dressing rooms back to the racks out front. I can't do the four-inch-heel thing anymore. Not all day. Although going to flats is going to make me feel like I'm a hundred and five."

"Don't think about that tonight. You're here to have a good time."

Her mother looked smug as she spoke. No, smug wasn't right. She looked *knowing*.

Their server appeared with drinks that Sage hadn't ordered.

She set a glass of white wine in front of Joanne and a margarita with a tequila chaser in front of Sage.

Her mother waved to the cocktail. "I ordered for you, darling. I thought you might have had a tough day."

Sage eyed the drinks. "I still have to drive home, Mom."

"Oh, don't be a party pooper. You can Uber home if you have to and pick up your car in the morning."

Uber? Why couldn't she just drive home with her mom?

But before she could ask, her mother raised her glass. "Thank you again for the spa week. You changed my life."

Sage touched her margarita glass to her mother's wineglass, then took a sip. The drink was perfect—sweet and tart, with a bit of saltiness from the rim. She was tempted to down the whole thing, but knew she had to pace herself. Maybe she could text Adam to come join them. She'd told him she was having dinner with her mom, but didn't think he would mind a last-minute invitation.

"Things are going well with Thomas," her mother said. "I'm thinking about moving in with him."

Which was so very like her mother. It had been all of what? Two weeks? Sure, why not move in? But what she said instead was, "You said he lives in Escondido. That's a long way."

"About ninety minutes when the traffic is light. He has a big house and a pool. It's lovely there and we want to be together." Her mother looked at her. "Sage, I can give you a couple of months to figure it out, but then either you're going to have to pay more or I'll need to rent out the place."

Sage hadn't seen that one coming. While technically she could afford to rent the whole house, doing so would mean no monthly savings deposit.

"You could get a roommate," her mother offered. "I'm not trying to be difficult, but if I move in with Thomas, I need to take advantage of that time away from the house. I need to bank as much money as I can." She pressed her lips together. "I'm not a young woman anymore. I need a nest egg."

"I get it." Sage understood the problem, even if she didn't like it. "I appreciate you giving me two months to decide what to do."

"Think about the roommate option."

Sage nodded. She didn't love the idea, but it might make the most sense. She could move into the master suite and rent out her room. There was also a third bedroom, mostly empty, that could be converted into a second rental.

"Or you could go live with Adam."

Sage looked at her mother. "I'm not going to ask to move in with Adam."

"Why not? He obviously likes you."

Sage wasn't going to bother trying to explain that she wouldn't do that to him. She wasn't trading sex for a place to live. Not anymore.

"I'll come up with something."

Her mother looked past her and smiled. "Right on time." She rose and waved. "Over here."

Sage turned, then nearly fell out of her chair when she saw Jordan approaching their table.

Her first thought was to run. She hadn't talked to him in years and while she'd seen him at the reunion, it had been from a distance.

"Mom, what did you do?" she asked, coming to her feet.

"I'm saying thank you."

Sage was still processing that unpleasant nugget when Jordan walked up to her, pulled her close and lightly kissed her on the cheek.

"Hi, Sage. It's nearly seven and everyone else in this place looks like they've had a hard day, while you look amazing. How do you do that?"

She honest to God had no idea what to say to him. The shock was too great. She studied him, taking in what was the same and what was different from the last time she'd seen him. Sure, they'd been at the reunion a couple of months ago, but really the last time she'd truly studied him had been at his wedding to Daisy.

He looked older, but in that great way handsome men seemed to age. There was a bit of tension in his shoulders, but otherwise, he was much as she remembered.

"This is a surprise," she admitted.

He grinned at her. "For me, too, but when your mom called and invited me to dinner, I had to come." He kissed her mom on the cheek. "You look younger than I remember. How is that possible?"

Joanne patted him on the shoulder. "You're such a sweet liar. All right, you two. Have fun."

Sage took a step toward her. "You're leaving?"

"I am." Her expression turned sly. "Have fun, darling. Don't worry, I won't wait up."

She walked away, leaving Sage alone with Daisy's husband. Indecision pulled at her, but her shaking legs made it impossible to walk away. She collapsed in her chair, then reached for the shot of tequila and downed it in a single gulp.

"At least now my mother's mysterious behavior is explained," Sage said more to herself than Jordan. "She was acting strange since I arrived at the restaurant."

Jordan sat across from her and flagged down their server. "Scotch on the rocks. Make it a double."

Sage raised her eyebrows. "So we both risk Ubering?"

"I live right around the corner. I walked."

Which made the choice of restaurants both more and less odd. She would guess that somehow her mother had figured out where Jordan had moved to and had chosen the restaurant for the location. But what was her end game?

Sage told herself it didn't matter. She was stuck for at least half an hour. She would talk to Jordan, remind him of his duty to Daisy, then hightail it out of here.

He leaned across the table and grabbed her hand. "How long has it been? Years, right? You were at the reunion, but we didn't get a chance to talk."

She carefully pulled her hand free. "We spoke briefly at your wedding. On the day you married Daisy." She emphasized the name.

"That was a while ago. How have you been?"

"Fine. Busy. I'm back in LA. Obviously."

She pressed her lips together to keep herself from babbling. What was wrong with her? She wasn't nervous—she didn't care about Jordan. Maybe it was just being so close to him after all this time. The situation bordered on surreal.

He stared into her eyes. "You look great. Seventeen-year-old Sage knocked my socks off, but the grown-up version is even better." He gave her a lopsided smile that unexpectedly kicked her in the gut. "How is that possible?"

"Each full moon I sacrifice a live chicken to the gods of the underworld and they reward me with everlasting beauty."

He laughed, a deep, full laugh that spoke of genuine amusement. She found herself joining in. Their server dropped off his drink.

He held it up. "To old friends."

Okay, that she could deal with. "To old friends."

twenty-four

Two hours and Sage wasn't sure how many drinks later, they were still at their table.

"It's not all Daisy's fault," Sage told him. "You're half the problem, possibly more."

"She doesn't love me anymore."

Sage rolled her eyes. "I know that's not true. She misses you desperately. I would know—I hear about it constantly." Not exactly what Daisy had been saying, but close enough. "She's caring and loyal and fun at a party. What do you want from her? What aren't you telling her?"

"She makes it hard."

"Isn't that a good thing?" Sage teased, then could have cheerfully slapped herself. Adding a hint of sexual innuendo to the conversation wasn't a good idea with any man, but certainly not with one she'd once, possibly, been in love with.

His gaze sharpened, as he studied her carefully, as if trying to figure out what she meant.

"That came out wrong," she said quickly. "It's the drinks. I take it back. What I meant is how does she make it, ah, difficult?"

"I don't want to talk about Daisy anymore."

"Yes, you do. She's your wife and you love her."

He looked away. "I miss my kids."

"If you moved back home, you could see them every day. Come on, Jordan, why won't you tell me what the real problem is? You have to know, because if you don't, moving out was the dumbest idea ever."

He drained his drink. "She doesn't need me. I think she likes having me around and she wanted to get married, but she doesn't need me. Not to take care of her or pay for anything or rescue her. I shouldn't have married her."

Sage shook her head. "That's your self-pity talking."

"Ouch. You always gave it to me straight. There were no games with you, Sage. I miss that. I shouldn't have let you go."

"You didn't let me go. You dumped me."

His gaze met hers. "No, I said we were too young to get married back then. I still wanted us to be a couple."

"Okay, yes, that's what happened, and you were right. We were too young. It wouldn't have worked between us."

"I disagree. I don't regret putting off the wedding, but I do regret losing you. I should have explained myself better. I should have followed you to Paris when you took off."

Something she'd wondered about, from time to time. What *would* have happened if he'd shown up in her tiny apartment and had declared undying love?

"None of that matters now," she said. "We took different paths and now you're married to Daisy, who loves you very much."

"Not anymore." His gaze was steady. "I don't think she was ever in love with me. She loved the idea of me, but not who I am."

Sage fought against a sinking feeling in her stomach. "Don't say that. I don't want you to break Daisy's heart."

"What about my heart? And why do you care about her? You two always hated each other."

"Not anymore. We're friends now." More than friends, she thought. Sisters. "I'm on her side."

His smile was bitter. "Everyone is."

"Don't say it like that. You're not a martyr."

"I'm sure as hell not the man."

"You're being—"

But that was as far as she got. Without warning, he leaned in and kissed her, really kissed her with intensity and yearning and tongue. In a single heartbeat she was swept back to a time when Jordan's kisses had been able to rock her world. When he was all that mattered and she'd wondered how she would ever find the strength to leave him.

Her body responded instantly, with her nipples tightening and heat settling between her thighs. The need to take and be taken nearly stole her breath away.

Shocked and afraid, she pulled back. They were both breathing hard.

"Another round?" their server asked.

Jordan pulled a credit card out of his pocket. "We'll take the check."

Relief eased some of her tension. They were going to do the right thing. Say good-night and go their separate ways. Hopefully he would simply walk away, rather than stay with her while she waited for her Uber. She wanted to avoid those awkward minutes of conversation. Enough damage had already been done—better to avoid the chance to do more.

He paid the bill, then stood and held out his hand. "Shall we?"

She took it and they walked out. Sometime while they'd been talking, the sun had gone down. The sky was dark, the air still, but warm. She felt every one of the four or five drinks she'd had, probably because she'd forgotten to eat, or drink water. Come morning, she was going to have a heck of a hangover.

"Jordan, I—"

He cupped her face in his hands and kissed her again. In that second before she parted her lips, she knew she had a decision to make. That once again, she was clearly at a crossroads—to do what was smart and sensible and right, or to roll the dice on the exciting, stupid and self-destructive choice.

She'd always been able to see these moments clearly, to understand there would be consequences, and yet every single time, she'd picked the wrong one. The bad one.

What would Daisy do?

The voice in the back of her head whispered the question. That was what she was supposed to ask herself. What would Daisy do?

Sage felt a bubble of hysterical laughter build up inside. She knew exactly how to answer that. Daisy would take Jordan home and screw his brains out.

Sage came awake to a pounding headache and a sense of dread. She was afraid to move, afraid to open her eyes. Not just because she was concerned she might throw up, but also because she didn't know where she was or what had happened the previous night.

There were vague memories and hazy images, but nothing she could specifically recall. Finally she let her eyelids drift open, then wished she hadn't.

She wasn't at home and she wasn't at Adam's. The unfamiliar bedroom was sparsely decorated. She turned her head to the left and saw her clothes on the floor. Worse, there was an open condom wrapper on the nightstand.

Slowly, carefully, she sat up, then swung her feet to the floor. Her stomach lurched but stayed in place. The pain of the headache increased. She was naked, she was in Jordan's bed. Because it had to be Jordan. The last thing she remembered was walking home with him and into his place.

She'd slept with Jordan. Worse, she'd slept with Daisy's husband. Daisy, her sister, her friend. She'd taken everything precious to her, she'd ruined it, and for what? Nothing. Nothing worthwhile. Nothing meaningful. It had been an act of destruction, nothing more.

What about Adam? Oh, God, no! How was she going to tell him?

She heard a groan, then felt movement on the bed as Jordan sat up.

"You okay?"

She didn't turn around. "No."

How could she be? The hangover didn't matter—it was everything else.

He got up and walked into the bathroom, then returned a few seconds later and handed her a robe. He'd pulled on sweats. She wrapped the robe around herself and stood, facing him.

He looked bad. His skin was gray and he had dark circles under his eyes. Not so much the charming seducer now, she thought bitterly. Instead he looked like what he was—a weak man who blamed others for his own faults. The only problem was, she was just as guilty of their crime.

She walked around him and into the bathroom. After locking the door, she used the toilet, then washed her face and rinsed out her mouth.

When she returned to the bedroom, Jordan was sitting on the foot of the bed, obviously waiting for her.

"Want me to make coffee?" he asked.

"No."

She collected her clothes, then started getting dressed. With every passing second, her sense of doom increased. She cared about Daisy. She'd begun to think of her as family and now all that was lost. Just as awful, she'd screwed up a perfect relationship with Adam.

Why was she so stupid? Why did she always do this? What the hell was wrong with her?

"We have to talk."

She pulled her dress on over her head, then smoothed it into place. "There's nothing to say. It was a mistake. I'm sure we both feel that way. You wanted to get back at Daisy, and who better to do that with than me? But why did I do it? I don't care about you. I don't even know you. So why did I do this? Why did I totally mess up my life?"

She slipped on her shoes. "Don't worry, I'm not expecting an answer."

"You can't tell her." He spoke flatly, without emotion. "She can't know, Sage. The truth will destroy her."

Something else she hadn't considered. What happened now? Did she lie and keep the secret to herself or did she admit to the truth and leave broken hearts in her wake?

"It was a mistake and we're both sorry," he continued. "That's all that matters."

"You're right about that," she told him. "We're both sorry. Too bad not talking about it doesn't make it go away."

She found her handbag, put on her sunglasses, then stepped out into the early morning light. It was barely after six, but the sun seemed to bore right through her eyes and into her brain. She ignored the pain and walked purposefully to her car.

Twenty minutes later, she was home. She hurried inside, hoping Adam hadn't noticed she'd been gone all night. She went directly to the kitchen, only to find her mother was already awake, sipping coffee at the kitchen table. Sage poured herself a cup, then leaned against the counter.

"You're up early," Sage murmured.

"I wondered when you were going to get home." Joanne's tone was gleeful. "You spent the night with Jordan."

"Apparently."

"I'm so glad. I was hoping it would work out. Just like old times."

"It's nothing like old times," Sage snapped. "It's a nightmare and it's all my fault." Her eyes began to burn, but she blinked away the tears. "I screwed up, Mom. I've hurt Daisy and I've hurt Adam. How could I do this to them?"

"Darling, you've never been able to resist Jordan."

Not exactly helpful. "Why couldn't I have been strong last night? I was so stupid and for nothing. Nothing! I don't want to get back together with him. The man cheated on his wife with the one person he thought would hurt her the most and I was a willing party. Who does that? Worse, I'm her sister."

"Stepsister," Joanne corrected. "*Former* stepsister."

"You're wrong. I'm her sister and I love her and look at what I did to her." The burning increased and this time Sage couldn't stop the tears from trickling down her cheeks. "I hurt her and she's never going to forgive me. I've lost her."

The enormity of that truth made her start shaking. She had to put down her coffee and clutch the counter.

"I destroyed what I had with her and I destroyed what I had with Adam. It's all gone. I had everything I've ever wanted in my hands, and now it's gone and it's only my fault."

She ran into her bedroom and closed the door, then sank onto her bed. She pulled her knees to her chest and gave in to the sobs, knowing that her pain affected nothing. She'd taken a hammer to her carefully constructed life and shattered it into pieces too small to ever be made whole.

After returning from dropping off the kids, Daisy stood in the doorway to her dad's bedroom. "Do you really have to go back so soon?"

Her father looked up from his open suitcase and smiled at her. "Is that a whine I hear in your voice?"

"Yes. I like having you around. It's only been a couple of weeks."

Wallace walked over to her and kissed the top of her head. "I need to get back to my patients. I'm going to let my practice know that I'll be moving back, but I'm going to give them time to replace me." He grinned. "It shouldn't take long. Who doesn't want to live in Hawaii?"

"There is that." She told herself not to get too hopeful. "You're really coming home to Los Angeles?"

"Yes. I'm going to find a nice condo somewhere near a golf course and think about retirement."

"You always think about it, but you never actually do it."

He winked. "Maybe that's the secret to how young I look."

She laughed. "I'm sure it is." She watched him fold a couple of shirts. "You're always welcome here, Dad."

"I appreciate the offer every time you make it, but that's not happening. I need my own space and you need to figure out your life. Having me here is a distraction."

She didn't like to admit it, but she knew he was telling the truth. "You mean Jordan."

"Yes, your husband. Any thoughts?"

Daisy leaned against the door frame. "I don't know. We can't go on like we have been. We either have to commit to making it work or we need to be done."

"Which is it for you?"

"We should make it work."

"Should or want to?"

"I don't have an answer to that," she admitted slowly. "Dad, is it possible I'm not in love with him?"

Her father looked at her. "Only you can answer that."

"He says that's what's wrong. He says I don't care about him anymore. He's trying to get my attention because I'm done with him and us and I'm just going through the motions."

"Is he right?"

"I don't know, which makes me wonder if not knowing is its own answer. I'm tired of fighting. I'm tired of not knowing what his latest complaint is. But if he's right, then everything wrong is my fault and I don't like that."

"It's never one person's fault. If you love him, you need to fix the marriage. If you don't, then you have to decide if you want to stay with him anyway."

"Is there a third choice? I'd really like that instead."

"You can make any choice you want. Whatever you decide, I'll be here for you." He smiled. "As will your sisters."

She felt her mood lift. "Yes, I have them. Both of them."

Her father smiled. "That makes me happy."

"Me, too. I can't explain it, but I'm happy they're both in my life. Sage and I had a great time in Miami. I love Cassidy. It's like we've made a family together."

"Makes my heart even more happy. Now give me ten minutes and you can drive me to the airport."

"I'll meet you downstairs."

Daisy sat at the top of the stairs and considered her options. Despite what Jordan had said, she was fairly sure she still loved him. He frustrated her and sometimes it felt as if they couldn't find common ground, but they'd been married over twelve years and they had a couple of kids together. That had to count for something.

If she could wave a magic wand and fix things, she would want them back the way they'd been in the beginning, when they'd spent all their time together and their future had been so bright. The last couple of years had been anything but that. So how much of the problem was Jordan and how much was her? Did she love him?

"I have to," she whispered.

There'd never been anyone else. Not seriously. She'd been in love with Jordan since high school. That hadn't changed. Sure, she'd grown up and she was a different person than she had been, but so what? They were a team. Lovers, parents, friends.

Although thinking those words made her wonder if any of them applied to their current situation.

Sage stepped out of the shower and dried herself off. She still felt hungover, but the headache had faded. Not surprisingly, her sense of anxiety had only grown.

She dressed in jeans and a T-shirt, and didn't bother blowing out her hair. She'd already called in sick to work. The truth, for once, although her illness had nothing to do with a virus and everything to do with the destruction of her life.

She went into the kitchen, where she found her mother waiting by the blender.

"There you are. I thought you might need this."

She flipped on the machine. The sharp, high-pitched whirring sound nearly split open Sage's skull, but she knew it was for the greater good. The pinkish-gray drink was a combination of coconut water, protein powder, and fruit. Not her favorite way to start any morning, but today it sounded more disgusting than usual.

But Sage knew the drink worked. The coconut water had electrolytes and would help hydrate her. The fruit would give her a little sugar high, while the protein powder would stabilize her blood sugar. In an hour or so, she would try real food, but for now, getting this down would be enough.

Joanne poured the drink into a glass and handed it to Sage.

"I'm going to take a trip with Thomas for a couple of weeks," she said. "When we get back, I'll move in with him permanently." She smiled. "Clock's ticking on your two months."

"Thanks, Mom," Sage murmured, trying to sip the drink without gagging.

She hadn't had time to consider her future, nor did she want to now. While getting a couple of roommates to help cover costs made the most sense, how could she make any decisions until she figured out how much damage she'd actually done?

Her mother patted her arm. "You're making way too much of this. What's done is done. Move on."

"I ruined everything. Moving on isn't going to be easy."

"Why does anything have to change? Just go on the way you were before." Joanne smiled. "You think Jordan is going to rush to tell Daisy what happened? If he does, he's an idiot and not worth your time."

"I can't lie to her. I can't have that between us."

Her mother's expression of sympathy hardened. "You've already slept with her husband, Sage. Don't you think at this point, the lie is hardly the point of things?"

The tears returned. "I didn't want to hurt her."

"Too late." Joanne's smile returned. "All right, I'm off to pack. I assume you'll be moping around the house today?"

"I need to see Adam."

"To tell him? Sage, no. While I don't agree with you, I understand you think you made a mistake. Fine. Punish yourself, but don't draw him into things. He'll never be able to handle it."

Her mother moved in front of her. "You're his princess, the dream girl he never thought he would have. That puts you on a very high pedestal and while it's lovely to be so cherished, the perch is also precarious. One wrong move and down you fall. Never forget that while you're the one all broken on the ground, he'll be the one who's angry at having his dreams shattered, even if he gave you a little push to send you tumbling. Men are fickle that way."

"Adam's not like that."

Her mother patted her shoulder. "I hope you're right and I'm wrong. It's just I've been doing this longer than you and they never get over being played for a fool. My advice—don't say a word. Eventually you'll stop feeling guilty. Besides, you're not just keeping quiet for yourself. He doesn't deserve a broken heart."

Sage told herself that her mother was only trying to help. From Joanne's perspective, she was giving sound advice.

"Thanks, Mom," she murmured.

"You're welcome."

Sage retreated to her room, where she choked down the rest of the protein drink before stretching out on her bed and trying to figure out what to do next. Extending her mother's odd analogy about lying shattered on the ground, she supposed the only thing to do was to start picking up the pieces. And that meant telling the truth.

She brushed her teeth, drank another glass of water, then went next door and knocked on the door. Adam answered a couple of seconds later, smiling when he saw her.

"Hey, you," he said, pulling her close and hugging her. "I was just thinking about you. How was your night?"

As he spoke, they went inside, his arm around her. His body was warm and familiar, his house welcoming. She looked around at the casual furnishings, the comfortable sofa, the dining room he rarely used. Everything about this place reminded her of Adam and whenever she was here, she felt comfortable and safe. As if she belonged. She'd had that, and more, with him, and she'd blown it because she was stupid and self-destructive.

She stepped in front of him and placed her hands on his chest. He smiled at her.

The affection and trust in his eyes stabbed her through the heart. She wished there was a physical manifestation for what she was feeling because the blood pouring out of her would be a distraction. Then she wouldn't have to tell him.

She fought to find the right thing to say, the least hurtful phrasing so he wouldn't cast her aside, only she didn't think those words existed. Which only left her with the truth.

"I slept with Jordan."

She watched as confusion was replaced by a cold blankness that scared her more than anger could have. He took two steps back and half turned away.

"I'm not even surprised," he said, his tone more disinterested than hurt.

"I'm sorry," she said quickly. "I didn't mean to, I swear. There wasn't a plan. My mom wanted me to meet her for dinner, but then she invited Jordan. We had a drink and then that drink became several…"

She trailed off when she realized how ridiculous and pathetic her excuses sounded.

"I'm sorry."

He looked at her, his expression closed and judgmental. "You could have left. You could have walked away. You could have said no. You could have called me to come join you. You could have said you were seeing someone. You could have not been interested in the first place. Am I missing any of the other options?"

She ignored the tears in her eyes. "Adam, please. I was wrong. I know I was wrong. I'm so sorry. I can't figure out what happened."

"You mean aside from the obvious?" He swore. "I knew you were going to screw up, I just didn't know how."

"I'm sorry."

"Stop saying that."

He was so quiet, she thought, wrapping her arms around herself and trying to stop crying. If only he would yell—she could understand that. She could yell back and they could talk about it. But this quietness—she didn't know how to deal with it.

"I didn't mean to hurt you. I was stupid, I know that. I don't even know why I did it. I don't like him or want to be with him. He's some guy I used to know. You're the one I—"

He took another step back. "Do not tell me you love me. Do *not*."

She hadn't known what she was going to say, but in that moment, she realized it was true. She did love Adam. She probably had for a while.

She wanted to crawl into a corner and wait for this all to be over, but there was nowhere to go. Worse, if she left now, if she didn't fight for him, she might lose him forever.

"I should have known," he said, walking the length of the living room. "I should have guessed. It was all too easy, you and me. We were getting along and the sex was great and you don't trust things working out because they never have. You're always waiting for the bad thing and if it doesn't happen on its own, you make it happen." He stopped in front of her. "Like with Ellery. Why did you leave him?"

"He loved me too much and I couldn't love him back."

"No, you left because you cheated and you couldn't stand to see him so wounded. You *cheated* because you couldn't love him back. You are one broken person, Sage." He grabbed her upper arms. "Why couldn't you believe in us? I'm strong. I don't scare easily. Why did you have to do it?"

He released her and turned away. "I'm such an idiot. I knew the second I saw you were back that I was screwed, but I didn't care. Because I'd always had a thing for you and grown-up Sage was even better than the girl I'd known all those years ago. I took it slow, I was careful. I did my best to figure out where it was going to go bad, so I could protect myself."

He walked to the other end of the room. "I was in love with you, but I knew better than to scare you. So I kept it to myself and started planning our damned future together." He walked over to a small table and pulled open the top drawer. He threw a folder on the floor.

"I was going to suggest you enroll in the UCLA teaching program and move in with me while you were going to school."

His pain surrounded her, sucking the very life force from her body, leaving her nothing but a shattered shell.

"I was going to ask you to marry me."

Her tears turned to sobs—the ugly kind that made it impossible to catch her breath. Several minutes passed as she tried to get herself under control, so she could gasp and then, finally, breathe again. Through it all, Adam stayed on the other side of the room, watching her with cold, lifeless eyes.

"Adam, please," she whispered.

"No. I won't play your games and you don't know how to do anything else." He walked to the door and held it open. "You should go now."

She nodded slowly and did as he requested. Once in her house, she curled up on her bed. She heard Adam drive away. Not long after that, her mother called out that she was leaving and would be in touch.

Sage rolled onto her back and stared at the ceiling. She opened her hand and closed it, unable to comprehend that everything she'd ever wanted had been within reach, and she'd thrown it away without considering that once lost, it was gone forever.

twenty-five

Daisy drove to Sage's house. Her sister's text had been brief, but determined. **I need to talk to you away from the house. Please come by. My mom's out of town.**

Mysterious and a little scary, Daisy thought. She and Sage hadn't talked in a couple of days. She'd texted her to tell her Wallace was leaving, but Sage hadn't answered. Daisy had found herself making excuses for that to her father, which just showed how far they'd come.

As Daisy pulled into the driveway, she was once again reminded of their very different circumstances. She'd grown up in Bel Air, in a fifteen-thousand-square-foot house, with servants and more money than she could ever spend. Sage and her mother had moved to this small house in a nice enough neighborhood, but they must have both been in shock by the changes. Not just when Joanne and Wallace divorced, but when they got married. Moving into their exclusive world couldn't have been easy.

She knocked on the front door. When Sage opened the door, Daisy couldn't keep from gasping.

"My God, what happened?"

Sage was pale, with shadows under her eyes. Even though it had only been a few days since they'd seen each other, she seemed to have lost weight. Her hair was dull, her mouth turned down.

Daisy hurried inside. "Are you sick? Did you get in an accident?"

Sage stunned her by bursting into tears. Daisy instinctively reached for her, hugging her tight. A thousand thoughts crowded her mind. Had Sage been attacked? Raped? Did she have cancer? Had Adam dumped her?

"Don't be nice," Sage said, stepping back and wiping her face. "Don't be nice. I couldn't stand it." Her mouth quivered. "Daisy, I'm sorry. I'm sorry. You have to believe me. You're my sister and I love you and I'm sorry."

Worry morphed into fear. "You're scaring me. Tell me what happened."

Sage's face crumbled. "I slept with Jordan."

She kept talking, but Daisy couldn't hear anything but a kind of buzzing sound. Her body stilled as the room around her blurred. She briefly wondered if she was going to pass out, but she was able to breathe and the blood didn't seem to be rushing from her head.

She could see Sage's lips moving. Her body language was pleading, as if she were trying to make her case. Daisy felt her heart shatter and waited for the resulting pain, but oddly, there was nothing. It was as if a protective wall had gone up between her head and her heart. Sage had slept with Jordan. Her stepsister had slept with her husband. They'd been naked together, having sex. Two of the people she trusted most in the world had betrayed her—doing the one thing that was sure to devastate her.

"I'm so sorry," Sage kept saying. "It was a huge mistake. I can't explain how it happened. We got drunk and then he kissed me. I was upset about stupid stuff. I was scared about my life and things going so well and I guess I needed to break everything. I can't explain it, but I'm sorry."

She wiped her face. "Daisy, please say something. Hit me. Kick me. Just talk to me. I don't want to lose you. We just found each other and now I've screwed that up. I'm sorry."

Daisy felt Sage's pain and knew it was genuine. Under other circumstances, she might even be happy to know Sage was suffering, but not right now. Right now she had to be somewhere else.

She walked out of the house without saying a word. She got in her car and drove a couple of blocks before pulling into the parking lot of a fast food place. She paused to see if she was shaking or about to have a panic attack, but she seemed fine. A little numb, but fine. Every instinct warned her that the crash was coming, but not just yet. She still had time.

She pulled out her phone and stared at the clock. Jordan should be finished with his surgeries and in his office, making notes. She texted him, saying she was going to stop by for a few minutes, then tossed her phone on the passenger seat and drove to the clinic.

She was careful to keep her attention on the road and her mind clear. She didn't want to get in an accident. Fortunately, the numbness continued, allowing her to breathe easily and drive with clarity.

She pulled into a parking spot and turned off the engine, but couldn't seem to move. She looked at the front of the building. She'd been the one to help Jordan refurbish the office, when he'd first bought the practice. Together they'd chosen the waiting area chairs and the paint color. She'd sent their family gardener over to spruce up the little planters by the door.

She picked up her phone, but still didn't get out of the car. Instead she remembered when she and Jordan had decided it was time for her to get pregnant. How she'd been so excited and scared and how, two months later, when she'd missed her period, she'd just known it had happened.

She hadn't said anything to him—not until enough time had passed for her to take a pregnancy test. When she'd shown him the stick, he'd grabbed her and spun her around, laughing and telling her how much he loved her.

Other memories flashed through her mind. Their first date, that first trip to Hawaii, when they'd finally made love. Ben's birth, getting pregnant with Krissa. All pieces that made up the mosaic of their life together.

A knock on her window startled her. She jumped and turned to see Jordan standing next to the car.

"You okay?" he asked, his expression quizzical. Not guilty or ashamed, just confused. "Why are you just sitting in the car?"

Instead of answering, she unlocked the doors and motioned for him to join her. He walked around her SUV and sat in the passenger seat.

"What's up?" he asked, when he was next to her. "You were just sitting here, staring. You feel all right?"

He sounded normal, she thought. Not like Sage, who had obviously been suffering. Not Jordan—for him, this was just another day.

"I'm fine," she said automatically, then realized it was a dumbass thing to say. She wasn't fine—far from it—but social niceties apparently lasted forever.

She was grateful that the numbness continued, that she could speak without disappearing into the pain. The downside of that was she had no idea what she felt. Shock, of course, and betrayal, but what did she want from Jordan? Him punished? An apology?

She opened her mouth, closed it, then surprised herself and

possibly him by saying, "I'm getting a lawyer. You should do the same."

His instant shock should have been gratifying. He physically flinched, then angled toward her.

"Daisy, no. Don't do that. We can figure it out. I believe that and I think you do, too. We belong together."

"Really? That's what you have to say? After all the time you've been gone, you think we belong together? We've been to therapy twice and you never said that. You've been difficult, reclusive and you've accused me of not loving you."

She stared at him, the truth slamming into her so hard, it forced its way past her numbness. Dark and scary, yet oddly freeing. Yes, it was awful, but to finally know what was happening made everything more clear.

"Oh my God! It's you! *You* don't love *me* anymore," she said, finally understanding the truth. "You want things over and you didn't know how to handle it, so you made it about me. You want it to be my fault."

The realization was so blinding that for a second, it was all she could see. Maybe she was done with this marriage as well, but that didn't matter now. He'd been gaming her from the beginning.

She felt the first whispers of hysteria and carefully slowed her breathing. She'd gotten this far—she was going to hold it together until she was home.

"Please," he said, reaching for her hand. "Don't do this. I love you."

"Something you should have thought of before you slept with Sage."

He went pale as his eyes widened in disbelief. "She told you?"

Until that second, she hadn't known there was the tiniest flicker of hope inside of her. Hope that he would be devastated by what he'd done, that he would beg and promise and plead. Hope that somehow he understood he'd crossed a line and that he had been forever changed by his actions, made better somehow.

But those three words—no, not the words, the tone—showed her the real ugliness. That he'd never planned to own up to his actions. That he'd intended she never know. He was willing to let her go the rest of her life unaware that her own husband had played her for a fool.

Questions crowded into her mind. How exactly had he seen the situation unfolding? Were they going to get back together and have Sage be a part of their lives? And then what? Would they spend Christmases together? Would he and Sage keep the secret, maybe smile behind her back, or meet up somewhere every now and then for another go at it?

"It was a mistake," he said into the silence. "One I regretted as soon as it happened. We were drunk and it didn't mean anything."

"It means something to me," she said quietly, looking out the front window rather than at him. "I loved you and married you. I trusted you."

"So you finally got what you wanted," he said bitterly.

She spun to look at him. "What did you say?"

"You got what you wanted. You've been looking for an excuse to dump me for a year and you finally have it."

"I never wanted to dump you, Jordan. Don't try to make this about me. I'm not the one who cheated."

"It's not about the cheating. It's about how you've treated me. You don't see me anymore."

She hadn't known he was so emotionally weak, she thought in surprise. She hadn't ever seen it and no one had warned her. He was making this all about him. He was twisting the circumstances and in a few weeks, his sleeping with Sage would be her fault.

She still didn't know what had gone wrong or if they'd been doomed from the start, but none of that mattered. The way forward was clear.

"I see you now," she told him. "I only wish I'd figured out who and what you are a long time ago. We could have saved ourselves going through all this."

They stared at each other until Jordan got out of the car. Daisy started the engine and drove home.

As she entered the familiar neighborhood where she'd lived all her life, the shield protecting her began to crack. When she pulled into the driveway, she began to tremble and her breath caught in her throat. She was running out of time, but she needed to hold it together for a few more minutes.

Once in the house, she went upstairs and into the play-room. Her children were there, both reading. Krissa's book was in French.

"Hi, Mom," Ben said, catching sight of her. He frowned. "Are you okay?"

"I'm not feeling well. I think I ate something that didn't agree with me. I'm going to go lie down. Please ask Esmerelda to get you dinner."

Krissa ran over and hugged her. "Want me to get you some ginger ale, Mom?"

Daisy stroked her soft hair. "Maybe later."

She felt more cracks forming and knew she had to get out of there. She kissed both her children, then hurried to her bed-room, where she managed to crawl onto the bed before the sobs began, ripping her into pieces as the pain washed over her.

There was so much hurt, twisting through her, stealing her breath and making her wonder how she was going to survive, knowing what had happened. Jordan was gone and her marriage was over. It had been dead a long time, only she hadn't known. She'd been trying to revive a corpse.

As for Sage, that she could barely comprehend. Had any of it been real? Daisy had been so sure they'd found something special together, something that would last. But she'd been wrong and now there was nothing.

She cried until there were no tears left, then lay in the dark, not sure how she was going to pull herself together enough to fake it for her kids. Because she had to. The divorce would be tough on them and she had to be their safe place. Somehow, for them, she would dig deep and get through it. Just not tonight.

She had no idea how much time had passed when she heard a knock on her bedroom door, followed by the sound of it opening as Cassidy stepped inside.

"I heard you weren't feeling well," she said quietly. "Esmerelda wanted me to see if you felt up to eating anything."

"I'm not hungry." She couldn't imagine ever being hungry again.

"Is it food poisoning?" Cassidy paused. "Can I turn on a light? I can't see anything and I don't know my way around this room."

Daisy wiped her face, then sat up and switched on a lamp on the nightstand. In the seconds it took her eyes to adjust, she heard Cassidy gasp.

"You've been crying and you look awful. What happened?"

She was going to have the say the words, she thought grimly. Probably more than once. She would have to say them and deal with the consequences. Because what they'd done was about more than them and her—it was about the entire family.

"Sage slept with Jordan."

Cassidy's reaction was nearly comical. She drew back, almost stumbled, then ran to the bed and pulled Daisy into a hug.

"Oh, God, I'm sorry."

Despite the distance and the trouble that had existed between them, Daisy found solace in Cassidy's embrace. Her sister hung on tight, pressed right up against her, holding her as if she would never let go. For a few seconds, she was able to breathe again, to imagine a time when the world wasn't dark and terrifying.

"I can't believe it," Cassidy admitted.

"Me, either."

Cassidy drew back a little, her mouth twisted, her eyes wide. "But why? She loves you, I know she does. We've finally figured out how to be sisters—why would she screw with that?" She pressed her lips together. "No pun intended."

Daisy managed an almost-smile. "I don't know, but she did, and it can't be undone." She drew in a breath. "It's over with Jordan. It was bad enough when he walked out with no explanation, but this is too much." She wiped her face again. "She told me. She just said it. No excuses, just the truth and then she apologized. He wasn't going to tell me. He was going to pretend it had never happened."

"I hate him."

"Me, too. I look forward to not feeling anything for him, but that's not today." She swallowed as she realized the question of loving or not loving him no longer mattered. If only she'd figured that out sooner.

Daisy sighed. "You know, in some ways, it hurts more about Sage. I thought she'd changed. I thought, like you said, we'd found something together."

"We had. I don't get it, either. She really messed up. There's no excuse for what she did. I'm seriously mad at her."

"Thanks for taking my side."

"I love you, Daisy. I'm glad you're my sister."

The tears started up again. "I love you, too." She managed a wobbly smile. "Please don't sleep with Jordan."

Cassidy hugged her again. "I won't ever do that. I'll mess up in other ways, but not that."

"At least you have a plan."

Cassidy got a box of tissues from the bathroom. She brought them back to Daisy and took a couple for herself.

"What happens now?" she asked.

Daisy blew her nose. "I call the family lawyer and get a recommendation for someone to handle the divorce. I'm going to have to tell the kids. I don't trust Jordan not to blurt it out the next time he sees them."

"Is he going to get a lot of money?" Cassidy asked.

"Not really. My inheritance and trust aren't community property. I earn more than him, so I'll be paying child support, even if we share custody. But I don't care about that. We'll split the money in our joint accounts."

Which all sounded so easy, but she knew it wouldn't be. A divorce. She was getting a divorce. Honestly, she never thought they would end up here.

"I want to call Sage," she said with a shrug. "Stupid me, huh? I keep wanting to talk to her."

"You trusted her. Of course you want to talk to her."

"Yeah, I trusted a lot of people I shouldn't." She stood up. "I need to arrange to take a few days off work, then go talk to the kids."

Cassidy grabbed her hand. "Want me there with you? If you think it would help?"

"Yes, please. I'll tell Esmerelda first, so she can be with us, too. I want them to feel supported and know there's stability in their lives."

Cassidy hugged her again. "I wish I could make this better."

"Me, too, but don't worry. I'll get through it and I'll be fine."

Maybe not today or tomorrow, but eventually. Broken

hearts healed and life moved on. That was what Sage would tell her, and then her sister would make her a drink and say something funny.

"If it was just Jordan," she began.

"But it's not."

"No. It's not."

twenty-six

Sage had never felt so alone—not after any of her divorces, not even when she'd left her life in Rome and had flown home with nothing but a couple of suitcases and a nest egg that mostly consisted of designer handbags.

Her mother was in Escondido with Thomas. Adam had left shortly after her confession and hadn't been back. She couldn't talk to Daisy and when she'd texted Cassidy a couple of days ago, her sister had bluntly told her that no one wanted to talk to her.

At work, Sage went through the motions because she couldn't afford not to, but she had lost all will to move forward with her goals. The steps required seemed insurmountable.

She arrived home a little after seven. After checking out the contents of the refrigerator, she decided she wasn't hungry and sat on the sofa in the dark. A few minutes later, her phone buzzed with an incoming text.

Daisy wants a divorce. Her lawyer's already been in touch. Can we talk?

She stared at the message, not sure where Jordan had gotten her number and not caring. Why would he even be surprised that Daisy wanted a divorce? He'd slept with his wife's stepsister. Who did that?

She tossed her phone on the sofa as she realized one of the answers to that question was her. What she'd done was worse, because she and Daisy had just found each other.

Sage?

She grabbed her phone and quickly blocked him, then went out to her car. She drove directly to Daisy's house and rang the bell. Esmerelda answered.

"Go away," the housekeeper said firmly, blocking the entrance. "No one wants to talk to you. You're a bad person. I thought you'd changed, but I was wrong. Go away."

Sage stared into unforgiving eyes. "I need to talk to Daisy."

"She doesn't want to see you."

"Please. I have to see her. I'm not leaving until I do."

"I'll call the police if you don't leave."

"Esmerelda, please. Just let her know I'm here and I'd very much like to talk to her." She hesitated. "Tell her I'm sorry."

Esmerelda snorted. "Because that matters." She slammed the door and shut off the porch light.

Sage sank onto the top step, prepared to wait. The evening wasn't that cold and she had nowhere to be.

Time passed slowly. Sage thought about that first, serendipitous meeting, only a few months ago, when Krissa had been sick and Daisy's car wouldn't start. She remembered the shock of Cassidy's accident and how she'd spent so many nights here when her sister refused to stop texting. How over time, she and Daisy had discovered that maybe they could be friends and how they'd come to depend on each other.

Sage had blown it all for a one-night stand with a guy she didn't even care about.

"I should probably get therapy," she murmured aloud. "Find out why I'm so self-destructive."

She sat there, ignoring how her butt was sore and starting to get numb from the hard porch step. At some point she would have to give up and go home, but for now—

The front door opened and Cassidy stepped out.

Sage stood and faced her.

Cassidy shook her head. "She doesn't want to see you, Sage. You hurt her."

"I know and I'm sorry. That's what I want to tell her. That I'm sorry and I wish I could take it back."

"That's not good enough. She's divorcing Jordan. The kids are upset and it's going to take a while for everyone to process. You hurt them. All of them. Not just Daisy, but Ben and Krissa."

Something Sage hadn't thought about. Her mouth began to tremble as tears filled her eyes. "No. Not them. They have to be okay." She twisted her hands together. "I don't know what to do. Cassidy, you have to help me."

"I don't know how." Her sister stared at her. "Why'd you do it?"

"I don't know. I got scared. Everything was so good and it's never good for me. I guess I wanted to control what the bad thing was going to be. I know how to be when things are bad. That's all I know."

"You picked a hell of a way to screw up your life."

"I know. I miss her and I miss you and the kids and everything."

Her voice was pleading, her tone desperate, but Cassidy was unmoved. "She doesn't want to see you." She sighed. "I guess you and I could hang out sometime, but we'd have to meet somewhere else. I get my cast off tomorrow and I'll need some physical therapy but then I can drive and meet you."

Sage moved forward, intending to hug her, but Cassidy pushed her away.

"Don't do that. I'm not ready."

The verbal slap caught her off guard. Cassidy had never done that before—if anything her sister clung to her too much. She was the one Cassidy called whenever she was down.

"But I was here for you," she managed, barely able to speak. "All those nights."

"I know and I appreciate that. But jeez, Sage. This was bad and you were wrong."

She turned and went into the house. The door closed and Sage heard the dead bolt being engaged, and then there was nothing.

Two weeks after finding out about Jordan and Sage, Daisy was almost sleeping through the night. She'd met with her lawyer twice, and together they'd drawn up a temporary parenting plan. She would have primary custody of the kids, with Jordan seeing them every other weekend and on Wednesday nights.

Ben and Krissa were a little quiet but seemed to be processing the changes in their lives. She'd found a highly recommended child psychologist and had scheduled appointments for each of them. Their teachers and school counselor had been told what was happening. So far they were both doing fine in their classes and with their friends. The biggest problem, as far as Daisy was concerned, was they kept asking about Sage.

"Why can't we see her?" Krissa had demanded that night at dinner. "I want to show her how much better I'm reading in French."

Ben had wanted to tell her about his science project. "She gets that stuff, Mom."

Cassidy had saved her butt with a quick lie about how Sage

was out of town, but would be back soon. Daisy knew she was going to have to come up with something to explain her absence, although she had no idea what. The truth wasn't an option.

Of course they missed their aunt—Sage had become a part of their lives. Even more troubling, Daisy had to admit she missed Sage, as well. Finding her after all this time had seemed like some kind of miracle. To lose her again—especially over something so stupid and tragic—was almost more than she could stand.

Daisy got the kids settled with a movie for the evening, then retreated to her office to review the paperwork from her lawyer. Not that she was in the mood—but the sooner they got everything settled, the sooner she could try to move on with her life. But before she could even boot up her laptop, Cassidy joined her.

"Have a second?" her sister asked.

"Sure. How's your leg? You barely have a limp."

Cassidy sat in one of the chairs on the other side of the desk and stretched out her leg, now free of the cast. "I'm feeling good. Stronger."

"You look good."

Cassidy sighed. "You know she still stops by every day."

"Esmerelda told me."

Daisy wasn't sure what to do with the information. Most of her wanted to see Sage and find out if they could work things out, but the little girl who had been rebuffed so many times, all those years ago, couldn't find it in herself to consider forgiveness.

Walking away made the most sense. Forgetting her. Only she couldn't do either, apparently, because even now, when she should hate her, she missed her. Desperately.

"I've been thinking about her a lot," Cassidy said. "How

she was just getting her life together when she had to go and screw it up. It doesn't make sense to me. You and she were tight and she had Adam, and now it's all gone. And for what?"

"She panicked," Daisy said before she could stop herself. "All her life, she's always lost the thing that mattered most. First her dad, then Wallace. Her home here, her dreams of being special. She walked away from Jordan, when I'm pretty sure she loved him. But instead of talking it over and maybe realizing they *were* too young and should wait to get married, she ran."

"You're being generous in your assessment."

Daisy managed a smile. "I can be generous from a distance. I'm not sure I would be so kind if she was in the room."

"You would be. You love her."

"I do. More fool me."

"It sucks."

"It does." Daisy thought about all that had happened. "I think this is the first time she's tried to fix things. Before, she always ran away. She never fought for what mattered to her. At least that's an improvement."

Cassidy nodded. "I watched the two of you. When I was first brought here, you circled each other like wary adversaries. But then it all changed. You started to like and trust each other and then you started to care. It was nice. I'm sorry it ended."

"Me, too."

"I miss her."

Daisy sighed. "I'm still not there yet."

Cassidy surprised her by smiling. "You're so lying. You miss her a lot." Her mouth straightened. "I'm going to be moving out, you know."

"What? No. You can't leave." Daisy wasn't sure she could take one more change in her life.

"I have to. It's time."

Daisy knew that was true, but she didn't have to like it. "Where are you going?"

Cassidy looked at her. "To Miami. I'm going to see Desean."

"Wow. I didn't see that coming. Does he know?"

"No. I'm going to show up and see what happens."

"To what end?"

Cassidy smiled. "I'm going to face my fears. How's that for shocking? Watching all this play out, seeing how strong and brave you are and how the kids are coping, it finally occurred to me that I'm being a total coward. He's a great guy and I love him. Maybe it won't work, but maybe it will, right? I mean, it has to work for someone, somewhere."

"Good for you. I'm really proud of you."

"Thanks." Cassidy sighed. "I'm scared, though. What if he won't give me one more chance? I dumped all over him a bunch of times. If I were him, I'm not sure I'd take me back."

"That's in the past," Daisy told her. "You made a mistake and you get that now. You're sorry. You want to make things right—he has to see that."

"You don't."

At first Daisy didn't understand what she was saying, but then she got it. "You and Desean aren't me and Sage."

"Why not? You love each other and you want to be close. Sage messed up in a huge way, but she gets it and she's sorry. Doesn't that mean something?"

"Fool me once," Daisy told her.

"Be the bigger person."

"I can't trust her."

"You *won't* trust her. There's a difference."

"Taking her side?" Daisy asked.

"No. Trying to figure out how to hold my family together."

Cassidy stood. "I have an early flight to Miami so I'm going to go pack."

"Need a ride to the airport?"

"That would be nice."

Daisy smiled. "Text me after you see him, so I can know what happened."

"You'll be the first."

Adam was finally back. Sage had seen his car in the driveway when she'd gotten home from work. Her heart had instantly quickened as hope blossomed inside. Maybe now she could talk to him and explain how sorry she was. Maybe now he would listen and at least consider forgiving her.

She hurried through the house to the patio. The tightly coiled worry she'd carried for the past couple of weeks relaxed when she saw him at his usual desk, typing away. She stepped out of her shoes before walking across the grass to their low, shared fence.

She knew the second he sensed her presence. His entire body stiffened, as if he were bracing himself for something. Then he looked at her.

His stark expression was like a punch to the gut. There was no welcoming smile, no hint he was happy to see her. His eyes were unreadable, his jaw set. She could tell he wasn't looking forward to any part of the conversation they were going to have.

"You're back," she said softly.

"I ran out of places to go."

She winced. "I'm sorry I chased you from your house. I'm sorry about a lot of things."

He leaned back in his chair. "Do we have to do this?"

"Please, Adam. Hear me out. I need to tell you how much I regret what I did to you. To us. I was a fool. There are a thousand reasons and not one of them makes a damn bit of difference."

She blinked away the tears. She wasn't going to try to play him. She wanted to be honest in every way possible, no matter how much that left her vulnerable. She'd had two weeks to think about what she wanted to tell him—as this might be her only chance, she was determined not to blow the opportunity.

"I screwed up," she told him. "There's no excuse for my behavior. I betrayed you and I betrayed us and I lost something that matters to me. I lost you."

The threat of tears increased, making it difficult to speak, but she willed herself to stay strong—mostly because she didn't want him to think she was looking for sympathy.

"I love you," she whispered, then cleared her throat and repeated the words. "I love you. I didn't know that until I lost you, which makes me even more ridiculous. It's a pretty basic emotion—why couldn't I have figured it out before I messed it all up?" She swallowed. "I know it's too late and you don't care how I feel. I'm not expecting anything. I just wanted you to know that you mattered so very much and I will always regret what I did and how I made you feel. That's the worst thing, even more than disappointing myself. I hurt you and I have to live with that. I'm sorry."

She pressed a hand to her mouth as she tried to stay in control. "You are an amazing man. You're smart and kind and affectionate and you get me. Even when you don't like who I am, you still get me. That's so rare. I hope you get over me a lot faster than you think you will and that you find someone who deserves you."

He stared at her without speaking.

She tried to smile. "I'm moving. Living next door would be too hard on me and it doesn't seem fair to you, so I'm going to go. My mom is moving to San Diego with her new boyfriend and she'll be renting out the house."

She couldn't control the tears anymore and they spilled onto her cheeks. She brushed them away.

"Goodbye, Adam."

She hurried inside, pausing only to collect her shoes, her bag and car keys. There wasn't any food in the house and while she wasn't eating much these days, she knew she had to at least pretend everything was all right.

But instead of going directly to the grocery store, she found herself in a familiar Bel Air neighborhood. She parked in Daisy's driveway, then walked up to the big double doors and rang the bell. Seconds later, Esmerelda answered.

"You're back," the housekeeper said.

"I am. I'd like to see Daisy."

Sage expected to be turned away yet again, but Esmerelda surprised her by holding open the door.

"You can come in."

Sage stepped into the house, not sure what had changed, but happy to have the opportunity to talk to Daisy.

"Wait here." Esmerelda pointed to a spot on the rug. "Don't move."

"I won't."

Sage wondered how long Daisy would keep her waiting, but it was only a few minutes until her sister appeared in the foyer. Like her, Daisy was pale and looked tired. She seemed more guarded than angry, which Sage hoped was a good sign.

"I'm sorry," Sage said quickly, in case Daisy changed her mind and threw her out. "About everything. I was completely and totally wrong. I hurt you, I hurt your kids and I hurt myself. I was stupid and thoughtless and scared and I reacted in the most destructive way I could. I don't have an excuse, I just want you to know that I understand I'm to blame and I will regret what I did for the rest of my life."

Daisy looked away. "Cassidy's gone. She went back to Miami a couple of days ago. She decided she was running from the best thing that ever happened to her, so she talked to Desean and told him she wanted one more chance."

"I didn't know. What happened?"

Daisy looked at her. "He took her back. They're moving in together and based on the brief amount she's texting me, I'm guessing they're having a lot of sex."

"I'm glad for her."

"Me, too, although it puts me in a bind. Come on."

Daisy walked into the family room and crossed to the wet bar. She pulled a bottle of wine from the cellar and opened it. Sage hovered, not sure what to make of her sister's actions. She was hoping they meant Daisy wasn't going to throw her out, but knew there was a fifty-fifty chance Daisy was only opening the wine so she could throw a couple of glasses in Sage's face.

Daisy carried two glasses to the coffee table and sat on one of the sofas. Sage sat across from her, both anxious and hopeful.

"Jordan and I are getting a divorce."

Sage held in a moan. "No. Please don't say that. Daisy, I'm sorry. I'm—"

Daisy held up her hand. "Stop apologizing." She picked up her wine. "It's not your fault. I'm not saying you're not some whore bitch who slept with my husband, but the divorce isn't about you. We've had problems for a long time. Jordan and I..." She sipped her drink. "It's been over for a while—I just didn't know. I thought we were in a rut, but instead we'd drifted apart. Somewhere along the way, I stopped loving him. I didn't see it, but he did. Probably because he'd fallen out of love with me, too. We couldn't have made it, even without you screwing up."

Sage ignored the "whore bitch" comment, figuring she'd earned it. "That has to be hard. I'm sorry you're dealing with all that. How are Ben and Krissa?"

"Managing. They miss you."

Gratifying words. "I miss them, too. And you."

Daisy wrinkled her nose. "There is that." Her gaze sharpened. "Dammit, Sage, what were you thinking? He was my husband! You don't sleep with your sister's husband. I'm pretty sure every cultural group on the planet would consider what you did incredibly shitty."

"I know. It was awful. I'm a horrible person."

"You screwed up big time. You broke my heart."

"I did. I was wrong. I wasn't thinking and I was scared and I reacted. I did the only thing that would totally ruin everything I've worked for. I just found you and now you're gone."

The tears returned. She was getting sick of them, but with everything happening in her life, she wasn't sure they were going to go away anytime soon.

She wiped her cheeks and squared her shoulders. "I know you said not to keep apologizing but I am sorry. You are someone I care about so much." She hesitated, wondering why it was harder to tell Daisy than Adam. "I love you."

Daisy stared at her. "You have a hell of a way of showing it."

"That's very true. I just wanted you to know how much you mean to me. You and the kids. I'm going to miss you so much."

"Miss us? Why?"

"I'm moving to Dallas. I can't stay here and live next door to Adam. It's too hard on me and it's not fair to him. I thought maybe starting over somewhere else would be easier for everyone. I have a friend who lives in Dallas. I can rent a room from her and find a job, then look at getting my teaching credentials there."

Daisy set down the glass and glared at her. "You're running away? Haven't you learned anything? It gets a little hard and off you go? You love me? Hardly. If you loved me, if you cared about us, you wouldn't disappear at the first sign of trouble. You'd fight for us."

"I'm hardly running at the first sign of trouble. I slept with your husband, Daisy. That's not a little thing. I have no idea if you'll ever forgive me or if seeing me hurts you. I don't know—"

"Then ask!" Daisy's voice rose with each word. "Ask me what I want. Ask me if I'd prefer to have you halfway across the country where I'll never see you and my kids will forget who you are. If you want to be my sister, then be my sister, but don't you dare cut and run."

They stared at each other.

"I don't understand," Sage admitted. "You want me to stay?"

"Didn't I just say that?" Daisy snapped.

Sage pressed her lips together. "You're not being very nice about it."

"I don't have to be nice. As you just pointed out, you slept with my husband. You're going to owe me for a very long time."

Sage wondered if it was safe for her to hope—just the tiniest bit. "I'm good with owing you."

"You also have to be a decent human being. No more sleeping with Jordan. And you have to love my kids."

"I already do. I've missed them."

"Like I said, they've missed you. It's been annoying."

Sage stood and moved around the coffee table. Daisy rose

and reached for her. They held on to each other for a long time. Sage felt her broken heart begin to heal.

"I'm sorry," she whispered. "Daisy, I'm so sorry."

Daisy drew back and shook her head. "No more apologies on that subject starting right this second. Those are house rules. Not the only rule. There are others. I'll get you a list."

"I'm not here often enough to need rules."

Daisy surprised her by flushing slightly and stepping away, as if she were nervous. "Yes, well, about that..."

Sage went cold as she realized she'd totally misunderstood what her sister was saying. "You don't want me visiting? We're not going to be friends?"

"What? No. Of course we are. I was just going to say that you could, well, the house is really big, so if you wanted to live here, I probably have a spare wing."

Sage blinked in surprise. "You can't mean that."

"I can and I do. It makes the most sense. I've been doing a lot of research on your teaching credentials and while the UCLA program is great, you couldn't start for over a year. But if you want to do the one at USC, it's a lot online and I think my dad could help get you in." She smiled. "If you're still interested."

Sage felt the room start to spin. It was probably a combination of not eating, shock and the two sips of wine she had. Before she could figure out if she was going to fall, Daisy had her on the sofa and was shoving her head between her knees.

"Breathe," Daisy said firmly. "Cassidy is finally back on her feet. I'm not interested in you getting a head injury."

"I'm okay." Sage straightened. "I haven't been eating much."

"Me, either. Want to raid the kitchen?"

Sage nodded and stood. The room remained still.

They made grilled cheese sandwiches and a salad. When

they were seated across from each other at the table, Sage smiled.

"We'll have to work out rent payments. How much do you want?"

Daisy rolled her eyes. "You're not paying me rent. Why would you even ask that? You're a freak, you know that?"

"Not nearly as freakish as you are."

Daisy picked up her sandwich. "We really are going to need rules for the kids or they'll bug you all the time."

"I look forward to it." And winning over Esmerelda. "You're giving me a second chance. I'm not sure I deserve it."

"You don't," Daisy said cheerfully. "But it's what Cassidy told me. I have to be the bigger person."

Sage felt her lips twitch.

Daisy glared. "Emotionally, not physically. Have I mentioned how annoying it is that you're so skinny? It's one of the things about you that makes me crazy."

"I only love you." Sage reached for her wine. "Now who's the bigger person?"

Daisy reached across the table and grabbed her hand. "Welcome home, Sage."

twenty-seven

Despite how much she'd learned and how far she'd come emotionally, Sage could still fit everything she owned in her car. It took a little pushing and shoving, but she managed to get all her clothes, shoes and handbags into her trunk with just enough room for a few personal items she wanted to keep.

Her mother was going to lease the house furnished. It was close enough to UCLA to command a high rent and Joanne already had several interested parties.

Sage walked through the house one last time, checking for anything she might have forgotten. Then she went out onto the front porch and locked the door behind her. As she crossed to her car, she glanced at Adam's house, wishing she could...

No, she told herself. There was nothing she could do. She'd said what she needed to and now she had to let the man be. It was the right thing to do. She could miss him all she wanted, but she wasn't allowed to do anything about it. One of her four zillion regrets was that he was suffering, too. She'd only meant to be self-destructive, not pull other people into the mess that was her life. Unfortunately, she'd hurt too many of those she loved and she was going to have to live with that.

But she'd been given a second chance with Daisy. She didn't know why, but somehow her sister had found it in her heart to forgive her and offer her a place to stay. No, not that, she thought as she drove into Bel Air. Daisy had offered her a home.

Sage didn't think, if the situation had been reversed, that she would have been so generous. But she was grateful to be given the opportunity to belong and this time she vowed she would get it right.

She arrived at the familiar mansion and parked in the driveway. After collecting a couple of suitcases, she walked toward the front door, half expecting to be turned away. But Esmerelda was there, offering a tight smile.

"You're here. Let me take those bags. You go get your other things. You're in what was Cassidy's room."

Sage stared at her. "I thought you hated me. Why are you being nice?"

"If Daisy can forgive you, it's not my place to be angry." Her expression softened. "The children love you and you love them."

Sage relaxed. "Saved by the babies."

"You are."

She left the suitcases for Esmerelda, then returned to her car to carry in a load. She'd barely grabbed a tote bag full of shoes when Daisy appeared at her side.

"Hey. You made it." Daisy reached past her for several coats on hangers. "Is your mom already gone?"

"She moved out last week."

Daisy took a shopping bag full of sweaters and turned toward the house. She hesitated and stared at Sage.

"What?" Daisy asked. "You look weird."

Sage managed a strangled laugh. "I feel weird."

"Okay, then." Daisy tilted her head. "What's wrong?"

"I'm feeling emotional about all this."

"I'm a saint. Get over it."

Sage didn't laugh. "You've been really good to me. I'm so sorry I—"

Daisy shoved everything back into the trunk, put her hands on her hips and glared at her sister. "No," she said forcefully. "Just no. It's done. We're family and we're going to make it work, but if you constantly apologize and walk around looking guilty or sad, we'll never get past what happened. You were wrong. Very wrong."

"I was."

"And you're never sleeping with Jordan again. Not even if he's the last man on the planet."

"I swear."

Daisy smiled at her. "Okay. Then let's try to fake normal."

Sage fought against tears. "I love you."

"I love you, too. Now come see what I did with your room." She picked up the totes again. "You were saying you wanted flocked wallpaper, right?"

"I can't wait to see it."

They went upstairs and turned toward what had been Cassidy's suite of rooms. Sage expected to find the same furniture and paint color, with maybe a fresh throw rug, but instead the entire space had been redecorated. The drapes had been replaced with white shutters and the walls were a pretty pale gray. A sofa sat across from the fireplace, with a couple more chairs to form a seating area, but what captured her attention was the desk under the window.

It was big, with drawers and a bookshelf on the side. A desk lamp sat on top, along with a basket filled with office supplies.

Sage let her suitcase drop and crossed to the desk.

"For when you start classes," Daisy told her. "The kids helped me pick out everything, so I think your pencils all have unicorns on them. Sorry."

"Everything is perfect," Sage whispered, then looked at

the wall. Several Ben and Krissa originals had been framed. "I love the artwork."

"It's impressive. They picked those. After getting them up on the wall, I decided to get you some original art, as well. My choice is in the bedroom."

Sage walked through the open doorway. The king-size bed was back with a new duvet cover. There were shutters in here, too, along with a chaise and a big dresser. A pretty painting of a water garden with lilies was above the bed, the blues and greens of the—

Sage gasped, then moved closer. Her heart thundered in her chest.

"No," she breathed. She spun to face her sister. "That isn't what I think it is. It can't be."

Daisy smiled. "A painting? It is, as a matter of fact. The artist is some French guy. I thought you'd like it, what with having lived in Paris."

"It's a Monet."

The smile turned into a satisfied grin. "Huh. Are you sure? A Monet?"

"You're insane. I didn't even know you had one."

"I have two. I love his work. And don't get crazy. I didn't buy either of them. My mom did. She was a fan."

"You put a Monet in my room."

Daisy smiled. "On loan. Don't get any ideas."

Sage flopped back on the bed and started to laugh.

That night, after the kids were asleep, Daisy and Sage sat out on the patio. Dinner had been a loud, raucous affair, Daisy thought happily. Having Sage back in their lives gave the kids a sense of continuity. She and Jordan had pretty much fleshed out the parenting plan, and now Sage was going to be around. They could settle in for a happy summer.

"You get unpacked?" Daisy asked. "Do you need more storage bins or bookshelves?"

"I have unpacked and there is closet space to spare." Sage smiled at her. "I'm loving my Monet."

"I'm glad. So, what are you going to do until school starts in September?"

Sage frowned. "What do you mean? I'm going to be working. I have a job."

"I know, but you're not going to have much in the way of expenses and you don't love working at the boutique..."

"I'm keeping my job," Sage said firmly. "And I'll be working as many hours as I can, so I can save money. I appreciate you letting me stay here, but I refuse to mooch off you."

"So touchy."

"I'm a little fragile, yes."

"Apparently." Daisy reached out and touched her sister's hand. "What about Adam?"

Sage flinched. "What about him?"

"You should talk to him."

Sage shook her head. "No. I can't."

"You fought for me. You should fight for him."

Sage looked at her. "It's too soon. He's in a lot of pain still, and so am I. Getting in touch with him now would be too much like harassment. He needs time to decide if I'm worth it."

"You are."

"He may not think so. In a few months, I'll talk to him."

"You're very wise."

Sage smiled. "Not yet, but I'm trying."

The late August afternoon was perfect—sunny and about eighty-five degrees. Daisy relaxed in her lounge chair, shaded by a large umbrella, while Sage, Cassidy and her dad played with the kids in the pool. Beside her, Desean sipped his lemonade and grinned.

"Is it always like this here?"

Daisy laughed. "Are you asking about the weather, the company or the fact that we're all being incredibly lazy today?"

"All of it, but we can start with the weather. I have to say, I don't miss the humidity."

"It makes the summer much easier to deal with," Daisy told him.

He glanced toward the pool, where Sage was clapping her hands as Ben jumped off the diving board.

"You like living with her?"

Daisy smiled. "I do. She's very easy to be with and the kids adore her."

Sage had been in the house nearly three months. She was still working at the boutique to save money but she would quit in a couple of weeks, when her classes began. Daisy was surprised how quickly they'd fallen into a comfortable routine. Sage usually dropped the kids off at camp and Esmerelda picked them up. Wallace had moved back to the mainland five weeks ago and was staying in the house until his new condo was remodeled.

Dinnertimes were loud and lengthy with the five of them discussing everything from pop culture to who had the best curveball in the league.

"You miss him?" Desean asked.

Daisy didn't have to ask who he meant. Cassidy had warned her she discussed everything with Desean.

"No," she said quietly. "I don't miss Jordan, and isn't that sad? We were married nearly thirteen years. I should still love him and want him back but I don't."

She'd spent a lot of time trying to figure out what had gone wrong in her marriage. She knew much of the blame was hers. Like her father, she'd withdrawn from the relationship, leaving Jordan feeling that he didn't matter. She still wasn't sure when the love had started to fade. Part of her was afraid it hadn't been that strong to begin with. Maybe her initial attraction had been more about his failed relationship with Sage than she would like to admit. Not her finest hour, but she was trying to learn from her mistakes.

"Jump!" Wallace called, holding out his hands.

Krissa looked doubtful but threw herself into the pool. Her grandfather caught her and swung her in the air. She laughed loudly.

"You have a nice family," Desean told her. "Thanks for letting me be a part of it."

"I'm glad my sister was smart enough to agree to marry you. We're happy to have you join us and I'm so proud of her for risking her heart." She faked a stern expression. "Don't even think about breaking it."

"I won't. She's the one. I'm going to be there, no matter what."

Daisy hoped that was true. Love was a tricky thing—hard to find and easily lost. But when it worked, it was the best. Her sisters had taught her that and it was a lesson she was never going to forget.

Sage sat in her car for so long, she was afraid the neighbors would call the police. At some point she was going to have to suck it up and be brave. That was her new thing— to be a trustworthy adult who kept her word and followed through. No more lies, no more deceit, no more pretending she couldn't do better.

"I'm here to do this," she said aloud and got out of her car. She raised her head slightly as she walked purposefully to Adam's front door and knocked.

A frightened voice in her head screamed she could have texted and asked if this was a good time. He might not be home. He might have a woman over. There were a thousand reasons to put this off.

She ignored the voice and waited. When the door opened, her breath caught. Adam looked good in cargo pants and a T-shirt. He needed a shave, but in a sexy kind of way. His blue eyes were clear, his hair a little too long.

"Hi," she said, trying to smile. "I wanted to stop by and ask if we could talk for a few minutes. It doesn't have to be now if that doesn't work for you." She shrugged. "I promise to be calm and reasonable. No tears, no drama."

"You were never dramatic and you didn't use tears to get what you wanted."

Which sounded nice, but he spoke without moving to let her in the house.

"It's been a long time," he said.

"Four months." Two weeks and three days, she added silently.

He stepped to the side and held open the door. She walked in, then let him lead the way to the family room.

The house was exactly as she remembered, with the stack of books on that one end table and the TV remote in its tray.

He motioned to the sofa. She perched on the edge of a cushion and took a deep, slow breath. She could do this. She was stronger than she'd been before, with purpose and a sense of self. Whatever the outcome, her victory was in the telling. She didn't need Adam to forgive her, even if she wanted it more than she could say.

He sat across from her, looking stiff and uncomfortable.

"How's work?" she asked.

"Good."

"You married?"

He laughed and relaxed. "No. I'm not married."

"Me, either." She smiled. "Just clearing the air on that one." She cleared her throat. "So Cassidy and Desean are engaged. They visited last month and it was really fun. He's great with the kids. I can't wait for them to have a few of their own. Oh, I'm enrolled at USC to get my teaching credentials."

"Go Trojans."

She paused, not sure what other information he would want to hear. Telling him that Daisy and Jordan were getting a divorce could make things awkward. Not that she wasn't going to mention what had happened before, because she was. It was just that—

"Sage," Adam said, drawing her back to the conversation. "Why are you here?"

Right. That. "I want to apologize again for what happened with Jordan. I was completely in the wrong and I hurt you. I regret that and I take full responsibility for my actions."

She looked at the floor, then at him. "I'm not going to defend what I did or try to explain why I did what I did, because that doesn't matter to you. I was wrong and I think I've learned from the experience. I feel different. Stronger." She brightened. "I'm living with Daisy, if you can believe it. It's fun and the kids…"

She exhaled. "Sorry. I need to get to the point." She looked at him. "I still love you, Adam. I'm in love with you and I'd like another chance to prove myself. As a woman, not a girl." She smiled slightly. "I'm almost forty, and someone once pointed out that means no more girl talk from me."

She watched him, hoping for some hint as to what he was thinking, but his face was carefully blank.

"I'm going to screw up," she added. "If you give me that chance. I'm not especially good at relationships. But I'm getting better and when I make mistakes I own up to them and work hard not to repeat them."

She had more to say, but wasn't sure it mattered. Adam looked past her toward the door, as if willing her to leave.

Disappointment crushed her like a heavy weight. It took all her strength to stand.

"I can see there's no going back," she said, telling herself she was going to keep her promise to herself and not cry. "I understand. I probably don't deserve your forgiveness. You were a good friend and I'll always treasure the time we had together. Thank you for that."

She walked toward the door, her back straight, her head high. She'd done the right thing and she could be proud of herself for that. No matter how much it hurt, she wouldn't regret coming here. She'd been honest and shared her heart. Daisy had promised, whatever the outcome, it would be a growth experience.

At least this time, she wouldn't be suffering a broken heart by herself. She would be surrounded by her sister and the kids and the dogs and cats and even Esmerelda.

"Sage, wait."

He came up behind her and turned her until she faced him. His gaze searched her face.

"Dammit all to hell," he muttered before cupping her face and kissing her.

She felt the need and hunger in his touch and flung her arms around him. He dropped his hands to her waist and pulled her close, all the while his mouth never leaving hers.

"I've missed you," he said when they finally paused to breathe. "Every damned day. I nearly called you a thousand times, but I wasn't sure about what you said before."

"That I was sorry? I was. I am. I hurt you and I hated that I did that."

One corner of his mouth turned up. "Not that part. I wasn't sure you meant that you loved me."

"I do, Adam. I love you."

"I love you, too."

She held in the need to do a little dance. "For real?"

"Yes. For real. How could I not? You're irresistible."

"I wish, but it's nice you think that about me." She looked into his eyes. "Adam, I'm working hard on being a better person. I'm seeing a therapist and I'm in an emotional support group. I'm working through my problems, but it takes time."

He smiled. "As long as you love me, take all the time you want."

She wasn't sure how he was able to forgive her, but she would be grateful for the rest of her life.

"Thank you. So we can start seeing each other?" she asked.

"I'd like that. Very much." He grinned. "Want to start seeing each other right now?"

She laughed. "Yes, I would."

He took her hand and tugged her down the hallway. She followed eagerly, ready to be back where she belonged—in his arms and in his bed.

"Daisy said to tell you that if it works out between us, she's expecting you at dinner tonight. We eat at six, because of the kids."

He glanced at the clock. "That only gives us four hours."

She laughed. "Poor us. We'll just have to make do."

★ ★ ★ ★ ★

the **stepsisters**

SUSAN MALLERY

BOOK CLUB DISCUSSION GUIDE

mira

Bel Air Cobb Salad
(recipe follows)

Berry Bellinis
(recipe follows)

Note: These questions contain spoilers, so we recommend that you wait to read them after you've finished the book.

1. What was your first impression of Daisy and Sage? Did your feelings about either or both characters change as the story progressed, and if so, in what way? What happened in the story that made you see them differently? With which sister did you empathize most strongly? Why?

2. Susan Mallery is best known for writing grab-you-by-the-heart romances. With *The Stepsisters*, she set out to write a love story of a different sort—the story of two women falling into friendship and sisterhood. What were the turning points in Daisy and Sage's relationship?

3. How did the sisters' understanding of their childhood change throughout the story?

4. Why do you think Daisy reacted so emotionally to the tie-dyed shirts? What did they represent to her?

5. Although Cassidy wasn't a point-of-view character, she had a fully fleshed-out character arc. Discuss how Cassidy changed from the beginning of the book to the end, and what effected that change.

6. Even if you didn't agree with Sage's actions, did you understand why she did what she did? Why or why not? Did you understand why she needed to do that for the story to work? Why or why not? Would you have forgiven her if you were Daisy? If you were Adam?

7. What were the themes of *The Stepsisters*?

8. Families today are arguably more complex than at any time in history. How did *The Stepsisters* reflect that reality? Did you see any similarities to your own immediate or extended family?

9. Cassidy and Sage both feel that their mother, Joanne, truly loved Wallace. Do you agree? Why or why not?

10. Were you satisfied with the ending? Why or why not? What alternate ending could you imagine?

11. What did you think of Daisy's house? Would you want to live in a house that big, that required servants to keep it running both inside and outside? Why or why not?

12. If you were a trust fund kid like Daisy and Cassidy, would you work? Why do you think they chose to work?

Just for fun... Pop Susan Mallery an email via the Contact page at susanmallery.com, under the Members menu, and tell her you'd like to hear the juicy secret about this book. (If you're not a member yet, you can join for free.) She's not going to share it publicly, but she will tell every reader who contacts her privately.

Bel Air Cobb Salad

Per main dish serving:

2 cups organic salad greens
1 slice of pancetta, browned and diced
½ cup grilled chicken breast, diced
¼ cup blue cheese crumbles
1 hard-boiled egg, halved, then sliced
1 small carrot, diced
¼ cup jicama or celery, diced
1 green onion with top, sliced
½ heirloom tomato, diced
¼ avocado, sliced
2 tbsp candied walnuts*
Blue cheese dressing**

Fill bowl with salad greens. Add the remaining ingredients, except dressing, in stripes across the top of the greens. Drizzle dressing in zigzags across the rows.

*Candied Walnuts

1 cup walnuts, broken into ¼-inch pieces
¼ cup sugar
1 tbsp butter

Preheat a nonstick skillet over medium. After it's preheated, add all the ingredients. Stir constantly for about 5 minutes. Remove from pan immediately and cool on a cookie sheet lined with parchment paper so walnuts don't stick together in clumps.

**Blue Cheese Dressing

¼ cup blue cheese crumbles
¼ cup mayonnaise
½ cup Greek yogurt
2 tbsp fresh chives
Juice of 1 lemon
Sea salt
Freshly ground pepper

Put all the ingredients in a food processor and blend until smooth.

Berry Bellinis

1½ cup mixed berries
¼ cup sugar
1 bottle sparkling wine, chilled

Place the berries and sugar in a food processor or blender and pulse until smooth. Taste and add a little extra sugar if necessary. Strain if desired. Put about 1 tbsp of the berry puree into a champagne glass and top with sparkling wine. Serve immediately.

#1 *New York Times* bestselling author
Susan Mallery delivers a warm and witty new novel
about two sisters at very different moments in life, their
parents' vow renewal and wedding, and a Christmas
they'll never forget.

Enjoy this preview of
The Christmas Wedding Guest

one

"It's a vacuum," Reggie Somerville said, trying to sound less doubtful than she felt. "You reinvented the vacuum?"

Gizmo stared at her, his hurt obvious, even behind his thick glasses. "It's a *smart* vacuum."

"Don't we already have those round ones that zip across a room?"

"They're not smart. They're average. Mine is smart."

Reggie was less sure about the vacuum's intelligence than her client's. Gizmo had a brain that existed on a different plane than those of average humans. His ideas were extraordinary. His execution, however, wasn't always successful. A basic knowledge of coding shouldn't be required to work any household appliance—a fact she'd tried to explain to him about fifty-seven thousand times.

She eyed the triangular-shaped head of the vacuum. The bright purple casing was appealing and she liked that it could roam on its own or be a regular stick vacuum if that was what she wanted. The printed instructions—about eighteen pages long—were a little daunting, but she would get through them.

If the trial went well, she and Gizmo would discuss the next steps, including her design suggestions. Once those were incorporated, they would start beta testing his latest invention. In the meantime, she would be doing a lot of vacuuming.

"I'll get you my report in a couple of weeks," she said.

Gizmo, a slight, pale twenty-year-old who lived with his extended family just north of Seattle, offered her a small smile. "You can have until the first of the year. I'm going to be busy with Christmas decorations for the house. We started putting them up just after Halloween and it's about to get really intense. I've worked out some of the kinks from last year, so the animatronics look more real. It's taking a lot of time. My grandma's really into it."

"Sounds like fun."

"We're launching the Friday after Thanksgiving, but we'll be upgrading everything through December. Come by close to Christmas. You'll be blown away."

"I can't wait," she said with a laugh.

She and Gizmo talked for a few more minutes before she walked him out of her home office. When the door closed behind her client, Belle, her one-hundred-and-twenty-pound Great Dane, poked her large head out from behind the desk.

"You didn't come say goodbye to Gizmo," Reggie said. "I thought you liked him."

Belle shifted her gaze to the purple vacuum sitting in the middle of the area rug, obviously pointing out that potential death still lurked.

"It's not going to hurt you," Reggie told her. "It's not even turned on."

Belle's brow drew together, as if she wasn't willing to accept the validity of that claim. Reggie tried to keep from smiling. Belle made a low sound in her throat, as though reminding Reggie of Gizmo's last invention.

"Yes, I do remember what happened with the dog walker robot," Reggie admitted.

The sturdy, odd-looking robot had started out well enough—walking a very concerned Belle around their small yard. Unfortunately, about ten minutes in, something had gone wrong with the programming and the robot had started chasing her instead. Belle, not the bravest of creatures, had broken through the screen door in her effort to escape the attack, hiding behind Reggie's desk for the rest of the day.

Gizmo had been crushed by the failure and had needed nearly as much reassurance as the dog. Sometimes, Reggie thought with a sigh, her job was the weirdest one ever.

"I'm going to leave this right here," Reggie told Belle. "It's turned off, so you can poke at it with your nose and get used to it."

Belle took two steps back toward the desk, her body language clearly saying she would never get used to it and why couldn't Reggie have a regular job that didn't threaten the life of her only pet?

"Or you could sit on it," Reggie pointed out. "The robot weighs about ten pounds. You're more than ten times that size. You could probably crush it like a bug."

Brown eyes widened slightly and filled with affront.

Reggie held in another smile. "I'm not commenting on your weight. You're very beautiful and way skinnier than me."

She settled on the sofa and patted the space next to her. Belle loped all of three strides before jumping up and leaning heavily against Reggie. The soft rose-colored sweater Belle wore to protect herself from the damp cold of mid-November looked good on her dark gray fur. Reggie put an arm around her dog and pulled her phone out of her pocket. A quick glance at the screen told her she'd missed a call. From her mother.

She tried to ignore the sudden sense of dread. Not that she didn't love her parents—she did. Very much. They were good people who cared about her. But they were going to insist she come home for Thanksgiving and Christmas, and she couldn't think of a single reason to refuse.

Last year had been different. Last year, she'd stayed in Seattle, with only Belle for company, enduring the holidays rather than enjoying them. She'd given herself through New Year's to mourn the breakup and subsequent humiliation that went with the man of her dreams proposing on the Friday after Thanksgiving, arranging an impromptu celebration party on Saturday and then dumping her on Sunday.

After sharing her happiness with nearly everyone she knew, having her friends coo over her gorgeous ring and ask about wedding plans, she'd had to explain that Jake had changed his mind. At least that was what she'd assumed had happened. His actual words, "I can't do this. It's over. I'm sorry," hadn't given her much to work with.

Hurt and ashamed, she'd buried herself in work and her life in Seattle. She hadn't returned home to Wishing Tree even once since it had happened. She'd told herself she was healing, but Reggie knew the truth was less flattering. She was hiding and it was time to suck it up and get over herself. Thanksgiving was next week. She was going to go home, like she did every year. It was past time. Besides, it wasn't as if she was still mourning Jake. She'd moved on and now it was time to demonstrate that to her hometown.

"At least that's the plan," Reggie told her dog and pushed the button to phone her mother.

"Hey, Mom," she said when the call was answered.

"Reggie! It's you. You'll never guess. It's so wonderful. Your dad and I are getting married."

Reggie blinked a couple of times. "You're already married. Your thirty-fifth wedding anniversary is coming up next month. I thought we'd have a party or something." She and her sister had talked about the possibility a couple of weeks ago.

Her mother laughed. "You're right. Technically, we're married. We eloped, and I have to tell you, I've always regretted not having a big wedding. Your father pointed out I've been upset about that for the last thirty-five years, so maybe it was time to do something about it. We've decided we're renewing our vows with a big wedding and a reception afterward. It'll be the Wednesday before Christmas."

"You're having a wedding?"

"Yes. Up at the resort. We're inviting everyone. It's been so much fun, but the planning is getting a little out of hand. I was hoping you could help me."

"With your wedding?"

"Yes, dear. Are you feeling all right?"

"My head's spinning a little."

"I know it's a surprise, but I'm so happy. You're coming home for Thanksgiving, aren't you?"

"I am."

"Good. So I was thinking you could just stay through Christmas. There's plenty of room down in the basement for you to work. You could handle your business in the morning and help me in the afternoon. It's only five weeks, Reggie. You have a job that lets you work from anywhere."

While technically true, Reggie wasn't thrilled at the thought of packing up her life for over a month and moving in with her folks.

"What about Belle?" she asked, hoping bringing up that subject would help shift things.

"You know we love her."

"She's afraid of Burt."

"Oh, they're fine together. It's all a big game."

Reggie thought about how Belle quivered with fear every time she saw her father's small dachshund in the room. Burt was normally good-natured, but he'd never taken to Belle and spent most of his time running after her and biting her ankles. Belle, for her part, tried to keep out of his way, frequently traversing a room by going from tabletop to sofa to chair, often with disastrous results.

"I want her to be a flower girl," her mother added. "We'll get her an adorable dress and she can have a basket of rose petals hanging around her neck."

Reggie rubbed her dog's back. "She'd look good as a flower girl."

"See? Say you'll come home and help me with my wedding, Reggie. I need you. Dena's busy with school and she's developed terrible morning sickness. I have no idea where she got it from. I was fine with both my pregnancies, but she's wiped out. You've been gone too long. It's time to come home."

Almost the exact words Reggie had told herself, minus the wedding guilt.

"Mom," she began, then held in a sigh. Why fight the inevitable? Once she was home, she would be happy she'd done the right thing. Plus, it was Wishing Tree at Christmas—nowhere else in the world came close to that little slice of magic.

"Sure. I'll be there. Belle and I will drive over the day after tomorrow."

"I'm so happy," her mother squealed. "Thank you. We're going to have so much fun. We haven't had the first snowfall yet. Maybe you'll be home for that and you can go to the big town party. All right, now that I know you're going to be home for the holidays, I have yet another favor to ask you."

Reggie wasn't sure if she should laugh or moan. "What did you do?"

"Nothing, really."

"It has to be something or we wouldn't be talking about it."

"Yes. Good point. Dena's class is going to do a knitting project for their holiday charity this year. Normally I'd be happy to manage it for her, but this year with the wedding and all, I just don't have time. I was hoping you could do it for me."

Reggie closed her eyes. "Mom," she began, then stopped, knowing she was going to say yes in the end, so why fight it?

Every year students at the local elementary school came up with several charity projects to do in December. Since Dena, Reggie's older sister, had started teaching there, the family had also gotten involved. For the past couple of years, Reggie's mom had been in charge of that project, organizing supplies and students, paving the way for their good deed.

"This is why I've avoided coming home," Reggie said weakly.

"No, it's not. You avoided coming home because Jake Crane was too stupid to realize what he had with you. I hope he spends the rest of his life regretting his decision and fighting a very painful rash."

"Go, Mom."

Her mother laughed. "I can be supportive."

"You always are." Reggie smiled. "Fine, I'll be the knitting queen."

"Wonderful. I'll email you the information you'll need to get up to speed. You're going to have a great time with the kids. In the meantime, think about wedding favors. Something we'll make ourselves so it will be really special. I was playing with the idea of painted coasters, or we could make soap. I've always wanted to learn how to do that. We could go botanical or floral."

They were going to make soap? "You know you can buy really cute little soaps, Mom. They sell them online."

"I'm not buying the favors. I want this to be a project for us to do together. Anyway, I'll see you soon. Let me know when you leave Seattle so I can start worrying when you're not here on time."

"How about if I just show up unexpectedly so you don't have to worry at all?"

"Where's the fun in that? I can't wait to see you. I'll give Dad your love."

"Thanks, Mom. And congratulations on the wedding."

Dena Somerville had known being single and pregnant would offer challenges, but she'd never thought she would be sick every second of every day. *Her* mother had always talked about how easy her pregnancies had been and the fact that the women in their family popped out babies with barely a pause in their days.

Sitting on the floor in her bathroom, leaning against the wall, while wondering if she was done throwing up for this hour, Dena decided either her mother had been lying or Dena had been adopted.

It wasn't supposed to be like this, she thought, turning over the damp washcloth on the back of her neck and wishing she could magically transport herself eight weeks into the future, the time her doctor had promised the nausea and subsequent vomiting would finally end. Alas, she had yet to figure out how to move through time at will, so she was stuck with the unpleasant reality of knowing that, in an hour or two, the waves would return and three times out of five she would oh, so elegantly puke with little or no warning.

What really got her was the fact that she'd had a plan. A good plan, a sensible plan. A plan that could almost be called superior. She'd always been the girl with a plan and she'd always done the work to make it happen. She didn't believe in luck or fate—she put in the time and effort required, even when it was hard.

She'd fulfilled her childhood dream of being a teacher and she loved her job even more than she'd thought she would.

When her grandmother Regina had passed away, dividing her estate between her two granddaughters, leaving stocks and bonds to her namesake Reggie and the Wishing Tree B&B to Dena, she'd moved into the spacious apartment above the old carriage house and had spent her summers updating the place.

Although Dena had been less than successful in the romance department, she'd kept putting herself out there. She'd signed up for a dating service and had traveled to Seattle every other weekend for five months in an effort to meet *the one*. She'd used three different dating apps, had told anyone who would listen she was on the market. She'd gone on group dates, blind dates and double dates.

After two years of honest effort, she'd accepted that she wasn't likely to find Mr. Right, or even Mr. Good Enough. At that point, she'd had to start asking herself the hard question: Did giving up on love also mean giving up on having a family? The answer had come quickly enough and it had been a big fat no. She loved kids and she wanted kids of her own.

Being a logical, fact-driven person, she'd taken an entire year to research IUI—aka intrauterine insemination, or what her sister referred to as the turkey baster method of getting pregnant—and another six months to make the decision to have the procedure. She'd scheduled the first such that her due date would align with the end of the school year, thereby giving her the whole summer to spend with her baby.

She'd picked out colors for the nursery, she'd investigated the best day care options, and she'd typed up notes for when she sat down with her family and told them what she wanted to do. She had a wonderful support system, including her parents, her sister, Reggie, and the staff at the B&B, all of whom had become like family to her. She'd even managed to get pregnant right out of the gate.

She'd tried to think of everything, but she'd never considered the possibility she would be laid low by morning sickness.

The combination of the cool, damp washcloth and the cold tiles beneath her butt seemed to ease the nausea enough for her to risk standing. When she was on her feet, she paused to see if her stomach would punish her, but all seemed calm. With a little luck, she would get through the next couple of hours without the need to barf.

Tightening the belt on her robe, she walked to her balcony and stepped out into the freezing, dark morning. As always, the sharp, cold air shocked her lungs and made her shiver, but the last whispers of nausea faded in the chill.

It was barely six in the morning and much of the world was still asleep. This far north and only a month from the shortest day of the year, daybreak was nearly two hours away. She looked up at the bright stars twinkling overhead. Although it was cold enough to snow, the weather had been remarkably clear. The mythical first snowfall had yet to occur.

Soon, she thought with a smile. Soon there would be snow and the celebration that went with it, because Wishing Tree was that kind of town.

She glanced toward the main building of the B&B and saw the kitchen lights were on. Ursula, their gifted but snarky chef, had already gotten to work on breakfast. Once that meal was done, she would put together box lunches for any guests who had ordered one. That endeavor was followed by batches of cookies, brownies and scones that they sold in the lobby every afternoon. Ursula's last task before heading home was to create appetizers for their evening wine and snacks event.

Sometimes she made little quiches or put together a really great cheese plate. Her stuffed mushrooms were popular, as were the crab puffs. And the wine. All beautiful Washington wines from the great wineries: L'Ecole, Painted Moon, Northstar, Lake Chelan, Doubleback and Figgins.

"Ah, wine. How much I once loved you," Dena murmured, then laughed. At least she could still eat the food—or most of it. Soft cheeses were a no-no and these days olives made her gag, but otherwise she was all in.

A light clicked on, illuminating the back patio of the unit below. The ground floor of the carriage house had been split into a storage room for the B&B and a stand-alone suite for guests who preferred something more upscale and private. The space came at a premium, but they rarely had trouble filling it—especially during the holiday season.

The current resident, a ridiculously good-looking guy who had arrived two days ago, was booked through the day after New Year's. Dena was nearly as excited about the thought of all those weekly charges filling up her bank account as she was by the eye candy. Most of her guests were couples and families. Attractive single men didn't often find their way to her B&B.

Not that his marital status mattered to her. Not only had she accepted that love wasn't in her destiny, she was pregnant, and getting involved with a guy made no sense. Oh, and there was the added fact that, based solely on looks, he was miles out of her league. Still, an expectant mother could look and admire, she thought with a smile.

So far, he was a quiet neighbor who didn't slam doors or play his TV too loud. Last night she'd heard music coming from his place—a song played several times in a row. The soft rendition had lulled her to sleep, so she wasn't about to complain.

The cold seeped through her bathrobe and made her shiver. Dena sucked in one more breath before heading inside to start her morning. She brushed her teeth, then dressed quickly. Once in the kitchen, she ate the only breakfast she was able to keep down these days. An avocado and egg salad sandwich on rye bread. Possibly gross in most circumstances, but her doctor had given it a thumbs-up.

She glanced longingly at her coffee maker, thinking how incredibly close the two of them had been, back before her life had been defined by something the size of a lima bean. Not that she had regrets—giving up coffee was so worth it for her baby's sake, but at least she'd known that deprivation was coming. It was the morning-slash-afternoon-slash-early-evening sickness that was going to do her in.

But for now, her tummy was quiet, so she filled her water bottle, retrieved her lunch from the refrigerator and headed downstairs to her car. If she could get a little cooperation from her body, she was going to have a good day—mostly because every day she was teaching was a good day. Plus, there were so many things to look forward to. On Friday she would be announcing the charity project chosen for the third-grade class, then next Monday they would have their monthly career day presentation. If she remembered correctly, they were hosting a plumber, a veterinarian and a Christmas tree farmer. So many possibilities, she thought as she walked to her car. She was, in every way possible, the luckiest person on the planet, and she had the life to prove it.

Need to know what happens next? Preorder your copy of
The Christmas Wedding Guest *today!*

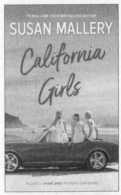
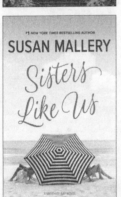